47 SECONDS

47 SECONDS

JANE RYAN

POOLBEG
CRIMSON

Published 2019 by Crimson
an imprint of Poolbeg Press Ltd
123 Grange Hill, Baldoyle
Dublin 13, Ireland
E-mail: poolbeg@poolbeg.com
www.poolbeg.com

1

A catalogue record for this book is available from the British Library.

ISBN 978-178-199-775-8

Printed by Liberduplex, Barcelona

About the author

Jane Ryan studied with the Institute of Chartered Accountants in Ireland and has worked in the technology industry for over twenty years. She lives in Dublin with her husband and two sons. Her stories are published online with Creativewriting.ie and in print. Jane was shortlisted for the Hennessy Literary Awards and her latest short story appeared in an anthology entitled *Strange Love Affairs*.

47 Seconds is her first novel.

Acknowledgements

This book is in your hands because so many people believed in me and helped me. My first reader was Karen Whelan, then my beloved sister-in-law Teresa Ryan, and along the way my book club readers Deirdre Kelly, Gillian Matthews and Anne O'Malley. My thanks also go to all the Willow girls and Cliona, Ruth, Jeanne, Sinéad, Aoife, Niamh, Helle, Ellen, Liz, Sharon, not forgetting Dervil. If I am to be judged by my friends, let it be these wonderful women.

To Larissa – everyone should have a friend like Larissa.

To my brother David, a man of action, compassion and ideas. To Maebh, Peter and Paul.

To the team at Poolbeg who put shape and form on this novel, in particular Paula Campbell for her belief in *47 Seconds* and me, and Gaye Shortland for making the unintelligible telligible – you see what she was up against.

Thanks to Vanessa Fox O'Loughlin, Sinéad Moriarty, Fenella Garvey and Ann Lalor for their advice, time and generosity of spirit.

To the serving and non-serving gardaí who answered endless questions, listened to ridiculous scenarios without complaint and gave technical advice. In particular, Detective Garda Damian Healy, a very sound man who gave me an insight into the complex world of policing in Ireland.

I owe a great debt of gratitude and love to my husband Ron and my boys, Adam and Conor, for just being.

Lastly, to Mum, the finest woman I have ever known, who faced Alzheimer's with such bravery and grace.

For my mum and dad, Pat and Peter Ryan

PART 1

devil

ˈdɛv(ə)l
verb
gerund or present participle: **devilling**

INFORMAL•DATED
to act as a junior assistant for a barrister or other professional

CHAPTER 1

BRIDGET

Respect was everything. Conditioning less so. There I was, jaw pumped on nothing, words chewed until they split, husks of anger supressed then broken, granular in my mouth, sitting on the grooves of my tongue until they felt like hairs in my mouth and I spat.

'*The Park!*'

'Don't you roar at me, Bridget Harney!'

'Sending us to the other side of the city to investigate a container of tampered-with pigmeat! We might as well paint *bacon* on the side of the squad car.' I threw my hands in the air and stomped on the accelerator.

'*Careful!*'

My partner, Kay Shanahan, a usually smiling woman with a mop of dark curls, was rummaging in her outsize handbag.

'Are you searching for a sweetie for me?'

Kay's look of chagrin would have been comical if I wasn't so worked up. She tried to style it out by jiggling to some undanceable music playing on the radio and let her bag fall to the floor.

We were making our way to Dublin Port in fits and starts. Traffic swayed and choked all lanes – no way was I putting the lights on or using the bus lane for pigmeat.

'Why aren't Irishtown looking after this?' I asked.

'Short-staffed, there's a match in the Aviva.'

'Midweek?'

'It's soccer. The November "friendlies". PSNI gave a heads-up that some thugs are coming down for it. Irishtown have been pulled in to assist Donnybrook, might even be a couple of other stations on call.'

'Soccer hooligans aren't the reason we're on this, Kay. "Got a call from the Park," Joe says, "Assistant Commissioner looking at this," Joe says.'

My face scrunched as I mimicked my immediate superior's squeaky blue-tit voice.

'Calm down, Bridge! And don't get arsey about orders from the Park. Why can't you be a bit more political? Anything from Garda Headquarters gives us a chance to shine.'

'More political? You mean brown-nosing?'

'*Watch the road! You nearly rear-ended that car!*' Stress was heightening her strong Kildare accent. 'Let's just get to the Port in one piece, right?'

'What does it say on the report?'

Kay looked at her scratched screen and used two pudgy fingers to scroll down. 'Container belongs to Doyles' Irish Meats Group. For export to the UK –'

'There's your answer right there. Guy who owns Doyles' is a big political donor.'

'You don't know that.'

'Okay, but I'll bet you that half-eaten KitKat stashed in your bag that the Park got a call from Leinster House.'

'And I'll bet, Bridget Harney, if you don't stop chopping lanes you'll be trying to talk your way out of a multi-car collision.'

I stayed in the inside lane and switched to Lyric FM, Kay's favourite station.

'Milky Moo?' said Kay.

She'd unwrapped it and was enticing me by moving it under my nose, an oblong of sweetness on blue-and-white paper. I don't have a sweet tooth but sugar calms me.

'Go on,' I said.

'Keep your hands on the wheel.'

Kay popped the treat into my mouth and I sucked on the creamy whiteness. It helped me summon the grace to stay within the speed limit as I turned off just before the yawning Port Tunnel into the main gate of Dublin Port.

The flinty-smelling air signalled our arrival. As part of the port-city integration, Dublin Port Company had opened up areas of the port to the public and beached an ancient crane, that looked to be riddled with bullet holes, outside the front door. It was painted powder blue. I was unsure what message was being conveyed, but it was easier than ever to walk into the port.

A Harbour Policeman waited for the barrier to rise and waved us through, then checked our ID and give us a map of the area.

'Off Tolka Quay Road, towards the East Wall. I've drawn a route on your map. Yard gates are open so you can drive right in, there's a small portakabin onsite and one of my colleagues will be waiting for you there.'

I thanked him and made for the fields of landed cargo, Kay navigating with the map. Just as he'd said the gates were open and we pulled up just inside.

As we got out my hand went for my Trinity College scarf and

hesitated of its own accord, but the bitter cold made my decision for me. I wound the scarf around my neck, taking care to turn the sky-blue and red stripes in, leaving only the coarse navy woollen side on view. For some people the scarf was a sign of privilege. I knew the lads in the squad had some choice pejorative language for me when I wore it. Assuming they knew what *pejorative* meant.

'Hello,' said a lanky man in a Dublin Harbour Police uniform with a backside shiny from wear.

'Detective Garda Bridget Harney and Detective Garda Kay Shanahan from the DOCB.'

We showed our identification. I pocketed my badge and looked around while Kay chatted to him and read his report, asking questions and generally acting like he was an interesting conversationalist.

'What're two Drugs and Organised Crime detectives doing here? Is this gang-related?' he asked.

He had bulgy, barfly eyes.

'What's it to you which division investigates?' I said.

Kay glared at me and took the lead. 'Our agri-food sector is very important to the economy – lots of important people looking at this. Where's the container bound for?'

'Doyles' Irish Meats Group, West Midlands – around Walsall, near Birmingham.'

'Right,' said Kay.

'And no one heard the seals being broken or noticed any intruders?' I asked.

'No. Though we've put in a load of new checks because of Brexit.' He gripped his clipboard, from which he seemed to take his authority.

'A load of new checks?' I said. 'Where? And the Port is busier than ever, isn't it? You'd never hear the doors opening unless you were standing here. I can hardly hear myself speaking with those gantry cranes.' I looked around pointedly. I was still annoyed about the case assignment and this fool was getting the brunt of my anger. My hair was whipping in the wind, irritating me, so I pulled it into a ponytail using a wide elastic band.

The Harbour Policeman stared at my boobs while I had my arms raised, a hello-baby smile hanging around his mouth. I was tall, with breasts that had sprouted overnight to Double D when I was sixteen – that and a stupid Cupid's bow mouth gave me a pin-up look.

'You've got something to say?'

He gulped and ran a grubby finger around the inside of his shirt collar.

'Dublin Port has applied for new planning permissions, in case of a hard Brexit. Checks will be live this time next year . . . end of 2019 . . .' He went a dark, beetroot red.

'By the way, who did you ring first, us or Doyles'?' I asked.

'I'm obliged to ring Doyles' the moment anything happens with their containers – it's in the contract.'

I would have said more but something navy streaked out of a container row. A stick man-boy kicking up yard debris as he flailed past.

'*Wait! Stop!*'

I sprinted after him but he was halfway towards the gate before I'd run five yards. He turned and I caught a flash of yellow school crest on his fleece just as a discarded lump of cement caught my left foot. I staggered forward like a clown in oversize shoes, trying to maintain my balance, and landed on my palms. The boy was facing me, his phone lens trained on my efforts while he continued to back away on the uneven surface, sure-footed as a Dublin Bay crab.

'You wouldn't know what you'd trip over in a freight yard.'

My jaw tightened and I bit off an expletive.

Stephen Lowry from the *Daily Journal* smiled as if remembering something pleasant.

I got to my feet in one movement and was glad there was some distance between us. The urge to punch his smug face was intense.

'Christ! How did he find out about this?'

Kay had reached me, her exertions shortening her breath. 'Easy, Bridge . . . don't lose it. Say nothing or he'll start his Lowry Investigates rubbish.'

'He'll never do that to me again.'

'*Don't rise to him!*'

Kay's voice was a squawk as I moved forward, trying to contain my panic with movement and an outward show of confidence.

'Why are you here? You're trespassing! I could have you tied up all day in Harcourt Square for coming in here without authorisation.'

'Freedom of the press, Detective Harney. And what are you doing here? Selling black-market pig carcasses? I'm sure if you get into trouble your daddy the Judge can bail you out.'

He was sneering. The injustice of his comments must have blinded me – how else could I have missed the boy still recording? I was running towards Lowry, teeth bared – too late the magnesium flare of a phone's flash winked in my peripheral vision.

I halted. 'You stay there, Lowry – I'll want to talk to you after this – and who's the Saint Gerard's kid?'

The boy blanched, the phone still aloft but the light now dead.

'Transition Year student on work experience with the paper. I wouldnt be too high-handed with him, Detective Harney. His family are nearly as well connected as yours.'

The boy's slim fingers tapped and conjured.

'Hope the Dublin Port free Wi-Fi's on the blink,' said Lowry. He showed me two rows of ridged teeth, his attempt at smiling.

'*Come on, Bridge!*' It was a hiss from Kay.

Of course, she was right. I could pick up Lowry and his video producer later.

'Where's the container?' I demanded.

'It's over here.' The Harbour Policeman pointed to a crumpled-looking iron container, the size of a mobile home, with broken Department of Agriculture and Custom's seals and a black triangle of open door.

We walked over to it.

'Did you open that door?' I glared at him.

He started to stutter, his Adam's apple bobbing out dots and dashes.

'No! No! The boy and that man must've done it. I didn't open that door – we never touch the containers if the seal is broken! Bloke here lost his job last year because a side of beef went missing. We ring the gardaí straight away. Honest.'

'Well, that's reassuring.' I didn't work to keep the sarcasm from my voice.

Kay pulled the door open wide to give us some light. It screeched across the metal base of the container.

'How often do you come down here? And I'm not talking about the sign-offs on your roster. Where's the CCTV?'

I looked around the yard at the bushels of weeds at the base of the containers and the clotted gravel.

'Not every yard has CCTV – there's over five hundred acres of landed cargo in the Port.'

'That much?' said Kay.

The Harbour Policeman looked pleased. 'It's much bigger than you'd think. We patrol this area every half hour by van and there's some cameras over there,' he pointed to some spires with bubble eyes nearly half a kilometre away, 'but they have some blind spots.'

'We'll still need to see it.' I said. 'You say you patrol every half hour? On the half hour? Quite the routine you have going there.'

'Easy, Bridge,' said Kay. 'We'll take it from here, Dave, and thanks.'

He nodded at Kay and threw a reproachful look at me as he left.

'How do you know his name?'

'It's on the report he gave us, Bridge. Would you ever make an effort with the likes of him?'

'He looks the type to cool his coffee with Powers.'

'I know, but most of those Harbour guys applied to join us and were turned down. Give him a break.'

'Doesn't even have the wit to vary his routine,' I grunted and snapped on a pair of blue gloves. I had them stashed everywhere, pockets of jackets, glove compartments, back-seat footwells.

I side-stepped into the container and felt that tight shiver of excited fear. Something had happened here, even if it was just tampering with pigmeat. The breath froze in my lungs. The container had the refrigeration turned off, but it would be hours before it reached zero degrees, never mind the jolly twenty that was room temperature. It was dark. Nothing but a wedge of grey light from the open door.

The dead pigs were a shock. In the dim light they looked like victims of a massacre, hanging there naked and headless. I put a hand out to touch one and the marbled flesh felt unsettlingly human. They swung back and forth as I moved through them and I was grateful there was no smell, but the sub-zero air lodged in my lungs had me doubled over in a coughing spasm. Putting a hand out to steady myself I caught the ribcage of a pig – it was razor-sharp and tore through my glove. Red spots beaded on my finger. It throbbed and I cursed myself for contaminating the scene – the last thing I needed was another bollocking from the Technical Bureau.

'Who told Lowry about this? How did he get here so soon?'

Kay wasn't listening to me. 'Bridge?'

She had her torch between her teeth, its white beam thick with frozen motes. She had her hands either side of an open pig's ribcage, her forehead creased. Attached to the same hook as the pig, was a human hand. It gripped the hook the same way a mother held onto a child that was being torn from her. My eyes moved down the arm that lay within the pig itself and the severed flesh where a shoulder should have been.

'I'm gloved.' I had pulled a second glove over my bleeding finger.

Kay looked at me like I was an idiot – of course I was gloved – it was a crime scene. Lucky her mouth was full of torch.

In the weak light the arm was porcelain and defenceless-looking. With pulpy fingernails and a reddish-yellow flower tattooed on the soft part of the inside arm. I took the torch from Kay's mouth and she gave a hard shudder that had nothing to do with the cold. She pressed the radio at her shoulder and was rewarded with a burst of unnerving static in the near-darkness.

'Container must be thicker than I thought,' she said.

'Call it in from outside – and ring Joe. We need to close the site fast – I'm thinking we close the whole Port?'

'Port Authority won't like it, but yes. All five hundred acres.'

She paused, then asked tentatively, 'Is it clean-cut?'

Her question bounced off the frozen blocks of pig. In the near darkness the metal hooks creaked, adding to my unease. The thought of other body parts or multiple victims hidden in the meat stayed unspoken between us.

'Not sure.' I strained to see. 'Can't tell – we'll have to wait for the State Pathologist. Come on, get the Tech Bureau here and call for uniforms to cordon off the site.'

Kay shoved her way past carcasses and made for the door.

'*What do you think you're doing?*'

It was the Harbour Policeman outside, shouting at someone.

'*You can't come in here! This is Dublin Port Company! You have to have a permit!*'

We stuck our heads out of the container and saw two middle-aged men with cameras at the top of the row. They looked put out.

'Jesus Christ, more reporters?' said Kay.

'Somebody must have rung them, told them they'd have an exclusive. Bet they're hacked off to see each other.' Pissed-off reporters was beginning to look like the high point of my day.

Kay fumbled with her phone. 'It's up on the *Daily Journal* website already! Yes, he's been inside the container – he's shown the arm.'

'Well, let's not give the reporters pictures of the cops looking at their camera phones – they'll make it into a dumb meme.' I sounded snarky, taking my anger at the situation out on Kay and my radio, punching the button on my shoulder and nearly knocking the radio out of its mesh pocket. '*Control and any units nearby, assistance needed to secure Dublin Port. We have a severed arm in a container.*'

A female voice acknowledged my request but told me I'd have to wait for uniforms.

'Get a call in to Raheny — go out as far as Howth if you have to,' I said. 'I need the Port sealed off. We have outside activity and the site will be contaminated.'

I'd said enough on the radio, not wanting to give the scanners any reason to congregate, but that stable door was hanging off its hinges — the boy and Lowry had taken off with their scoop and I was losing control of the crime scene. All I could do was wrap my tattered dignity about me and order the Harbour Policeman around.

'Dave! Move those reporters out of here! They have no authorisation!'

Bolstered by my badge, shiny-suit Dave seemed to light up and menaced his way over to the reporters, pointing towards the site entrance.

'*Watch the blonde — she's got a temper on her!*'

'*Who does the arm belong to?*'

I bared my teeth at the catcalling reporters, cursing Lowry and feeling like the baited fool I was.

Kay's voice floated towards me — in the commotion I'd forgotten her. 'Bridge?'

'Hold on, I'm coming!'

She was back in the container and I knew she'd be forming her own honour guard for the dead arm. I sidled back in, past a massive pig. We stood there with a shard of light from the open door making Halloween props of us all.

'You call Joe?'

Kay nodded and rubbed a greasy fingerprint off the front of her phone. 'Hope it's just some loon messing with dead bodies.'

'It's all right, Kay. For the moment that's all it is.'

I saw the hurt on Kay's face.

'It's not though, is it?' she said. 'Looks female. Someone's daughter.'

I put my arm across Kay's shoulders. 'We'll help her. We'll find out who did this. Come on, let's close up the scene. Do we call any of the Cigiri?'

Kay looked uncomfortable.

'No, Joe will have called the Technical Bureau and he'll be hacked off if we escalate it.'

'While you're at it call him again and ask him to pick up that boy and Lowry, no need to be gentle. Uniforms will be here in a bit to cordon the site off. Dave's coming into his own out there.'

Kay couldn't muster a smile. 'This is the first case we've been lead on.'

'Don't worry. Just tell Joe what's happened and ask him to give whatever Cig he wants the heads-up as well. Don't use the radio.'

Kay sagged as she walked out of the container, holding her battered mobile.

I looked at the bare arm. 'I'm sorry.'

I could pretend I'd seen it all before, that this was just another dead body part but something so fragile, so mutilated, hurt me cell-deep. My breath formed a white funeral veil in the freezing air. Outside the swollen sky capsized and it sounded like raindrops the size of a child's fist were beating at the iron container.

CHAPTER 2

Vans from television and radio were perched outside the Drugs and Organised Crime Bureau in Harcourt Square as reporters scuttled around in the rain. The microphones, cables and cameras strapped to their bodies made them look like shiny cockroaches. By the time I had a chance to look at Lowry's upload he'd done a voiceover in his best 'our intrepid reporter' style, telling the viewers they were looking at a severed arm stumbled upon by two DOCB detectives. Worse, the news networks had picked it up off the *Daily Journal* and it was now on a steady loop. No doubt the switchboard in Harcourt Square would be flooded with calls from families of missing persons – hope and dread in the same moment. The State Pathologist had taken the arm and the Technical Bureau were still at work, mapping the scene and running forensics – nothing more would be heard until both departments had finished their work.

It was a lovely idea to think that all the crimes in Ireland, above the pinching of a bottle of milk, were solved by twenty 'fellas' in a murder squad. A cabin fever of bogmen in tweed suits with notebooks. Romantic and useless, a portrayal of an Ireland that never got past *The Quiet Man*. The truth was rather more brutal. With nearly five million people living in Ireland, organised gang crime, drugs in most secondary schools, human trafficking and over three thousand kilometres of coastline, the notion of a Murder Squad was as antiquated as the notion that most gardaí had wellies in their car smelling of cowshite.

'*Harney!*' yelled Sergeant Joe Clarke. A man with the consistency of slime, slipping through your fingers if a straight answer was needed, but able to assume any shape at the sight of a superintendent.

'He sounds more bilious than usual — trouble at home?' I said to a detective with half his body inside a cavernous filing cabinet. He straightened, grinning, and asked if my scarf was choking me yet because, if it wasn't, Joe would. I put my hand to the comforting weight of the wool and feigned indifference.

Other than Joe's roaring, the squad room was quiet. Some of the team had opened an incident room and started to work-up a board with areas for victim identification, suspects, witnesses and crime-scene mapping. It was decent of them and a sign of respect. A grin started to pull my face up until Liam O'Shea, a bog-baller with a square face and hair fleeing the scene, all but knocked me over in an effort to avoid me. I could feel the heat off his face. He looked embarrassed when I winced, pain flaring in my side from where I'd taken the tumble in the freight yard.

'Sorry, Bridge. Are you okay? Don't lose the head, will you?'

It was a bit dramatic for just bumping into me.

'*Bridge!*' It was Joe again.

'*What?*'

I sounded pissy, but I could be like that. And stupid. A kind of immature bravado made me slow-walk to Joe's office in front of my colleagues, even though I could hear how irritated he was becoming.

Joe's face looked like he had a bad case of sunburn, which was unlikely in mid-November.

'You're on the television! Bloody Sky picked up the feed off *Dailyjournal.ie*! Yourself and Shanahan blundering around like two bickering auld ones at bingo. What the –?' Joe's anger seemed to struggle as he wasn't prepared to use curse words.

'Sarge, first off, I contaminated the scene. Kay did nothing and neither of us saw that boy –'

'Of course it was you, Harney! I don't need to be told that! Shanahan hasn't had a thought in years you haven't put in her head and I told that to the Super from the Tech Bureau when he rang me ten minutes ago, looking for your head on a plate, John the Baptist style. And I'm tempted to give it to him.'

I swallowed and tried to strengthen my voice. 'I understand your initial reaction but, Joe, I don't think this is the crime scene. It's not like the pig ate the arm.'

'Jesus, she's a pathologist as well! You're a real one-man band, Harney, and lucky that we answer to nobody but the Commissioner. Otherwise there's a row of Supers across I don't know how many stations looking for your body parts. You're off the case. I'm moving it to O'Shea and team.'

'*What!*' It exploded out of me. 'Are you serious?'

He held up a hand. 'My mind's made up. The press are involved. Lowry of all people! He'll be doing the big man on the *One O'Clock News*. You know what they're like in here if the media show up and that's down to you.'

'So you gave me this political pig-pie and the moment you find out it's something more you want to take me off the case?'

'Nobody stitched you up, Bridge.'

'I never said I was stitched up!'

'There's talk of a leak —'

'You think I leaked information to the media? Prove it!'

One of Joe's eyes had a tick. A kind of furious, popping movement that increased the more riled he became. It was building.

'Would you listen to the way you speak to your commanding officer, Detective Garda Harney? I don't need to prove it. We have a contaminated crime scene. Not to mention the TV cameras and reporters outside.' He puffed out his chest and repeated his words. 'TV cameras and reporters.'

'Are you serious, Sergeant Clarke? I'll go to the Cig with this.' I pushed the words out of tight lips.

'You be careful, Detective Garda Harney — threatening to go above my head on this! A Cigire's time is valuable — this is a matter I'll handle.'

'Not if I think you're being unfair. I can take it to the Workplace Relations Commission.'

'That's your answer to everything, isn't it, Bridge? Take it legal. Rubbing everyone's face in your barrister background. I'm taking you off this case because you've contaminated a crime scene and I've had complaints about you! About not sharing information with your management or colleagues. That's not going to work on a case the media are already poring over.'

'Cite them! There's nothing in my personnel file about that.'

I knew I sounded aggressive, but I was reeling. I'd no idea how to rescue the conversation. Joe taking the case from me wasn't a scenario I'd prepared for. I sat down and put both my hands on his desk, palms turned upwards in a gesture of supplication, and willed this conversation to come back down to earth. Where was my Verbal De-escalation Training when I needed it? It was only a month since I'd taken the course, but all I could remember was, 'How did that make you feel?'. You didn't have to be a genius to know that wasn't going to work.

'Would you listen to yourself? "Cite them." You don't seem to understand, Bridge. I assign the detectives here. You should've stayed chasing tuk-tuks for street coke or in the Sexual Assault Unit if you can't accept a commanding officer's decision! The only reason you're in this unit is your ability to present a case to the Director of Public Prosecutions.' Joe stopped speaking and rubbed an eye with the heel of his hand.

I stood up and my right leg moved forward with my weight pushed back onto the left leg: a fighter's stance.

'I didn't mean that, Bridge.' Joe suddenly looked old. 'You get great results but, you know, not everyone sees things from your perspective. O'Connor is looking at this.'

The particles in the air around me stopped moving. Detective Superintendent Niall O'Connor was a dangerous man who spent his time looking for an angle. On a good day he unnerved me, on a bad day he made me stupid and reckless.

'Why?' My body collapsed into the chair. 'He's not in our chain of command.'

Joe looked at his phone for a beat then shrugged – rumours ran rife a couple of years ago, about internal meetings being bugged by a new phone system. I had no idea if they were true, but Joe seemed cagey.

'You're off the case, accept it.'

'Can't do that, Joe. I'll take it to the Garda Sergeants' Association.'

I stood up again to show him I was serious. A breath of air puffed by me as Liam O'Shea opened the office door – it lifted a twist of hair off my forehead. Otherwise there was complete stillness in the office and surrounding squad room. I could feel eyeballs crawling across my back.

'Bridge,' said Liam O'Shea. He rested a beefy shoulder against the peeling doorjamb and pulled off some of the old veneer. It made a satisfying *tssssk* noise as it came away. 'Joe can probably talk the Tech Bureau down, but you know what the brass are like, particularly after the whistleblower and those *Prime Time* specials. They don't like reporters anywhere near the place.' He angled his head to catch my eye.

Joe moved from foot to foot, his bulk rippling, and I had a moment of sympathy for Mrs Clarke.

'So I'm the scapegoat? No way I'm putting up with that. I'm keeping this case. Have you ever taken a case off any other DOCB detective?' I glared at a silent Joe. 'I didn't think so.'

Kay barrelled in the door.

'Let's get a cuppa, Bridge, eh?' she said.

The air in the tiny office thickened with our exhalations.

'Come on, Bridge. Pick your battles,' said Joe.

Part of me wanted to give in, the part that wanted people to like me, the part that told me if I did what other people did I'd fit in. But then there was the set of their faces. All lined up against me. I could never back down in the face of so much opposition.

No one in the squad room could meet my eye as I left, making for the bathroom, my flat feet smacking against the scarred wooden floor, Kay in my wake.

The cleaners had just been in to give the ancient porcelain sinks a wipe. I looked in one of the streaked mirrors. My left eye was bloodshot.

'You okay, pal?' said Kay.

'No, I'm not! He's going to take us off the case and thinks women should be working in Vice because proper coppering is for lads.' I sounded petulant, even to my own ears.

'Joe never said that.'

'"*If you can't take a commanding officer's decision go back to the Sexual Assault Unit!*" And I quote.'

'Okay, that's what he said, but that's not what he meant. Joe thinks the world of you – some Super on the sixth floor rang down looking for the best detectives to go to the port and Joe sent us.'

'You're not seeing this for what it is.' I couldn't understand why Kay was so calm. It was as if I was running at full pelt for the bus, only to have the driver shut the doors in my face. 'If he thinks the world of me why is he taking us off this case?'

Kay looked like my question was rhetorical and said nothing.

'Why do I bother? Do you know every law firm in Dublin has female senior partners and managing partners? I could be working as a corporate lawyer in James Cox or Waterson's making a fortune and writing my own hours. Toughest thing I'd have to do is a share option agreement.'

'For greedy people you'd despise, Bridge. And you knew when you came in that the Force was decades behind, even by government standards.'

She rustled in her suit-jacket pocket and found two Murray Mints, putting one on the cracked countertop. I snatched it up and sucked out my aggression.

'And that's okay, is it?' I said. 'Jesus, Joe thinks 1970 was thirty years ago.'

Kay gave a tight grin. 'It's because Joe's so close to collecting his pension that he's careful.'

'So that's why he's taking the case away – because he's halfway out the door? Humiliating us in front of everyone. No wonder they all feel they have license to make fun of us.'

'Ah Bridge! You're the posh, horsey-faced bird and half of those fools in the squad room fancy you, so of course they bait you.'

'The ancient courtship ritual of the Irish male?' The mint was reducing in my mouth and I slurped at the sharp sweet menthol taste.

'See? That's the kind of stuff gets them all hot under the collar.'

Kay could always get me to smile, but it didn't change anything.

'I'm sorry . . .' It echoed around the tiled bathroom. 'I shouldn't have mouthed off at Joe. I don't want you to be penalised because of your association with me.'

My eyes dropped to the floor, a pattern so old it was back in fashion. The lukewarm heating wasn't dulling the nip in the air.

'Don't be a lemon – I'd follow you to the North Pole to look for Santa, Bridge. And Liam O'Shea will never take the case, no matter what Joe tells him to do. The lads accept you as one of them, no matter what you think. I would imagine Joe's praying you don't report him to the Garda Sergeants' Association. They'd hang him if they thought this had anything to do with gender.'

I rubbed my stinging eyes. 'Only because I could go to the media and there'd be a feeding frenzy. Maybe I should leave Joe hanging. Or just bloody quit the DOCB, get a posting down the country.'

'Hey! C'mon.' Kay handed me a paper tissue. 'Don't let them get to you. No more talk of quitting.'

Realisation dawned stupidly on me. 'Who gave the case to Joe?'

Kay shrugged her shoulders. 'It won't be on PULSE – the Park have started to use a generic field when they assign a case.'

'Joe mentioned O'Connor was looking at this. I bet he wants us off this case.'

Kay's body tilted forward, her small face alert. 'Jesus, Bridge, please be wrong about that.'

CHAPTER 3

DECLAN

Just off the M6 past Leicester, was Orton Way, turn left again and you were in an old cul-de-sac with no signs or branding, where three titanic industrial buildings with copper roofs the colour of acidic moss sat. Nothing out of the ordinary at ground level, but each basement housed a generator with boneshaking capability and eardrum-splitting whirring. No conversation was possible there when they were running. It was the shiny steel ball bearings that made all the noise. That's how I started in Lydia's old man's business, gave guided tours of his first facility, impressed potential customers with my knowledge of electronics and the possibility of feeding the National Grid. All of which I learned in five minutes from a Caterpillar salesman.

Old Man Burgess knew nothing about technology. He left school at fourteen and was cleaning windows when he saw a bloke fixing boilers. He started as an apprentice and built up a business then sold it off to Centrica. A real rags-to-riches story he never tired of telling anyone who'd listen. He stumbled into the whole data-centre thing in the noughties and would make up what he didn't know. He was car dealer selling cut-'n'-shuts as new, but the punters believed him. Success begets success – to hear Burgess you'd think he coined that phrase.

My Maserati had a customised paint job, James Bond blue. It was mixed in Maserati's headquarters in Modena. Cost well into four figures, but I wanted it to stand out from all the footballers' cars that littered Birmingham. I parked it outside the main reception area of Burgess Data Centre. I'd come straight from the gym and my hair was damp. I slicked it back and stood to my full height beside the car. The air was ice-pick cold and my nuts contracted up into my abdomen.

Some big lad with a bad haircut drove into the parking lot and got out.

'Can I help you?' I bit off every word, so he'd know there was no help for him here.

He closed his car door with a zealous clunk and flashed a West Midlands police badge at me. That caught my attention in a most unpleasant manner. The policeman pulled his belt up around his paunch with the other hand. I flexed my fingers to stop them making fists.

'Just wondering what was located here, sir?'

'Burgess Data Centre.' I shoved a smile on my face. 'Is this an official visit, officer?'

His curious expression told me my tone was wrong.

'Sometimes the alarm goes off and the alarm company calls the police,' I said.

'Why would that be, sir?'

I had overexplained and wanted to end the conversation. 'Lot of important client data held here.'

'Is that so?'

'Yes, officer, but it's all confidential. I can't show you anything.' I was babbling again.

'This place is hard to find, no signs or logos,' he said.

'It's supposed to be, Officer . . .' My nerves were showing, I couldn't remember his name even though I'd seen it moments ago on his badge.

'Chris Watkiss, sir.'

'Is there anything else, Officer Watkiss?' Panic was making me abrupt so I stopped speaking, not wanting to sound hostile.

We stared at each other during the silence.

'It's Detective Watkiss and no, sir, just curious.' He grinned, his front teeth like tombstones.

I watched him get back into a tired-looking Alfa, a 5500, my least favourite model. Its rear wheels scattered gravel on his way out and I stood there, transfixed at the sight of nothing. My breath coming in small, frosted puffs. Only the morning cold touching my legs through my suit pants brought me back and I forced myself to focus on my upcoming sales meeting as I walked into our high-tech reception.

The glass curtain-wall had recessed lighting and there was a desk made entirely from Nero Marquina marble, which made the whole area look futuristic. I caught my reflection in a mirrored surface and felt calmer. Our new receptionist eyed me up. I caught her gaze, held it, then closed my fist, letting her know her behaviour was inappropriate. Life had taught me it wasn't smart to soil your own cage. Unfazed, she fluffed dry-looking platinum hair. As always, I bolted up the stairs, leading by example. The movement calmed me. I took points off sales jocks who took the lift instead of the stairs and I wouldn't hire fat people. I got rid of a few butterball Burgess supporters when he retired.

My suit strained against my muscles as I checked the offices along my corridor. A quick head-bob in each doorway to find out who was at their desk, who was already on their way to a customer meeting, or who was late. This was my domain and I liked my employees to feel that.

My first meeting was at eight: sales and finance. I gave the sales guys a good bollocking, which is what they needed every Monday and twice on a Friday. My secretary knocked on the door and asked if she could bring in refreshments. I gave her a brusque nod and she put down coffee with a plate of nutty protein balls, but I didn't let anyone eat. The finance team looked harried as I checked the upcoming end-of-quarter exceptional expenses, closing the meeting early, too irritated to continue when I saw that Mike Burgess had taken a chunk of money out of the business.

After the meeting I checked my mobile. There was a breathy voicemail from a reporter who'd interviewed me a couple of weeks before, for a *Data Centre E-Zine*. She wanted a call back. I'd have to call her but couldn't face it right now so I sent a text instead, promising a call later in the week. She was a stupid woman who pushed harder the more I pulled away.

A bank of screens sat to the left of my desk. Sometimes I watched a match, but usually they were tuned to news stations. It looked great when clients came into my office, as though I spent my time analysing world events for opportunities and threats.

Sky News flashed in the corner of my eye. Breaking news . . . *Some butcher in the West Midlands could have been in for a grisly shock as a container of pigmeat from Doyles' Irish Meats Group, destined for distribution there, was found to contain a severed human arm. Fortunately, the arm was discovered before the container was shipped from Dublin. Viewer discretion is advised . . .*

The room fell away from me.

Pinpricks of light punctured my vision and danced off the flat, depthless screen. The remote lay within reach and I grappled with it, my slick fingers unable to get purchase. Some blonde woman cop was waving hands the size of shovels at a man, yelling at him to move off. The segment ran in a loop and the amateur footage showed the arm, hand gripping the pig hook, a flower tattoo on the lower inner arm. I hit pause on the remote, but shock got the better of me and I slipped off my chair. The knotted carpet weave burned through the backside of my trousers.

I looked up. Straight into the eyes of my secretary. The sight of her terror, at being caught seeing me on the floor, brought me back to myself.

She retreated rapidly.

I phoned Lydia.

'Turn on the news!'

'What? Declan, are you okay?'

'Just switch it on or Google "Dublin docks severed arm"!'

'*What!*'

'Just do it or you'll miss –'

'Oh Christ . . . '

'Are you okay?'

'Are you?'

'I don't know.'

'Maybe it's not her?'

'It's her, Lydia. Look at the tattoo.'

CHAPTER 4

SEÁN

Saint Martin's Gardens was my compound. A teardrop-shaped cul-de-sac off the East Wall Road built by Dublin Corporation, twenty-five two-up-two-down houses. No one got a house in the Gardens unless I said so. Didn't matter that the Corporation owned it. Anyone we didn't want we burned out. I kept the place well. Had the houses painted and dealers weren't allowed to live here. I didn't even keep our own stash here. With all the empty 'apartment' complexes NAMA was saving for the next building boom, there were plenty of places for me to set up my drug supermarkets. I didn't need to bring it home.

It finished raining. The air had a stiff quality after the downpour. I stood at my lintel and looked at the two teddy-bear pups playing in the front patch of garden. They dug at a piece of grass and I let a roar out at them. Poor little feckers cowered. I'd fostered them from the pound, two pit bull brothers. They'd been badly treated. I couldn't abide a person who was cruel to a dog. I remember being inside the house one evening and heard what I thought was a dog going under the wheels of a car. I'd run out to beat the head off the driver, but it turned out to be a shooting. One of my lads playing with his silencer. Blew a hole in his leg. Unfortunate.

'Lorraine!'

'Yes, Seán?'

She wore her bleached-blonde hair tied up in a wagging coil on top of her head. Saw some bird on the *X Factor* with her hair like that. It looked stupid, but Lorraine wasn't the brightest. She was loyal though.

'Will you get the bottles ready for the dogs? I'll feed them.'

The low winter sun came out, reflected in the window across the road and blinded me. I saw sunspots when I blinked – made me feel vulnerable. Someone could get the drop on me if they worked that out.

'Where's Gavin?' I said.

'Dunno, think he's in Number 7.'

'Riding again.' That irritated me, he was supposed to look after my protection detail. 'Where are the other lads? They should be on patrol – what am I paying them for?'

Lorraine ran out of the kitchen with two warm bottles of milk. They had that powdery, baby smell. I flipped them over and tested the heat of the milk on my wrist. Couldn't be too careful of the pups' mouths.

'*Wake up, yis lazy fuckers!*' Lorraine banged on the connecting wall.

'Don't swear, Lorraine. It lets me down and you let yourself down.'

'Sorry, Seán. I'll-knock-in-to-the-lads-next-door-get-'em-goin'.' Lorraine's words were clumping together like overcooked pasta. A sign she was nervous.

'It's all right, love.' I pulled her into an embrace and kissed her temple. This was as physical as I liked to get with Lorraine. Her skin was a clammy velvet.

'Yes, Seán.'

'You go and get the lads now.'

'Yes, Seán.'

She ran out the door in those stupid pink fluffy slippers she bought online. She was so thin her thighs were as skinny as her calves and she had a clickety-clack look to her. But I liked that and Lorraine knew her place.

The walls between these houses were made of thin, grey plasterboard – despite my adding premium insulation, every sound leaked. The lads had started to move around next door and Lorraine was screaming at them, her guttersnipe accent as audible as her intent.

I left her to it and turned on the telly. The sales guy had tried to sell me a fifty-two-inch television, but I wanted one with a sixty-five-inch curved screen. 'How big is your room, sir?' he had said. I'd smacked him in the mouth. A shiny red droplet appeared at the corner of his nose and he hadn't asked any more questions. He was right, though – the front room was so small I had to knock into the kitchen and get a custom-made semicircular couch for the window. So I didn't get screen blindness from being too close.

The pups sat on the maroon leather waiting for their milk. I shoved a bottle into each of their greedy maws and baby teeth gnashed on silicone teats, their ears pinned back and little beady eyes glinting with delight. It made me smile.

The docks flashed on the screen, yellowed with winter sun. The camera swung to a container and there she stood. Bridget Harney. That entitled bitch who wouldn't defend an innocent man over a misunderstanding. More information scrolled across the bottom of the screen about the gardaí investigating a container of pigmeat they said was tampered with. I laughed so hard I knocked the pups off the couch. They yowled, but I couldn't stop laughing. Some rent-a-cop in a polyester suit was trying to look important and Bridget Harney was running at a reporter. She stumbled over a block hidden in the overgrown gravel. I was holding my sides and snorting. She looked ludicrous as she staggered forward in giant steps, trying to regain her balance. When she fell I gave her a standing ovation.

'*Go on, Bridge!*' I said to the television. I hadn't enjoyed anything as much in a long time.

I might buy a Lotto ticket, then again I might not. Gambling was for mugs.

CHAPTER 5

BRIDGET

'How was your weekend?'

Such a simple question. It was from Kay, sitting at her side of the desk and smiling at me. There was no agenda.

'Quiet, but good,' I lied.

It was the same as every weekend for the last two years. Forty-eight hours drenched in adult nappies and wrestling with a fifty-nine-kilo woman who would go as stiff as an ironing board and scream when I tried to change her. Who walked in endless figures-of-eight looking for her own mother, a lost child – and who knew what else her rotting grey matter told her to search for? When Nata had come in this morning I'd charged out of the house and gulped the outside air with a mixture of relief and shame. This was my mother. Had I been this ill, she would never have left my side.

'Any news on the arm?'

'No,' said Kay, her mouth going down on one side.

Joe had relented, making sure I knew on what end of the wedge I stood, and we were still on the case. Whether my various threats had worked, or he had always intended to give us a second chance we didn't know.

One of the lads was devouring a bacon sandwich, the crispy meat crackling, at his desk just behind my back. My breakfast-less stomach yipped and saliva filled my mouth at the salty aroma.

I didn't see Paul Doherty. Kay did. I felt a thwack on my shin from under the table and reared up, about to throw out expletives by the lorryload. Kay threw her eyes at Paul and my gaze followed. He wasn't gorgeous by any stretch. His hair was grey with the memory of its darkness held in his salt-and-pepper beard. His eyes were too brown and hopeful for my liking. But he'd walked by, and ten minutes later I was still telling myself how I could never find him attractive.

'Bridge? Want to go for a coffee?' said Kay. She jiggled her wide hips.

I nodded and Liam O'Shea looked up. His desk looked like it had been hit by a Post-It sandstorm and I recognised Kay's handwriting on some.

'Get us a cappuccino, will you, Kay, if you're going to the Ritzy? And, hey, is there anything new on Venus de Milo?'

'You think that's funny?' I roared, annoyed that anyone would defile my case, but it was misplaced anger. The source of my irritation was the delay from pathology and forensics. 'Your chances of getting a coffee just fell by ninety per cent. Want to keep your mouth shut and hang onto that last ten per cent, O'Shea?' I glared at him.

'Okay, Bridge, take it easy.' He raised both hands.

'Don't talk with your mouth full, Liam,' said Kay and winked to take the sting out of her remark.

'When you're back, Kay,' said Liam, 'you might give me a dig-out with some births, deaths and marriages stuff? Have a look on the data portal thing? Need to find a missing person. Please.'

'Will do, Liam.'

We clattered down the cement backstairs of Harcourt Square into the soot-smelling air that was waiting for snow. A courier on a bike flashed by us, his sinews and bone melded with the gun-metal grey frame of his bike. I rounded on him.

'Watch where you're going! Idiot!' I yelled.

He gave me the finger as he weaved off the path and into traffic. I couldn't help but laugh. He was dexterous. My nose was already watering against the cold and I pulled my Trinity scarf across my face.

'Is everything okay?' said Kay.

'Course, why wouldn't it be?'

'You lost the head with Liam.'

'Did I?'

'Ah, Bridge, you know you did. I thought you were going to thump him. Liam was only asking about the case. It's not a sin to be interested. But, hey, did you see yer man, the new shrink? Won't mind the annual psych evaluations with him. Nice to see a good-looking fella. Particularly as they're so rare in the Square.'

I duffed her lightly on the shoulder. 'It's not that. I don't like Liam O'Shea giving orders. He's the same level as us. And I'm not up for our girl having nicknames like Venus de Milo.'

'I know, that was disrespectful, but it's just banter.'

'Oh yes, the great Irish "banter".' All manner of insults and sins were permitted in our squad room and labelled banter.

'Liam wasn't giving orders, Bridge. He's a good bloke and you rise to him too quick. But I know you, lady, you're changing the subject. You liked the shrink, I saw you looking at him.'

'So?'

'So? What's with the tone?'

'You wouldn't get it. And Liam's a lazy git, always looking for help with the systems. Using you.'

I knew I'd hurt Kay's feelings and I didn't like myself for it, but I detested when she talked about men – it only ended with me getting vexed. I focused on work, put my juice there, kept the team clearance rate in the black – fair enough not all of them would make it to a conviction but our names in lights on the PULSE dashboard was down to me.

Kay folded into herself like a concertina. 'What's wrong with helping a colleague?' She had her back to me. 'Nice to be able to call in a favour once in a while.'

'A favour? From Liam O'Shea? What use would that be?'

Kay turned up the collar on her navy suit and said nothing. We walked in silence towards the Ritzy, a café that had been in the shadow of Harcourt Square feeding hungry gardaí forever. It had wooden cladding someone thought was a good idea in the eighties. It wasn't, but the aroma of baked bread and melting cheese drew the punters in, despite the décor.

'Toasted special and an Americano?' I looked into Kay's face and tried to get a smile from her.

She found a table at the back without answering me.

I ordered, then sat facing Kay. She was fiddling with the sugar, flicking grains off the table. Target practice.

'Look, I'm sorry,' I said. 'I ... I ... hate letting my guard down, you know?'

'Oh, I know, Bridge.'

'I don't want to be evaluated by a psychologist. That's all. I shouldn't have been snotty when you said he was good-looking. He is, but I loathe psychological evaluations. I don't see why we have to have them. I don't want someone prying around the basement in my head.'

Kay blinked.

I hated the silent treatment.

'Come on, Kay.'

The waiter put our order on the table.

I wolfed into the crunchy, toasted bread and Kay bit through a string of melted cheese.

'You know, Bridge, most people don't see psych eval as someone prying around their basement. And, by the way, we have them bi-annually now.'

I paused mid-bite, but Kay chose to ignore my horrified face.

'I'm not looking forward to mine,' she said, 'but I'm not dreading it either. Most people see it as a chance to talk about the challenging aspects of the job. A help.'

My eyes found the ceiling.

'Don't throw your eyes up to heaven at me, Bridget Harney! And while we're on the subject of help. I don't mind helping the other lads. I'm good at research, maybe even the best in the squad, so I like helping them. Being part of the team.'

'You don't need them! You have me.' I couldn't understand why Kay would choose the lads over me.

Kay's eyes widened but her voice stayed low. 'It's not them or us. I know your conviction rate is fantastic. So do all the other lads.'

'Like O'Shea? Whose last case was thrown out at petty sessions? The idiot all but gave his perp an inducement to confess. This isn't television, Kay.'

'And you certainly told him that.' Kay kept her voice steady and took another bite of her sandwich, leaving teeth marks in the soft cheese.

'You think I humiliated O'Shea?'

'You don't?'

'It wasn't aimed at him. He broke Judges' Rules, and I had to show Joe that we know not to do that.'

'Bridge, Joe knows you have the legal stuff nailed. How do you think the rest of the squad see us? The team treat me like your apprentice.'

She had worked herself up until her face was a blotchy purple, but she had a point. I hated when Kay called me out like this. Truth was she kept me grounded, but I didn't tell her that. Instead I rounded on my one supporter.

'Do you think two female detectives in the DOCB are anything other than window-dressing? That's why I have to solve this severed-arm case. This isn't a community station where everyone's equal and willing each other on. This is the DOCB and it's full to bursting with career police. Male career police.'

'I know that! I was in the room when the Commissioner gave the recruiting speech!'

'Then support me and stop muttering! How many female detective sergeants are there in the DOCB?'

Kay's shoulders sagged. 'None. But I would like to remind you that we were promoted to detective four years after graduation – that's a stellar rise by anyone's standards. We got into the DOCB two years later.'

I opened my mouth but Kay held up her hand.

'I'm not saying it wasn't difficult for women years ago, but a lot has changed and I want us to be part of a team. Be able to call for help if we need it.'

'I don't need help and you can think again if you expect me to ask for it. Nothing gets done unless I do it myself.'

Kay brushed off the crumbs on her suit, the noise of clanging cutlery suddenly intruding.

'I gave up the law to do this, Kay. And people like Lowry called me "an overprivileged dabbler" when I did.'

'Jesus, did you memorise that article?'

'My father's never forgiven me. I have to make detective sergeant, if only to show him I made the right choice.'

'Okay, but you don't have to be so angry about it. You weren't always like this. You used to be a great laugh when we were training in Templemore. Are you still doing your night jogs?'

'No, and since when am I not good fun?' I didn't want Kay's answer to that. 'I can't jog any more, in case Mum needs me during the night. And we're not in Templemore, that time's gone. You do realise we have over 500 – active – gang death threats in Dublin city alone?'

'Don't lecture me, Bridge. And since when is it up to you to sort all of them out?'

'How many relate to Seán Flannery's crime family?'

Kay shrugged. Her boxy-looking jacket made her look stubborn.

'My tout tells me over thirty per cent. Either issued on his orders or ratified by him.'

Kay paused and put her cup down carefully. 'Your tout? Are you running someone outside the Covert Human Intelligence System?'

There was a lousy silence. I had opened my mouth to answer when she raised a hand.

'You know what, don't tell me – it's just another thing I'd have to lie about if Joe asks.' She made a pinching movement with her fingers, like she was trying to snap something. 'How good is this information? Most of the threats come from the two main feuding families. Flannery doesn't figure at all. In fact, no one rates Seán Flannery except you. He's not even a small-time enforcer — he lives in a corporation house, doesn't have a car or a driver's licence and is rarely seen outside.'

'That's subterfuge.'

'It isn't, Bridge, it's just his shitty little life. You're obsessed with Flannery, have been since you joined the Force.'

'No, I'm not!'

'And if I know you're obsessed with Flannery you can bet your tout does too. Do you ever wonder if he's simply telling you what you want to hear? Touts always need a few quid.'

I stayed silent. I had tried to convince Kay on any amount of occasions of Flannery's cunning but I had clearly failed.

'Either way, why does it have to be you that stops him?'

My eyes cut to the left, not because I wanted them to, but because unconscious memory took over. Every time I spoke about Seán Flannery I was back in Cloverhill Prison, looking at his shark-bite of a smile. In my hand a picture of a damaged eleven-year-old girl I had failed.

'It just has to be me, Kay.'

CHAPTER 6

The squad room air wobbled with the smell of stale vegetable soup. I hoped someone had left their flask open rather than eaten and exhaled. There always was the question of what end it came from.

'All right, lads, Tech is back!' I called out louder than was necessary and felt heat flood to my neck.

It was my first time to address the squad as lead detective and I wanted to sound enthusiastic, not hard of hearing. I clicked on the whiteboard, and mercifully it came on first time. I'd uploaded everything the Technical Bureau sent me to a memory stick. I clicked the icon and held my breath. My first slide had the Garda navy background with no info visible. In the sudden dark, the squad room took on the appearance of a night club. The lads laughed like I was the comedy act before the floor show. I scrolled down to my second slide where I knew I had a white background and the information flashed up on the screen.

Biúró Theicniúil – Garda Technical Services Bureau and Forensic Science Ireland covering crime scene mapping, fingerprints, DNA recovery.

State Pathologist's Office: post mortem.

All information will be on your dashboard on Police Using Leading Systems Effectively: PULSE.

I had spelled everything out on the slide to look as professional as possible, but I'd inadvertently switched on the overhead projector and stood in a blinding haze.

'Deer in the headlights eh, Bridge?'

The lads jeered as I fumbled with the laptop, trying to cut the wireless connection with the overhead projector. If I'd been trying to light up the overhead and the whiteboard at the same time, I'd never have managed it.

'Settle down!'

It was Joe Clarke's high-pitched voice that sliced through the laughter. He leaned against his office doorjamb and slurped his tea.

'Someone get her a cuppa,' he said in a no-nonsense voice.

Joe's comments were helpful, but God hadn't made me the type to look grateful. Liam O'Shea stomped up on a table and cut the projector's power at source. Normal light resumed. Kay plonked a mug of mahogany-coloured tea in front of me and I had the shakes. I held it two-handed to keep the tea from slopping out.

'Right, can everyone see?' I said.

Most heads moved in the affirmative, not all eyes looking at me yet.

'First off, I'd like to thank Kay for all the work she's done on this with me.'

Kay went a surprised pink and I had a moment of unease, wondering if I'd ever thanked her before, publicly.

'Crime scene is back. It's quick so I'll take that first.' I didn't wait for questions.

I was dismayed at how light and nervous my voice sounded. I'd taken off my scarf in an attempt to look more open and had hung it over the back of my chair. I missed it now. The rough feel of the wool, the comforting weight at my mouth. I felt bare.

'Crime scene was mapped for presentation in court, when it comes to that, but it's a clean scene –'

'Professional or rubbed down, Bridge?' said a voice and derailed me like a flagman with a stop sign.

'Questions at the end, you know that, lads.' It was Joe again.

I didn't know what to make of the white-knight act and locked eyes with Kay. She was willing me on, I could see it burning in her. I swallowed and thought of the times I'd faced ill-tempered judges, lying defendants and bored jurors.

'It's more than rubbed down. The whole site was clean, which means whoever did this used masks, hazmat suits and placed the arm. If you were expecting the luminol to light up like Funderland, you'd be disappointed. Just stray prints, fibres and hair follicles we have no matches for. We're checking with the Doyles' workers who loaded the pigs and my guess is we'll get matches there. Whoever did this had time with minimal interruptions, which isn't as unlikely as it sounds. That yard is at the back of the docks, the East Wall end, and only has two lads in a van patrolling it. They have a solid routine which anyone watching them for a few days would figure out.'

Joe nodded at me.

I was warming up and my vocal chords had found that depth I remembered from the courtroom.

'In conclusion, I would say it's gangland. It has the hallmarks of a well-thought-out professional job.' I raised my hand into a fist and listed off items by raising a finger for each one. 'Preparation – surveillance – protective clothing – forensic awareness – confidence. Usually reserved for big cash and jewellery jobs.'

My hand was in a high five. I'd found my groove.

'Question is why? Why did this girl merit so much attention?'

The air in the room was heavy, but the team's faces were tense with effort, no one getting up for water or toilet breaks. The mouse clicked as I scrolled down to the next screen. A picture of the detached arm on a stainless-steel pathologist's workbench. Kay closed her arms over her chest. I wanted to do the same but stayed the impulse.

'Pathology send their apologies about the delay, but the arm was frozen solid and you can't just thaw out an arm. It had to be defrosted by emersion in saline at a constant temperature of 37 degrees Celsius or much of the tissue would've been damaged. The external exam shows a severed arm, weighs 6.5kg, female, white, visibly small bone structure. Extrapolated weight according to pathology, 57kgs. Nails are manicured – however, the manicure had decomposed as the fingers were soaked in acetone, we assume to remove any traces under the fingernails. There is a tattoo of a yellow-and-red orchid on the lower inner arm – a standard pattern, but right now one of the only identifiers we have. The arm has a coating of fake tan and was cut,' I looked down and consulted my notes, 'just above the humerus at the glenoid cavity. Not a clean, surgical cut, but done by someone who knew where to cut to minimise the amount of bone they'd have to saw through. Someone with time. The cut is jagged. Pathology believe a small power tool was used. Port-mortem lividity suggests the arm was severed after life was extinguished.'

There were a few sighs, but the relief was short-lived.

'Tox screen is clear but analysis shows she was pregnant.'

Silence.

I sought refuge in the coils of steam that rose from my tea.

'Time of death is thrown off by freezing but pathology says she was murdered in the ninety-six hours between the 3rd and 6th of November. They can't be any more specific than that. Manipulation of a corpse is all we'd get in court, based on what we have, and there's no murder scene, but I believe we'll turn up the rest of this girl at some point.'

All eyes on me now. Kay made a circling motion with her forefinger and mouthed 'keep going' but I was in fact done.

'Bone-density scan puts our girl's age at somewhere between twenty-two and twenty-five,' I concluded and scanned the room. 'Right. Are there any comments or questions?'

'Are we looking for a sex worker?' Question number one from Liam O'Shea.

'We can't tell anything from the arm. There's nothing that would give us a hint of where the victim worked or lived.'

Raised eyes and accompanying groans, but one pair of eyes were shining at me. Kay gave a thumbs-up.

'Good summary,' said Joe. He cleared a wad of phlegm from his throat. 'But limit resources on this to two weeks. It's grains of sand stuff.'

I acknowledged his comment with a curt nod.

'All right – if there's no further questions I'll divvy out the workload,' I said. 'Liam O'Shea, take missing persons please. Widen the net to six months looking at runaways, strays, office workers on late-night drinks. Split the city into zones and start with East Wall – maybe she was local to where she was found. Use O'Keefe and Walsh to help you.' I pointed at two lads standing at the back of the room and they shifted from foot to foot.

'Right, Bridge,' said Liam.

'Kay and I will see if the victim's tattoo is exclusive to any salon. Maybe she put it up on social media? Or the salon put it up on Instagram? We'll check with Ruhama and the couple of Irish girls still working the street, see if we can find anyone who might recognise the tattoo. See if any of the girls are worried about someone who's gone missing recently.'

I clicked off the whiteboard.

'Profile is up on the DNA database for anyone who wants further details.' I plucked the memory stick out of the whiteboard to signify the end of the session.

A couple of the lads said, 'Thanks, Bridge,' and I tried not to look pleased.

The pressure in the room changed as the lads opened doors and started to leave the briefing. A white breath of air came from outside. I could feel it cooling the ruddy skin on my face.

Kay was beckoning to me, her eyes hopping out of her head.

'Well done, you!' she said in a half-whisper, half-shout. 'Come on, we'll get a head start and I'll help you update the dashboard on PULSE.'

'Thanks, Kay. Is that lad you were on the course with still based in the National Central Bureau?'

'No, he's moved. Gone in as detective sergeant to the embassy in Madrid.'

'Bully for him, but no good for us. Do you know anyone else in Interpol?'

'No, and they're a difficult shower to deal with at the best of times. You want to put her up on their database? You don't think she's local?'

'I don't think anything, other than this is the first case we're lead on and I'm going to check every system and every possibility. But she could be from a pop-up brothel.'

'They're like a plague,' said Kay. 'Does Joe still have that pal in the Protective Services Bureau? They'll have an idea who's actively trafficking girls.'

'Yes, I sent him an email about it, but his contact says it's like whack-a-mole at the moment with brothels moving location every week.'

I pulled a rickety old chair over to her side of the desk. It protested when I put my weight on it. A sickly-sweet violet smell was pssshed into the squad room.

'Christ, what's that?' I reached for my scarf, wrapping it around my mouth and nose, flying-ace style.

'Joe was told the smell is awful in this squad room, so he bought a few aerosols.'

'Wish he hadn't.'

Kay fired up the ancient terminal she and I shared.

'Is this the only terminal with access to the DNA database? What happened to the app?' I watched as Kay punched clunky grey buttons the size of marshmallows.

'Bridge, take that scarf out of your mouth. Do you ever read your emails? Last set of outside developers got the app interface wrong – same crowd that are responsible for the lost breathalyser tests. Now we're back to hardwired networks. This links directly into Forensic Science Ireland and you can upload to their main server.'

In a few clicks Kay had the interface up.

'I'll put a flag on it, so if I get any sight-of-file requests the system will notify me with an email.'

I must have looked like a dog who thought he'd seen his owner throwing a treat, only to find it was sleight of hand.

'How do you do that, Kay?'

'Here.' Kay pointed to a miniscule box on the bottom left of her screen. 'It's new. If you tick this box on your profile and you receive a sight-of request, PULSE will generate an email to your account.'

'Will it show the police force and the detective who asked for the files?'

'Don't know, I've never had one, so it'll be interesting to see how it works, but the lead times from Interpol are awful. They're taking longer than ever to respond and the UK have started to bypass them, going straight to the Park.'

Joe was standing to my left, watching us.

'Hiding behind screens, your generation. Time was we just picked up the phone to one another.'

'You can't do that any more,' said Kay. 'Audit trails and GDPR —'

'We didn't have the luxury of time! You could get a call with a code word and it was all go. You had to be able to make a decision.' He gave an awkward swing of his body, throwing his foot forward, and made for his office.

'Is he okay?' I kept my voice low.

'Wife's still in their place in Spain, finds the winter too harsh here. No early retirement for Joe.'

My mouth formed a silent O.

'Come on.' Black-and-white cross-hatching pulsed across the bottom of Kay's screen. 'This could take twenty minutes, maybe more to complete. Will we go down and see if the bread machine in the canteen is fired up? I'd love a bit of fresh brown soda.'

I didn't need to answer. I reached into my drawer for my fine-cut homemade marmalade, a perfect accompaniment to brown bread, and popped the lid. Bitter orange filled the air.

CHAPTER 7

'Your mother's evening meal is ready,' said my father.

For the Judge, Mum had gone from 'Elizabeth' to 'your mother' with the onset of dementia.

'Come on, darling,' I said to her as though she were a small child and the look of innocence in her eyes was that of a young creature. 'Dinner's ready.'

She gave me a bird's wing of fingers and rings with which to pull her up.

'Did you have a good day, Bridget?'

'Yes, Mum.'

'Do you have any friends at the station you'd like to ask over?'

'Not tonight, Mum.'

'Well, your friends are welcome here anytime.'

'Thanks, Mum.' I kissed her temple. She smelled of lavender and bergamot soap with a hint of the cinnamon apple tarts she had spent her life baking.

We walked to the huge kitchen and into an arched alcove my father's mother had referred to as the 'small dining room', a pleasant savoury steam from Nata's dinner tickling our noses.

'Umm, yum,' said Mum and took a baby's-mouth breath. 'Did you have a good day, Bridget?'

'Yes, Mum.'

'Do you have any friends at the station you'd like to ask over?'

'Not tonight, Mum.'

I smiled at her lovely face and prayed that her memory would come back, or that this vile disease would just halt and leave her alone. I promise I'll never ask for another thing. I'll never ask for a lucky break or a Lotto win. I'll never want direction on a case or a piece of crucial evidence to land in my lap. I'll never even ask for Seán Flannery to make a slip-up, I'll get him on my own, if you just give me back my mother. Even for a day.

I steered Mum to her seat as Nata served up the rich goulash. I tasted a barbeque smokiness on the air and it made me realise how hungry I was. She had puréed Mum's dinner into a manageable mush. I looked at Nata, this stout woman with her broad face, and mouthed my thanks. She nodded and retreated to the kitchen area. I knew she would soon slip on her coat and head off for the night, closing the door soundlessly on her way out.

We had a quiet house. This was my father's domain and he had an aversion to raised voices, other than his own. He sat in his usual place. At the head of the table.

'How do you think your mother is faring? Well?' He picked up his spoon, rubbing the already clean utensil in his napkin. He scooped up a small amount of sauce from the side of his bowl and carefully blew on the steaming stew. His fastidious movements were hypnotic.

I looked at Mum. 'How are you doing, Mum?'

'Good, or at least not so bad today. How are you, Judge?' My mother had started calling him Judge instead of Vincent and he hadn't stopped her.

He didn't answer her. He took a pinch of salt from the cellar on the table and sprinkled the grains on his food. He was a vigorous man with a head of thick white hair. He exuded strength and energy, even at seventy-four. I was told I took after him. I hoped not.

'I think we need more carers. It's important your mother isn't left on her own.'

'She isn't, is she? Are you, Mum?'

'I went to the Merrion Centre today. Nata took me and we had our lunch out.'

'Your mother went to the Merrion Centre last week,' said my father. 'She went to the day care centre today. Nata took her to the one in Blackrock.' His voice was flavoured with impatience.

I stayed silent while he chewed his food. There was no point in trying to anticipate him. He regarded me as a baffling perversion and it was mutual.

'So you've had a good day, Bridget?" he asked then.

'Fine,' I answered guardedly and waited for the inevitable attack.

It came.

'Studied law at Trinity and Kings Inn, then became a bangharda?' he said. 'I ask you, who does that?'

My father's tone was conversational, even lively, as though wondering about a tricky crossword clue.

'You know, Judge, that police officers are all called gardaí now. The term bangharda or 'woman guard' was phased out in nineteen-ninety as it's sexist and demeaning.' I kept my voice low and my tone sweet, as if this were the first time we'd had this exchange.

'They used to look like navy-clad airhostesses when they came into the courtroom. Much better than the clumpy trousers and stab vests they wear now.' He let out a small sigh. 'I'm not trying to wind you up, Bridget — it's just the way I remember it. And I think if you had just let me help you a little in the law —'

'Please don't, Your Honour.'

'Am I not allowed to be afraid for you? You're armed, Bridget.'

It felt like a criticism. 'Were you going to say something about Mum's trip to Blackrock?'

He gave a small sigh. 'I believe your mother might be happier if she had a carer in the evening time. Someone to put her to bed and help with her medication. You being a detective doesn't allow for consistency in arrival times and your mother's having increasing difficulty at night with the bathroom.'

Mum looked at us as though we were an abstract painting she was viewing in a gallery. She'd lost the ability to work out the Judge's code. Alzheimer's will do that to you. Mind you, I was struggling and allegedly had all my faculties.

'Are you having problems sleeping, Judge?' I said. It was pathetically passive aggressive, but as close to defiant as I could get with my father.

'I manage.'

'You're sure?'

He didn't answer. There wasn't much more to say, so we ate in silence. I walked to the kitchen counter and filled a jug with water, more to give myself time to work out what my father meant. The Judge's words would never give him away. I cut hard limes into quarters and their biting, green smell perfumed the air. Some 'Adventurous Over-Sixties' holiday flyers were pinned to the gingham kitchen noticeboard, nestled beside Mum's meds timetable. A jaunty chap and his lady looked out at me from an arctic background. It made me mad. Not the proper adult anger that fuels debate and opinion, where someone's behaviour might change. But the choking, childish rage built on injustice. It was so unfair that my mother couldn't remember what it was to have a good conversation, yet here was my philandering father planning some type of getaway.

I went back and sat down on the horsehair-stuffed chair too quickly and was rewarded with a single wiry hair piercing right through to my thigh, the short pain in tune with the thought of my father's planned tryst. I derided myself for my cowardice. I should have spoken up for my mother, but my father liked nothing better than 'a measured debate', which anyone else would have called a row. I would end up snuffling back stupid tears and he would raise his eyes to the ceiling and start counting to ten.

My father ate bread and marmalade at the end of dinner. Every dinner. It was a habit he'd picked up years ago from his parent's undergardener, with whom he'd shared many meals and jars of conserve in this old kitchen. Of course, for the Judge routine was everything. Now, the marmalade was in a crystal cut-glass pot with a small silver lid. Some grovelling junior counsel had commissioned it when my father took the bench. It had his initials engraved on the lid and my father didn't like anyone else to use it. So I did.

I took some of the bread and mirrored his meticulous buttering. No edge left without a yellow coating. We were in sync. I took the marmalade first and lifted the jar out of my father's reach. He pursed his lips but said nothing. I took the engraved lid off, making sure to leave buttery fingerprints on it. I stuck my knife into the thick, jelly jam, fished out a chunky piece of rind and popped it into my mouth. It tasted like sunshine, fermented under glass. My father sucked air in through his teeth. I moved the marmalade to my left, out of his reach.

'Would you please pass the marmalade, Bridget?'

'Oh sorry, Judge, I didn't know you wanted it.' I sent the jar whizzing down the conker-coloured table.

'*Oh sorry, Judge, I didn't know you wanted it,*' said my father *sotto voce*.

CHAPTER 8

It had been a tiring, unproductive day — nothing but circular conversations and dead-end leads on the severed arm. Joe didn't appear to be fully reconciled with me leading the case and the press were still crawling all over the station. To top it off, I'd been drafted into the bureau's first wave of mandatory psych evaluations. I could sense Joe's hand behind that.

When I arrived home the main hall was in darkness, with just one floor lamp left on, to take the edge off the gloom. My mother was sitting in her armchair in the small sitting room, the open fire crackling in the grate beside her, a rich peat smell from the burning turf. Mum was wearing her nightdress and a heavy wool dressing gown with a fluffy nightcap pulled down around her ears. She looked like a little merino sheep.

I dropped my coat and bag, popped a kiss on her head, then made for the drinks cabinet and a glass of peachy Albarino.

My mother was looking down at the floor, her forehead

knotted, perhaps looking for her beloved collie. I couldn't face telling her the dog had been dead for over a decade. I took a mouthful of my wine and let the mineral aftertaste sit on my tongue.

She looked up at me.

'Who are you?' She was beaming at me. 'You're a lovely girl.'

'It's me, Mum. Bridget.'

'Bridget?' She turned my name over in her mouth. 'Bridget.'

'That's right, Mum.'

'You're a policewoman.'

'That's right, Mum, a garda.'

She nodded and looked right into me. 'You're a detective. A good one.'

It was her rare moments of clarity that sliced me. Her eyes clouded.

'Did I have my breakfast, Bridget?'

'Yes, Mum, it's bedtime now. Are you hungry?'

'No. Should I have breakfast?'

'Not now, sweetheart. Would you like some toast?'

'I don't know.' She gave a wide yawn, her shrivelled toothless gums reminding me of tinned pink grapefruit segments.

'Come on, let's get you up to bed . . .'

She followed me out of the room and up the stairs like an obedient child. I pointed her towards the cavernous room she shared with my father, although he slept in his dressing room now. So, as well as losing the story of her life, he wasn't even in the bed as a bookmarker — no one to help her find her place.

I watched her walk into her own room with the timid politeness of a stranger finding themselves in family quarters, then followed to take off her dressing gown and settle her in. I'd moved out of the main house when I joined the gardaí. Painted up one of the old outhouses and fired in a potbellied stove. I was happiest there, but I'd had to come back into my father's house when Mum's short-term memory turned out to be full of holes.

I opened the double door to my old room.

When I think of it now, I realise my bedroom was quite a grand space for a child. An upstairs room at the front of the house, permeated with the smell of cloves from stargazer lilies that sat on a table on the landing. My home was a pastel-blue Georgian pile – on over an acre – it was a showstopper and if you lived in South County Dublin, you knew our home. People would look at me and gasp, 'Oh, that house!' I was born in the eighties, but my room didn't reflect that. It had a period feel to it with powdery cornicing and a chandelier that looked like it was spun from sugar. A large fireplace dominated the room – if not lit on a winter's night you could suffocate from the cold. As a child I would look out at the garden, into the playing pitches of the school next door, and on to the city beyond, as the parquet floor touched the whorled pads of my bare toes. A door led on to the corridor and my parents' bedroom suite on the other side of the landing. What I remember most about my room was feeling lost in it, I scrunched in a corner with a doll's house and a bald Teddy, who despite his tired appearance was as brave as a lion. Much braver than I. The wind rattled my windows at night as it blew down Cross Avenue, banging to get inside and gobble me up.

My bed was an enormous pink four-poster confection – a little like a French fancy. As a child, I thought I was a guest in this house and that the room was simply waiting for me to grow up – move on. So that it could get back to the business of hosting weekend guests, who affected a world-weariness on arrival but were, as I saw on many occasions, intrepid night explorers.

My phone vibrated, scratching against my unfinished glass of wine. A text from Kay asking me over to her house for dinner tomorrow. I closed my eyes, so grateful to Kay Shanahan and her hygge home. The thought of her company was the only thing that would get me through my psych evaluation in the morning. I took my over-the-ear headphones out of their foam case and stripped down to my underwear. With the volume turned up as far as it would go I immersed myself in a hard-rave, free-form mix I'd taken from Spotify. I threw my body around my room in an imitation of dance, until I was slicked with sweat, wave after wave of eardrum-splitting music giving me release.

CHAPTER 9

The beech trees some viceroy had planted on Wellington Road would be stencilled black against the sky in a week or so, as winter breezes stole their leaves. I walked quickly, the wine from last night and the anxiety about my upcoming meeting mixed in my empty stomach. I was glad for the sharp morning air. On the way to Paul Doherty's clinic, a childhood memory surfaced, of visiting this road when my father's sister was alive. She had looked down her knife of a nose at my mother and said, 'You can't expect to keep a man like Vincent if you don't look after yourself.'

It was early, but I'd told Paul seven o'clock was the only time I could manage this week. That wasn't true, I just wanted to get it over with. Light hadn't broken through the morning darkness, blinds were still drawn but family life was resuming: a type of Chinese shadow play. I followed the directions Paul had sent me and arrived at his practice in a mews in Wellington Lane – it looked like his home as well. A neat two-storey in a straw-coloured brick with an airy extension and a sign for his practice. I hit the wireless bell and was surprised by the tinny Westminster chimes, too late realising I might be waking a family.

'Morning, Bridget,' said Paul. He rubbed his hands together against the cold and his breath fogged between us.

I wore my Trinity scarf high up my face like an outlaw, the wool side turned in and absorbing my breathing. It gave me a closed-for-business look.

'Come in, come in.' He backed down the hall and into an open-plan space.

'I didn't disturb your family, did I?'

'No, no. Just me here.'

That told me a little, but not enough. I looked around for pictures of a wife or children, but the only framed pictures were of Paul with an older couple and judging from the likeness they were his parents. The other picture was him with a group of scuba divers all suited up with wet heads. I got ready to quiz him about diving, but he forestalled any questions by gesturing to some chairs beside a red stove.

'Bit of a cold snap,' he said.

The stove wasn't lit but radiated heat from the previous day. He had a tray of tea things and hot toast pooled with butter waiting. The room was neat to the point of a mental disorder.

'Thanks, Paul, this is nice.' I blushed, thinking I sounded like I was on a date. 'I mean, there's no need for all this – just for me – for just meeting me.' Too many words in my mouth getting backed up.

He looked at me, a curious stare. 'It's no bother, Bridget. I'd do this for any early meeting.'

'Call me Bridge.' I was an ugly crimson colour, my face

reflected in an edgy waterfall mirror on the back wall.

The sun started to come up, giving the room a less intimate feel and I was thankful for that.

'You went to "Trinners for Winners".' He nodded at my scarf. 'Me too.'

He would have read about my education in my file. I didn't like that he had information on me while I knew nothing about him. He was gorgeous-looking though, there were no two ways about that, and if I couldn't tell anyone I could at least admit it to myself. He had a few years on the clock, but that only made him easier on my eye. I smeared my toast with a fine-cut marmalade and inhaled the citrus tang heightened by the warm bread.

'Nice.' My mouth was full – not such a good look for a grown woman. 'It's Little Chip, isn't it? I prefer it to Old Time Irish. Did you buy it in Donnybrook Fair on Baggot Street?'

'Yes.' He smiled at me. 'Not many people can tell the difference.'

'I can. Little Chip is more like a jelly and is sweeter while Old Time Irish is thick-cut, a little more pith in the flavour. But both beat all the Bonne Maman conserves and other brands that have flooded the market. Nothing as good as homemade though. I make my own.'

I had hoped to come across as an interesting person with a hobby but sounded more like a lunatic with a marmalade fetish. I shrugged and stopped shovelling food into my face. Paul handed me a napkin and I dabbed the melted butter off my lips.

'You know why you're here, Bridget?'

'Yes, but is it professional to have this meeting outside of Harcourt Square?'

'Yes – I've cleared it with your management.'

Was he talking about that buffoon Joe Clarke?

'Last year a number of your colleagues said they didn't find Harcourt Square conducive.'

'Conducive to what?'

'Unburdening yourselves, I suppose. It's a tough job and not getting any easier . . . some of the things you experience are hard to . . . assimilate.'

I nodded. In previous years the psych eval had been a tick in the box. I was aware that outside pressure, fuelled by commissions and independent reports complaining about working conditions, meant that new approaches had to be taken. This must have been one of them.

'You had a colleague you graduated with, Jeanne Healy, who went missing. Does that still affect you?'

I was glad I wasn't holding anything. I might have dropped it. I knew Jeanne going missing right after graduation was on my personnel file. I'd assaulted another officer whom I suspected wasn't telling the truth about his association with Jeanne. Kay had to pull me off him, but I still managed to fracture his jaw.

'Bit strong as a starter for ten, isn't it?'

'Sorry about that, Bridget.'

'No, you're not!' I grinned, believing he had a flirtatious tone in his voice.

But he'd shifted into work mode and frowned, unimpressed with my interruption.

I was mortified.

'This is a working session,' he said, 'and I need to find out if any of your past arrests or associations are clouding your judgement. For instance, on the last psych eval, it's noted that you are something of a maverick. That you don't work well as part of a team – and there's a note that you've had a recent clash with your commanding officer – do you have issues with authority?'

'Oh, for God's sake!' They say attack is the best form of defence and I was disgusted at myself for letting a pretty face unhook my armour. 'Spare me the Psych 101 speak! Of course I have problems with authority – that's what gives me an edge as a detective! If you take everything at face value and question nothing, you're no use at detecting. Surely you have a manual on that, Dr Doherty? Or is this your first time working for the gardaí? I'd have expected better from a chap who has his shingle out on Wellington Lane. Perhaps you should stick to those personal sessions with the bored housewives? Cops are tough and it's unlikely they'll be having a cry-in at the shrink's. And why do we have to have bi-annual evaluations? Is it optional?'

I knew I'd gone too far. He didn't say anything for a bit, just sat observing me. I didn't feel judged but I think he might have.

'No, it's not optional. And the evaluations can be quarterly if senior management deem it necessary. Do you always go straight in?'

His voice was noncombative and that surprised me. But I wasn't going to let him see that.

'Look, it's not you,' I said. 'We live in a culture that lionises "what you see is all there is". So Joe Public has no interest in all the intelligent sifting we do for complex cases – like behind-the-scenes work on gang crime or the weeks, sometimes months, needed to piece it all together. If it's not up – pouting on Instagram – it doesn't exist.'

I was on my soapbox again and trying to step off. Judging by Paul's face I wasn't doing too well.

'Why so angry?'

'I'm not angry.' My fists tightened. 'But I have to ask, what would you know about what we face in the DOCB? You have to be tough to survive in there.'

'I see, Bridget, that you have 10.5 on the shuttle tests, firing-range accuracy off the charts and you were one of five selected to represent your trainee class in the elite course run by the Defence Forces. Impressive stuff.'

I tapped my right foot and tried to siphon off my annoyance at his blasé comments.

'We have tough jobs. We see pain, violence and hardship. It does change your life, it does make normality a little less likely. It even stops relationships – that's why a lot of mules marry other mules.'

'Mules?'

'It's our nickname for gardaí.'

'Apt term.'

'Have I passed?'

'We're not finished.'

'I passed last year's eval conditionally, and that's fine for me.' I wanted to be gone now. I'd let a stupid crush colour my judgement and misread his signs. In fact, there were no signs to misread, which left me feeling like an idiot.

'Okay, but continuous assessment is what we're driving for and clear passes at each evaluation.'

'How many of us get clear passes? Remember, I work with these lads, we're all in the same boat and I don't know anyone that isn't stressed. You saw me and Kay on Sky News with a severed arm, right? Hardly the pressure of trying to finish the monthly accounts now, is it?'

I knew I sounded crabby.

'Were you upset that the press found out about the severed arm? Were you hoping to keep that a secret until you had further time to investigate?'

'Aren't you supposed to start all your sentences with "how does that make you feel?"'

'Do you want me to do that, Bridget?'

I rubbed my eyes. The skin felt rough and grooved. I was weary from dreams of dismembered girls. I looked up at the clock on his wall. Just after eight.

'I have to go. I've got to get into the station – most of the team are out training so it's a skeleton staff.'

'That's probably enough for now anyway.'

Paul walked me to the door and shook my hand. His grip was warm and strong. I wasn't sure, but it felt like his fingers tightened for a second longer than was necessary.

'I'm on your side in this, Bridge. I just want to make everything easier for you.'

He'd called me Bridge, giving me a smile that was real and gentle, not some lit-up tooth-bleached-neon thing. I tried not to think about it for hours after.

CHAPTER 10

The emptiness of the squad room was peculiar on a workday morning. Most of our squad were on a technical training: miscellaneous forms of trace evidence. Kay had left a half package of Wine Gums open on her side of the desk. I went for the sticky sweet black one and lobbed it in my mouth then took my chair. Joe started speaking in that overbearing tone he used when he felt everyone should be at training but somehow had legitimately managed to avoid it.

'Don't think because you're here that this training doesn't apply to you.' He pointed a stubby finger at me then moved it over the remainder of the squad. 'You lot think you're the mutt's nuts because you get first dibs on the Technical Bureau. You'd wrap the whole city in a bag and fire it off to forensics if you could. Trace-evidence training reminds you to look at the crime scene with your own eyes, be responsible for evidence-collecting in your own right.' He rose onto the balls of his feet and stretched his neck.

I knew what was coming. 'Lion hair,' I mouthed to the rest of the squad, while rolling the gummy sweet around my mouth. One of the lads let out an involuntary snort.

'The less common the material, the more valuable is the evidence of its occurrence as a contact trace. Let me give you an example. The finding of lion hairs on the shoes of a man suspected of breaking into a house containing a lionskin rug may strengthen suspicion, because lion hairs are rare in this country. Each contact leaves a trace. The finding of lion hair at a secondary location will provide useful insight into a culprit's movements.'

'Unless of course he's a lion tamer.' I should have just left it.

Liam O'Shea looked like he might choke.

Joe glared at both of us and abruptly changed tack. 'The jokers – O'Shea, Harney! Call here about a robbery in Dalkey, being handled out of Dún Laoghaire Garda station. Be appreciative of the cooperation coming from Dún Laoghaire. They flagged it as a possibility to us. Might be organised crime. Armed burglary, husband and wife tied up during the raid. O'Shea, you take the lead –'

'You give us the nicest things, Joe,' said Liam.

It was juvenile but I laughed. More to cover my frustration that Joe hadn't assigned the lead to me, but I didn't deserve it after the lion-tamer crack.

'Look lively, the pair of you! Burglary happened weeks ago. Watch out for anything peculiar with the family and try to show the team from Dún Laoghaire we're professionals.' Without another word Joe huffed back into his office.

Liam and I took a car that had taken a few punches chasing a suspect into Sheriff Street earlier in the year. It was dung-brown and had a fist-shaped dent in the hood that belied the speed of its customised engine. We were not above subterfuge when it was needed.

'Will you drive, Bridge? This is your neck of the woods.'

The road to Dalkey was narrow and tortuous. Little old ladies with steel-grey perms on their way to Mass vaulted over bridges at breakneck speed, in jeeps the size of tractors, inches from our bumper. Then beamed and raised an index finger from the driving wheel in salute. The roads tightened even further as we neared Coliemore Harbour, but the air had the clean, bitter taste of the sea. It was all around. Along with the trophy homes, high walls and unchecked expectations.

'How's the severed arm case going, Bridge?'

I tensed, waiting for some smart remark.

'I'm serious. I thought it was a difficult case to get for your first time as lead. I never found anything in the missing persons that was of help. That arm had cold case written on it from the start. Tough break.'

My fingers were gripping the steering wheel, but I heard a genuine tone in Liam's voice. I didn't answer him immediately, mostly because I had only one setting with my male colleagues: defensive. I tried extending a branch.

'Remember that body, or the bits of body to be accurate, that was found in a canvas bag in the Royal Canal last year?'

Liam nodded.

'I think that was Seán Flannery,' I said. 'The guy in the bag was a known associate of his.'

Liam's mouth started working before he spoke. 'If I remember correctly the dead man lived in the East Wall – it's a bit of a stretch to say he was a known associate of Flannery's because he lived in the same neighbourhood. Look – if I can give you a bit of advice . . .'

I gave him a sidelong glance, not knowing what to expect.

'Maybe stop looking for Flannery everywhere? Lads in the squad are always ripping the piss out of you for it. They say you see him under your bed and the like.'

I was sure they said much more, but there was something warm, possibly even gratitude, forming inside me for Liam O'Shea's honesty. He looked as uncomfortable as I felt.

'Nice out here, Bridge. Lots of money.'

I grabbed at the change of subject. 'Or a lot of people trying to look like money.'

'There's dough out here all right, but there's all sorts moving in. One of the Limerick gangs has a money man in Dalkey.'

'Is that so? One of the lads in the regional squad give you that? I'd love to get a hint of where — any of the organised crime families stash their money men.'

Liam gave a twist of smile. 'Have a look at this place. Talk about the real deal.'

He was right. The house was called Tallulah and the automatic gate was open. The owners were expecting us. We drove in, catching glimpses of the Victorian castellated façade of the house, behind trees with trunks the width of a bull's back. The winding drive was long and the property large enough to disguise a carport. I found it when I went snooping around. That and a yacht the size of an articulated truck, docked in their own part of the coastline. I wandered around to the house. It was painted a chartreuse green, a ridiculous shade on a house this noble and put me in mind of an older woman who gets talked into a new hairdo, decades too young for her.

'This place is a summerhouse?'

'Yeah,' said Liam and looked at his phone where he'd stored the email Joe sent him. 'A second residence.'

'Did Joe send you an email with all the particulars?'

Liam nodded.

'Send it on to me, please.' My tone was collegiate, but Liam pretended not to hear. 'Ah Liam, would you just send it on to me? Bad enough Joe keeps me on a need-to-know basis, without you doing it too. I don't need to meet complainants with no clue as to what happened.'

'I'm the lead on this, Bridge, and don't forget it. Also, you bollocked me last week about messing up Judges' Rules. I know I got it wrong, but would it have killed you to say it to me in private?'

'Sorry,' I said, somewhat chastened.

We sounded like teenage siblings having a row and after a couple of guilty swipes with his thumb, my phone pinged.

A uniformed garda opened one of the double doors. I didn't recognise her, but the 'F' on her shoulder numbers told me she was out of Dún Laoghaire Garda Station. Liam was over faster than I'd seen him move in a while. Badge out and hand proffered. She filled out the navy uniform well and I presumed from his enthusiasm he was still single.

'Detective Garda Liam O'Shea and my colleague Bridge Harney from Harcourt Square. We were asked to come by –'

'She gets the picture, Liam.' I was all up for helping Liam's love life, but I had limits.

'I don't see anyone from the Tech Bureau – have they been and gone?' I said.

'Yes, about an hour since. Our Super in Dún Laoghaire didn't think it was necessary to bring in the Square, but one of the drug-squad detectives called you.' She eyeballed me. Gutsy.

'And that's your considered opinion as well? That the Square aren't needed,' I made a show of looking at her epaulettes, 'Garda FT 507?'

'We're well able to handle crime in our locality,' said the garda. She stretched her neck upwards.

Liam muttered.

'The T is for traffic, isn't it?' I said. 'This is a bit of a step up for you.' I wasn't having some traffic gal tell me how to do my job.

'If it's a question of jurisdiction –'

I cut her right off. 'You've been watching too much CSI. If anything looks like it might be related to organised crime the Square are brought in. You might want to go back to your Crime Investigation Techniques manual and refresh yourself on chain of command. Where are the owners of the house?'

The sea filled the next couple of moments, the only interruption being Liam clearing his throat and his silent desire to apologise for my behaviour.

The garda pointed to the interior and looked as if she would accompany us.

'You wait here, in case your Cig comes. Liam, you come with me.'

Which he did, with all the grace of a police dog leaving a fruiting female, but he said nothing.

We wandered down a hall, past double staircases and entertaining rooms. Crushed velvet couches sat beneath windows and low, open shelves were higgledy-piggledy with edgy ornaments. A coffee table was laid out with an arc of books. I checked them out – some were first editions. What kind of person put first editions on a table in sunlight?

Liam was impressed, but there was a staged feel to it. A forced elegance that was nothing to do with the owner's taste.

'Hello, sir,' I said to an older man who materialised from a side room. He had suspiciously black hair.

'Mr Burgess?' said Liam.

'Yes, I'm Mike Burgess.'

He had a Brum accent and a lumpish gait, as though his own legs were busy and he'd been forced to borrow someone else's. A faded bruise on his cheek had a ridged centre which I guessed was the result of stitches.

'Detective Garda Bridget Harney and Detective Garda Liam

O'Shea from the Drugs and Organised Crime Bureau. Did you get that in the raid?' I pointed to Mr Burgess's cheek and showed him my badge.

'Yes, buggers punched me in the face. I'd swear the lad who hit me was wearing a ring.'

I took a closer look, hoping to find a crest but couldn't see anything other than discolouration and the wormlike scar. I looked at my notes.

'Says here your wife was also tied up?'

'Yes, she's in here. This way.' He was brusque and marched off, motioning us forward with a liver-spotted hand. 'You know, we've answered a lot of questions already. My wife was distressed and I don't want anyone disturbing her any more.' His jaw shot forward as a warning to use our time well.

He directed us to a small room with two wingback leather chairs around an unlit fireplace and a forest-green tartan on the walls. It was a pleasant enough room, but scores of porcelain dolls dotted in every space made me feel as though a miniature army was watching. It was disquieting and I guessed this was the Burgesses' true taste.

'This is my wife, Anne.'

Anne Burgess must have been good-looking when she was young. Her face bore the echo of a beauty that would have been hard to let go of, but her burgundy hair was a shade too dark and her Botox a twist too tight.

'Mrs Burgess.' I offered my hand.

She looked at me as though I were the help who had left smudges on the silver teaspoons. My hand was left unanswered, in mid-air.

Liam took over, assuming the manner of a civil servant addressing a District Judge. I'd seen him do this before and it worked well with a certain type. He'd pegged the Burgesses. I retracted my offending limb and stood to the side.

'Mr Burgess, first off, why didn't you report the burglary? It happened on the 25th October and today's the 23rd of November. Nearly four weeks between the robbery and report. Why?'

'There wasn't much taken.' Burgess looked at his wife before he spoke. 'We didn't want anyone to know we'd been broken into. No one else's business.'

'All right,' I said, 'but why report it now? Why not leave it, if as you say not much was taken?'

'Anne and I were afraid they might come back if no one starts looking for them.'

'Them, Mr Burgess? Did you know them?' said Liam.

'*No!*' It was a shriek from Anne Burgess. She looked severely rattled.

'Okay, let's start from the beginning,' said Liam. 'What happened on Wednesday the 25th of October? You were both here?'

A look passed between them I couldn't interpret, but I had the feeling Anne Burgess was livid. Her mouth was puckered as though she was chewing a sloe berry. She didn't speak.

'We'd been at De Ville's and had a late supper. Do you know it?' said Mike.

We shook our heads and I marvelled at a Brummie picking up the parochial self-importance of this seaside village.

'We had one or two drinks and rather than walk home we used a taxi. There was no obvious sign from the outside that anything was amiss. The gate was closed, I keyed in the code and we opened up. That was 11.46 p.m.'

'That's very specific,' said Liam

'I have an account with my taxi and it gives the exact time of drop-off on the receipt.'

'Useful.'

Anne harrumphed as Liam asked another question.

'What alerted you to the presence of raiders?'

'Well, at first nothing,' said Mike. 'The house was as we left it. Some lamps were turned on. We had left —'

'Stop!' Anne raised her hand as though to halt an oncoming car.

Mike waited before he spoke. 'My wife is just trying to protect us.'

'It's not like anyone else has our best interests at heart,' said Anne, the side of her lip giving a soft upwards snap when she spoke.

A woman accustomed to being listened to.

'The insurance company will find out that we never turned on the alarm,' said Mike. 'All this stuff is online now. You can see on the app the alarm was off.'

He paused. He met Liam's eyes. Liam said nothing.

Anne Burgess was restless, didn't know where to put her hands and they kept fluttering up to her neck.

'We went upstairs, I turned off the lamps,' said Mike. 'They were waiting for us in our bedroom. It was fast. In the half-light I saw nothing. They were all masked and wore boiler suits. Only one man spoke — he shouted at me for the code to the safe. Another two men tied Anne up and gagged her.'

Anne reached for Mike's hand. Her knuckles were a clenched white, with insect-like bones just visible under the skin.

'It must have been difficult.' Liam was sincere, but Anne looked like she might slap someone.

'What kind of an accent did the raider who spoke have?' I asked.

'Dublin. It was muffled because of the masks, but I'd say a hard Dublin accent,' said Mike.

'Did you notice anything about the raiders — height, any hair showing, wiry, heavyset?' I asked.

'No, they were all in boiler suits with hoods pulled up. They wore masks and gloves.' He looked down and his eyes bulged back and forth under his lids. 'They were all around the same height, now that I think of it. Is that helpful?'

Not especially, but I couldn't say that.

'It's all useful,' said Liam.

'Any smells? Chemicals, bleach?' I looked at the staring porcelain dolls for inspiration. 'Hardboiled sweets, mint, crisps? Sweat?'

A wrinkle appeared on the bridge of Anne's nose, otherwise her face was completely still. It was disconcerting.

'No, which was odd,' she said. 'A man put his hand over my mouth. I remember the coarse feel of his glove, but no smell. Other than a new plasticky odour.'

Liam raised an eyebrow at me and I moved on.

'The crime report you filed states that the safe in your bedroom was behind a picture – did the burglars seem to know where it was?'

'Well, I can't see how,' said Anne. 'But they took the painting of my daughter off the wall, which has no value other than sentimental – but they wouldn't have known that – and so they found the safe. They told us to hand over cash, jewellery, anything they could carry. They had black bags in our bedroom, full of the house silver and had pulled paintings out of frames. Nothing of value, we only have reproductions over here.' She sounded indignant, like she wanted to vent. 'Is this modus operandi typical of any criminals you know?'

'It sounds professional, Mrs Burgess, and as in the UK there are any number of gangs that operate like this here,' I said.

'Do the paramilitaries still exist?' Mike asked.

'Not as units,' said Liam, 'but individuals have expertise and loan it out to gangs or sometimes take on a job themselves. If there's enough cash involved.'

'They were waiting for us!' said Anne. 'In our house, from

God knows what time! My husband was beaten and I was bound. You're sitting here asking questions like we're on trial!'

'Easy, Annie, they have to ask their –'

'Don't you "easy Annie" me!' She rounded on him, nails like talons. An old rook cawing at a rat lurking around her nest. 'This is all down to you! You insisted on buying this god-awful parody of a castle and sailing over here . . .' She stopped speaking and I sensed she was furious with herself. Her breath came in quick little puffs.

Mike Burgess looked cowed.

'I want them to leave,' said Anne, as though we weren't in front of her.

Liam and I stood in the Burgesses' silence. It was like standing in fog, but I knew if we kept quiet it would clear.

'What else do you want to know? Be quick.' Mike's voice was a rumbling bass.

Liam looked at his notes. 'And home is Newnham House in Newnham on Severn? That's near enough to Birmingham, isn't it?'

'Off the M5,' said Mike.

'I was in Birmingham last year. Lovely city,' I said. I had the idea of agitating Anne, see what I might get out of her. The locked-down body language she displayed was a message to her husband I couldn't interpret, but she was seething.

Anne gave me a long, appraising look.

I cleared my throat, suddenly tight from her excessive scrutiny.

'It's over an hour and a half if the traffic's up,' said Mike. 'It's a big area. When I retired we moved to the coast. I like to sail, hence here.' He indicated his current surroundings. 'Family who owned it before us got burned in the property bubble, so we picked it up after a bit of bargaining. They had the safe put in. It was a good one – the robbers couldn't open it. Put a gun to Anne's head.'

'Yes, but you hesitated, didn't you?' Anne's spite peppered the air.

Mike coloured and his big body climbed in on itself. 'I didn't know what to do! I was frightened and I fumbled, that was all, and he decked me in the face for it.'

Anne turned her back to her husband.

'It's not unusual to freeze in a situation like that,' said Liam. 'In fact, it's more usual to freeze than to have your wits about you.'

'What kind of gun was used?' I said.

Mike raised his heavy shoulders. 'Don't know. Handgun.'

'What was in the safe?' I looked right into Mike's distressed-asset-buying eyes.

'Not much, couple of thousand in cash and Anne's emerald ring. A diamond bracelet and earrings.'

'Can you be exact about how much money was in the safe?'

'Six thousand tops,' said Mike. The lie stained him, same way hair-dye leaves a tell-tale trace on your forehead.

'And that's not a great deal of money and valuables to you? Not worth a report to the gardaí?' I said.

'No, it's not a great deal of money, Garda Harney!' Anne snapped at me with teeth the size of piano keys. 'We're wealthy and the idea that we allowed ourselves to be robbed isn't something we want to get out. Imagine if our daughter were kidnapped! Or if we were attacked again in our home in Newnham simply because word got around that we're an easy target?'

'It's a plausible enough reason, Mrs Burgess, but something doesn't sit right with me.' I looked at each of them in turn.

'You'd better watch your tone,' said Mike.

'Or what?' I didn't know what the undercurrent I sensed meant, but I was curious.

Anne put a hand on her husband's sleeve and they gave me a hard stare apiece.

'Can you show me the safe, please?' said Liam after some moments had ticked by.

Mike trundled out with Liam in his wake.

I was left in the small reception room with Anne and her anger. I noticed some Staffordshire dogs stuck in between all the dolls and Ladro ladies.

'They are rare, aren't they? The Staffordshire dogs.'

'Yes, it was our thing, collecting porcelain. Everyone has a thing when they're first married – my daughter and her husband work out together. Are you married?'

I didn't answer but my bare ring finger made her garrulous.

'Not to worry, you've a little time left. Mike and I would go around flea markets, I would spot an original, or something that was valuable, and Mike would zone in on the stallholder, convincing them that what they had was tat and buy it for a song. Good times.'

Anne was lost in memory as she looked at their collection. She wore an expensive perfume I couldn't place, but it had opening notes of mandarin orange and plum. It was a strange sensation, watching Anne, as she watched those staring dolls.

The garda from Dun Laoghaire had left and I had a moment of conscience when I saw Liam looking for her. We walked in silence to the car, our ears cocked in case any stray conversation floated towards us from the Burgesses.

I took one last view of their property, from the house down to their personal jetty. The sea was an ice-green topped with foamy white peaks. It crashed onto the rocky shore with a primal rhythm. I was pulled towards it and repelled when the sea had done with me.

Liam revved the car and a rainbow of diesel fumes surrounded me. 'Get in the car, Bridge. You zoned out a bit there.'

'Sorry.' I sounded foolish. I got in and belted myself into the passenger side.

'What do you make of that pair?'

I eased the seat forward a notch. 'Hard one. Alarm was turned off – no way insurance will pay up on anything. So no financial gain. You were on the last two high-profile robberies – is it reasonable for people to go out and leave their alarm off?'

Liam nodded. 'A lot more than you'd think. It's not broadcast as it suits the insurance companies because they don't have to pay up. Still, it happens, particularly in quieter neighbourhoods when people are popping out for a few hours. But Burgess is lying about the amount of money he had in that safe.'

'You got that?'

'Ah yeah, Bridge. I've done this sort of thing before.'

'So if you have a wad of euros, sterling or bearer bonds in a safe, you'd turn on the alarm, right?'

'They're an elderly couple, Bridge – they may have just forgotten and are ashamed to admit it.'

'That's reasonable and the robbery's too clean. Too organised.'

'So you're ruling out Mike and Anne Burgess as suspects?'

'Well, it's hardly likely, is it? No alarm on, so no insurance pay-out and where are those pair going to find a villain to rob them? Donedeal.ie? No, this was a gang.'

'All right, it has the signs of organised crime. Do you like someone for it?'

It was hard to get one over on Liam.

'It could be Flannery – it's his MO – particularly the no-smell thing.'

'That why you asked about crisps and mints?'

'Yes, Flannery makes them wear full hazmat gear under the boiler suits. All odours and fibres kept inside.'

'How do you know that?'

'One of the jobs he pulled two years ago, the jewellery heist in Munster Bank, the wholesale place.'

'Bridge, that was the Dunnes. No way has Flannery the wherewithal to do a job that size.'

'That's what the brass think because he's not flashing his cash around town or holed up in Marbella. Flannery's too clever for that. Larry Dunne and one of Flannery's lads had a fight and were caught on CCTV, pulling off each other's masks and boiler suits – you could see the hazmat gear on underneath.'

'Bridge, it was Larry Dunne went down for that job. He was the main player.'

'No, Flannery organised that job with the Dunnes' blessing and on condition he took Larry Dunne. The Dunnes had wanted Larry out of the picture for some time.'

I could see Liam's mind working by the creases in his face.

'Yeah, I'd heard Larry was a cokehead and they wanted him gone, but who told you they picked Flannery for the job?'

'The other man on the job, Jim Redmond.'

'Then why didn't he give Flannery up? Would have shortened his sentence.'

I shook my head. 'Flannery told him he'd get a payoff at the end of the sentence if he stays quiet, but if he talks Flannery told him he'd cut up his kid.'

Liam looked like he had no words.

'Redmond is still serving his sentence, but he asked for me last year, told me he was terrified that Flannery would kill him in prison. Wanted protection.'

'What did you do?'

'Initially we put him in the vulnerable offenders unit, but he hated being in with sex offenders and agitated to be moved again. And he was still scared out of his mind that Flannery would come for his kid.'

'Jesus.'

'Still think Flannery's just some small-time enforcer? Remember there's still over half a million in gems and gold unaccounted for from that Munster Bank robbery. I'd say that's what Flannery got for framing Larry Dunne. If you look at the CCTV, Redmond literally starts in on Dunne for no reason.'

'But Dunne didn't testify to that.'

'Like a Dunne's going to co-operate with the gardaí. And anyway tests showed he was high as a kite during the fight, probably didn't know what was going on.'

'So was Redmond moved again after that?'

'Yeah – he was moved to Shelton Abbey.'

'Bloody Butlins?'

I smiled. 'I reckon it was on the cards for him anyway, given his good behaviour.'

Liam opened his mouth to say something but changed his mind. Instead he looked around, and I could swear he was deliberately changing the subject. 'There are still questions around the Burgesses. I wouldn't write them off yet. Who gets robbed and doesn't ring it in? I'm not buying that about not making themselves a target.'

'I don't know. They're rich for sure and Anne Burgess is one of the angriest women I've ever met. Maybe she's forcing him to come clean because she's scared the daughter might get kidnapped? It happens. Just doesn't get reported.'

'All right, I won't rule out organised crime – the Dunnes would have the resources for this or even the Mulvihills in Limerick. This kind of crime is on the up.'

I eased a knot in my temple with my forefinger. 'Christ, it's a growth sector.'

CHAPTER 11

Dublin's South Circular Road was never in darkness, even in the depths of November. It had seen many changes over the decades. In the sixties, it was the upper-middle-class quarter of Jewish doctors and jewellers. Now it housed working families, university students, Muslims and socialists. The old synagogue was a night club and a stone building at the other end of the road had a new sign, Mosque Atha Cliath. Which I thought catered for a niche group. I'd never met any Gaelic-speaking sons of Islam, but I loved their optimism.

'Mammy, Bridge is here!' Kay's middle child, Dan, was five and heralded my arrival. His grinning round face stared at me through the front door, his nose squashed against the clear glass panel. I loved that Kay didn't have frosted glass. She lived her life in the light.

A small dog yapped from inside. Kay came tumbling out of the kitchen with the baby on her hip, all but falling up the three wooden steps to the main hallway.

'Come in, Bridge, and welcome,' she said as she opened the door and pulled me into a hug with her free arm.

'Grab the dog!' yelled Kay's husband Matthew. He barrelled past us out onto the path and scooped up the fluffy pup. 'He's a right Houdini! Evening, Bridge. Lovely to see you.'

Matthew was a huge man encased in hair. He looked like a Yeti, but Kay loved him. Sometimes a look passing between them would pierce me, bringing my paltry personal life into sharp focus. We walked to the kitchen through the obstacle course of laundry baskets, shoes, hurleys and a woebegone tricycle.

I took the baby out of Kay's arms. He had a sweet, biscuity smell and I tried not to hold him too close, tried not to shower his round, delicious face with kisses, tried not to pretend he was mine.

'Take a seat, Bridge. Matthew, will you take Jamesy off Bridge? She's not here to babysit.'

I relinquished him, whispering in his ear I'd feed him his tea when Mummy had it ready.

'Pop yourself up on that stool, Bridge.'

I perched myself on a counter stool. Kay had three despite the fact the family always sat at the kitchen table. I think it was her nod to interior design, that and sheepskin rugs dotted around the sanded wooden floorboards. It was worlds away from the Judge's home. Lists of instructions for where to put schoolbags and whose day it was for table-laying or dishwasher duty were written on Post-Its stuck to the fridge door. Kay had a wood-fired Aga with bubbling pots on top, steam lifting the lids into a jingle and luscious food smells tickling my nose. One in particular.

'We're having bacon?' I said.

'Matthew's idea of a joke – poor man has no sense of humour.' Kay poured red claret into a bucket of lead crystal and handed it to me, then got one for herself and sat on a stool beside me.

'To us, Bridge. The pig-rustlers!'

I found it in myself to laugh – with Kay around everything seemed possible.

'Don't ever change this house, Kay.'

'With a roof that leaks and only one bathroom? We can't afford to move, though Liam's just been promoted to vice principal.'

'Congratulations! When did this happen?'

'Last week but there's feck-all of a pay rise. You don't know how lucky you are with no mortgage to pay.'

'I'm thirty-five and live with my parents.'

'You've said before, spoiled wench.'

We snorted with laughter.

'Saw one of your legal brethren in the paper recently,' she said. "His estimated earnings are well over three hundred thousand.'

'Who?'

'Freddie McHugh SC.'

I nodded. 'I know him to see.'

'The money you'd make in this climate as a barrister! I'd freshen up this place for sure if I'd a few quid.' She gave a wistful look around her kitchen.

'Is your integrity worth a few tins of paint? Some of those chaps making the big bucks have clients who raped vulnerable women.'

She looked chastened.

'And lots of them are on buttons,' I said. 'The law is clubby.'

'Yes, but with your dad's connections?'

'Precisely. They're my dad's connections and I was never going to use them. I'd do it on my own or not at all.'

'So you're just stubborn, that's why you left, eh?' Kay's dark-lashed eyes sparkled at me.

I looked up at the watermarks that needed painting over and hoped my words wouldn't stain Kay, same as some leak had marked her ceiling.

'I was a bit . . . soiled after the Nash case. The panic defence.'

Kay's face was a question mark, her eyes darting to the left as she attempted to access memory. 'Remind me?'

'Nearly ten years ago. The assault on the trans girl? Landmark case in Ireland. I used that made-up-bullshit "panic defence".' I swallowed and pushed the images from my mind.

Kay nodded. 'It wasn't your fault. You had to do your job.'

'I got him off. I think that's why Richie Corrigan brought me Seán Flannery.'

Kay shivered and hunched into herself. 'That Flannery freaks me out. Any time we've met him he never takes his eyes off of you. Fragile-looking . . . almost beautiful. Maybe that's what makes him so strange.'

Kay had put her finger on it.

'That's what I thought the first time I saw him in Cloverhill Prison. He was on remand. Richie Corrigan was my instructing solicitor.'

Kay's mouth puckered as though she were sucking on something sour.

'Richie Corrigan was all chat, telling me what a huge opportunity he was giving me. Told me Flannery had a terrible upbringing, children's homes and the like. Victim of the system but had pulled himself up, didn't trust authority, but when all was said he was essentially a good person. Richie never showed me the file, kept it in his sweaty paw until Flannery came in. When he walked in, the first question I asked him was why he had dismissed his last counsel. Do you know what Flannery said to me?'

Kay shook her head, her glass half-raised to her mouth.

'His last counsel had wanted him to plead guilty. But how could he? It was consensual, she was asking for it – not that he was ever going to admit that in open court. The 'she' was eleven years old. I couldn't defend him, couldn't even stay in the same room as him. And I wouldn't stay in an establishment that gave a monster like Flannery the presumption of innocence.' I looked up at the ceiling stain – it was getting fuzzy. 'Doesn't matter though, I still failed that child. And Flannery walked of course – girl and her mother were too scared to proceed.'

'Bridge, why didn't you tell me before? How long have you been carrying that around?'

Our conversation was cut off as her tribe piled into the kitchen demanding food.

We ate in a tight circle with the two older children shovelling food in enthusiastically, with a constant chorus of demands, complaints, instructions and announcements – mostly from Kay's seven-year-old daughter Sheena, who was thinking of running for public office.

'Mammy, Jamesy is making a mess.'

'Mammy, can I have water?'

'Mammy, the dog's chewing the skirting board again.'

'Matthew, cut that up a bit smaller, will you?'

'Mammy, Dan's choking.'

'Matthew, give him a solid pat on the back . . . use the flat of your hand.'

I spooned buttered mash into Jamesy and watched with wonder as he stuffed his fat fists into his mouth, gurgling and giggling in equal measure.

When Matthew had taken the tribe up to bed for the usual routine of singing, toothbrushing and storytelling, Kay and I sat by the Aga.

She opened the ceramic door and put a few green sticks into the oven – they popped as the flames swallowed them. The wind rattled at the windows and she turned down the main kitchen lights, striking a match to a few tealights and putting them in rinsed-out jam jars. I was as happy as I could be and wanted to preserve this moment, put it in a snow globe. Safe under glass. All I'd have to do is shake it when I needed respite.

'You okay?'

I nodded.

'Have you given any more thought to the case?'

'I think it's Flannery, Kay. And before you tell me I'm a fanatic or seeing Flannery everywhere, this is the kind of thing he does. Cold, planned actions. What we don't know is why.'

'So you're determined to investigate him?' Kay opened a second bottle of wine, dumping almost half of it into the glass in front of me. 'That tout gave you Flannery for the severed arm?'

I nodded. 'But it's not just the tout – I know he did this. That arm is a message to someone and that's Flannery all over. No one believes me. If anything, the lads think I'm some kind of joke where Flannery is concerned – but I'm going to get him.'

I was blathering, half hoping Kay would tell me she could see some type of logic in my declarations.

'Well, sláinte!' Kay raised her glass.

'Saol fada agus bás in Éirinn!' I held up my glass and marvelled, in that hazy state before real drunkenness sets in, at the intricate prisms some blower had created from sand.

'Long life and death in Ireland? We just might get that death in Ireland if Seán Flannery's the criminal you think he is.'

I took another mouthful of the soft wine and slipped off my shoes, looking around for my Trinity scarf. Kay saw me eyeing it on the coat rack by her back door.

'I put it there for safe keeping in case one of the kids wrecked it. Do you ever wash that muffler?'

'I have it dry-cleaned every few weeks! And it's not a muffler, Shanahan. You'd know that if you'd had a lady's education.'

Kay snorted. 'Some lady you turned out to be.'

I laughed, mainly because she was right. 'I'm a real disappointment to my parents.' I meant it to come out as a witty rejoinder, but somewhere between the thinking and saying truth came out.

'Never to your mum, Bridge.'

A pocket formed in the back of my throat. I couldn't swallow and we sat looking at the fire for a time.

'You still don't believe Flannery is behind the severed arm, Kay?'

'I believe you believe he is and that's enough for me. Can you imagine Joe's face and that sleeveen Niall O'Connor if we solved this case?' She threw her head back and gave a growl of laughter. 'Do you know he's conned some young one into marrying him? And she's a right *leanbh*. That's wife number three. Did you know he has two sons in private schools? Since when are the Christian Brothers not good enough for the likes of him!' She gave a small hiccup. 'Pardon. What was I saying? Oh yes! I believe you. You've done a huge amount of work – good work.' She gave me an over-serious nod. 'You brought those strip clubs in Leeson Street and Dame Street to a standstill and they were big earners for the gangs, not to mention refill posts for the tuk-tuks.'

'We've done that, Kay.'

'No, Bridge, that was you. You ran Operation Nightingale, and that tip line's been in place for nearly a year. All those girls got out because of you. What about women in the Rape Crisis Centre? Or Ruhama? They've said to me you're an angel.'

My face knotted into itself, the praise resting like a crown of thorns.

'You're too tall for an angel, unless it's one of those big fighting bastards.'

'Archangels.'

'That's the one!' Kay took another mouthful of wine.

I smiled. 'I have to follow Flannery, Kay. You understand that, don't you? Doesn't matter where it leads. I'm not going to give up – not this time, Kay.'

'Plus, it'd be something else you've given up, and your dad would never stop reminding you.'

I didn't quite follow Kay's logic but was too drunk to disagree.

'We can't have that.' I burped, a big man-sound, and a miasma of fermented grapes sat in the air. 'I'm going to find out what happened to that pregnant girl and rub Sergeant Joe Clarke's face in it and all the lads on the squad who think I'm chasing shadows.'

'And who knows? Land Flannery and you could become the next Garda Commissioner.' Kay listed to the left as she stood up, trying to find solid ground for a toast to my career prospects.

'Ah Kay, don't wish that on me! Didn't you see what they did to Nóirín O'Sullivan!'

'Good point – let's go outside for a sneaky fag.'

PART 2

endpoint

ˈendˌpoint
noun

1. Either of two points marking the end of a line segment
2. The final stage of a period or process

CHAPTER 12

DECLAN

No noise apart from a revved engine which drifted up from the pavement below and had the purist pop-pop of a vintage 911. The sudden silence it left behind had a thickness at that hour of the morning. We were twenty minutes from the city centre in a brand-new penthouse that looked out onto St Paul's Square. The only real noise up here was the wind. The prices had kept families out, so it was mostly professionals and footballers. Lad next door was a recent signing for West Brom.

I was in that dream state before being fully awake, a growing erection tugging at my conscious mind. That female reporter kept popping into my mind's eye when I wasn't controlling my thoughts, her suggestive eyes and curvy body enticing me. She had told me she liked my footballer's thighs and dark, brooding profile. She had licked her lips when I pulled my earlobe, a stupid gesture I made to cover my embarrassment. Then I twisted my wedding band around my sweating ring finger. Rather than deter her it seemed to spur her on.

A pebble of guilt stuck in my throat and I turned to my sleeping wife.

'Lydia?' I nuzzled into her back and lifted her bright rope of copper hair. She wore a matching white lace bra and satin thong. She looked chaste and pure as she slept. I drew little circles down her bare back and watched as a smile started to form on her features.

'That's nice, Dec.'

'Dec' was a sign I was getting it right, that things were going back to normal. I unhooked her bra and squeezed her nipple between my thumb and forefinger. The grooved skin tightened. I reached over, unable to stop myself, and sucked.

'Umm, Declan . . .' She turned onto her back. 'Do that thing, with your mouth.'

I travelled down the smooth whiteness of her body.

'You still going to that cardio class?' I said.

Lydia's body tightened but I liked the feeling and focused on her stomach, kissing my way to her nest of spicy, ginger hair. That reporter tart licking her oversize bottom lip appeared in my mind. I closed my eyes and focused on Lydia's sweet smell, burying my nose in her rich, musky odour.

Then she surprised me by telling me to stop and sit in the chair. It faced the window — we were too high up for anyone to watch us, but there was always a chance.

Lydia took what looked like a studded table tennis bat and leather stays out of a drawer and began to tie my arms and legs.

'This is new . . . where did you get those?' I worked to keep the shock out of my voice. The leather was tough and pockmarked, like it had been bought at some discount erotica store. I couldn't picture Lydia in that kind of shop. We weren't a sex-toys couple and had laughed about it only recently, after a dinner party with friends, amused that the most unlikely of people were buying beads and vibrators online.

'We don't need stuff like this, babes.'

She knotted the leather stays – not too tight, but I was bound.

'You don't speak.'

'Lydia, I'm not into this.'

There was an uneasy quiet, of wind stilled and imagined ears cocked. I pulled against the stays as embarrassment mixed with humiliation, but I was still hard. I didn't want to focus on that too much.

'Just go with it, Dec. We need a change after all the . . . hassle. We can't always do the same stuff. Do we need a "safeword"?'

'What!'

'Calm down, Declan.' Lydia was giggling, a soft fuzzy sound.

'Okay, babes. Put on some music, will you?'

'No.'

Instead Lydia oiled her hands with something from her dressing table – it had a heady, forest-floor smell. She warmed it between her palms, then rubbed it on my cock in long, quick strokes. She twisted the delicate skin at the top of my shaft with every stroke. The effect was like micro-needles and getting more intense. I groaned. She upped the tempo of the strokes and all but pulled me off the seat. She put one foot on the seat arm and spread herself, rotating her hips like a belly dancer. My hips danced off the seat, desperate to ejaculate.

'Jesus, Lydia! Where did you learn to do this?' My voice was hoarse.

She tugged harder and rubbed a rhythm into my shaft that my breathing began to follow. I wouldn't be able to hold back if she kept going this fast. I was giving into the temptation of an easy climax. That reporter slut appeared behind my eyelids and this time I didn't banish her.

'You okay, Declan? Your face is all creased.'

'Yeah, babes.' I was going with it, picturing the dark-haired reporter watching Lydia working on me. I looked into Lydia's clear blue eyes. 'I love you, babes.'

Lydia pinched the top of my dong, right under the hood, catching the pulsing blue vein. I groaned. My erection faded and she slapped my thighs with the studded paddle. I yelped.

'Thought you might like it.' She gave me a dirty smile and put one hand on my forehead, pushing me back into the chair.

I was ready again in seconds.

'Come on, baby!' I was pleading. Aching for relief.

'Not yet. You've been naughty, haven't you?' She hit me full on the shaft with the paddle. I nearly orgasmed.

'Fuck . . .' My breath was coming in ragged heaves.

She oiled my cock again. Four hard pulls and I was close. Heightened by her first orgasm denial.

She straddled me.

'Is it safe, baby?'

Lydia didn't answer but pulled a rubber onto my erection and lowered herself onto me. Squeezing me. I writhed against the bonds. Ecstasy pumping through me. I was still trembling from my climax when Lydia orgasmed. She sat on top of me, spent, my chest lifting her up and down as my breathing regulated itself. Something flitted across Lydia's face and I gave an involuntary jerk as she pulled off the used sheath.

As she made for the bathroom my phone buzzed beside the bed, an old-school clanging ring. I could see it was Ava.

'Untie me, babes, I have to get that!'

Lydia came back, still with that strange look on her face and I wondered if I'd said the reporter's name out loud as I orgasmed. My insides contracted.

The phone rang, impatient to be answered, but Lydia paused.

'Come on, Lydia, please.'

She whipped the stays off and I grabbed the phone.

'How's Daddy's girl?' I grinned into the phone.

Lydia rolled her eyes but I knew she liked Ava.

'I'm good, Dad. How're things with you and Lydia? I'm not disturbing you, am I?'

'No, pet. It's Saturday morning – it's all good.'

Lydia threw a towel at me as she walked towards the bathroom. 'Ask Ava does she want to come over for brunch this morning? Around eleven? I can make those American pancakes she likes. Be lovely to have something other than porridge for breakfast.'

'Did you hear that, Ava? Fancy coming to ours?'

'I'd love that. Dad, please don't tell Lydia, but Mum isn't crazy about me spending time with you guys. She thinks I'm like your new toy.'

A knot formed in my chest. 'You're fifteen, Ava, you don't have to tell Cheryl . . .' I stalled, 'Cheryl' sounded cold, 'don't have to tell your mum everything about us. We have our own relationship, right?'

Quiet on the phone.

'Look, I know we've only been in touch for a while, pet, but I'm going to go to a solicitor and get proper access.'

Still silence.

'It'll be fine, Ava pet.'

'I don't want Mum to feel left out, or as if she has to compete with you and Lydia. She doesn't have your kind of dosh.'

'I know, I'll do it right.'

We said our goodbyes and I sat thinking for a time about Ava, what a good kid she was and how much contact I might get with her.

Lydia came out of the shower — the heat of the water had given her a kind of nimbus.

'Cheryl being a bitch again?'

I nodded. 'I'd say she's guilt-tripping Ava.'

'Just pay her off, Declan. I'll talk to Dad and see if we can take money from the business. I guarantee, if you wave twenty grand in front of Cheryl's face she'll be down at her solicitor's before you can say "money-grabbing-bint".'

'I know — it's just, what will that do to Ava?'

Lydia raised her slim shoulders. 'Only reason you met Ava was that eviction. If Cheryl hadn't needed money she wouldn't have gone to see your mother. And I can't imagine that conversation was a barrel of laughs. I'd say Ava's been through enough. You need to stop the rot, Declan.'

CHAPTER 13

BRIDGET

The squad room was icehouse cold, something about the heating pipes not working properly. They rattled and clanged like an inmate before slopping out but gave off no warmth. I was trying to stoke up my body heat with coffee.

'We've got a hit! A sight-of request, Bridge! Bridge?'

It was Kay, high-pitched with excitement.

A mouthful of hot coffee scalded my throat as I gulped it down. 'From where?'

I hurried over.

Small trident-shaped patterns appeared at the sides of Kay's eyes as she squinted at a screen filled with confusing grey panels.

'How is this supposed to be user-friendly?' she said. 'I could batter those computer consultants. It's a request for sight of DNA file HS230405 — that's our girl. FLINTS? Who's that?'

Liam O'Shea got a whiff of the excitement — he and Kay were looking at me like little birds with their mouths open.

'Force Linked Intelligence Systems. It's the system the West Midlands Police use.' I had dipped my mouth into my scarf to help me think.

I glanced into Joe's office. He was sitting rigidly at his computer screen, most likely transfixed by the same information we were.

I signalled Kay to follow me outside.

'Ah wait, girls!' said Liam O'Shea to our retreating backs.

Once outside the squad room I pulled out my mobile. 'Need to call Yvonne Walsh in Forensic Science Ireland.'

I punched in Yvonne's mobile number. An artificial dial tone, the only point of which was to give comfort to the listener, beeped in my ear. Kay elbowed me and I put the call on speaker.

'Hello?'

'Hi, Yvonne, Bridge Harney here from Harcourt Square.'

'I was wondering when you'd call. Got a sight-of and you're referred to as the lead detective on it.'

Yvonne snorted down the phone and Kay joined in when she saw my pained face.

'It's file number HS230405 and the severed arm.'

'I know, Bridge. I'm looking at it right now. It's not every day we get a severed arm.'

Nails clacked at speed on a keyboard at the other end.

'It's a request for the DNA profile. We've sent that and the full forensic case file over to the West Midlands Constabulary, including photographs and physical description. They should be back to us in four hours or sooner.'

'Four hours?'

'Or sooner. We've a new service level agreement with the UK, as part of forensic policing procedures around Brexit. If either side request a sight-of for serious crime it's given priority.'

'Can you see the name of the officer from the West Midlands who requested it?'

'No.'

'Right, thanks, Yvonne.'

'Bridge? I'm on a temporary contract here – if you get a chance, will you put in a good word for me?'

'For sure and thanks again.'

I was a bit of a heel agreeing to put in a good word and should have been more honest with Yvonne. A good word from me was as likely to get her contract terminated early as extended.

When we went back into the squad room Liam was nodding towards Joe who was standing up and all but saluting as he spoke into the telephone receiver. At first I thought he might have wind – the contorted expression on his face spoke of gas – but as the minutes passed he reddened like a schoolboy who had just won the class-captain election.

'It's the Park,' said Kay, punctuating each word with a tap from her pencil. 'Must be an Assistant Commissioner – he's pulling in his gut like he's on parade at 0700. Could be the sight-of request.'

'Either that or he's up for the Scott Medal for Valour, which would be a travesty,' I said.

Kay had taken a mouthful of tea and choked.

'Bridget Harney!' said Joe.

Joe was shiny-faced with self-importance as he waited in his office.

'That was the Assistant Commissioner in Garda Headquarters from the Park.' He had to stand to deliver the news, as though he couldn't be contained in a chair. Similarly, his uniform faced the same struggle and hummed on his waistline.

'You've had a match on the DNA profile of the arm victim.'

Excitement pulled my insides up and I went to stand beside

Joe, on his side of the desk. 'Well? An ID? Who is she?'

'No, not an identification as yet.' Joe's shiny face dulled. 'The other arm. Found in Centenary Square in the centre of Birmingham. West Midlands saw you and the arm in the Docks on television and it prompted a sight-of request for our file on the girl.'

'How did they get away with dumping the other arm in Centenary Square?' I asked. 'That place is thronged, isn't it?'

Joe held up a meaty palm. 'You can ask the West Midlands Constabulary all about it when you land in Birmingham. The Park has other concerns and frankly so do I. You know we are struggling politically with the UK right now.' He would have written the words in the air and highlighted them neon green if he could. 'This is a cross-borders operation and you need to be as sharp as they say you are. Bloody gleaming with cooperation. You won't be able to do enough for the lead detective . . .' Joe looked down at his desk, deep in paperwork, 'Detective Chris Watkiss. Have you got that, Harney? This operation is as much about diplomacy as it is investigative. Brexit and the politicians have caned us rightly this last while. Nothing but bad feeling in the media. We need a success, so that police on both sides know there's respect. That we're above the politicos and the hacks. And, God help us, Harney, with your size tens it's falling to you.'

'Thanks, Joe.' I did my Best-Bangharda-in-Ireland face, but Joe knew. I was somersaulting inside.

CHAPTER 14

DECLAN

2002

She was so small. Even her name sounded small. Cheryl. Tiny and beautiful. I didn't have any other words and was stuttering out the same ones over and again. They were stuck to the roof of my mouth like Sunday Communion. I wanted to touch her shiny hair and lick her smooth skin that looked as creamy as Walker's toffee. But I wasn't sure how to say it in a way that would get her clothes off. I was clumsy around Cheryl, everything about her made me ache. I might love her. My mam's *Woman's Own* said a woman liked to feel special, that no other woman could take her place, but I didn't know what that meant. My mam was always saying Dad kept putting her in her place.

Cheryl laughed at me and her cheeks turned pink. Perspiration gathered in the crooks at the base of my fingers. It happened whenever I was excited or scared.

'Your fingers sweatin' yet?' said Cheryl with a smile so knowing my cock jerked. She grabbed my middle finger and put it in her mouth, the soft grooves of her tongue swallowing the beads of perspiration.

'Fuck, Cheryl, you're a dirty bitch,' I said.

She released my hand, then turned up the CD player and Nelly sang to Kelly the way I wanted to sing to Cheryl. When I touched her, sparks ignited. The sting was all over my body. But my mate Shabba said if you tell girls you love them they go off you, or move on to your mate. Or worse, if they think you're a sad sack, on to a bloke they know you don't like. Shabba was like five years older than me, so he knew the score. I pulled back. Cheryl looked confused, maybe even upset. Did that mean she liked me? I didn't want to upset her, but Shabba said if they get upset or think you might leave them they'll do anything you want. Including a blow job. And I wanted a blow job from Cheryl. I wanted a blow job from any girl, but especially Cheryl.

We were in Shabba's brother's flat. He had two girlfriends and three kids, but I didn't know which of the girls lived in this flat. It was two blocks away from our tower – my mam said it was where all the knackers live. She used the wrong words all the time and made me call her 'Mam' instead of 'Mum'. Knackers meant balls, not scumbags, but I'd never told my mam that. She'd kill me for saying 'balls'. Everyone in Lozzell Grove called me Paddy or Micka, but they dragged it out like 'Mick-kaa'. Made me sound like a retard. My mam said Cheryl came from the poor part of Lozzell Grove. Not that I thought there was any difference. It all looked like shit to me.

'What's wrong?' said Cheryl. 'Why did you stop?'

I put my hands behind my back and crossed everything. Hope tore me up inside. I knew if I could find the right words she'd get naked. Shabba said when you think you're going to make a tit of yourself in front of a girl, say nothing. I started to say a Hail Mary in my head and told myself to stay quiet, something about the delayed gratification my O-level Humanities teacher kept banging on about.

'Is it your 'mammy?' Does she not want her precious Irish boy going with – what does she call me? A coloured girl?'

'It's not that, Cheryl, and I'm not Irish. Just my mam. That's why she says stupid *tings*.'

I did an impression of my mam's h-less accent to make Cheryl laugh, but even her smile turned me on. I lunged across the room at her and grabbed her. We toppled over one another and dissolved into hot, fuzzy giggles, her brown eyes wet with tears from her hiccupping laughter. It was better than music. My boner prodded her blue fatigue trousers. I licked the exposed skin under her crop top. She was better-looking than that bird from All Saints.

'You know I don't care what my mam says – she's ancient and has no clue what's going on.'

I touched the sweatband around my head, Nelly-style.

'You've got a bandage on your face – did something happen?'

'Nah, just for the look.'

She kissed me. Her mouth fitted onto mine and her perfect tongue searched me out. I could hardly breathe when she stopped. Fuck Shabba.

'I love you, Cheryl.'

She smiled and peeled off her top, pretty fingers unhooked her bra. Her skin was like golden treacle. Her hands pulled at my pants and everything started to melt into her softness, my body pulled in an arc by her sweetness.

CHAPTER 15

BRIDGET

2018

Birmingham International airport was a wonder of concrete and steel. A wonder that no one bothered to put any effort into its design. The freezing, gritty wind found my face every time. I would imagine I looked watery-nosed and tangled-headed when Chris Watkiss first clapped eyes on me. I'd sent him over my Garda profile. I wouldn't have done this for just anyone, but Joe had been clear. Every cordiality had to be offered.

He pulled up to the set-down area just beside Departures and turned to talk to the airport traffic policeman on duty. They looked in my direction and Watkiss waved a bear paw at me. I snapped my telescopic handle into my carry-on and picked it up. It was a pricey piece my mother bought as a gift on my ascension to the bar. It was too much then and still looked pretentious. I had brought it out of habit and hoped it didn't make me look precious. I muscled my way over the scrubby green verge to the set-down area.

He took my carry-on. It looked like a handbag in his fist and his wedding band looked like it would fit around my wrist.

'Hallo, Detective Garda Harney, this is us,' he said and indicated to the front passenger seat of a big Alfa Romeo.

'It's Bridget, but everyone calls me Bridge, DC Watkiss.'

'Bridge it is then and I'm Chris.' He continued talking as he got in. The car had a clean, male smell. 'I can take you t' station or we can go right in and I'll show you where arm was found.'

He skipped certain words and his voice had a rich northern burr. He was what the lads at home would have described as a bit of a unit.

'If we can go straight to the scene that'd be great. Do you have any questions for me? Or may I ask you some?'

'Whichever comes easiest, lass.'

He had an open grin and I instantly took to him.

'Our arm had no identifiers on it other than the tattoo. Yours?'

'Nowt, not even a matching tattoo. Arm was clean, only fibres on it were from inside of packaging. A right dead end.'

I was a bit flattened and sat contemplating what I'd achieve on this trip.

Chris didn't say much, but he drove like a man who knew Birmingham and its rat-runs blindfolded.

'Right, we'll park here, it's a bit farther off than I'd like, but you can see the city's got her skirts up. They're redeveloping Centenary Square. I hope it's worth all this ruddy inconvenience.'

He had a point. The walkway through Paradise Forum was closed and Centenary Square was all but covered over, inaccessible from pedestrian level. New hotel carcasses surrounded both squares. With their open steel skeletons and flaring welding tools, the overall effect was that of a massive pathology lab.

Chris shouted over the vibrating drone of earth-movers and hammering builders.

'*It was found in there!*' He pointed at an area completely

squared off with hoarding. He came up close and spoke in my ear. 'The *Birmingham News* were tipped off by phone. I'd say immediately it was thrown in – it was still frozen. If they had waited the rats would have got it. Follow me – we can get a better view from the second floor of the library.'

I followed him to a building, with shining discs and intricate ironwork. The light bounced off the exterior, giving the illusion of supple movement. It was like walking into the belly of a golden cowfish, but he was right. Up on the second floor we had a perfect view of city and the intricate domed white building at the centre of the wooden panels.

'It's called the Hall of Memory,' said Chris. 'It's a World War I memorial.'

'And the arm was dumped in there?'

'No, not in the Hall itself, just thrown over the hoarding. Forensic Science Investigators came back yesterday with profiling and the bone analysis. Took longer than expected as the arm was –'

'Frozen.'

'Aye, that's right. Same as yours. It isn't possible to search the site – we mapped it but look around. With the building work and machinery, there's too much cross-contamination.'

'You think whoever put it here had forensic smarts and knew we'd never be able to sift the site?'

'Either that or it's just a good place to hide it away. City's been turned upside-down in the last couple of months, dead quiet at night though. Surveillance cameras have been knocked out by JCBs, and even if they weren't, it'd be nothing to cut the power supply. The network is unstable with all the movement. Some cameras work and some don't. Still, we got a view from the library's internal and courtyard cameras.'

My face must have looked hopeful.

'Got nothing. It was a courier. He was given instructions to take it to Centenary Square and throw the package over the hoarding.'

'Are you serious? The courier service told him to do that?'

'No. Someone approached him in the street and asked him to do it.'

'Any description?'

'Not much, courier's just a lad.' Chris looked down at a tatty moleskin notebook. 'Chap by the name of John Willis. He's eighteen and I would imagine whoever picked him was looking for a greenhorn. Willis told us a guy approached him on the street, wearing a hoodie with a surgical mask. He gave Willis a note. Note said it was a Med School sponsored Charity Challenge. That the bearer of the note had to get a package to Birmingham's Centenary Square without speaking and without being seen. Specifically, to throw it over the hoarding. Gave Willis money and Willis was happy to do it for him. Thought he was helping out.'

'That's ridiculous.'

Chris shrugged. 'Courier's an idiot.'

'Do we still have the note?'

Chris shook his head. 'Willis binned it.'

'Anything in the wrapping?'

'Nothing. Only that it was so clean it's a professional job. This isn't the Burger Bar boys.'

'Burger Bar? That one of your gangs?'

'Aye, we've a few. Nothing but lads who think they're top boys stabbing one another in night clubs. They wouldn't have the smarts for this.'

I stretched my neck around and took in Birmingham from a height. It was packed with new developments, much of them looking more for investment than beauty, but it had the air of a place that was thriving.

'City looks like it's going places.'

'It's doing well enough, but so are the villains. Don't like this dismemberment stuff – it gives the estate boys something to aim for. Come on, let's get lunch and I'll take you over Station after. We can have a look at our missing girl's file. You have anyone you like for this?'

'No, there's too many, Chris. One woman was missing for a couple of weeks but she's turned up. Got herself a new boyfriend.'

'Waste of police time.'

'True, we've had an increase though in missing persons. You seeing anything like that?'

'Aye. Same. It's the sex industry – gone online and indoors. Girls running away from pop-up brothels.' Chris was solemn-faced at the thought of all the unaccounted-for women. 'Come on, it's Friday, let's get ourselves a pie for cheering up.'

He had an innate decency and I couldn't refuse him, even if a pie wasn't my idea of being cheered up.

Out of sight of the building works Birmingham looked good. The old part of the city had a sturdy, high-Victorian feel to it. As we passed them, Chris told me the history of the imposing council offices and the art museum named for the city, all built by town elders and the prosperous merchants of the nineteenth century.

We sat down over pies in the aptly named Pieminister, on a stony street near the museum. It was a bright, clean place and the smell of roasting meat and garlic made my mouth water. I picked up the menu with real interest, looking at their signature pies.

We ordered and settled in to discuss the case. Chris was obviously like me – if something was top of his mind he couldn't focus on anything else. He spoke through a mouthful of Deerstalker Pie, a train-wreck of mashed potatoes, bacon and venison.

'Pathology put time of death in that same ninety-six hours as your lot did,' he said. 'I'm looking at missing persons from last summer up until now. Mind you, helps that she's young – it will narrow down the search. What do you think it looks like?'

I could sense he was being diplomatic. A red weal of sorrow formed inside me and I put down my fork. Its clattering joined the sounds of the other satisfied diners.

'Working girl. Pop-up brothels all over Dublin so I would imagine they're here too.'

Chris nodded his tufty head. 'Aye. Bloody Airbnb is like trip advisor for nonces.'

'Girls are trafficked in and try to escape. I would imagine some industrious pimp made an example of her.'

'Poor lass. That's my best guess too.'

'But why dump an arm in Dublin then Birmingham?'

'Makes no sense.' He shook his head. 'It's one of the reasons I like the East Europeans for this. We've a couple of gangs taking over the cabs around here. App-based taxis that deliver more than you've asked for. They're big into massage houses and brothels. They like a bit of gratuitous violence, as if there's any other kind. Could be they're expanding across the pond. You seeing any of those gangs in Dublin?'

'Yes, we're seeing some East Europeans, but it feels more like individual criminals getting involved with local boys. Maybe that's the link?'

'Maybe. We've a couple of wrong 'uns in the area that Interpol are interested in, but they haven't put a foot wrong so far.'

'We may never find the rest of her,' I said.

'No, but we might get lucky if we keep looking. I've found over the years the harder I work the luckier I get.'

'Someone famous said that.'

'Aye, Chris Watkiss.' He belted out a laugh that could have started a regatta.

CHAPTER 16

DECLAN

It was early, but the sky had the look of a losing prize fighter so I headed back into the kitchen. The porridge I'd left steaming was ready to eat. I should have covered it with chia and flax seeds, but no one was looking so I went for a layer of runny, sweet honey. It tasted forbidden and rich. I moved to the living room, attracted by a glossy brochure with bright aquamarines and turquoise, glinting up at me from the coffee table. I was half-hoping to see some all-inclusive holiday package. We needed something like that. Lydia was exhausted and I was becoming short with her and everyone else for that matter. A smile started to snake up my face until I read, in subtle print, *Are you having fertility issues?*

Lydia crept up on me, her footsteps lost in the deep, smoke-coloured rug. I jumped when her cold hand found the underside of my fleece.

'Come back to bed.'

'I want to, baby, but it's Saturday, need to drop my shirts into the cleaner's and I have to get to the gym.'

My phone rang. Lydia saw who it was before I did.

'Cheryl? Why's she ringing here? Hundred per cent she's looking for money.'

'It might not be money. Ava says she's been down lately.'

'Cheryl's a bird from Lozzell Grove you shagged when you were a kid. Now she thinks you've a few quid and is always calling here on some pretence. Does she think you're going to go back to her?'

Lydia had a point: unwanted women hung around like out-of-contract footballers.

'You're interrupting my weekend, Cheryl.' I sounded harsh and wanted to knock her back in full view of Lydia, but she talked over me.

'She's gone! The little rip said she was staying at a friend's house last night and would call me the moment she left the party. She knows I worry –'

'What? Ava? Whose party? Have you tried her phone?'

'Oh, why didn't I think of that? Nescafé Dad! Of course I've rung her phone! And when did your accent get so posh? Tackin' lessons, are ya?'

'Cheryl, you sound drunk.'

She was wailing now. It was like listening to a blender. Lydia cocked her head as I pulled the handset to a safer distance.

'Do you have any of her friends' mobile numbers? Their Facebook accounts? Cheryl? Cheryl!'

She was blundering around in the background, as though looking for something. 'Ava's new boyfriend – a big Villa supporter – he goes down the Spotted Dog or the Drayton Arms.'

'What would she be doing in those dives?'

'How do I know? She's fifteen, an adult.'

'Fifteen is not an adult, Cheryl, you stupid –' My control was swinging away from me and I worked on the breathing exercises my personal trainer had taught me.

Lydia was following my conversation, tracking me with her eyes.

'She might have lied to me about staying with a mate, might've bunked into a rave. I saw a flyer for one in Floodgate Street in her room.'

'Why the hell are you letting a fifteen-year-old go to a rave, Cheryl?'

Lydia was shaking her head and mouthing to me, 'Not now.' She pointed to herself and then in the rough direction of Cheryl's flat.

'Right, I'm going to drop Lydia over to you and she can go through the stuff in Ava's room, see if she can work out where Ava might have gone. Don't you know any of her friends? Zoe? That girl Audrey from school?'

'Who? Are they new friends?' Cheryl was burbling down the phone. 'Hang on – me phone's beeped – how do I look at a text and keep talking?'

'For the love of – there should be an info line at the top of your screen – tap on the message icon and it'll come up.'

'It's Ava! She's fine! She's with Katy. Oh, thank God!'

'What the hell is wrong with you, Cheryl? What kind of fucking pathetic excuse for a mother doesn't know who her daughter is staying with?'

Lydia grabbed the phone off me and hung up. 'Don't go off at her or you'll never see Ava again.'

I stood beside the coffee table with nowhere to put my frustration. The infertility brochure caught my eye.

'And what's this?'

'This isn't the time, Declan – you're up to ninety.'

'I'm a father, I don't need fertility treatment!'

'I know, but I've been off the pill for a year now and nothing. Please, Declan.' She made a sound, somewhere between a hiccup and a sob. 'All my friends have babies. Can we at least discuss it? Maybe something is wrong? It's years since Cheryl had Ava.'

'Have you ever thought something might be wrong with you?' It came out as much more vehement than I had intended. 'I'm going to the gym.'

I grabbed my car keys but couldn't shake my anger at Lydia.

'You think you're entitled to anything you want, don't you? That Daddy's money can buy you a husband, a fancy flat, a life some of us only caught glimpses of?'

'Oh, please don't start your Lozzell Grove council-estate-boy act. You went to Five Ways same as me.'

'Except it took me two buses and over an hour every morning to get there. And my mum had to clean the corridors,' I said.

'Oh, your sainted 'Mammy' who smoked cigarettes in the girls' toilets when she was supposed to be mopping?'

'Don't you disrespect my mother!'

Lydia crossed the floor but I pushed her away and bit down the impulse to smack her. Instead, grabbing my gym bag, I made for the front door. That reporter tart flitted into my mind – at least she knew how to be grateful.

CHAPTER 17

BRIDGET

1991

I had fallen into a bed of spiny thorned roses in the back of our garden. My mother roared out my name.

'Bridget!'

The pain was almost worth it to hear her coming to my rescue. I could smell the sweet oil of the rosebush, even as it ate at me with its thorns. I looked into my mother's oval face. Her big, red hands pulled at the stems until blood stippled both of us, like one of my toothbrush-splatter pictures.

'I have you, little one. I have you. My brave girl.'

I sobbed until my breath came in great, shuddery heaves and Mum gave me two Junior Disprin that fizzled their way down my insides.

I lay in my bed surrounded by Mum and we watched *Rosie and Jim* on the television Dad bought me as a 'sorry present', after he left us for two weeks. Mum looked like she'd fallen into a rosebush when Dad left.

Mum and I cuddled down in the bed and watched our show.

We counted three big bandages and five small bandages on my arms and legs. Mum told me it was lucky that tomorrow was Saturday and I could rest, but I wanted to go riding. Mum didn't think that was possible, so as a treat she brought Dotty up to my room. Dotty jumped on my bed and pushed her wet muzzle into my face. Everyone knows collies are the cleverest dogs in the world. I burrowed into her soft black-and-white fur and listened to my mum telling me 'Sleep, little one, go and visit the stars'.

I'm not sure what time I woke up. Dotty was gone but my curtains were closed and the house was quiet. There was a seam of light as bright as the stitching on my jodhpurs under my door. I used it to find my nightlight. I didn't like the dark but wanted to go for a wee. I didn't like my bathroom at night either. The light-switch had a long cord that hung from the ceiling. Richie Corrigan said it looked like a noose and tied my favourite dolly to it. Said my dad would find it funny. I wasn't sure what it had to do with my dad but Richie told me it was our little secret. Richie scared me. He and his wife were always coming to our house for weekend parties. She told me to call her Beatrice, but I didn't like her and said, 'Yes, Mrs Corrigan'.

I thought parties were supposed to be fun, but Mrs Corrigan spent her time singing warbly songs and trying to sit on my dad's knee. She was drinking a rotten-looking water that went cloudy when my mum put ice into it. Why did my mum have to keep getting up and refilling Mrs Corrigan's glass? Why couldn't she get my mum a drink? Mrs Corrigan stank of aniseed balls and smiled when she spoke to me and Mum. Except it didn't feel like a smile. Mrs Corrigan said things about my mum's clothes, like 'that green is such a difficult colour to wear'. I didn't know if she was being nice or not, but everyone laughed. I told a girl at a party that her dress was a difficult colour to wear, because I wanted to make her laugh. But she cried, and Mum took me home early with no birthday cake.

CHAPTER 18

BRIDGET

2018

It was a bar-room brawl of an evening. We rocked from side to side as the pilot made a fitful descent, as though he couldn't decide whether to land or keep going. The passengers clapped, a big *bualadh-bos* sound when he finally threw the plane down.

Kay was waiting for me in Arrivals. She'd made a placard with a picture of a stick *bangharda*, including the dodgy peaked hat, and was dancing from side to side, oblivious to the staring onlookers.

'Just a heads-up. Joe will want you in at cockcrow on Monday. Needs a report on your diplomatic mission to Birmingham.'

I had expected no less. I knew Joe would want an update, yet I hadn't rung him from Birmingham. It was small-minded of me.

'Want to come over to ours for tea?'

I shook my head and pulled my jacket around my body. The air was damp. Aer Lingus hostesses walked by in their green uniforms, pops of colour in a dank night-time Dublin.

Kay drove me home. 'I got some pictures of Anne Burgess's jewellery from their insurance company.'

'Anything?'

'Not much – earrings, necklace and two diamond rings, one with an emerald centre. Nothing she'll ever see again, either on some lackey taking the ferry to England or being broken up over here. But Anne Burgess had an Iranian blue gemstone ring. It's set in gold and I have hopes for that. It's rare. Thieves mightn't realise what they have. It doesn't look much in the way of bling, but it's flawless.'

I must have looked confused.

'It's that duck-egg colour. Did your mum have one? Apparently they were all the rage back in the day.'

I had a vague memory a baby-blue domed ring with diamonds surrounding it.

'Anyway, they're in demand now,' said Kay.

'You've been chatting to your pal Mr Welby?'

She grinned. 'No, it's just my innate knowledge of fine gems. Course I have. He said he'd keep an eye out for me. If he hears anything, he'll let us know.'

'If he hasn't bought it himself and passed it on.'

'Ah, Bridge, benefit of the doubt and all that. He deals in estate jewellery.'

'Now there's a useful term to explain a lack of provenance.'

'What are Mr and Mrs Burgess like? I haven't met them yet.'

'They're like any couple married for over three decades. Gloriously unhappy and trying to do as much as they can on their own, without looking like they're trying to get away from each other.'

'Jaysus, Bridge! You've a queer view of marriage. I can't wait until Matthew and I are retired. Driving our kids nuts and messing around with the grandkids. Bring it on.' Kay wiggled in the driver's seat at the thought. Her hair was in a messy ponytail with strands escaping the elastic band and a chewed pencil peering out, looking like it was making a break for freedom.

'Maybe for you, but I'd say Mike Burgess has given his wife a tough enough time. He's a big lumpy thing. Hair dyed off his head but thinks he still has it. She could have been Miss Birmingham 1960. Still has traces of it, but not going gracefully.'

'That's tough. Better born with a sense of humour.'

We laughed.

'Anything going on for you, Bridge – Miss Best Arse in Trinity? Nobody to have a drink with at the weekend?'

I thought about her question for a bit. It was Friday night and a downpour had washed the pavements – the city had a clean, hungry look. I wound down the window and felt a wire of electrical current in the air. Perhaps I should go out tonight? Go to a club, find someone. Find release. The prolonged nasal call of a seagull, hanging in the air, brought me back.

'That was a long time ago, Kay. I'm focused on Mum and the job right now.' I said it with a finality that closed the conversation.

CHAPTER 19

Monday brought me through the swing doors of Harcourt Square, that bore the black scuffmarks of a thousand standard-issue garda shoes. Roll-call voices boomed from the squad rooms, as different divisions sounded off.

'*Anseo!*' said Liam O'Shea, in imitation of a primary-school boy.

'Always the comedian, O'Shea,' said Joe. 'Bridge.' He threw his head in the direction of his office.

Somebody shoved up a screeching metal window and the outside air rushed into the vacuum. He got a round of applause. I'd never seen the windows opened before.

'Close that,' said Joe. 'You'll ruin the air conditioning.'

Kay mouthed 'man-cold' at me.'

I walked into Joe's office. It was like stepping into a eucalyptus sauna. A humidifier blasted out menthol vapours – it mixed with his exhalations and the steam from a brackish-looking drink on his desk. The overall effect was eye-watering.

Joe shut the door quickly behind me.

'Sit down, Bridge. You're not going to like this . . .' He let out a huge *yessuhing* sound and the air around his nose and mouth misted with water droplets.

I hugged my scarf to my mouth. 'You're right, I don't,' I said with a grin.

'What happened with your man Watkiss?' he said with a scowl.

'What?' My head jerked up and the scarf fell away from my mouth. 'It was all good. I saw the site, arm belongs to our girl, obviously. Exact match –'

Joe held up his hand to stop me. 'Yes, but we knew that. You were supposed to add value. As Watkiss himself said, she's a prostitute. Allegedly, you agreed with this prognosis, including his assumption that it was European gang-related. So your trip was just a jolly at the taxpayer's expense.'

'Chris said that?' My jaw-muscles tightened and I shoved my chin back into my scarf to hide my irritation.

'No, his Cig.'

'They don't call their inspectors Cig, Joe. That's Irish.'

'Figure of speech, Bridge. His inspector reckons he's as bad as you are, spending hours on missing working girls who are trafficked in and out of the UK at a rate of knots, wasting his own time rather than bumping it over to Interpol. And not only that but Chris's Cig put the complaint through the Park. We don't need them looking at our expense sheets, or we'll be sharing pencils before you know it.'

Relief flooded. I wasn't wrong about Chris. It was the brass jumping all over us any chance they could manufacture. 'Well, I hope you told Chris's inspector we'd keep looking into this on our side.'

'I didn't get to speak to Chris's Cig. I got a message from Superintendent O'Connor.'

Joe let that sit between us.

'We're handing this over to Interpol and Chris Watkiss will be told to do the same.'

I walked out of Joe's office in protest and left him calling after me.

Kay grabbed my coat and slung it at me. The noise of the squad room was rising faster than a barrister's fee scale and I pretended not to hear Joe's harsh voice.

'I told you, Bridge! We gave you two weeks for this and it's nearly up.'

Kay gave me a quick half-smile. 'C'mon. Got something on the Burgess ring, told you I would.'

We clambered into a squad car, not caring that it was badged, and made our way into Dublin's city centre.

Welby's jewellers on Clarendon Street was located outside a church. It was said the original Mr Welby was a pawnbroker, who took a man's best suit in on a Monday and the woman of the house retrieved it with her man's weekly earnings on a Friday, so he could wear it to Sunday Mass. Assuming she got the weekly earnings. Time had moved on and the current Mr Welby sat behind his antique counter, encased in his shop of glass. Platinum and diamonds glinted from the surrounding shelves, caught by clever lighting.

He stood to receive us. A gentleman with a fine plume of grey hair and a cloud of cologne that had seen its best-before date — even his steaming coffee couldn't counter the aroma. In the small shop the smell threatened to overpower me.

'Ladies,' he said, 'you're punctual.'

'Interested in this one, Mr Welby,' said Kay.

She had a way with him. I believed he was a huckster and he sensed it. I watched as he weighed the information he was going to give us against what it would yield him. He flicked an old sovereign over his knuckles – it got lost in the bones and pleated flesh of his hands, then reappeared between the pads of this thumb and finger. I wasn't much on parlour tricks.

'My lady friend runs a shop on Instagram, if you can believe that.'

Kay joined in. 'Oh, I can, Mr Welby.'

'Here,' he said, as he flashed a top-of-the-range mobile and double-tapped a purplish icon. Several small pictures flashed up. He pinched the screen. 'That the ring you're looking for, Kay?'

Kay looked at me. 'Bingo, Mr Welby! Where's this lady located?'

He flicked through his contacts and pointed at her name. 'Shall I?'

'Please,' said Kay.

He tapped the screen and waited.

'Darling lovey, it's Welby,' he said in an affected voice. 'I've got some lovely girl guards here. Enquiring about your ring. Would you be an angel and talk to them?'

He passed the phone to me.

'Give it to the Alpha, why don't you?' Kay gave a staged sigh.

Mr Welby snorted out a few puffs of air, in between reaching for his steaming latte. He plopped saccharin tablets from a Tic-Tac-like dispenser into the creamy foam. One for each word. 'Not – too – many – questions, Detective.'

I had expected this. There was a price to be paid for dealing with Welby.

I started without ceremony. 'Where'd you get the ring?'

'It was an estate buy, a nice young man who was hired by the family. A sudden death. I believe the family are traumatised, so I won't mention any names.' The caller sounded fussy and put emphasis on the wrong words like some dodgy panto dame.

'Right,' I said.

Kay glared at me and flapped her hand upwards, in an effort to get me to increase my level of charm.

'Of course. I understand that and applaud your discretion.'

The words stuck in my throat, claggy as one of Welby's paste diamonds. I hated fences, but the nameless person on the end of the phone was just a tag-along, not worth the paperwork of an arrest.

'Did you buy it up front or are you waiting to sell the ring and then settle up?'

It was a dig and the caller knew it. If it was a legitimate sale the jeweller would usually put the piece on show, either online or in their window and barter with the owner when the piece found a buyer. If the caller had paid cash, cents on the euro, it was stolen.

'You know I paid cash for it, detective.' The caller dropped her fake accent and the facade.

'Fine. Can you describe the seller?'

'Hard-faced, somewhere in his twenties, wore a hoodie.'

Sounded like half my mug-shot file. I was getting tired of this.

'If that's all you have why shouldn't I pull you in? You and Welby both.'

Silence. On the phone and in the shop.

'There's blood on the underside of the ring. Caught between the setting and the stone,' said the caller.

CHAPTER 20

I waited a couple of days for the blood tests, but with nothing forthcoming Kay and I drove out to the Garda Technical Bureau Headquarters. It was currently being merged with Forensic Science Ireland, with the possibility of being privatised, according to the Garda newsletter, and the teams involved were working out 'creative tensions'. Which was shorthand for the Superintendent in charge of the Technical Bureau was in a knock-down, drag-out brawl with the Director of FSI for the top job. Housed in Garda Headquarters in the Phoenix Park, any detective thought twice before coming here without informing their direct superior. So I'd broken that tenet of the Conduct Code. It was beside Dublin Zoo, which predated the Force, but Garda HQ was the lion's den.

'You sent the ring in the internal post, right?'

'Course I did,' said Kay.

'And they confirmed delivery?'

Kay nodded. 'By email.'

'Okay then.' I wiped my sweaty hand on the leg of my trousers and held the steering wheel with the other. 'But I don't like coming here unannounced.'

'Don't blame you.'

'Thanks, Kay.'

I huffed for a silent moment. 'It's just that they take so long.'

'No, they don't.'

'They do! Last time I sent documents for handwriting examination they took over four weeks. I could have done it myself faster! I had to go up the line and threaten to go to an external source.'

'I remember,' said Kay.

I coloured at the rebuke I heard in her voice and tried to talk over it. 'I have to know if we can get a match on the blood.'

'I agree you do, but I'd be eating a bit of humble pie here, Bridge, if I were you.'

A white-coated girl greeted us as we signed in at reception, looked into lenses and were reminded not to smile.

'Christ, she's young,' said Kay, as the girl sashayed in front of us. 'And when did Tech get so cool-looking?'

The girl looked back at us. 'You usually don't look at us in the white hazmat suits, Detective Garda Shanahan.'

I clamped back a laugh and Kay threw a filthy look at me.

'You can work out of the hot-desk area,' said our guide. 'Log in using your own credentials and I'll check to see if the results are ready, Detective Garda Shanahan.'

Kay gave her a contrite, 'Thank you.'

For all the bland sameness of the outside, the interior was a riot of colour, with foosball tables, lit cube areas for meetings and a row of cherry-coloured partitions with desks and laptops. It was more like a hipster tech company. I felt old.

'They spend their time viewing dead things on petri dishes,' I said. 'I thought it would look like the inside of a vocational school.'

'They need the colour. I wouldn't begrudge them a thing.' Kay was salivating as she looked at a new Dell XPS 15. 'Beats the humpty-dumpty terminals we use.'

She logged in and, from where I was standing, she looked like a concert pianist as her fingers flew across the keyboard.

At least an hour had passed since we'd arrived. Kay was still absorbed in the intricacies of the forensic database, looking up old cases like she was searching for ex-boyfriends on Facebook.

'What are they doing?' I said.

'Most likely doing the actual blood test – will you get us a couple of coffees?'

I grunted and went to a vending machine that had an impressive range of flavoured coffees and any amount of herbal tea bags on a table with milk and stirrers.

'*Bridge!*'

I was across the room in a flash, coffee machine forgotten. I hunted on the screen she'd brought up. A one-hundred-per-cent match on the blood lodged in the underside of Anne Burgess's ring. It flashed up in large type, surrounded by graphs that looked like sound waves, showing blood markers, chain reactions and unique identifiers.

Lorraine Quigley

Seán Flannery's girlfriend.

Hope thrashed around inside me like a fish on a hook. I rose onto the balls of my feet to contain the exhilaration.

'He'll have an answer for this, Bridge.' Kay was trying to warn me.

'Don't bring me down, Kay. This is the first mistake he's made in years.'

'True.'

'Let's go and see if Mr Flannery is receiving. Shall we?'

'Joking aside, Bridge, you can't pick her up. You know that, right? You can't bring Lorraine Quigley in unless you can charge her immediately. And there's no guarantee she'd be safe on remand. Dochas Centre's full of women from East Wall.'

'We could put her on that women's wing in Limerick prison. The one that looks like it's from the Famine? No one would expect her to be there.'

'She'd be dead within an hour.'

I put a hand through my unruly hair. One piece at the back refused to sit down. 'I'll do it some other way. I can put her in a safehouse. I'm bringing her in.'

I punched out a text to Joe Clarke, asking him to request the Emergency Response Unit from Superintendent O'Connor.

'While we're at it, I'm going to get a sample of Seán Flannery's hair.'

'Oh? And how's that going to happen?' said Kay. 'Is Mr Flannery going to let you comb his hair? Maybe you'd take a comb from the DNA kit, the specialised ones that have the cotton wool on the teeth? Perhaps he'd give us a urine sample while he's at it? And a dental imprint?'

Kay's voice sounded like she was sucking on a helium balloon.

'Take it easy, Kay, your voice is getting all tight. We need more information on Flannery. Think about it – all we have are fingerprints and DNA from a swab taken eight years ago when he was on remand. The file on Flannery isn't even a centimetre thick. We have his birth cert, his exit interview from Saint Augustine's home for boys and his 1997 Leaving Cert results. On the processing side we have two ancient counts of receiving stolen goods, both of which he beat and a caution for domestic abuse from 2000. He's only spent a week in prison and that was on remand in Cloverhill where I first met him in 2009.'

'All that from memory.'

It wasn't a question.

'Kay, I can quote DPP V Cash, chunks of the McFarlane case, not to mention the snails-in-the-bottom-of-ginger-beer-bottles. The few pages on Flannery are nothing. We need his hair. Better than skin.'

'It'd be better if I get the sample. Flannery never takes his eyes off you. I'll manage to get a brush or something while you're distracting him with Lorraine.'

'No, out of the question.'

I knew by Kay's face I'd phrased it wrong.

She was tapping a long pencil with an eraser at the top. In quick staccato rhythm. Her jaw was so far forward she looked undershot. Too late I noticed the hot-desking area wasn't empty but quiet. Everyone was listening.

Kay walked out, towards a long white corridor with double doors for non-gender-specific toilets. A cleaner with a yellow Rubbermaid trolley was mopping the floor.

I trotted behind Kay with my tail down.

'What's up, Kay?'

Kay glanced at the cleaner and waited for her to finish, thanking her as she went out.

'I don't like the way you speak to me. It's bloody patronising!' It came out of Kay like an explosion. 'Please don't say to me, in front of everyone, that my voice is getting tight because I'm worried. Of course I'm worried! You're trying to lift samples during a raid. From a man you believe hacks up body parts — while picking up his girlfriend. Jesus, Bridge! Could it be any more dangerous?'

Kay was out of breath. I stood looking at the mottled blue tiles on the floor like a mutinous teenager.

'You never see anything from someone else's point of view! I offer you a good plan and you dismiss it out of hand, in front of the whole of the Tech squad.'

'It was hardly the whole of the Tech squad, Kay. Just a couple of punters using the hot desks. Twenty at most.'

'Are you serious?'

I was being reductive – in my defence, it was unintentional. 'Sorry.'

And I was sorry. It hit me like a smack across the back of the head. Kay was frightened. I didn't have anyone except a mother who was starting to forget me. Kay's world was bright and shiny, living in a redbrick house on the South Circular Road. Her life began when she got home.

'If I'm asking too much you can step out and let Liam O'Shea take your place. I should have thought of it earlier. Of course you're worried – you have Matthew and the kids to think about.' I looked up to the ceiling. The neon-strip light made a tiny scratching noise at one end. 'Starter's about to go on that light.' I was blinking.

'Come here, you daft cow!' Kay muscled me into a bear hug. 'You've no fear, that's what it is. The rest of us quake in our boots at the thought of going into situations where we need firearms, but not you. You're a brave woman, Bridget Harney.'

'Or stupid.'

'That and all. Come on, let's go back to the Techies and tell them we've made up.'

It was lunchtime now and most of the administration staff was on its way down to the canteen. Kay got caught in the throng and her voice floated back to me.

'So Flannery was in Saint Augustine's? Awful stories in the news about what happened there in the nineties. Did a wing of it burn down?'

I caught up to her and we moved further into the building.

'Yes, burnt to the ground in 2000. I reckon it was some of the inmates.'

'You mean Flannery,' said Kay with a single raised eyebrow.

'Well, it's likely, but the investigation file is pretty sparse, something about faulty electrical wiring. Come on, let's follow our noses, Kay, and get a free lunch.'

I could smell lemongrass and coconut milk.

'Don't try to distract me, Bridge. I'll get a brush or comb, maybe even a hair from some clothes or the sofa. If we get in, and there's every reason to believe we won't, warrant or no warrant. You distract him when we're inside. Chances are he'll never take his eyes off you anyway.'

Kay patted her pockets for her Post-It pad. She took it out and made scribbly notes while we walked. I knew from old they were tasks that would be assigned to people, when Kay had worked out the details. She was all about logistics.

'Are you sure you want to do this, Kay? Flannery had that girl cut –'

'This your idea of a pep talk?' Kay held up her hands. 'It's better if I do it. If it looks risky I'll abort. You don't know the meaning of the word. And remember, I'm not going near Flannery without protection. So you'd better get the lads with the MP7s.'

Kay smiled at me and I had the same sensation as at my childhood confessionals: forgiveness, at a price.

'Why is hair better than skin?' Kay's eyes were quizzical.

'Hair's better. That'll give us tox. Drugs and medicines leave a footprint in hair. Skin sheds too quickly to be of any use. Flannery keeps his hair relatively long for a man, about six maybe seven inches, that's one year of growth. A single follicle will give us information on whatever medicines or drugs Flannery's taken in the past year. I don't believe Flannery's on recreational drugs, he's too clever, but I'd love to know if he's on any prescription medication. He's a terrible colour and his hands are always shiny. The way I see it, the more we know about Flannery the better we can tailor a trap for him.'

Kay pulled her shirt cuffs down from her sleeves and checked her cufflinks – they were made from dainty, navy knotted thread. I gave them to her last Christmas.

'All right, I'll get it.' Kay stood off from me in a way that told me there was no arguing with her. 'And another thing, you'd better have the Super line up a safe house or Lorraine Quigley won't last a day when we release her.'

I nodded. 'I'll get it sorted. I'm not letting this go, Kay. It's too good a chance.'

My phone pinged with a text from Joe Clarke.

Superintendent O'Connor has denied your request for ERU.

CHAPTER 21

SEÁN

1992

Bullock Harbour sounds like it is. A baby bull of a thing that fell asleep beside the sea. Sister Assumpta and I arrived around ten in the morning. Sister Assumpta had brought a transistor from the Community living room and we were listening to Gay Byrne. Sister Assumpta loved Gaybo. We were going fishing for my birthday. We were going to sail out and cast off.

'Thirteen today, Seán, a man now,' she said.

I was so excited I nearly couldn't keep it in and legged it behind the nearest rock to have a slash. I messed around doing a break dance between the slabs of granite and touched the feathery grass that grew in the ridges with my bare toes.

'Do you know, Seán – that grass there will keep growing and one day dislodge the granite?'

'Ah, Sister Assumpta, that couldn't happen, not something as light as grass. It's too green to break stuff like granite.'

She laughed at that and my insides contracted with pleasure.

She was a big, broad woman with a thatch of blonde hair she pinned into submission under her habit. Except on days like this – when she took her headgear off and put her face up to the sun. I mimicked her and raised my face, letting the warmth of the sun fill me.

The man in Bullock Harbour knew us and gave Sister Assumpta the loan of a red, scratched-up dingy. There was a kind of stillness in the air that you only get once or twice during a Dublin summer. We sailed out onto the flat sea and caught glittering mackerel. While I rowed back Sister Assumpta snapped the fishes' necks, then opened them out like books. Blood bloomed around her fingers as she flicked off the jewelled scales with her nutbrown hands and they landed on my legs. She said I looked like a merman.

We made a fire, of seaweed and sundried grass. It crackled and gave off blue, salty smoke. Sister Assumpta put the mackerel in a small skillet she brought just for this purpose. We spread pats of butter on the hot flaky fish and ate it with our fingers.

Later, I went swimming in a spare pair of underwear Sister Assumpta had brought for me. She scooped up the polar seawater and soaked my back with it. My teeth rattled from the cold.

'Does it hurt, Seán?' Her voice had a grainy sound to it when she saw the marks.

'It fucking did –'

'Don't use bad language, Seán! No matter what! It lets me down and you let yourself down. People will think less of you.'

I was from a place where pregnant girls ran pale-faced through the convent gates – people thought less of me as it was.

I nodded. 'It's not that bad, now.'

Sometimes I wished Sister Assumpta was my mother. Or that my real mother would descend like one of those archangels sent to Earth to sort out serpents and demons. That would show Father O'Mahony I had someone on my side.

'How did my mother die?'

I wasn't sure if she heard, but I didn't want to ask her again in case she was annoyed and would cut our day short, so I changed the subject.

'We could go for a walk on the pier in Dún Laoghaire? Get an ice-cream in Teddy's? My treat, I've money with me – I did jobs for the other lads and they paid me.'

She said nothing. I was sure she'd say we had to leave. That I'd ruined everything. A needle threaded itself down the inside of my gut and I prayed to Father Mahony's God that I'd put up with everything he told Father O'Mahony to do to me, if Sister Assumpta wasn't mad or upset.

'You'll make a great sailor one day, Seán. And you can fish. You could get a job on one of those big boats in Donegal, the ones that go out to sea. That'd be the life, wouldn't it?'

'None of them fishermen swim, Sister Assumpta, in case the ship capsizes. They all want to drown. I wouldn't want to die at sea.' I looked at her, willing her to answer my question.

'Or you could crew on a boat? On a big fancy yacht? You're a good sailor, Seán, and you've a quick mind.'

She glanced down at the cooling frying pan where the fish bones and butter had fused together into a burnt caramel.

'Your mother isn't dead, Seán. She left you in Saint Patrick's because she . . . couldn't cope with having children.'

'She's alive?' I wasn't sure if said it out loud. 'Who is she?'

'I can't tell you that, Seán. I'm not allowed.'

The ground whizzed up towards me and my nose made a crunching noise as it connected with the harbour stone.

CHAPTER 22

BRIDGET

2018

My laptop screen blacked out. A white dialogue box appeared and effectively shut me down. **You need to update to Windows 10. Free up 8Gb space**, it told me in a pompous, mechanical manner.

'How many times does this flipping thing have to appear before IT do something about it?' I was roaring, like some lonely bovine separated from the herd.

'Just click "not at the moment" on the bottom of the screen. They'll get around to it when they get around to it,' said Kay.

'Yes, but it's annoying . . .' I stopped speaking. I sounded like whinging toddler, without any of the sticky-fingered charm. 'Fancy a walk?'

We left the station and clattered down the front brick steps. Kay missed her footing on one of the uneven ledges. Her head shot forward in an attempt to regain her balance and she staggered like a three-legged turtle.

'Who makes steps without a lip? And out of bloody bricks? I ask you, did they just get any auld eejit to design this place?'

'Stairs have lips, Kay, steps have noses. Really.'

She joined in my laughter.

I wrapped my jacket around my body and pulled my scarf halfway up my face. There was a hard, brittle smell as though one more frost and the air might break.

'I should've worn a coat,' I said.

Kay looked like she was wearing a giant packet of marshmallows, but it looked warm. Behind Harcourt Square, down the corkscrew of Clonmel Street were the Iveagh Gardens. We stopped by a coffee cart and bought two coffees, I inhaled the toasted-bean smell. It reminded me of a gentle boy who would wake me by putting a mug of freshly made coffee on my side of the bed. A lifetime ago.

Kay slurped on her cappuccino. The sweet steam of the cart disappeared as I lengthened my stride and she worked to keep up.

'What's up, Bridge?'

'Just irritated is all. Can't get this girl out of my mind.'

We fell into silence. The Iveagh Gardens were bestowed by the Guinness family to the city of Dublin in the nineteenth century. The city would have been served better if they had donated alcohol rehab centres, given how much of their product we still drink. We sat on a wrought-iron bench dedicated to Samuel Beckett, who spent his life asking rhetorical questions. The cold was encapsulating, so I squirmed over to Kay to get some heat. I worried the information I had about the girl back and forth, like a hangnail.

'Who chops the arms of a pregnant girl?'

'You channelling your inner Sam?'

I waved Kay away. 'What's one arm doing in Dublin and one in

Birmingham? It has all the signs of a brutal gangland killing, but to what purpose? And it's too clean. Most of those lads are hopped up on something before they can get this psychotic. Machine guns are their weapons of choice and they spray bullets like a dog pisses. And they wouldn't have the wherewithal to start freezing and chopping.'

'Maybe there's a cleaner guy? Stick the body in a deep freeze and call in the disposal man.'

'Sounds like Flannery.'

'Bridge, everything sounds like Flannery to you.'

'Well, they hardly googled Forensic Cleaning Ltd, did they?'

We lapsed into silence. The sounds of the city were muffled by the cold, dense air.

My phone rang, startling us.

Chris Watkiss's name flashed on the screen.

'Chris? How are things?'

'Good, Bridge. All well your end?'

'Grand — what can I help you with?'

'Got a favour to ask. Lass I have on my missing list might be in Dublin. Contactless payment on her Barclay's debit card on the 8th of November four minutes past seven in the evening. Farringtons' Supermarket on East Wall Road at Cash Point 5. I need the store CCTV footage if there is any — can you get it for me?'

My eyebrows drew in. Kay's head turned to one side in response.

'I'm sure I could, but I'd need a warrant and it would be quicker if you kicked it off from your end. Then it would come from the Park to me. Any reason we can't do it that way?'

'We can, but this is a punt. I think this girl might be our severed-arms victim.'

My insides tightened. 'Why didn't you tell me this when I was over with you?'

'I wasn't sure, Bridge. Girl's gone missing before, but she's the right age and went missing in the time frame.'

'Did you get a DNA profile?'

'No. Look, I've been wrong about this one before. Last time she went missing she took herself off to London with a boyfriend and told no one. Was a real Seventy-two when she was a teenager.'

'Seventy-two?'

'Game of Seventy-two. Think it started in Toronto. Kids go missing for seventy-two hours, no contact with family, phone switched off. Idea is to get us to chase our tails. Extra points if we make tits of ourselves by going public.'

'So no one will authorise resources on her?'

'I used up all my favours getting her bank account tracked.'

'Okay, send over the details and I'll see if I can call in a favour, but I can't promise anything without a warrant. What's her name?'

'Emer Davidson. Flatmate reported her missing so I went by her office last week to see if I'd catch her or chat up the security guard. No one there except a prick in a Maserati. He wasn't giving anything up.'

Kay waggled her fingers at me in an attempt to join the conversation.

'My partner's here, Chris. I'll update her and call you by close of business.'

'Ta muchly, Bridge.'

A tone in Chris's voice had me running back to the office at full pelt, outpacing Kay on every stride as her breathing rasped behind me.

'Slow down, Bridge!'

I was in the front doors before Kay got to the compound. At my desk with Chris's email on the screen before she flopped into her seat.

'It's a contactless payment from a point of sale terminal at 19.04 on Wednesday 8th November, just outside our time of death.'

Kay, still short of breath, nodded.

I rang a college pal who headed up legal for Farringtons' Supermarkets.

'Brian?'

'Speaking, Bridge Harney, Where have you been, Miss? When was the last time I clapped eyes on you?'

'Yonks, sorry, but you still have me saved on your mobile.'

Kay snorted at my use of 'yonks'.

'And I know by your voice this isn't social,' he said. 'What'll it be?'

'I need CCTV at your till points in East Wall Road, 19.04 on 8th November, please. Cash Point 5 please if you have specific cameras for each lane.'

'That's what I like about you, Bridge, balls of steel. Why would I do that? Is there something in it for me?'

'A like on your Facebook page, making a married father of two look like he's a police-girl's pin-up?'

'I'd prefer a couple of points lost off my licence.'

'Jesus wept! They monitor calls in here, Brian.'

He guffawed down the phone. 'Go on, send me over the details of what you need.'

'Gmail to Gmail – that okay?'

'Oh, it's like that, is it? All Special Branch?'

He was laughing, but I noted a boyish excitement in his voice.

'What's it called now?' he asked.

'Special Detective Unit.'

Kay eyed me.

'You'll have it within the hour,' said Brian. He sounded like he was part of a *Hardy Boys* adventure.

'I'm impressed, Brian.'

'You should be – we've spent a fortune updating our CCTV systems – surveillance is real time now, there's nowhere in any store that isn't covered and it's all online.' There was real pride in his voice.

When I hung up Kay turned towards me, a small smile playing on her lips. 'What's with the reference to SDU?'

'Ah, he was so excited I had to give him something . . .'

True to the efficient Brian I remembered, I had his email forty minutes later.

'Kay, how can I watch this video and share it with Chris at the same time?'

I knew calling our IT support line was a waste of time. I'd yelled too often at them so they'd backlisted my calls.

Kay raised a single eyebrow. Her deft fingers flew over my keyboard and sent out a webinar invitation to Chris, giving him a local Birmingham number to dial into.

'Can't we Skype?'

'Get you, Miss Technical – no, we can't. I don't know what size file your retail buddy has sent over and I've no idea what blocks Chris's firewall might use.'

'How do you know this stuff, Kay?'

'Some of us listen to the IT support guys.'

I had the grace to look ashamed.

'Also, while you were clock-watching I checked our registers and databases – we've nothing on an Emer Davidson from

Birmingham. No one's come in through Dublin Port or the airports using that name in the last ten days. Doesn't mean she isn't in the country – she could have travelled under an alias.'

'Nice one, Kay.'

'Don't sound so surprised, Bridge.' She swung her butty little body in an excited curve – like me, Kay loved the chase.

She opened the bridge and I uploaded the file, texting Chris to dial in immediately.

'Hi, Chris, this is Bridget. Kay, my partner, is on as well.'

'Hallo, Bridge – hallo, Kay – nice to speak,' said Chris.

Kay was grinning and falling for Chris's northern charm.

We were all in place as the AVI file opened. It was clear and covered the entire check-out lane – the number 5 was visible in lit-up green. We watched as the girl put a couple of items on the belt and waited for her turn. She was scrawny and hunched over. Chris muttered his frustration. We saw the shiny blue Barclay's card as the girl waved it over the point-of-sale terminal.

'Chris, what do you think? That your girl?' I didn't like the thought of yet another missing girl. I wanted one of them to be found.

'Can you enlarge it? Doesn't look like her, but it's impossible to tell, she's all hunched over.'

As I was about to try the zoom function, the girl on the video looked up. Not much more than a child, but I knew her pinched face.

'No,' said Chris, almost drowned out by Kay and me as we identified the girl at the same moment.

'Lorraine Quigley!'

I was off my seat and pumping the air. Liam O'Shea twisted himself around in his swivel-chair to get a better look at me and all but choked on his phone cord.

'What are you so happy about?' said a disembodied voice in my ear.

I righted the microphone on the headset. On the video Lorraine collected her shopping and exited the aisle.

'She's wetting herself because it's not your girl,' said Kay. 'That's Lorraine Quigley, Seán Flannery's girlfriend. If she has your girl's bank card, chances are Flannery's involved.'

'Who's he?' asked Chris.

'He's nobody. Or at least we believe he goes to great trouble to make himself look like a nobody,' said Kay.

'Aye, they're the dangerous ones.'

'This may be the first mistake he's made,' she said.

'Right then, one thing is clear. This isn't Emer Davidson. She's still missing. I'll go around to her apartment and bag up a hairbrush or something and get her profiled. In the meantime, I'll formally connect your case file to mine and flag it on the national database. That'll give me something other than a runaway to catch my guv's attention.'

'Sounds good, Chris – but a word of advice?' I said.

'Go on.'

'Maybe just call it the database – don't use words like national if you can help it.'

'Oh, right.' His embarrassment travelled down the phone line. 'Sorry, was on a case with Northern Ireland recently. Probably shouldn't say Éire either.'

'Now you're getting the hang of it, Chris.'

I put the phone down and looked at Kay.

'This is it, Kay. Now Joe or Superintendent O'Connor can't have any reason to deny me the armed response unit to pick up Lorraine Quigley.'

Kay looked at me for what felt like a long time. Looking back, I wonder if she had a premonition of the lighted rag I'd just thrown into the munitions dump.

CHAPTER 23

DECLAN

2002

'I'm pregnant.'

Cheryl was looking at me with a kind of horror in her eyes. I looked at myself, reflected in Gregg's shiny counter. My mouth was open and full of sausage roll. I gagged on the pastry and spicy meat and tried to swallow.

'Calm down, Declan.' Cheryl handed me a tissue. 'Dry your fingers.'

I didn't bother with the tissues and gulped at a glass of water. It spilled down the side of my mouth. The shop was suddenly at an angle and the plastic chair toppled. I was on the floor with the kids around me laughing and pointing. I thought I might vomit down the front of my school uniform.

What was my mam going to say when she heard I got a girl in the club?

'Declan? Declan? You okay?'

Cheryl was beside me trying to rub my back through my coat

— the rapper chains under my school shirt were choking me.

I was outside and gulped at the misty air. Time separated into tiny puddles waiting to come together, just like the rain on the tarmac, unnoticed by anyone except me. An old Corolla's horn shattered the silence. All my hinges jerked, knees and elbows raised in a string-less dance. From a cold moment I thought it was my dad's car. If he found out, I was dead. I started to run home.

Cheryl called my name and for a time she seemed to be getting closer. But I was fast. My legs pumped and my trainers spanked the lumpy pavement, the pace turning my lungs an iron-red. I swerved to avoid hills of broken cement and kept pushing myself on. I was in a race and if I crossed the line of my front door I'd win — and all of this pregnancy stuff would disappear.

Now I knew I didn't love Cheryl. I wasn't going to be tied to her in some falling-down flat in Lozzell Grove for the rest of my life. Smoking spliff with Shabba and boosting cars. I was made for better than that. My muscles contracted and released as the motion of my sprinting increased. My breath tasted like I'd licked the inside of the kitchen bin. The harder I pounded my feet, the more it sounded like the beat of a train. I knew what I was going to do. I was going to pack a bag and jump the barriers at the Jewellery Quarter station. I'd go to London.

Our block came into sight, same as all the others. Twenty-four floors of families made from every combination possible. My family was somewhat unusual, being a mother and father with one child. 'Enfant unique' as my mother put it, when she was in her cups. Which wasn't so often and that was another unique thing in Lozzell Grove.

I peered through the bubble-wrap glass but couldn't make out any moving shapes inside. My key had been a sixteenth birthday present, which made little difference as most of us could open any front door with a piece of straightened coat hanger. I eased my key into the gold-coloured lock. Silence greeted me. The fart smell of broccoli soup hung in the hall, evidence that my dad had come home for lunch from his job in the plastics factory. After Cheryl's news, the smell of food sent my stomach into contractions and I doubled over beside our console table.

My mam was so proud of that table – she and Dad had to go to Wednesbury to get it – there wasn't an Ikea in Birmingham. No one around here had anything like it. I had a bedroom full of stuff from Ikea. I was the only person I knew with a CD player in their room. It was over at Shabba's brother's place and I wanted it back. I didn't want to leave home either. What was I going to do in London?

'Declan, alanna?' said my mother.

I hated the way she used Irish words, but not today.

'What's happened? You're the colour of cement. Why aren't you in school? Were you fighting? It's that bloody Cheryl, isn't it?'

At the mention of Cheryl's name, tears formed at the back of my eyes. Hot rocks lodged in my stomach and I reached out to my mam. She pulled me in and I pressed my face into her neck.

'She's pregnant, Mam.'

There was a moment of silence and my mother's breathing gurgled like Shabba's bong.

'That little nigger tart! How dare she try to lay this at our door. That baby isn't even yours, love! She's been catting around this estate since she was fourteen and thought she'd trap you, my beautiful boy! Well, she can think again. If she comes near this flat, I'll beat her black arse blue. And you'll have nothing more to do with her. I'm going to speak to your father.' My mother bit her lip and was quiet for a moment. 'I'll speak to Mrs Robertson too — she was always good to us when I cleaned for her. Thought highly of me and praised my work. Of course, I'm honest and never let her down.' My mam nodded to herself. 'Her husband was on the City Council.'

I could hear the capitals in my mother's voice.

'She'll be able to help us. Advise us on how to get you out of that school and into a decent grammar school. That one I'm cleaning at the minute, King Edwards up at Five Ways. I might speak to the head directly. Tell him you're being bullied. Yes, that's what I'll do. I'll leave Mrs Robertson up my sleeve until my back's against the wall.'

My mother spoke her plans out loud, her neurons unable to make connections in silence. I lay against her soft frame and buried my face in her safe smell.

I couldn't be a father. I was just a kid.

CHAPTER 24

BRIDGET

2018

Flurries of ice crystals circled me. They clung to my clothes and blew into any orifice they could find exposed. The tiny hairs inside my nose crusted with frost as I waited at Birmingham airport for a delayed Chris Watkiss. It wasn't helping my mood. Chris had confirmed that our severed arms belonged to Emer Davidson and had instructed me to get on a plane quick as I liked. I hadn't liked it much at all: the thought of bringing in Lorraine Quigley was the only thing I could focus on.

'*Bridge!*' It was Chris, big upper body half out his car window.

It took me out of my reverie pretty quick.

We were soon on the M6, ploughing our way into Birmingham city centre, but the traffic moved like stop-start animation.

'Ruddy Colmore Circus is a nightmare to get into. Flipping road works on the Coventry Road are a never-ending cycle – they resurface the road then a couple of weeks later they're back digging again.'

Chris didn't seem to need an answer so I let him rant. He'd

never seen Harcourt Square – its location didn't exactly scream fit for purpose.

'Might as well settle in for the long haul, Bridge. This bugger won't free up anytime soon. I could put the lights on if you'd like? Mind you, it's been done so often that folks here are wise to it and don't move over.'

'No, it's fine, Chris. You can update me now on where we are.'

Chris raised a straggly eyebrow and I realised too late how bossy I sounded.

'Sorry, that didn't come out right – but I'm a bit niggled that you never told me about Emer Davidson in the first place.'

'It was a hunch – told you that and this isn't my first disco. "Only a fool uttereth all his mind."'

It was a saying my mother used and, though I liked the concept, I didn't much like having it quoted at me.

Chris expertly palmed the steering wheel. The Alpha was an old sports model with an all-leather trim. The steering wheel looked like black liquorice that had been squeezed once too often. The car had a fresh, green smell and Chris must have seen me looking for the source.

'Wife puts curry leaves in a muslin bag.' He nodded at the panel in between us. 'Takes the pong out of the car. Married to an Indian girl. Swapna.'

He wrestled his wallet out of his pocket with his left hand, then flicked it open. A picture of a petite woman, wrapped in a rose-gold sari with a strapping girl on each side of her.

'Girls take after me.' Chris was in danger of spontaneous combustion.

It was hard not to smile with him. 'They're gorgeous girls.'

We drove in silence, but it had edges. I was quiet until I couldn't be any more.

'Sorry I sounded rude earlier.'

'Good of you to say. Mind, if Dublin's anything like Birmingham a woman detective would have to put her fists up plenty to be heard.' Chris shuffled around in the driver's seat, scratching off the wood-beaded cushion.

'That's for sure.'

'Okay – an update. When I collected Emer's hairbrush for DNA profiling I spoke to her flatmate. Not a lot to say. I'd imagine it was more convenience than friendship brought those two together, but she did say Emer had a married boyfriend. Gave her trinkets and such. Took her posh places.'

'Did the girl seem reliable?'

Chris raised his shoulders up to his ears in an expressive gesture. 'Aye, she were the one who reported Emer missing but I'd say she were more worried about the rent. I had a look at Emer's jewellery box – what I could see they're good quality. Or at least expensive-looking. And where's a girl like Emer Davidson going to get stuff like that? Her job didn't pay anything out of the ordinary.'

'You knew Emer?'

'No . . . well, yes and no. I know her type. Twenty-three years old but been taking care of herself for a long time. Brought up in Lozzell Grove, mother was unmarried but had a job. Which is unusual enough in those parts. Couple of anti-social-behaviour-orders against Emer, breaking into the local community centre, drinking and running away. All this, mind, at the age of thirteen. Would take off for days at a time. Mother never seemed too bothered and took up with a lad good bit older than herself. All three moved to Mijas outside Malaga when Emer was sixteen. Mother is still there, I rang her.'

'You told Emer's mother she was dead? With her arms cut off? On the phone?'

'No! I asked her to come home and identify some items

belonging to Emer. I wanted to go to see her, but my Detective Inspector Maitland is a right tight-arse – excuse the language – and wouldn't sign off on the expense. Flipping Ryanair flight for £56 return! Cheap as ruddy chips.'

'We've got a few of those,' I said, smiling.

'I got the embassy to visit the mother and break the news. She identified the arm by link-up.'

'Didn't want to see it in person? Is she going to come home and bury the remains?'

'No, like I said she's a tough old bint, waived all claim to the body parts. Emer left Spain when she was eighteen, mother hasn't seen her since or had any contact. Emer came back to Black Country a couple of years ago, had a couple of waitressing jobs, then got her feet under the table in Birmingham with Burgess Data Centre.'

As soon as Chris saw an opening, he revved the engine and screeched up an off-ramp.

'Sod this flaming traffic, Bridge. We'll go straight out to Burgess Data Centre and question Emer's boss, Declan Swan. He's the prick in the Maserati I was telling you about. Loves himself, pound to a penny he's the married boyfriend. Not only that.' Here Chris paused, wearing his best rabbit-out-of-a-hat face. 'Declan Swan is related to those Burgesses. That robbery of yours out in Dalkey. He's only the son-in-law. Got to be a connection there, right?'

Now I was freshly riled. Why hadn't he told me this before? How did he even know about about the robbery? Kay obviously.

'I'm not so sure. We like a gang for that, very professional job.'

'What's to stop Declan Swan hiring a gang?'

'In Dublin? How? Rent a crook.com?'

'All right.' Chris sounded huffy.' 'No need to get sarky, but it's worth looking at.'

'For sure. Did Kay tell you about the robbery?'

'Aye.' Chris seemed oblivious to my irritation. 'My DI wants an update, but we've precious little worth talking about – let's see if we can't add to our store of information by having a chat with Swan.' He grinned like a naughty boy caught checking his parents' liquor cabinet and swung the car onto Birmingham's ring road.

'Any social-media activity with Emer Davidson?' I was slow-breathing out my ire.

'She was on Facebook, Instagram and had a snapchat ID, but we haven't got her phone. I have her laptop back in the Circus – some of the technical lads are getting into it.'

'Will you update us on anything you find? Also Kay's handy at finding the black accounts.'

'Black accounts?'

'Accounts that a user has under a different name – usually to post dick or tit pics.'

'Classy.' Chris sighed. 'I hope my girls never get to that.'

'They won't.' I nudged him. 'While we're at it can we look at Declan Swan's social-media footprint, please?'

'Already on it. They're all private accounts and it's unlikely they'll give us permission, but we've asked, just to get the 'no'. One of the lads in IT is working on getting access. There's a video on YouTube about getting into private Instagram accounts. Apparently it's all the rage.'

'If Instagram couldn't be hacked we'd know all about it because hackers would be discussing it all over the Web.'

'You're not a fan, I take it.'

'Can't bear the thought of being profiled to the vanishing point.' I shook my head. 'I saw Emer Davidson's public account on Instagram. She was a beauty, but young-looking even for twenty-three. She looked more like a teenager to me.' I felt old and sad in the same breath.

'Aye – still she wasn't the type the keep her light under a bushel. Putting up photos of herself near naked.'

'I loathe the way these girls are convinced to exploit themselves. Believing their bodies are the only thing of value they possess. Hashtag-no-regrets my backside. They put up soft porn pictures of their own volition while every idiot ogles them. And that's a best-case scenario. Don't think it doesn't have far-reaching consequences for those of us that keep our clothes on. It plays to every male who believes women shouldn't have positions of power because we'll be unbalanced by our tits.'

'Right,' said Chris, clearly a bit taken aback.

'Sorry, I'll get off my soapbox.' When I was passionate about something I gave it everything, but judging from Chris's face I was coming across as unhinged.

A soft rain started to fall. Light drops speckled the window and were spread and thinned as Chris picked up speed. I got lost in the struggling raindrops as the acres slipped by and tried to break my mind's looping thoughts of Seán Flannery.

'You've not said owt for nearly ten minutes – everything okay, Bridge? Are you worried about Declan Swan? I can tell you now he's no match for you. Bit of a ponce if you ask me.'

'It's not that.'

My chin dipped into my scarf and I nibbled on the coarse grain of the wool. An old habit. A bad habit.

'Go on,' said Chris.

'I'm wondering how Emer Davidson is connected to Seán Flannery.'

Chris gave a gentle nod. 'The bank card? Maybe he had it and Lorraine nicked it?'

'That wouldn't be safe, he'd kill her. That card leads us right back to him.'

'Is she a junkie? She didn't look too healthy on the video. People on that crap don't think straight, Bridge.'

'Flannery must have taken Emer's handbag when he snatched her. But why would he do that?' My eyes were stinging with the effort of making the pieces fit.

'Easy, Bridge, you're getting a ways ahead of yourself here. It would hardly be clever if he'd killed Emer Davidson, then gave his girlfriend Emer's bank card. In fact, if it points to anything, it's more likely to prove he didn't know Emer. More likely his girlfriend bought the wallet and identity from a fence and Flannery never had owt to do with Emer.'

'I'm not buying that.' I held my hand up to ward Chris off. 'I don't know if she's on anything and she didn't look that lucid on the CCTV, I'll give you that, but I know Flannery's involved. He's involved in the Burgess robbery as well.'

'Do you have proof of that?' said Chris.

'No, but it's a micro-clean scene, which is how he operates. I know it's him.'

Chris's face had a set look to it, like he was struggling to keep his thoughts from playing out.

'You don't believe me?' I said.

'It's not that, Bridge. You may be right — but I think you're making some hasty assumptions.'

My mouth flew open.

'All right, all right, don't go off on one!' he said. 'Flannery's girlfriend had the card, so he's a person of interest for Emer's murder and with the Burgess-Declan Swan link it puts him in the frame for the robbery in Dalkey. However, I'd still look at other gangs. Those Dunnes are still active.'

'I know.' I could be magnanimous in victory and beamed at Chris.

'No need to look like Cheshire Cat.' He focused on the road

ahead, both hands gripping the steering wheel, leaving indentations on the soft leather.

He certainly knew a lot about the Burgess robbery. Suddenly I was angry again. 'So you've been in contact with Kay – without me knowing.'

Chris's eyebrows climbed all the way up his forehead.

Heat blistered up my face and I pictured Kay's wagging finger in an effort to stay calm.

'With the greatest respect, Bridge, you're not particularly forthcoming on the information front. Only reason I know about the robbery is because Kay sent me photos of jewellery belonging to Anne Burgess, in case I could get a match.'

'Well, I didn't know they were connected,' I said.

'But you expected me to know!'

I was putting Chris's back up and had to mollify him. 'Sorry, I'm just a bit out of sorts. It's good we're joining the dots before we go in to Declan Swan.'

'Did you just say "joining the dots"? Kay will get a great laugh out of your corporate-speak when I tell her.' He gave me a grin that showed quarter of an inch of pink gum over his front teeth but felt like sunshine.

We turned a gravelly corner into a nondescript industrial estate and pulled up outside a series of unmarked buildings, each with a domed roof of lichen-coloured copper.

'Here we are, Burgess Data Centre. A handy earner if Mike Burgess's most recent tax return is anything to go by.'

'You can access Her Majesty's Revenue and Customs?'

'Course I can! Can't you get into Revenue in Ireland?'

'No, well, possibly I could, but I'd have to be in the Criminal Assets Bureau and they won't give me resources for someone they deem low risk.'

'They reckon you're too keen on Flannery? And he's not worth a punt?'

I flushed, my face shining in the windscreen. 'He is worth a punt, he's just too clever to put his head above the parapet. Would you do me a favour?'

'I'm way ahead of you. Seán Flannery has no assets in the UK. Legal anyways.'

'Damn.'

CHAPTER 25

DECLAN

I would have put her in her early thirties, a real beauty in that cold calculated way some women have, but her hands gave her away. They were the size of shovels. I knew where I'd seen her before: Dublin docks.

Chris Watkiss introduced himself and I frowned in the act of remembrance, more to give myself time. Sweat beaded on the skin between my fingers. I stood up, splaying my fingers to air-dry them.

'Detective Garda Bridget Harney,' said the haughty blonde and offered me a strong hand to shake.

I almost didn't take it. She made me nervous straight away — something about the quality of her stare. I knew if she found out about Emer she'd get her hooks into both Lydia and me. I looked right into her green eyes and tried to get the measure of her. She had an expensive smell, some kind of floral concoction I would have associated with a more petite woman, at odds with the Amazon across the desk from me.

'Thank you for seeing us at short notice, Mr Swan,' she said.

I gave her a high-watt smile. 'It's no problem. I'm always happy to help law enforcement.'

I tried to recalibrate my inner cheese-o-meter. I sounded like a people-pleaser. I decided to show them my boardroom in the hope of diverting them. It was an imposing grey room with a burnt-orange woven carpet, a stark contrast I liked. Old Man Burgess had insisted a painting of him, standing on the 10th hole at the Brabazon, was stuck up on the wall opposite the door. He could barely hack around the par 3 Golfbug course without picking up, never mind a Professional Golfer's Association course.

I took my time leading them into the boardroom, to let the sweat that was building at the base of my spine run off. I gestured to some chairs and we sat in a L-shape at the top of the table. Chris Watkiss almost pulled the steel-framed chair apart getting it out from under the table.

'Can I get you anything? Tea? Coffee? A sandwich? I think my secretary got fresh scones this morning.'

'I'm fine, Mr Swan, thank you,' said Bridget Harney. 'This room has real flare.'

Chris Watkiss raised his eyebrows. I wanted to tell him he wouldn't know taste if it landed on his buds.

'That's very kind of you, Guard-ah Harney. Am I saying that correctly? What's a Guard-ah?'

'Thank you, Mr Swan. Yes, you're saying it perfectly and I'm a detective in the Irish Police Force – An Garda Síochána.'

I liked her quaint, multi-vowel pronunciation and hoped my interest was giving her a positive feeling towards me.

'Anyhoo,' said Watkiss.

It was a stupid expression, made more so coming from a man the size of a Shire horse.

'You called here, Detective Watkiss, a couple of weeks back. Didn't you?' I gave him a mate's grin. 'I remember, you have an Alpha in great condition. A 5500, my favourite model. Great pace when you need it and sleek design.'

He looked like a dog with two dicks.

'That's correct, Mr Swan.' He reddened, but his gaze stayed level.

I kept a small smile stapled onto my face. I needed to win him over, but there was something in the frank interrogation of his look that told me I'd failed.

'All right then, I'll continue,' he said. 'Detective Garda Harney is here to observe, nothing more. I'm here to ask you about Ms Emer Davidson, your employee, formerly of Carver Street.'

'Formerly?' My blood felt like it had curdled and my heart beat in single, painful thumps. I was glad I had sat down. 'What . . . what do you mean?'

'Surely you've missed Miss Davidson over the last number of weeks, Mr Swan?'

'Please, call me Declan. Mr Swan sounds like my father.' I didn't know what I was saying. The inside of my mouth was chalky and the words were sticking to each other. 'When . . . where did this happen?'

'Detective Harney found Emer Davidson's arm in Dublin a couple of weeks ago.'

'That was Emer?'

'Yes. Emer's second arm was found a couple of days ago in Centenary Square.'

'*What?*' It came out as a shriek. High-pitched and female-sounding, I couldn't believe I'd made it. The room was pulsing in my vision and the automatic room-scent dispenser hissed out a pump of lavender so strong my mouth tasted purple.

'It's in the *Birmingham News*,' said Chris Watkiss.

'I don't read that, it's not how I get my news . . .' I was talking too much. 'How did this happen?' Both detectives looked at me with steady eyes. They must do a course in this: how to make an innocent man feel guilty.

'You don't think I had anything to do with this, do you?'

'Why would we think that, Declan?' It was the first time she had asked a question.

A car alarm burst into life outside, the insulation in the building making it sound like a yapping dog. The noise droned on. Seconds ticked by and neither cop moved. The big lump crossed his legs – he was wearing some old-man type of corduroy and sounded like a deck of cards being cut when he moved.

He leaned in to the table. 'How long were you having an affair with Emer Davidson?'

It was an ice cube down my back. I quelled the impulse to dial my solicitor – that would make me look guilty. However, if I sat through much more of this, they'd put words in my mouth.

'You have no proof of that.' These weren't innocent words and a muscle bunched at the back of my neck, forcing my shoulders up.

Bridget Harney leaned in and eyeballed me.

'I think you might want to reconsider your response, Declan,' she said.

Watkiss nodded and I attempted a thousand-yard stare, but it was difficult to do with your system overloaded. My jaw tightened and my mouth tasted like I'd been sucking pennies.

'Emer's flatmate reported her missing some weeks ago, Mr Swan,' said Watkiss. 'I noticed you didn't mention to anyone that Emer hadn't turned up for work. Is that what a responsible employer does?'

It was the way he said 'Emer's flatmate'.

'I'm not anyone's keeper. If someone doesn't turn up for

work, they're fired. Period.'

'Fair enough, but there's no P45 filed for Ms Davidson by your organisation,' he said. 'So you didn't fire Emer. Why was she an exception, Mr Swan?'

I looked up at the ceiling and tried to swallow. 'I'm sorry, I think I'm trying to brazen out something you already know. Yes, Emer and I had an affair. I've never done anything like that before,' I was babbling, 'but Emer was from Lozzell Grove, that's where I'm from and when she applied for a job I wanted to help. And she was good at her job, we became involved, but I ended it months ago and when Emer left I assumed it was best for both of us. You're not going to tell my wife, are you?'

'How long did the affair last?' said Watkiss.

'Four months, maybe five, it started at a company sales conference. Please, does my wife have to know about this?'

The big lad looked hard-faced, like he'd heard it all before, but she seemed to mellow.

'No, not if it isn't material to our investigation,' she said.

'But you'd be in a sight of trouble if your wife were to find out, wouldn't you? All this,' he made a circling gesture with a hairy finger, 'is your father-in-law's. Belongs to the Burgesses. You're the lackey in a flash car and your wife has you by the balls. Have I missed anything, Mr Swan?'

'How dare you speak to me like that! I'm co-operating fully with you.'

'What do you have to co-operate about, Mr Swan?' said Bridget Harney.

She was a cold bitch and her question had a slaughterhouse feel to it, like I was next in line for the stun gun.

'I think you should leave. If you want to question me again make an appointment and I'll have my solicitor with me.'

'You do that, Mr Swan,' said Watkiss. 'We'll be back, with a warrant if needed and we might as well have a chat with your wife.'

The grey walls started to blur. Lydia couldn't be involved. Bile foamed in my stomach and I put a hand to my mouth to cover a belch. The air-freshener hissed again.

'Let's try and take this down a level,' said Bridget Harney.

I couldn't work out if she was talking to me or to Watkiss.

'Perhaps I might change the subject?' she said. 'What do you know, Declan, about a robbery of the Burgess house in Dalkey?'

'Mike and Anne's place in Dublin? They were broken into?' I was reeling like a rookie prize-fighter taking blows from a pro and wondering why my agent had ever put me in the ring. 'Mike never mentioned anything to me.'

'That's peculiar,' said Watkiss. 'Doesn't he trust you?'

I shot to my feet. 'Get out! I bloody mean it. And if you do come back with a warrant I'll have a barrage of solicitors waiting for you.' I was standing with my hands in fists on the boardroom table, leaning over in a Hitlerian triangle. Drops of my saliva sat on the polished wood like cuckoo spit. 'Move it or I'll have my father-in-law call Terry Pike! How would you like your life peeled back, Watkiss?'

'Who's Terry Pike?'

It was Bridget Harney asking Chris Watkiss. The question echoed around the marble-tiled staircase. They were clumping down the backstairs to the main exit.

'West Midlands Chief Constable. Who puts stuff this expensive on a backstairs? We've cement in the station at the Circus.'

'We do too, like a car park, but it shows how much money there is in this data-centre business.'

She sounded amicable.

'Wide boys get everything,' he said.

I had hidden microphones built into the stairwell and in the lifts during the original fit-out. It wasn't entirely legal, but I believed in taking every possible business advantage. It helped to hear what potential clients said when they thought no one was listening and it had become a habit. Now I listened to everyone.

'I think Pike's a member at the Belfry. You saw that painting of Burgess on the golf course? Ugly daub, but that's the Belfry golf club. I doubt there'll be any calls put in. All wind and pee is our Declan Swan.'

'Why did you try and rile him? He's not hiding anything. Or at least he came clean pretty quickly when we asked about Emer Davidson.'

'We knew she was having an affair.'

'With a married man – we didn't know it was Swan – well, you assumed it was.'

'And I was right.'

'That doesn't make him a murderer.'

He snorted. 'Don't fall for that schoolboy-butter-wouldn't-melt stuff. "This room has real flare, Mr Swan."'

She gave a husky laugh. 'Well, it did! You don't like this guy, do you, Chris?'

'He'd eat hisself if he were made of chocolate. Profile on him and Burgess's daughter in DLuxe magazine when they got married – apparently they were school sweethearts. One of the most expensive weddings in Birmingham, if my missus is to be believed.'

I could make out Bridget Harney's footsteps as she walked down the tiled stairs – they were lighter than Chris Watkiss's, who pushed each foot down like he was trying to fracture the marble.

'Do you like him for it?' he said.

There was a pause.

I was still in the same position as when they had left, leaning on the table, my knuckles hurting from the pressure I was exerting on them.

Then she spoke.

'I can't see him murdering anyone. Though the affair stands against him and gives him motive for murder. If Emer was blackmailing him she had no extra money in her bank account to show for it. Just some fancy jewellery.'

'Maybe they had a row? Emer threatened to go to his wife and he killed her?'

'Then hacked up her body and dumped one arm in Dublin and put another in Centenary Square?' she said. 'Why would he do that? And where did he put the rest of the body?'

'I don't know, but my gut's telling me it's him. Might have got someone to do his dirty work for him and they're blackmailing him?'

'Sounds like Seán Flannery.'

'Is Seán Flannery the only villain in Dublin, Bridge?'

Watkiss was laughing.

'It was just an observation, Chris.'

'Save your blushes, lass. I reckon you've got a point. We'll look into any connections. But is Flannery a gun for hire?'

'No, he's not. Or only to other crooks who might have something he wants like territory or drugs. I can't see Declan Swan working for the cartels.'

'He's too stupid,' said Chris Watkiss and belted out an oafish laugh.

The pumping power of my heart muscles seemed to have trebled, blood roared through my head. I wanted to run down to the foyer and tell them I'd nothing to do with drugs or hacking off arms and didn't know anyone called Seán Flannery, but I'd have to admit I'd been eavesdropping and my reputation for integrity wasn't riding high.

CHAPTER 26

BRIDGET

Saint Martin's Gardens was at some point a row of terraced houses with crisp paint and neat front gardens. Perhaps a row of box hedges punctuated by black gates.

Not any more.

Now it was 'The Gardens': houses with boarded-up windows, others with shiny stone cladding, some with single-parent families, still others with three generations under one roof.

I touched my gun. It was a standard issue to all organised-crime detectives: Sig Sauer. And my talisman. If I carried it, I wouldn't have to use it. That at least was the theory. There were five of us in the Garda wagon. One of the new lads had his stab vest too loose. I reached over and tightened the Velcro clasps.

'Has to be snug,' I said, which sounded ludicrous in the overheated quiet of the car.

He flushed a stinging red and his pimples pulsed. I should have said something to make him feel better but my mouth tasted like

I'd been licking batteries. The interior had the sharp musk of building testosterone. I was drenched in it and wanted air. I flicked down a window and flared my nostrils. The tarry smell of Dublin Port filled the car.

'What are you doing, Harney?' barked the Emergency Response detective driving. 'Get that window up.' Under normal circumstances he wouldn't have noticed the change in air pressure.

The red indicator signalled our approach to the Gardens. It made a ticking sound as we pulled in. *Tick. Tick. Tick.*

The car stopped. The estate was empty save for prowling teenagers. They flexed scrawny sinews, stretched themselves upwards and sniffed for our scent like feral dogs. Then touched spaces behind their backs that I prayed were empty. The air bristled with electricity when we got out. Pimples barged into me and static crackled between us like bee-sting. Someone laughed. The teenagers echoed the sound and it became a jarring pack call. My scalp tightened.

The pock-marked kerbs were lined with BMWs and Lexus jeeps. Gangsta cars. Hastily abandoned brightly coloured plastic trikes and unicorns were festooned around them like fairy lights. It told us of the human shield indoors. Seán Flannery knew we were coming. I tried to mould my face into casual boredom.

He was on his doorstep, his body propped against the rough lintel, a rictus of smile stretched over his teeth.

'Mr Flannery,' I saluted him.

He twitched in response, a lick of hate locked away in those dead eyes.

'You're all tooled up today, Harney. The lads with the MP7s. Frightened of the Gardens?'

'We've had a number of assaults on the gardaí here, some

leaving members of the Force in hospital for weeks at a time.'

'Members of the Force.' He pantomimed my voice and raised himself up on his tip-toes. He was shirtless, with flesh the colour of lard, but worked out. That surprised me – he had thin shoulders and I'd assumed he would have a starved, not toned quality to him. I found his nakedness in this cold unsettling, but it did reveal a network of red, wire-like streaks. Stab wounds. He was a survivor.

'Might I come in, Mr Flannery?'

'Why not?'

Getting Seán Flannery might have been what my life revolved around. But if he was my obsession, I was his.

'Don't put any gloves on now, Blondie.'

The game was on. I'd asked his permission to access his house, therefore anything I found was admissible in court – but, as I had no gloves on, anything I touched would be contaminated with my DNA and prints, therefore his counsel could say I planted it. Round and round we went.

'No gloves, Mr Flannery.'

'Call me Seán.'

I twisted my mouth up into a smile. His onlookers threw catcalls at us, but nothing else.

The Emergency Response unit with me requested orders.

'Tell the attack dogs to get back into the car,' said Seán. 'Just you.'

'And me, Mr Flannery,' said Kay. 'Don't want Bridge to get lonely in there.'

'Oh yeah, bring Dawn French with you an' all.'

I motioned the armed response unit to stand down and followed Seán Flannery into his castle. The house was clean. Anything that could have chrome applied was coated in it. A vulgar purple couch was stuffed into a front room he'd knocked through to the kitchen. The couch reminded me of a flabby intestine I had the misfortune of seeing at an autopsy. Two young pit bulls let out base, territorial growls.

It was force of habit, trying to see out of the back of my head, so I glanced around and when Kay wiped her hand along the collar of a thin anorak inside the door, my breath stalled. It was Seán Flannery's. I'd seen him wearing it. Kay moved her thumb against the brace of her fingers, like she had caught something.. She was doing it in plain view and at a normal speed. My heart careened around in my chest like an over-spun top as I blocked Flannery's view of her.

A little girl, eleven months old I guessed, was cooped up in a playpen. Her nappy hung between her legs and stank. She clung to the railings in her own filth and sobbed.

'*Lorraine! The baby!*' Seán lifted his voice over the sound of the child's crying. Nothing.

'*Lorraine!*' he tried again. Her lack of response obviously grated on him.

Wordlessly he looked at a lad sitting slouched by the door. The boy was like a spring and leapt to his feet, charging up the stairs.

Then he screeched. In that ear-splitting broken voice of a man-child.

'*Seán! Lorraine's dead! There's a fuc— there's a needle in her arm!*'

Seán Flannery didn't move, but his face cast itself into a sneer.

I couldn't look away from his lack of concern. This was his girlfriend.

Kay raged up the stairs, hitting every second step, her finger pressed into the button on her radio.

'Control, this is ERU three four — we need an ambulance to 54 Saint Martin's Gardens. Suspected overdose.'

Seán Flannery locked eyes with me.

'Seán, you have to let the ambulance through or the armed unit will come in and take Lorraine.'

I wanted to sound forceful, unafraid, but my mind was like a runaway train picturing bullets sinking into tiny limbs if guns were drawn. 'Please.'

I looked at the little girl in the playpen, still sobbing. I couldn't stand Seán Flannery's stillness any longer. I picked her up. She couldn't have weighed more than five bags of sugar and stopped crying immediately. I put her on my shoulder and pulled open cabinets and found white baby cream, wipes and a nappy.

'You looking in my cupboards, Harney?'

The nearness of him was like standing in a boiling wave of bluebottles.

'That's all you've got? Your girlfriend might be dead!' I spat the words out and turned my back to him to block his view and offered up a prayer for protection to whatever passed for the Almighty in the Gardens. The baby gurgled up at me and waved her little legs.

'Don't worry, Harney, she's too young for me.'

It was like putting my hand on exposed electric wire. The urge to do him harm was irresistible, but urges travelled like currents on the invisible circuit boards that connected adults to children. The child wailed, a sound full of fearful anticipation.

'All right, Lorraine love, take it easy. Down the steps . . . I've got you.' They were descending the stairs. Lorraine was a grey mass, slumped on Kay's shoulder. Kay spoke into her radio. 'Control, we're coming out with Lorraine Quigley and a baby.'

It wasn't a plan but something in the set of Kay's shoulders made me block Seán's view. All it took her was a second to swipe the anorak off the coat hook and shove it under her own puffer coat. She kept her focus on Lorraine and ordered me to take the child out to the car. Flannery didn't object and I wasn't waiting for him to.

The whoop sound of the ambulance filled the tiny cul-de-sac and their lights turned everything morgue blue.

Silence descended as Kay brought Lorraine out. The residents of the small terrace stood like sentries as they passed by. I hoped it was a guard of honour, not a reminder to Lorraine to pick a spot on the wall if she survived and was questioned.

I shushed the watchful little girl with fluttering words and kisses, then wrapped her in my scarf and coat. Medics put Lorraine on a gurney and strapped her in. I clambered into the ambulance with Kay, the little girl still in my arms. Neither of us made eye-contact. A medic plunged an IV into Lorraine's arm, the other closed the ambulance door and told the driver to move off.

'The anorak.' I held the child close to me and looked at the cheap, nondescript windbreaker, almost speechless at Kay's quick-smart thinking.

'Got you that hair you wanted – it's all over the collar. Flannery should've had a haircut,' said Kay.

CHAPTER 27

SEÁN

1997

There was always some congealed, past-its-prime pizza in a greasy box sitting in the admissions office in Saint Augustine's Residential Care Centre for young people. Leftovers from the rank-smelling night guards who never left their desks.

Ironically, my exit interview was in the admissions office. Saint Augustine's was big on irony.

'Have a seat, Seán,' said the newest administrator, the current incumbent in a long line of colourless little men who administered to the residents.

'You're eighteen now, officially an adult! How are you going to celebrate leaving us? I hear U2 have a concert coming up.' His face scrunched up in thought. 'PopMart, isn't it? *'Disc-o-theque . . . uh huh . . . uh huh!'*

He sang the lyric in a strained, tuneless voice and bobbed his head up and down like the music was playing in the background.

U2 were a load of wankers with bad hats that liked the smell of themselves. That's what I would have liked to say, but a reaction like that wouldn't get me what I wanted.

'Yeah, might go if we can get tickets. Or maybe me and the lads might go to see that *Men in Black* movie.'

'*Men in Black?* With Will Smith and Tommy Lee Jones? I'll have to catch that myself.'

He was grinning like an idiot now, thinking we'd bonded. As if I'm going to some UFO-loving-nerd's wet dream of a movie. Or like I have 'the lads' to hang around with — but these administrator types didn't like the idea of loners. Most likely I'd ask the man in Bullock Harbour if I could out take one of the dinghies.

'All righty, let's go through your aftercare plan? Not that you need an aftercare plan — you seem well set up.'

He flicked through a flimsy folder with an address and phone number of a boarding house I'd supplied him with. I had paid one month's rent in advance and that's all I intended to pay. I wasn't going to stay in that dive, but I was obliged to supply an address.

'You've a reference here from a Mrs Shelia Devereux of 3rd Avenue in Sheriff Street, a mother of nine and grandmother to your friend Gavin Devereux, saying she'll be in loco parentis. She didn't use those exact words, but it states she is happy to help you however she can.'

I nodded, an unexpected well of emotion rising up inside me at Granny Dev's kindness. Gavin had written to me asking if I needed anything — I'd asked for a reference but I hadn't expected anything.

'You don't need anyone in loco parentis . . . do you know what that means?' He gave a condescending smirk when I nodded. 'But it does help that you've ties to the broader community. The job side is strong too — you got a job, with a garage in Shelbourne Road.'

I smiled as though I'd won the lottery. It was a lock-up that ostensibly changed tyres and exhausts, but it was a chop shop taking in stolen cars. They needed someone who was good at electronics to disable the new onboard computers the expensive marques had. I'd heard about the garage through one of the lads who left Saint Augustine's couple of years back. He knew those of us getting ready to leave were frantic for a few quid. Otherwise you'd be on the streets.

'Yes, I got a job through the placement office.' Those fools couldn't place a mat on a table. 'They're decent blokes.'

The dry air in the office made me cough. The cantilevered windows should have let light stream in, but they were streaked with grime inside and out. Pretty much summed up Saint Augustine's. The administrator thumbed to the second and final page of the file.

'You got good results in your Leaving Certificate. If you like I can look at a bursary for third level? With your results you'd be in like a shot.'

'I'd rather go to night school. There's a tech in Ringsend does an Information Technology cert. I'm applying for that. Going to pay my own way.'

I'd practised saying that in front of the mirror to get my face just right. Not too cocky but not too humble either: steadfast, worthy. He lapped it up.

'Well, I have to say, as residents go you're a model. You've mingled well with your peers, we've had no disciplinary issues and now you find yourself on the cusp of life with a job and an education behind you. I think you might say Saint Augustine's has done well by you. In fact more, it's given you . . .'

I tuned out. How did he know what I'd been through? A priest's favourite from the age of nine, then into teenage dormitories where I fought for a bed, showers, clothes, food. I'd had my fists raised from the moment I came into Saint Augustine's. Nobody snitched, no one told this fool about the organised bareknuckle fights or that the security guards dealt weed and sometimes bet on the fights. I let him congratulate himself for a bit longer.

'I wish you well, young Seán.' He stood up and extended a moist hand. 'Is there anything I can do for you?'

I waited a beat. 'Yes, please, I'd like to say goodbye to Sister Assumpta, but I'm not sure where she's living any more. Could you give me her address?'

'Well, we're not supposed to give out addresses of the Religious. What with all the,' his hand batted the air, 'ongoing enquiries into activities in the past. Alleged misconduct . . .'

His voice trailed off and I put on my most harmless, bland expression.

'Were you close to Sister Assumpta?' he said.

'Yes, she was in the Mother and Baby home where I was born. She taught me how to sail.'

'That's important to you, isn't it, Seán?'

He was studying me so I kept my gaze soft, like I was twined in some soppy memory about Sister Assumpta and the ocean.

'I make a few quid crewing for boat owners during the summer. It was Sister Assumpta's idea. She was good to me. Kind. I wouldn't feel right leaving without thanking her. If I can't see her, would you perhaps give her a letter from me?'

I handed over a crumpled Basildon Bond blue envelope, full of false words of thanks. It was my insurance. It made me look genuine in the moment and, if he refused, he might read the letter when I was gone, believe it was real and give me the address at a later date. It was a gamble.

'Look, why don't I give you her address? I bet she'd be delighted to see you. See how well you've turned out.'

'Thank you, sir.' I returned his smile and watched as he rummaged in his desk drawer.

CHAPTER 28

DECLAN

2018

Some kind of migraine-inducing cold had set in. I craved heat. Carol Kirkwood on BBC One's *Breakfast* told us it was a cold snap, making it sound like a cheerful snack, rather than the hoar frost that adhered itself to everything. I was outside on the penthouse deck and imagined the capillaries in my lungs freezing themselves into a tangle as I breathed in. Lydia had gone in to her job in Bella's boutique in Birmingham city centre, selling tat to idle women whose brains had absorbed too much filler.

I didn't have the luxury of idleness and went back indoors to our safe. Similar to Mike's, it was behind a painting her mother had commissioned of Lydia. The painting swung outwards soundlessly and seemed to land in space, rebuking me. The pads of my fingers found the rubber-like buttons. I punched in the four-digit code and took out Lydia's attaché case, packed with her private documents. Lydia had been open with me when we married — her father had insisted on a pre-nuptial agreement.

Otherwise he wasn't going to settle anything on her.

'Babes, I'll sign anything, you can even draw up something that says no matter what I'll never get any of your money,' I had said. 'I love you.'

And I'd meant it, but till-death-do-us part didn't include either of us being charged with accessory to murder. I had to know how much money Lydia and I could take, or if it came to it, how much money I could lay my hands on. I was shivering, unsure whether it was cold or nerves, but I'd been jittery ever since the police had cornered me and sprung the news about Emer's second arm being found. I suspected that mightn't be news to Lydia, yet I hadn't told her about their visit. She'd been watchful for the last couple of weeks. It was no surprise. We were trying to carry on as though nothing had happened. My mind chewed holes in every idea I came up with for escape. Then there was Ava. She had promised me she wouldn't stay out at night again, but what would become of her if I up and left?

I was getting nowhere and sat on the bed dumbly looking at Lydia's briefcase for I didn't know how long. The thought of the bizzies coming to my door with a warrant was like a wire around my neck. Chris Watkiss had seemed so sure I'd killed Emer. An image of her floated up to me, the curve of her white neck, her startling blue eyes. I didn't know where the rest of her body was. My chest tightened and I closed my eyes against the pointless sorrow of her death. It would help no one.

The duvet bunched under my grip and cooled my fingers. I opened Lydia's briefcase. *Pop*. It sounded like a chicken's neck snapping. I splayed the documents that made me her agent and her savings-account information around like entrails and looked for the most delicate organs: her password information. I used our home laptop and the account was accessed after some simple steps and a random password her fob generated. Too easy for an account that contained over half a million pounds.

I closed my eyes against the temptation to run. Right now. To get on a ferry and sail on the channel's green-glass waves to something new, but I wasn't going anywhere empty-handed. A fledgling escape route led to a cul-de-sac as I looked at the highlighted information on Lydia's account. Old Man Burgess must have told her to put thirty-day unlocks on her deposit account. I couldn't withdraw funds without triggering something on Mike Burgess's end. My thoughts overlaid one another like twisted directions from a botched sat navigator. I kept coming back to Burgess Data Centre. The business had cash on deposit and more in the engineering service accounts, over four hundred thousand. I could break the penalty clause on that account – after much arguing Lydia had convinced her father to loosen some financial controls – but I could still only authorise one hundred grand at any given time. I needed more. I dialled Lydia's mobile phone and she picked up on the third ring.

'Yes, Declan?'

When I pictured Lydia at work, she was always deriding hapless men to her co-workers as they stood, stranded by dress rails, waiting on their wives. It was a place I avoided.

'Want to go out to lunch today?'

'Oh!' It was a squeal of delight. 'I can't remember the last time we went out to eat! Can we go to Adams, please? Oh my God, their smoked potato and guinea fowl and I'd have just enough room for the chocolate mascarpone mousse . . . heaven.'

'That's a bit of a calorie fest for lunch, babes, and it'll take around two hours. Does your boss mind you taking such a long lunch?'

'If I stopped buying all my clothes in Bella's, it would go out of business. Anyway, I'm only part time and I think I should give it up . . . I'm going to get tested . . . you know . . . so we can try. It mightn't be good for me to be on my feet all day.'

It didn't matter what I said. If Lydia got an idea into her head, it would stay there like a handprint in cement.

'Okay, babes. I'll see you at The Floozie twelve thirty sharp.'

She blew kisses down the phone.

I hung up and closed the laptop, taking care to delete my browsing history. Lydia was a sneak and constantly checked the proxy.

I needed coffee and headed for the kitchen. The local paper had been pushed in through the letterbox by the door man.

I looked at it, then tried to put it out of my mind, needing to slow things down, to give myself options and recognise if I was approaching the problem in a smart way. The headline wound its way across the paper, or perhaps it was just my eyes, as they skittered around the kitchen trying to avoid the picture. I turned it face down on the table, went back to the bedroom and focused on getting ready. I dressed for Lydia's benefit, in the sports jacket she liked and the shoes she bought me for my birthday, but my mind wouldn't stop yammering. I was being side-swiped by the repercussions of talking to the police, all the while I walked to our meeting place.

I sat on The Floozie's smooth stone bench and read the words carved into the mantel, something about glittering heart light, but nothing that could apply to my life. I folded the newspaper along its fault lines and put it into my jacket pocket. The paper was fresh and inky, might even stain the lining. An appropriate epitaph.

Lydia greeted me with a smack on the lips and she reached up to touch my hair. I was too keyed up and found her fawning attention tiresome, so straightened up, out of her reach. I told myself, if she suggests going on a holiday I won't take her money and leave, or if she says she's sorry and that we should start somewhere new, I won't take her money and leave.

'Did you make a reservation?' she said.

'Yes.' I nodded as though to prove the point.

We linked arms on our way down Waterloo Street. A vintage potato truck enticed the hungry with fluffy baked spuds. The smell of melting butter and roasted garlic was blowing towards us. My mouth filled with saliva but my stomach cramped. I had to get Lydia to convince her old man to up the limit on the financial controls in the business.

As though she were hardwired into me, Lydia looked up and gave me a smile that was more a baring of teeth. Her eyes never left my face.

'Did you enjoy looking at my bank accounts this morning, Declan?'

Lydia went straight for a nerve with a hollow needle point. I stiffened.

'Come on now, Declan. Why so tense?'

I said nothing, hoping we could continue to the restaurant in silence.

'You're not going to pretend you didn't hear me, are you? I think we might have played that game once too often. Do you seriously think I'd let you access my online accounts without knowing about it? Ever heard of audit trails? It's in the settings, ya yampy . . . but that's the problem with you. You're not that bright.'

'I don't use Brummie slang.'

'Oh, but you did, Dec man. Everything was bostin when you

first met me. Until you learned from us it wasn't the done thing.'
There was an entitled nastiness to Lydia.

'You're belittling me.'

'Oh! You feel belittled now, do you? How do you think I felt
when I found out about your little office girl?'

Lydia's face was full of petulance as she played her favourite
song, the same tune just different words.

'How many times do we have to do this, Lydia? I told you it
was nothing, a couple of drunken shags.'

'That's not what the private detective said. God, you're such a
cliché! What was it, Declan? Did she listen to your every word
like you were dripping gold? Did she keep herself prepped for
you? Waxed herself raw and always ready to suck your dick?'

'We've been over this, now you're being common.'

'Like your solicitor? You took a trip out to Marsden Green to
see that dandruff-encrusted little man, didn't you? I suppose he
told you our pre-nup won't stand up in court? Well, guess again,
Declan. All you've done is take –'

'You think everything is my fault, don't you? That you have no
part to play? As far as you're concerned I'm Dumb Declan, who
you planted in your fancy world and I should be forever grateful.'

'I think this is the longest conversation we've had in months
that isn't about Ava!'

I had to shut Lydia up, people were staring. I hooked her
elbow and steered her off the main drag.

'Where's this coming from?' I asked.

'Are you for real? You were looking at my bank accounts and
lying to me. Again. The receptionist told me two police officers
had been in to see you.'

I leaned down, inches from Lydia's face.

'They found another arm. Here. In Birmingham.' The paper

rustled and unfolded as I released it from my inside pocket. 'There's a photo. It's in that package.' I pressed down on the image and left ridges in the print.

Lydia crumpled in on herself. She looked lost.

'What's going on, Lyd? Let me help.'

She shook her head. 'You can't. It's Dad . . . he's being blackmailed.'

'About this?'

Lydia nodded. 'It's complicated – Mum said the less you know the better.'

She leaned in to me and blotted her face against the cloth of my coat. I hardly noticed, my mind spinning in circles trying to process what she'd told me.

CHAPTER 29

BRIDGET

2004

Quiet lived in our house. It was like a damp blanket draped over everything, so I heard my father's voice coming from his study. An exotic resin-type smell heralded his presence these days. I had checked his bathroom, curious about where he was getting this stuff. It was full of matching body cream, shaving lotion, a bristling badger-hair brush and aftershave. It looked like multiple gift sets and I sensed Beatrice Corrigan's fingerprints. I moved back and forth on the balls of my feet in an attempt to quieten my contempt.

'No . . . Beatrice . . . you're being ridiculous. It's not what you think, of course I'd know . . .'

I put my eye to the crack of my father's study door. The twill suit he wore had horse hair that padded out the shoulders, giving him a squarer shape under his new judge's robes. His hair was flattened from wearing his wig and it looked dyed to me. It was thick and blond with a couple of grey streaks — it looked plausible, but like everything about my father his artifice was well disguised.

'I can't have a scandal involving my family, Beatrice. Look what they did to David Blunkett and that woman from the Spectator! Peter Mendelsohn's making his life hell and they're just politicians – I'm in the Special Criminal Court . . . Yes, I know it's England but it's not that different here. Some of the chaps are talking about the Supreme Court. I can't have any blemish . . . calm down, please don't get upset, I hate to think of you upset . . . I know Richie is a beast . . . Of course my marriage is dead, but Bridget can be a difficult child . . . yes, she's twenty-one, I'm not using that as an excuse, but I cannot have a scandal! Beatrice, please! It will get better. I can sort everything out – I just can't . . .'

I had thought of my parents as two opponents in a tug of war, relishing their testing of mutual strength. When my father let go, the recoil must have been as painful as the kickback from a shotgun to my mother.

I knocked on my father's oak door. Three staccato raps.

'Just can't what?' I said. 'Just can't have your vulgar cliché hanging around outside the Four Courts when you do your Judge John Toler parade in front of the media? He was a very famous hanging judge in the 19th century, by the way.'

'I know who he bloody was, you pup! Get out!'

'Or what about ambulance-chasing-Richie? He's always the loose cannon – he might talk to the red tops. Tell them the Honourable Mr Justice Vincent Harney is open to undue influence from his blowsy mistress? And there's my mother. The elegant lady who stands beside you at Law Society dinners – remember her? Honestly, you disgust me.'

The words were wet sand in my mouth. Distress was making

my hands shake, so I knotted them together and must have looked like some childish supplicant pleading for intercession. I turned to leave and almost fell out of his study.

He restarted his conversation before I'd closed the door.

'I hope you didn't hear any of that . . . you're the wronged party here, I know that, my dear.'

I was glad I'd landed a punch but couldn't listen to any more. I didn't know how much my mother knew or tolerated. It was a conversation neither of us could start. At least there were no more house parties. He'd stopped that when a full-time Garda protection detail had moved into a hut in our garden. My mother organised a shed with a stove and basic catering facilities. To keep my father's protector warm and fed.

CHAPTER 30

BRIDGET

2018

'This place tastes like an armpit.'

'Have you licked many armpits?' I asked Kay.

'Enough.'

I took her at her word.

The air in the interview room in Harcourt Square tasted of dust motes that hung in the mean slashes of light thrown down by the ceiling striplights. The room was windowless which didn't help. Still, it had its uses.

Kay and I were waiting for Lorraine Quigley to be brought up from the cells for questioning. My phone pinged. I checked it out.

'Analysis came back on the hair and skin on the anorak from the Gardens,' I told Kay.

'And?'

'Most if it belongs to Flannery and they'll run a tox screen on the hair. Couple of different DNA signatures there as well and not ones we have on the system. Still, good to get more DNA from the Gardens — we might be able to match it to some old scene-of-crime profiles.'

'That won't tell us who it is,' said Kay.

'I know, but it all helps.' It was a field of dead runner beans, but I was the fool prepared to pop every withered pod in the hope of finding a shiny green pea.

A quick knock on the door startled both of us and a uniform brought Lorraine Quigley in. She was sober, having spent the last three days coming off her heroin high. Her hair was lank and clung to her face. She had delicate features that must have promised prettiness at some point, before poverty had shrink-wrapped her and given her a hard veneer. She stank of vomit, but I had long since become acclimatised to the odour of regurgitated station food. She was in pain. I looked at the cameras to signal I was starting the interview.

'This isn't a formal interview — you can leave any time you want,' I said. 'Would you like some tea?'

Lorraine nodded and I indicated to the uniform standing by the door to fetch it.

'Pot of tea for three, please, Ed,' said Kay and got a smile for her trouble.

She opened a bag of brioche buns from Bewley's café on Grafton Street, the ones with the swirl of almond in the centre. The smell of sweet marzipan filled the air.

'You're not going to try and eat something in this room, are you, Kay?' I must have looked appalled.

'No . . . well, maybe.'

The tea was brought in. The plain blue station delph clinked as the uniform dumped the tray on the table.

'This is nice.' Kay beamed at Lorraine like we were in a homey cafe. 'Go on, love – you've been a bit sick from all that stuff. Something sweet will settle your stomach.' She put a sticky bun on a plate and handed it to Lorraine.

To my surprise, Lorraine reached for a knife, cut the buttery brioche into chunks and offered them to us. I shook my head but Kay picked up a piece. She and Lorraine took bites of the sweet pastry and nodded in appreciation. It was a simple pleasure and I marvelled at Kay's ability to put anyone at their ease. I, on the other hand, tended to get the bad news out of the way first.

'Do you want a solicitor?' I asked.

'No,' said Lorraine. 'It was an illegal search so it doesn't matter what you found.'

I nodded. 'You're being recorded, do you understand that?'

Lorraine nodded.

'But I'm not cautioning you and we're not charging you with possession. Do you ever think about your baby when you're sticking that crap in your veins?'

I looked down at the social welfare blue-and-white form on my desk and read out: 'Marie Quigley is currently with the Health Service Executive in Glenageary for temporary fostering.' I waited for her response.

Her face formed a knot and some emotion I couldn't read moved across it.

'I'll get her back,' said Lorraine.

'Will you? I'm not pressing charges on the drugs, but no way am I allowing a child back into a house with a junkie mother and Seán Flannery.' I leaned in close enough to smell the sweet almond on her breath. 'You know what he is, Lorraine.'

She contracted into her seat and her little white hand shook.

Kay took a gulp of tea to wash the bun out of her mouth. 'Marie was in a dirty nappy, standing in her playpen. How many hours a day is she in there?'

Lorraine shrugged. 'Are youse a double act?'

'Don't be smart, Lorraine love,' said Kay. 'Social says Marie has bad nappy rash. And those pit bull pups have the run of the place. Does Marie like them?'

'Yes.' It was a squeak from Lorraine. 'But Seán doesn't discipline them enough. They snap at de two of us.'

'They'll do that until they find the pecking order,' I said. 'So right now Flannery is number one, the pups are number two. Where does that leave you and your baby?'

I had started to tee up the laptop and flipped open the CCTV footage of her in Farringtons'.

'That you?' I showed Lorraine the screen.

She nodded.

'Yes, it's me.'

It wasn't a statement I could use in court, but a punch of pure adrenaline went right through me. To stop myself from standing up I gripped the underside of the table until my thumbnails were pink. I had Flannery. At a minimum receiving stolen goods, but perhaps involved in Emer Davidson's disappearance. It was mouth-watering. I put my hands out flat on the table, amidst the possibilities and loose ends.

'The ring,' I said.

Lorraine's face drew in.

'Kay, bring it up on your Instagram please.'

Kay showed Lorraine a picture of Anne Burgess's Iranian blue gemstone in a delicate gold setting.

'Isn't it pretty?' Lorraine's voice was small. All her longings seemed to coalesce into that one whisper: to be someone who might own such a ring, to have a life that was clean, to have a chance.

'There were traces of your blood on the underside of the ring, Lorraine.'

She nodded. 'I only wore it for a day or two. Seán wanted it gone, said it was too obvious. I snagged the inside of my knuckle on a zipper, not a deep cut, but it bled like a bastard. The ring must have grazed the cut when I was trying it on.'

'So Seán Flannery had this ring?'

'Yes.'

Again that red punch of adrenaline.

Kay eyed me, warning me not to telegraph my hopes to Lorraine, but she had something else on her mind.

'How long will you keep Marie?' she asked.

'Where did you get that Barclaycard, Lorraine?' said Kay.

'Not saying. How long will you keep Marie?' Lorraine never broke eye contact with me.

'She's in a good place, Lorraine, safe and there's lots of . . .' said Kay.

Her voice fell away from me as I looked at Lorraine's face. Something wasn't right. Kay was strong with people, made them come out of themselves, but I had other qualities.

'That's up to us. How long do you want us to keep her?' I said.

'Six weeks.'

'Why would we do that?'

'Because I can give you Seán Flannery.' Lorraine's flat eyes flickered over me.

'That's easy to say,' I said. 'I'd want some proof before I'll sort out anything for baby Marie.'

The interview room had a heavy, soundless quality to it, on account of being surrounded by disused offices. Lorraine seemed to consider me in the stiff silence, put her head down and whispered into her hands when she did speak. I presumed it was in case Richie Corrigan ever asked to look at the video footage of our interview. She would be hard to understand.

'Seán took a million in bearer bonds from that safe in Dalkey.'

I listened to the point of strain and prayed what I heard was correct.

The silence was sliced open by the banging of a door. Richie Corrigan strode in like the big ham he was, using his most stentorian voice.

'How dare you take my client in for questioning, without alerting me!'

'Under section twelve of the Child Care Act 1991, subsection thirteen when a child is in danger –'

'Don't quote the law at me, Miss Harney. It was a temporarily incapacitated mother – there's no proof the child was in danger.'

'And you'd know all about taking care of children, Richie? Wouldn't you?'

Kay's head jerked up. Her hand hovered by her teacup and made that wagging-finger motion.

'You know, Mr Corrigan,' she said, 'that this isn't a formal caution and Lorraine here is free to go at any time. She is helping us with our enquiries.'

'It's fine, Kay.' I pulled my face into an imitation of a smile. 'Richie and I are like family.'

Which in some sad, twisted way was true. Richie Corrigan had been a part of my life since I could remember.

He sucked his gut in and sent a derisive flick in Lorraine's direction. 'We're leaving and if I find out there was any undue influence or harassment with my client, you'll be up in front of a judge before you can say –'

'Cuckold?'

Kay winced, but she was quick off the mark and scrambled out of her seat. 'Right, Mr Corrigan, let's get you out of here with your client, will we? Ed, help Miss Quigley and Mr Corrigan.'

Kay bustled Richie out the door. He was grumbling about mad dogs on leashes and Kay's strong Kildare accent floated back to me. 'It's probably safe to say that you and Bridge don't see eye to eye, Mr Corrigan.'

Lorraine was a heartbeat behind Richie. She swung around and locked eyes with me.

'Six weeks.'

Richie reared up and reversed back into the room.

'What's six weeks?' he said. A vein twitched in his eyelid, giving him a gargoyle look.

'The time it would take for a real detox,' I said, 'You need to get Lorraine to a good centre – the Rutland out in Scholarstown runs a six-week course.'

Richie's fleshy lips pursed and he left without any acknowledgment, shepherding Lorraine in front of him this time.

When Kay came back, she plonked herself down in the plastic seat and gave me a nudge with her elbow. 'You did that on purpose.'

'Course I did. Richie Corrigan is no fool. I had to rile him or he'd know what we were up to.'

'Why six weeks?'

'I don't know but Lorraine's up to something. Her eyes – she's not as wrecked as we think. That girl has a plan. Richie might even put her in the Rutland, he's not a complete bastard. Just weak. Either way, I'll get Marie's social worker to organise visits for Lorraine and I can meet her in the care home.'

'Jaysus, Bridge! Flannery will be all over that.'

'Kay, I'm hardly going to be parked outside waiting for her, am I? I'll be in the toilets and talk to her there. There's a nun there helps with the young mothers – Sister Catherine. I'll tip her off to Flannery.'

'Fair enough. Looking good though, isn't it?'

I grinned. 'For the first time in years. I know we've nothing that will stand up in court, but I'll get dates and times from Lorraine. We'll find out what Flannery's up to. He's involved in the Emer Davidson case, I'll bloody bet he is.'

'Steady. I know it's looks that way but we've no hard evidence. All we've got is stolen goods and a wodge of money in a safe. Circumstantial.'

'Don't you see, Kay? This is it. Flannery's involved in the Burgess robbery and this dead girl Emer Davidson. We now have leverage on Lorraine Quigley so Flannery's alibi is gone. If we dig around I'll find all sorts. I'm going to get him.'

I was soaring, lost in a vision of bringing a cuffed and hooded Seán Flannery into the Central Criminal Court, picturing my father as he watched the Six One news reporting my success. The faces of my colleagues acknowledging how right I was to never have given up pursuit of Flannery.

CHAPTER 31

BRIDGET

A bubble of noise, a mixture of siren blare and choppy voices, bounced up from the lane at the back of the station. Revellers who didn't realise the weekend was over or drunks who'd fallen asleep outside a Garda station. It would depend on the rostered duty sergeant, but they might even get breakfast on us. I hated Mondays – it was a day of reporting progress up the ladder. We all had to do it, anyone on an active case at detective level, right up the chain to the superintendents who ruled policing in Ireland.

Joe Clarke had left me a voicemail in which he sounded overexcited and squeaky, telling me to be in early. It nearly made me smile. Joe wasn't an early bird, I'd never seen him in before eight. Unsurprisingly the old marble reception desk, a repurposed relic from some Taoiseach's office in the eighties, was unmanned this early. Night shift had clocked off and those of us in this early had a routine of being quiet when we passed one another in the corridors. I was the only one in our squad room. I clicked on the coffee machine. It puttered to life.

Joe's office was empty. I stuck my head in his door, in part to let the stale weekend smell out, but also to look at what he was working on. Joe was messy and put me in mind of a teacher who left upcoming exam papers on his desk. So I contemplated his bare, cup-ringed desk in surprise.

'Harney! Do you have something for me?'

It was Joe, muffled against the cold in his full-length Garda coat and a blue-and-white handknit scarf. It sagged around his neck covering most of his face, leaving the top pink from the cold. He looked like boiled egg in an old-fashioned eggcup.

I moved out of his way and he unpeeled his layers at his desk. He never made eye contact with me and I stood on the shiny door saddle, waiting, a sense of unease building inside me.

'Give me a minute, will you?'

'Do you want a cup of tea, Joe?'

'Please.'

I got the tea and sat down, ready with my update, but Joe was building himself up to something. He paced in a tight line behind his desk, making me uncomfortable, more so as I believed he didn't realise it. He had the look of a traffic cop who'd lost his bike.

'You want an update on the Emer Davidson case for the Sergeant's meeting? We interviewed Lorraine Quigley —'

'I want you to listen first. This is a pre-disciplinary counselling meeting. You're a good one for terms and conditions, so it's important you understand that I'm going by the book on this.'

'What?'

I don't know whether it was shock or fear that made me think I was drowning, but either way I couldn't breathe. I opened and closed my mouth like a fish in the bottom of a boat. The room was too quiet — not even the air conditioning was on this early.

'Why? What have I done? What's happening, Joe?'

He made a tinny, strangled sound. 'I'm trying to get you back on track, Bridge. So that your performance can improve and create a better working environment for you. I have a duty of care to you and we need to assign specific, measurable, aligned, realistic and time-bound objectives for you.'

He said it like he'd memorised it. Now I knew why Joe's desk was so clean: he'd been in over the weekend to meet with Human Resources. Someone was coaching him.

'So what are the issues?'

'I'll tell you, yes, but there's a process.'

I sat quietly, absorbing his discomfort.

'I've never seen you like this, Joe.'

'That's Sergeant Clarke to you, Garda Detective Harney, during this process,' said Superintendent Niall O'Connor.

He was standing behind me.

I had my arms crossed and gripped myself tighter in an effort not to scream.

'Super, I didn't see you there.'

Superintendent Niall O'Connor was a tall man in his late fifties and, with a couple of ex-wives behind him, he routinely mistook his sense of entitlement for charisma. He was completely bald and it was said he buffed his head with a leather chamois before press conferences. Added to that, he was a person of barely contained violence. Some of my colleagues said he'd beaten suspects to a pulp in the nineties when looking for Johnny Adair. His mouth set itself in a flat line.

Joe reached into his pocket, took out a scratched key and fumbled, trying to open the lock of his pedestal drawer. After a few red-faced moments of rummaging Joe stood up, a buff-coloured folder in his hand. My name in large font on the front made me take notice.

'First, and this would be my main issue with you —' Joe stopped abruptly, as though trying to remember something he was told, and took a sip of his tea.

'Get on with it, man,' said Superintendent O'Connor.

The hairs on my arm stood on end as though wanting to puncture my shirt sleeve, but I tried to look like I was doing them a favour and had dropped into Joe's office on my way to another, more vital meeting.

Joe seemed to stretch upwards, his physique looking more taut. He was wearing full dry-cleaned-and-buttons-polished uniform and I cursed myself for missing that fact.

'You have exceeded your personal authority on many occasions. Let me give you an example. You are not senior to your partner, yet you routinely assign work for Kay Shanahan to complete. For instance, Kay has spent forty-two hours on research, building a profile for Seán Flannery. You yourself have spent zero time researching him. And I might add no one has authorised any resources on Seán Flannery.'

Joe passed over the first sheet in the folder to me, which thankfully wasn't as full as I expected. He waited for me to respond.

With Superintendent Niall O'Connor standing behind me, I knew who had coached Joe.

'I don't have the hours so I won't dispute your facts,' I said.

I glanced down at the sheet in front of me, listing all the systems Kay had logged in to, including Interpol's database, educational systems, debt registers, land registries, credit ratings and judgement's pending. All the systems the Gardaí had access to. She'd been thorough.

'Kay and I have a specific way of working, which uses our respective skillsets. It's one of the reasons we make such a good team.'

'Don't grandstand, Detective Garda Harney,' said Superintendent O'Connor.

I turned and looked him full in the face. 'I'm not, Ceannfort O'Connor.' Rumour had it Superintendent O'Connor didn't like his Irish title – he thought it sounded agricultural.

I turned back to Joe.

'I am entitled to rebuttal,' I said, 'or would you prefer me to stay silent?'

I hoped to bait him but, although he flushed, Joe seemed to have himself under control.

'Continue,' he said.

'I concentrate on preparing the legal side, making sure we have the paperwork in order, that process has been followed, that our casebook is in good order and is being managed, that our witness statements are usable. While Kay works the IT angle. It's proved more than efficient. Look at our conviction rate. I'm sure you have it in your dossier.'

I waited.

'That may be the case from your point of view,' said Joe and cast an eye over my shoulder, 'but I see it as an unfair distribution of work and it means your IT skills are not up to speed.' He stopped and looked as though he had received silent praise from behind my back. 'And your reporting is poor.' He sounded as if he were reading from an autocue and took another sheet from the folder, placing it in front of me.

It was my last progress report on Emer Davidson. It was succinct to say the least and had left out connections to the Burgess robbery and Lorraine's assertion that Flannery had stolen bearer bonds, but it had been uploaded onto all the systems.

'Are you trying to say my IT skills aren't fit for purpose? Perhaps you're using that report as an example?'

Joe went a stinging red.

'I make daily updates on PULSE. Police Using Leading Systems Effectively.' The daily updates were the only thing I could manage but Joe struggled with PULSE too and I doubted Superintendent O'Connor had ever used it. 'Why don't you bring up your dashboard and compare my usage with my peers? It's simple to do.'

It wasn't and I knew Joe would have no idea how to do it. The sheet with Kay's hours on it had been pulled by the IT helpdesk — their call sign was on the header.

Superintendent O'Connor tapped his foot on the hand-pegged wooden floor.

'Move on,' he said in a clipped tone.

'We have received a complaint from the West Midlands Police Constabulary,' said Joe.

My guts turned to ice. I dipped my face into my scarf and kept my eyes static. I knew this stare was unnatural and could disconcert whoever was trying to speak to me, but it bought me time to evaluate what was happening.

Joe made a scratching sound in his throat. I could fell irritation radiating off Superintendent O'Connor.

Joe tried again. 'They believe you are discounting a valid prime suspect, Declan Swan, in favour of Seán Flannery.'

He seemed to expand and fill the room or I was shrinking. An allegation like that could get me kicked off the Force. Ignoring a prime suspect was grounds for dismissal.

'What is the nature of the complaint and who is the complainant?' I reverted to legalese in my discomfort.

'I've just said. You are —'

'Neglect, wilful misunderstanding, unprofessional conduct,' Superintendent O'Connor cut across Joe. 'Do you need any more tenets that you've broken? This kind of biased behaviour is beneath any serving officer of An Garda Síochána and opens us up to serious censure from brother officers, the Public and . . . others.' He meant the media. 'We don't need to give you the identity of the complainant. If it were up to me, I'd have you suspended from duty, but Joe has asked that we follow a softer disciplinary procedure and appoint Kay Shanahan as lead on this case, while setting objectives for you which must be tracked at weekly meetings. Plus quarterly psychological evaluations with the department psychologist to help you with your authority issues.'

I opened my mouth, then shut it again. I'd been sucker-punched. Chris Watkiss had complained about me.

CHAPTER 32

The sky over West Midlands Police Headquarters in Lloyd House looked like someone had flung their old grey raincoat across it, stained in patches and faded to near white in others. I was keyed up and felt oddly exposed in Chris's domain.

He was wearing a floral knitted cardigan that had received a few raised eyebrows, but that didn't appear to bother him. 'Wife knits – can do all sorts,' he said as yet another person gawked. 'Could do you a Santa jumper, if you'd like? Only a couple of weeks away now.'

I batted the air, unable to contemplate Christmas. 'When are we meeting the Burgesses?'

'We'll head off shortly – it's about hour and a half to their place in Newnham on Severn. But first I think we need to get something off the table, don't you?' He gestured to a side office.

Two constables were inside, eating sandwiches and tomato soup when Chris opened the door. The room had a chummy, canteen feel about it.

'Out, you pair,' said Chris and gave them a wink.

I took a seat, flushing as I prepared myself for the coming encounter.

He slammed himself down into the chair opposite me.

'You've had a right gob on from the moment I collected you at the airport. What's up?'

'What's up? Are you serious?' My voice was too loud. I was too volatile and should have stayed silent, but I was nothing if not set in my ways. 'I'm under disciplinary proceedings because you reported that I'd discounted Declan Swan as a suspect in favour of Seán Flannery. That's what's up! And God knows what else you've said. So you might as well tell me now – I don't think I could handle more surprises from my management!'

'First off, I'm sorry you're in trouble but I'll come back to that in a moment,' he said. 'You have discounted Declan Swan, a man who was having an affair with the deceased that could've cost him his whole lifestyle. And who's my prime suspect, in favour of a man who's only link is a stolen bank card, which any barrister will get thrown out as circumstantial.'

'Declan Swan doesn't have the wherewithal for something like this. And if we're talking about biases, you should look a little nearer to home. You think Swan's a prick in a Maserati. Whereas a known associate of Flannery's was involved in the Dalkey robbery – the fence can identify him.'

This wasn't entirely true. Welby's friend had identified a thug in a hoodie, but I needed something to bolster my case for Flannery's involvement.

'Fair enough, but I don't need to tell you how quickly that will be thrown out of court. You say there was a million in bearer bonds in that safe, which Burgess never reported missing – if you really believed that you'd have told your brass.'

How did he know about that?

'Lorraine Quigley's an ex-junkie whose child has been taken off her,' he went on. 'She'd say owt at this point for leverage. Tell me you see that, Bridge?'

He was right. I pinched the bridge of my nose with my thumb and forefinger.

'I get it. Declan Swan has motive for the murder, an affair with Emer Davidson – but I don't have him down as a killer and hacking off body parts. He's too weak.'

'A cornered coward is dangerous.'

'True, but where's the connection to the bank card?'

Chris shrugged. 'No idea. I know you want Flannery for both, but he doesn't have motive for Emer Davidson's murder. He's not a hired gunman and what would he be doing in Birmingham? You've said he's wedded to that East Wall patch.'

I took a deep breath, trying to breathe away my discouragement at Chris's compelling logic.

He scratched his chin. It made a rasping sound. 'That Lorraine's rightly over a barrel, isn't she? Have you threatened her?'

I kept eye contact, but I didn't feel good about myself.

'I've done it myself, not proud of it,' said Chris. 'I've pushed buttons when I had to. Can't say I always got the truth, though.'

My hand came flat down on the desk with a thump. 'No one has played me. Seán Flannery is involved in this. I know it's him, I just need more time. And a little help wouldn't go amiss.'

I was lying but admitting to Chris that I had been played wasn't an option for me.

'Listen, I'm not saying there isn't a Flannery connection,' he said, 'but can we agree to find it together? And if I were you, I'd flag up Lorraine Quigley's accusation.'

I shivered but managed a nod. The room wasn't cold but I felt like I was coming down with something.

'You getting a cold? It's all that travelling in planes, there's always someone sick. I end up with the sniffles every time I fly.'

It sounded mildly ridiculous coming from someone as solid as Chris and I pulled a smile.

'That's better. Now, down to the other thing. I never reported you for discounting Swan – but hear me on this – your Superintendent O'Connor is a right bollocks and knows my DI Maitland. They were coppers together on a joint task force in the golden triangle of Dublin-Belfast-Birmingham during the nineties. Bombs and peace agreements. I don't have to tell you those kind of ties will bind. If your O'Connor wanted a favour, Maitland would be his man.'

'That gets you off the hook nicely.' I spoke without thinking and sounded puerile.

Chris gave me a crooked grin. 'Just give yourself a moment to think about it. I like the way you speak your mind, but it might be an idea on occasion to reflect.'

Heat pricked my face.

'Before you ask, it was Kay told me about the bearer bonds,' said Chris.

'I thought as much. How often are you and Kay in contact behind my back?'

I wanted to gobble the words back as soon as I said them. I'd made myself enough of an idiot for one day.

A small frown formed on Chris's open face. 'No one's in contact behind anyone's back! Kay and I regularly swap information. We're all detectives, Bridge. Why are you so bloody cagey?'

'Years of training.' I gave him a weak smile.

The chair seemed to catch me as I tried to get up and Chris put a steadying hand out for me.

'Ruddy barristers. Come on, little 'un. Let's get out to Newnham on Severn. You're in for a treat.'

CHAPTER 33

The city peeled out of sight. Chris drove so fast I thought I had imagined the noise and rubble of Birmingham. The M5 wasn't overloaded with cars mid-morning and wound into a smaller tributary road where we sped by fields full of sleeping crops, resting below the frozen brown earth. There was a comforting silence in the car and the motion made me nod off. I was so tired. Solid sleep had eluded me since my chat with Superintendent O'Connor and Joe Clarke. My eyelids closed and stuck together with sleep-wax like the frosted lumps of soil outside.

Cold air touched my face.

I jolted upright. 'What's up?'

'Relax, you've had forty winks is all. We're here now.'

Chris reached through the open car window and popped a button on the impressive intercom welded into the wall. A sharp beam of light, that could make its presence felt during the day, lit us up for a time.

'Burgess Residence,' said a polished-up Brum accent.

'Detectives Chris Watkiss and Bridget Harney to see Mike Burgess, please.'

Silence, then the light switched off abruptly and the massive wrought-iron gate wheeled itself back.

'You reckon the Burgesses are home?' I said.

'Aye, they're retired so chances are they're home. I didn't want to make an appointment, prefer to catch the likes of Mike Burgess on the hop.'

A winding driveway through an ornamental garden meandered up to the house. A boathouse the size of a four-bed family home sat at a short distance on the River Severn.

The house was a baroque mansion made from quarries of blasted sandstone, but rarely had so much money restored so poorly.

'What do you think of Burgess's country pile?'

'Some people shouldn't be allowed buy historic buildings,' I said. 'This should be taken back by the State and the Burgesses made to apologise. Publicly.'

Chris gave out his great guffawing laugh. 'Oh, I don't know. Out of Africa meets Mr Darcy?'

'Has Anne Burgess painted the pillars and inside of the porte-cochère banana-yellow? That can't be right, can it? Surely this building is listed?'

'Maybe it's heritage ochre.'

We had started to laugh again, but it was cut short by the sight of Mike Burgess standing in the mouth of his double-fronted entrance. The doors were held open by a man in full gloved livery.

'Does anyone other than the Royal family use uniformed butlers?' My eyes were out on stalks.

Chris snorted. 'Oh, our Mr Burgess fancies hisself all right. He's expecting to be on the New Year's honours list. Can't be knighted if you don't have a butler branded with your coat of arms.'

We bubbled with laughter as we got out of the car, but Mike Burgess was grim-faced as he walked out to meet us. The doors closed behind him.

'What do you want? You're lucky I'm seeing you without an appointment.' There was no trace of civility in his voice.

'Good morning, Mr Burgess, good intercom on that gate outside. Strong and secure. Pity you didn't have the same system in Dalkey, might have helped. Just a couple of questions, Mr Burgess. We're trying to solve your burglary.'

'Is that why she's here?' He pointed a stubby finger in my direction.

'Yes, Detective Garda Harney has some interesting news. Shall we go inside?'

'I'm happy out here.'

It was cold, but crisp. Mike Burgess was wearing a heavy coat as if he'd planned our interview would take place outdoors. He had a lit cigar in his hand. A big Cuban with a heady aroma. I breathed in. Burgess gave a small smile.

'You smoke?' he said.

Even with wind gusting up from the River Severn, the cigar smelled rich and loamy.

'No, but my father did when I was a child. Those big hard-to-get Havanas.'

'Man after my own heart.'

'That might just be the truth.'

Burgess frowned, not liking my tone, and reached for a gold lighter inside his coat pocket. It clicked on with a hiss of butane and a single blue light.

'Hard to keep that bugger going in this wind,' said Chris.

'You're – not – here – to – make – small – talk,' Mike said in between puffs.

'You're right, Mr Burgess. There was a million in bearer bonds in your safe in Dalkey. Why didn't you tell us about them?'

Mike eyed Chris up and down. 'That's not true. I don't know where you're getting your information from. Anne's jewellery was the only thing of value in that safe.'

Chris looked at me and I nodded – not that we had any code, but I was tacitly agreeing to go in whatever direction he wanted.

'A known criminal in Dublin has started to sell them. We have serial numbers that can be traced back to you.'

'I don't know what you're talking about.' Mike Burgess puffed out a great cloud of grey smoke. It hung in the air between us, just like his lies.

'You're not missing a million, Mr Burgess? It's a tidy enough sum. Unless you were involved in another robbery? Those bonds are yours, we can link you to them.'

Mike stared Chris down. 'I've told you. There was nothing in that safe except Anne's jewellery, so if you've anything on that let me know. Otherwise stop wasting my time.'

He quenched his cigar by flicking the top off and left the glowing ember at our feet.

He turned and walked back to the house without another word.

We had no choice but to retrace out steps to the car, where we sat looking at the house. Mike peered out at us, from behind a curtain that could have cloaked a stage. He was talking to his butler, a conversation I would have happily eavesdropped on given the opportunity.

'The townhalls on that boy,' said Chris. 'He's lying. Did you see the way he didn't flinch when I'd told him we had serial numbers on the bonds? Those bonds are real, all right. Anyone else would have wanted to see the numbers, check them out. He knows those serial numbers aren't in general circulation. And I'll give you another – he knows who has his bonds. Will we go and see what Declan Swan is up to?'

Chris started the car and did a three-point turn.

'Yes, but Chris, remember it was Lorraine Quigley who told us about the bonds.'

'True, I'll give you that, but maybe Flannery stole them on behalf of Declan Swan? This is an inside job, Bridge.'

'We're on the same page,' I said, more to mollify him than anything. 'While we're at it, can I have a look at Emer Davidson's flat?'

'Why not?' said Chris. He sounded magnanimous.

After I'd looked at the flat, we dropped Emer's flatmate back to her job in the Plucky Blackbird on Edmund Street. It was an old Victorian boozer, incongruous amongst the new apartment complexes and dug-up roads displaying innards of fibre-optic cables. We motored leisurely for once. We had no choice, as traffic choked our route towards St Paul's Square. Chris had rung Burgess Data Centre and was told Mr Swan was out.

'We'll try him at home. I wonder if he's receiving?'

I shared Chris's enjoyment. This was the kind of investigation I lived for, surprising people and getting them to pop out shiny pieces of information I scooped up like a magpie. It was how cases were solved. Chris made a call to his office and pleaded with one of the database administrators to run a query for him.

'Who owns the penthouse in St Paul's, Number 6 – is it Declan or Lydia Swan? Go on, flower, give us a tinkle back as soon as you have it.'

'I swear, Watkiss,' came a male voice from the car speaker, 'if you call me flower again I'll tell everyone about your salsa lessons.'

Chris snorted with enjoyment and hung up. I pressed the buzzer for the Swan penthouse and Lydia's voice crackled out at us from the intercom.

'Hello?'

'Detective Garda Bridget Harney and Detective Chris Watkiss to see you, and/or Mr Swan,' said Chris.

The buzzer rattled and I pushed the heavy glass door.

Lydia Swan was waiting for us on the uppermost floor, with her hip holding the front door of her apartment open. Her head held high and her lips tight, she had the look of a woman on the warpath.

'Is this a bad time, Mrs Swan?' Chris was asking questions before the lift doors had closed behind us.

'You've just been to see my father,' said Lydia.

'Did your father ring you?' I said. 'May we come in?'

Chris's phone bleeped. He read the text and passed the phone to me.

Swan penthouse is owned by Burgess Data Centre. Swans have no properties or assets registered in their names.

'He's fast, your flower,' I said to Chris.

Lydia Swan's eyes moved between us and she backed into her hallway.

'Come in, if you must. What do you want to know?'

'Might I have a glass of water, please?' I hoped the old trick of getting an unwilling host to open up by offering hospitality might still work.

She stalled, then shrugged. 'Still or sparkling?'

'Sparkling, if you have it.'

We followed her into the kitchen but, as we hadn't been invited to sit, we stayed standing. With something to do Lydia seemed to unbend.

'Ice?' she said.

'That would be lovely, thank you. Great-looking fridge.'

'Does everything: still water, sparkling, crushed ice.' Shards of ice came rushing out of the machine and sloshed into the clear glass Lydia was holding.

The apartment had a liquorice odour I associated with herbal shops. I guessed it was from the nutrient supplements and bags of trendy seeds on the counter top.

'Thanks.' I took a gulp. 'Tastes much better than Pellegrino.'

'Does it?'

She seemed pleased and I sensed we'd made a connection, so I started the questioning.

'We were out with your dad this morning. He was helping us. We're just trying to work out time frames around the robbery on the 25th October in Dalkey.'

Lydia nodded.

'Where were you and Declan on that evening? It was a Wednesday.'

'Here.' Lydia's eyes were as wide as they'd go. 'Both of us.'

'Young upwardly mobile couple like yourselves – not out on the town to a fancy restaurant?'

'No, Declan goes to the gym every morning and evening. I usually cook dinner. I think we had chicken or fish stir fry.'

'You've a good memory, if you can remember what you ate five weeks ago.'

She shrugged. 'Not so much. Declan is quite routine-orientated – he likes low-fat, protein meals mid-week, so it's stir fry something most nights and we only eat chicken breast and fish. Lately it's been all chicken because I can't stand the stink of fish around the apartment.'

'That's a bit restricting, isn't it? Mind you, means you can have a blow-out at the weekend.'

'We don't do blow-outs and no alcohol. We're trying for a baby.'

'That's wonderful news.' I gave her a broad smile. 'Did you know Emer Davidson was having an affair with your husband and was pregnant?'

It hit her as hard as I meant it to. Chris winced and I couldn't blame him.

Lydia Swan looked like she was going to fall to the floor. She staggered slowly over to a chair as if she were on a tightrope and the tiniest slip could land her in a broken heap.

'Declan's? He told me it was a couple of drunken . . . nothing important, she chased him . . .'

Her voice became lower on each word until she was whispering.

Chris grabbed a glass from the press and filled it with cold water. Lydia took a mouthful and I handed her a tissue. There were no tears, but I figured it was just a matter of time.

'Declan was with me on the night of the burglary, but he went away the following weekend.' She squinted over at a massive wall planner. 'There, I've written it in. "Lads' weekend – Declan." He left on Friday 3rd of November, but never told me where they were going.'

'Do you have any reason to believe he wasn't on a lads' weekend?'

Lydia gave me a level stare. 'You've met Declan, haven't you? He's more of a lady's man. He doesn't have anyone to go on a lads' weekend with.'

Chris and I walked back to the car, not speaking until the doors were closed.

'Has Lydia Swan just given us her husband for Emer Davidson's murder?' he said, breathless as a teenager after spotting a crush.

'Calm down, Chris.'

He looked like he'd been nominated for the Queen's Medal.

'All she's given us is that Declan Swan's alibi is suspect for the time Emer Davidson was murdered.'

'Ah Bridge, I can smell it! How in God's name did you get her to crack so fast?'

'It was all those tasteless dinners. Lydia thought Declan was saving himself for her, building up his swimmers so they could make babies. Whereas Declan was giving it all to Emer Davidson.'

Chris's laughter shook the car.

CHAPTER 34

A single porch light bloomed against the dark. However, it was never entirely black in Dublin, more of a navy with a band of amber light-pollution at the base. That was one of the things my mother missed about her country hometown. The comfort of pitch black with no edges or half-lit shapes to frighten you. A glitter glue of stars above your head, so you didn't feel alone. That was my mother's logic, at least at a time when logic was possible.

The main door creaked open, announcing my arrival home. Nata was in the hall, putting her coat on. I imagined she had been waiting for me, unwilling to leave my mother until I was back from Birmingham. Which meant the Judge wasn't home.

'Dinner for you in the oven, Bridge. Made enough for two, so you don't have to do your special eggs.'

I helped her with the sleeve of her coat. It was faux fur and I told her she looked gorgeous. 'Off on a date.' She gave me a wink.

'Hope he's worth it.'

'Why don't you go on dates? Nothing wrong with a bit of fun for you. You're a grand-looking girl.'

I smiled and told her I'd see her tomorrow.

'Dad?' I threw the question after Nata as she walked out the door.

She answered with a downturn of her mouth. 'Gone with a backpack. Full of energy.'

I couldn't keep Nata's gaze as a wave of tears rose in my chest. 'Does she know?'

'No, Bridge. She's away from that hurt now.'

I walked into the living room and looked at my mother. She was sitting under a brass lamp built in the Marshall Plan. Bronze and noble but worn from years of polishing and slapdash switching on and off.

Her walnut chess set was by her side. We would play games that went on for days when I was a child, but now it was a decoration to put in between us when the silence was too stark.

I went over to her and sat on the floor close to her, breathing in her aroma. She smelled of floral moisturising cream. For once, this vile disease had taken away pain rather than delivering it by the barrelful.

After a little while I showed her up her room. Her face creased with pleasure as she found familiar softness in her bed. I left her alone with her night light.

Kay tapped on the side door and grinned in through the glass, her breath frosting the pane.

'Smells good,' she said as I waved her inside.

'You sound surprised.'

She started to take off her woolly coat.

The kitchen was hot from Nata's work during the day and I'd

lit candles to give a bit of atmosphere. It lessened the barnlike feel of the place.

'I can never get over the size of this house, Bridge, in the middle of Dublin! It's like a hotel.'

I stirred the pot full of Nata's rich stew.

'What do you put in that? Oxtail? Roasted marrow?' She inhaled the savoury steam, almost sticking her tongue out to taste it.

'I could pretend, but I've no idea. Nata made it.'

'Thought so.'

Kay was smiling at me as she lifted crockery and cutlery off the kitchen island and laid the table. 'Not that I would've objected to your eggs but I'm so in the mood for stew. It's freezing out there.'

I dished up two massive bowls and added fluffy mashed potato, topped off with pats of butter. Kay didn't hold back and for a few moments there was nothing but the sounds of satisfied slurps.

'Thank you, Bridge. Nice to have it handed to you.'

'Good of you to come over. How's Matthew and the kids?'

'Doing a Dad's Night In, which means any food eaten will arrive in boxes on the back of a bike.'

I snorted. Kay hated fast food but her family lived for the nights Kay came over to me and they could dial out for pizza. It was the best part of my week too.

'How's your mum?'

'She's fine, gone to bed. She'll be well asleep by now.'

'At least she gets a good night's sleep. That's something.'

The softness in Kay's voice crimped my throat. She saw this and looked around the kitchen for something to talk about.

'Is that a brochure for a walking holiday in Norway? You thinking of going?' She squinted over at the noticeboard. 'Is it for singles? That's a great idea, Bridge.' She got up and walked over to the noticeboard. 'You know, I might come with you. God, can you imagine if I told Matthew myself and yourself were off on a singles holiday!'

'My dad. He's gone to give himself a break from my mum's care.'

Kay winced.

'Sorry, Kay, that sounded full of self-pity.'

'Don't be so hard on yourself. Is he gone with Richie Corrigan's wife?'

I put down my knife and fork and looked for something to do, a moment's composure. 'I meant to open a bottle of wine. I have no idea how to host.'

I pulled the cork from a bottle of Rioja. It released with a satisfying pop and I filled two glasses. We raised our glasses and I took a deep pull of the scented red berries and sweet spice wine.

'Yes, I think he's gone with her. Mum doesn't realise though.'

'That's a mercy.'

'It's the only one.'

'Why don't you take a break, Bridge? When was the last time you were away on holiday? I mean, on your own or with someone significant? You don't even go to the Galway Races any more! Christ, do you remember heading off to the Radisson Blu back in the day on a Friday night, all dressed up?'

I gave a small smile and tried not to think about my meagre personal life. 'It was brilliant but work's been so busy . . .'

'Ah Bridge, it's me! When was the last time you went on a date? Would you look at Tinder?'

'Has it come to that? Swipe left for a love life? Married losers looking for cheap sex.'

'They can't all be like that, can they? What about that fella, the son of a family friend, what was his name? The lad who lied about finishing his law degree?'

'Manus with the fanny on his face?'

Kate choked back a laugh and washed it down with a mouthful of wine. 'What about Simon? Do you ever see him any more?'

A tiny light flickered in my mind and I rushed to quench it. Too painful.

'He got married earlier this year.'

'You never said! I thought you two were good together.'

'So did I. But obviously not enough for him to make compromises on my being a detective and not a-stay-at-home-wife-who-polishes-her-degree.'

'Careful. You sound bitter, but that's all marriage is, Bridge. A series of compromises.'

'With a bit of sex, though.'

'Yeah, and that has its own set of problems.'

We laughed with glee and I clapped my hands, picturing poor Matthew in the hope of a shag.

'He's mad for it but I've told him there'll be no room at the inn unless he has the snip.' She made a scissors motion with her forefinger and middle finger. 'What about yer man Paul? The shrink guy.'

'No. No. Not work. I've too much invested there already.'

Kay put down her glass and tilted it slightly on the table's oak surface, until the wine reached the edge of the glass. Then she righted it. I watched as the wine sloshed against the sides of the clear glass, leaving legs of residue.

'Don't you think you might want to think about that more seriously?'

Silence.

'We've had this before, when Jeanne went missing.'

And there it was. All my failings exposed. Only someone who loved you could hit with such precision.

'You mean when I wouldn't eat, sleep or stop until Jeanne was found? When I clocked that guy who was making out with her and pretended he wasn't?'

'Yes, that's the time I'm thinking about.'

'Kay, that was years ago, we were training in Templemore. Things have come a long way since then.'

'Have they? You thought you were the only one who could find Jeanne. You wouldn't accept that she'd just run off. Left us behind. Jeanne wasn't cut out to be a Guard.'

'You're not bringing this up because of Jeanne.'

'No, I'm not. I'm bringing it up because I'm your friend and I'm seeing that obsessive behaviour coming out again. You're isolating yourself and you've a lot to contend with at home. Plus, I can see the only thing you want to talk about tonight is the case. Well, we're not going to, I don't care what new developments there are. What do you do for fun except hang around with me, a married auld one? Why don't you keep up with any of your Trinity crowd?'

'Kay, that was over a decade ago.' I picked at the cooling stew in front of me and popped a bright chunk of carrot into my mouth, still juicy.

Kay swirled her wine around and took an appreciative mouthful, making her go-on-twist-my-arm face when I held out the bottle. The inky wine glinted in the candlelight.

I found my mouth dropping to where my scarf would be had I not taken it off when I came into the house.

'I loved Trinity.'

'You don't say, Miss Trinity Scarf.'

I touched the leg of my wineglass, an impossibly thin stem that looked like it could never hold the bowl of full wine. Yet it did.

'I felt like I belonged there. That studying, debating in clean, straight lines was real life.'

'That why you wear the scarf? To remember happier times?'

'Some of the best times in my life. I might have even stayed, if Mum hadn't told me it would never be enough for me, that I was stronger than I realised and shouldn't hide in the shadows.'

Kay gave a sad smile. 'How long have I known you and I'm still finding out stuff about you?'

'I was always a bit . . . reticent.'

'Oh, I know, the lads in Templemore were always trying "to bring you out of yourself".'

I chuckled. 'You mean date me?'

'No, I mean get a good court out of you. We were all culchies or Northsiders and you were the posh bird.' Kay threw her head back, giving her growl of a laugh. 'You know, I think Liam O'Shea had a crush on you when you first came into the squad room.'

'That bog-baller?'

'He's a Kildare GAA All Star and I know by the stupid look on your face you've no idea how important or rare that is! Jesus, Bridge, that's as close to royalty as you can get in the Force.'

I wanted to laugh but thought of the squad room brought a spikey flare behind my eyes.

'Are you ever going to tell me what O'Connor said to you in Joe's office?' she said.

I raised my hand. 'I meant to, Kay – it's just I was so blindsided. Is it all around the squad rooms?'

'No one's saying anything. Just that I've been assigned lead. What happened?'

'I feel like *I'm* under investigation. They're giving me a load of guff about my IT skills not being up to par and that I don't update my management. Trying to make it seem like they're helping me. SMART objectives, my ass. The kicker was Chris Watkiss complained about me.'

'This is serious, Bridge. O'Connor's a blackguard, he knows that complaint will go down on your permanent record. That man spends his time kissing the Commissioner's arse and hogging the PR podium. Jesus, if I see him giving another press conference! And there's no way Chris Watkiss complained about you.'

'He didn't, we cleared that up in Birmingham. I think it was Chris's DI Maitland. Apparently he and O'Connor go back.'

'What did the West Midlands say?'

'Said I was discounting a valid suspect in favour of Seán Flannery. That I was making links to Flannery where none existed. But, Kay, I know Flannery's involved.'

Kay was silent and picked at the plate in front of her.

'I need you to look into any links between Emer Davidson and Seán Flannery. There has to be something. He must have met her somewhere.'

Kay swallowed. 'Bridge, I've spent quite a bit of time on this . . .'

'Forty-two hours.'

Kay made a wry face. 'That much? Certainly feels like it. Either way, I've found some stuff out about him, but nothing to connect him to Emer Davidson.'

'You need to try harder, Kay.'

'What?'

'I have to prove the connection. I know –'

'So you keep saying, despite no evidence we can give to the DPP, your immediate superior on your back, a complaint that you're ignoring a real suspect, a pre-disciplinary session and that ballbreaker O'Connor breathing down your neck!'

My nose started to run and childish, fat tears plopped down the side of my face. 'That's not the only thing. My mum's getting worse. She can't remember my name most of the time . . .'

'Ah, Bridge, love, why didn't you say?'

'I feel like everything's getting away from me.'

CHAPTER 35

Traffic lights clicked red and green for no one, going through their metronomic routine for cars that weren't there this early in the morning. A lone fox stopped in the middle of the road to look at me, then made his way to a bare-branch scrub opposite Brookfield Downs in Rathfarnham. The estate where Lorraine Quigley was waiting to meet me.

Number 4 was like all the other semidetached houses, other than this was allegedly owned by the Health Service Executive, its true purpose kept secret from its neighbours.

I sent a text as I parked outside, almost taking the backside off the pound car from a pillar that materialised too late for the sensors. An elongated, high-toned beep signalled my near miss. It was so loud I thought it might wake the estate.

Lorraine stood in the doorway, an orange dot at her lips, and scanned the estate.

'It's a bit early for that, isn't it?' I nodded at the cigarette.

Her face seemed to fold in on itself as she sucked the filter. Her cheekbones were knife-edges in her small face and her spindly arms stuck out of a cropped yellow sweatshirt, not designed for this cold.

'You're assuming I've slept. Come in, Detective Garda Harney.'

'Please, call me Bridge.'

I followed her down a short hall, carpeted in an outdated looping pattern that reminded me of every golf-club-Sunday-lunch my father had taken us to.

Lorraine had the kettle on and was warming cups for tea. 'Thanks for coming here so early.'

'It's no problem, Lorraine. Do you think you're being watched by Flannery?'

She nodded. 'Seán might be watching you as well. Don't underestimate him. He hasn't found me yet, but it's just a matter of time. Did you tell anyone you were coming here?'

'No.' I shrugged off my outer coat but not my scarf.

'That's like your baby blankie.' She pointed at my scarf. She looked so young when she smiled.

'It is a bit.' I pulled out a stool from under the kitchen bar and sat. 'Thanks for the tea.' It had a strong, dark smell. 'This is a safe house. You're the only occupant right now and this place isn't on any register or file. Why do you think Seán will be able to find you?'

'Because he's Seán Flannery. I ran out on his solicitor as soon as Marie was put into care. I took the SIM out of my phone, so he can't track me, but if he catches me . . .' She paused. 'How long more can you keep Marie?'

'As long as it takes. Have to say, you got clean pretty quick.'

Lorraine's eyes narrowed, as though she were weighing her

words. 'I wasn't using. I just made it look that way.'

'Well, at least you're being honest. Go on.'

'I'm an ex-junkie, but I got clean when I was pregnant with Marie. Been clean ever since. That's why I was so sick in your cells, because I was clean. My body reacted like a virgin when I took that half-mil of the bad thing. It had to look genuine in front of Seán.'

I didn't ask what the following days were like. An ex-addict given a whiff of heroin, then cutting it out. It would have been easier to swallow razorblades.

'Seán hates junkies. I knew he'd report me if I overdosed, then Marie would be taken into care. I just didn't figure on you showing up and being the ones to call in the overdose. You buggered it up completely for me. So the way I look at it, you owe me.'

I took a sip of my tea and stared at Lorraine until heat spread over her cheeks, but she was tough, never dropped her gaze.

'I might correct you there, Lorraine. I think you did figure on me showing up. In fact, you counted on it. You've been leaving a trail of breadcrumbs, haven't you? The blood on Anne Burgess's ring, Emer Davidson's bank card. All so we could pick you up in the Gardens.'

'How long did it take you to work that out? You think everyone around you isn't as smart as you are, don't ya? I needed the shades with guns to get us out of the Gardens. Can you imagine a social worker trying to get past Seán Flannery? You don't leave Seán – he's not into 'conscious uncoupling'.'

She gave a smoker's laugh, a clicking sound like a stick being run along railings.

'I bloodied up the ring and gave it to one of the lads to fence. I thought you'd pick me up straight away, but nothing. So I used the bank card in Farringtons', flipping looked right into the camera so you'd have no choice but to pick me up. I knew you'd come, just didn't know when, but I had the gear on standby for when you did come.'

Any anger at being played left me, the overwhelming feeling one of relief. Relief that Seán Flannery wasn't behind Lorraine's overdose. I might not survive the consequences of being manipulated by him.

'How did you get started with Seán?'

'I'm from Sheriff Street, it's Seán's territory. I got hooked on the gear when I was fifteen. He's the main man for drugs, can get you anything and he liked me, I made him laugh. I think he felt sorry for me when I got pregnant. I'd hang around him, run messages for him when he needed stuff. Give him an alibi, whatever he wanted, he said I was useful. Told me I could live with him after the baby was born.'

'He isn't Marie's father?'

'Christ, no!' Lorraine spoke through clamped teeth, lighting one cigarette off the other. 'Only woman Seán has a hard-on for is you.'

'I'm about twenty-five years too old for him.' I let that statement hang in the air.

'I believe you. That's why I wanted to get Marie out, but there's no proof and I've never seen Seán with man or woman. If anything he's asexual.'

My face must have registered surprise.

'For fuck sake, Bridge! You shouldn't let your middle-class prejudices define you. Some of us did listen, even if it was State school.'

I laughed and was rewarded with a grin, but it slid off Lorraine's face.

'That's all you're getting on Seán, though. Not until you've brokered a deal for me and Marie to be relocated. Out of the country. There's nowhere safe from Seán Flannery, not on this island. North or South.'

'I'm not going to make promises I can't keep. Witness relocation is costly and way above my pay grade.' And I'd have to talk to the likes of Superintendent O'Connor. 'But if you give me enough evidence to nail Flannery, we can look at it. I'd have to see what you have first, though.'

'Do I strike you as an idiot, Bridge? I've been planning this for months. I have information on Seán. Solid stuff. He has a place in Kilkenny, a farm, did you know that? Do you know where he goes to prep for a job? What his methods are or the equipment he uses? I can give you all that. There's a reason you lot can't get near him. He's smart, he's taken online courses in forensics, learned electronics in Ringsend Tech. Only takes big jobs. And here's another thing I know. If you can give witness protection to those arsehole Loyalist supergrasses, you can get witness protection for me and my daughter. Because what I can give you will put Seán Flannery behind bars forever.'

Lorraine was out of breath and I could barely breathe. It was tantalising, but impossible.

'Lorraine, I will never – read my lips – never, get witness protection for you based what you say you have. Do you have documentation? Emails? Irrefutable evidence other than hearsay? I've long suspected Flannery has a prep site for heists – that bank job he pulled last year didn't even make it into the papers it was so clean. Not to mention that Munster Bank didn't want to admit they'd lost a facility. But a couple of us had Seán under surveillance for weeks and got nothing. He didn't make any drops, go anywhere suspicious or make new associations.'

'He has a source in the Gardaí. A very high level informer.'

The room started spinning. 'What?'

'Have you never thought that was possible?'

I was the one answering questions now and if I weren't sitting I would have been on the floor. 'It crossed my mind, of course . . . but what evidence do you have? Do you know who it is?'

'He was keyed up one night last year, I think it was after that Munster Bank robbery. Seán was bragging that he was the king of this city, that he could do anything he wanted. Take anything he wanted cos he'd always have his tracks covered. "Fella far up the food chain is in my pocket."'

'Do you have a name. Or proof?'

'Course I don't! And I've no evidence other than whispered conversations on burner phones.'

Lorraine and I looked at one another, like two cats squaring off. Not unfriendly but not sure of each other.

'If you break Seán's alibi over this Emer Davidson murder,' I said, 'I can move on witness protection.'

She shook her head. 'The woman whose bank card I got? He's not involved in that. He found it in the safe –'

'What? That's ridiculous, he has to be involved in her murder.'

'He was involved in the robbery –'

'I know that!'

'For fuck sake, will you stop interrupting me! You know he did that robbery, you've tracked one of the fences he uses, but you'll never get to Seán. No one gives him up. And I'm not going to give him up either, until we're in witness protection.'

'I can put you into protective custody.'

'A place like here? I'm going to have to move in the next couple of days. He'll find out where I am. Protective custody is no good. I'm not breaking his alibi for the robbery unless I'm on the witness protection programme.'

'I can't put you in witness protection for a jewellery robbery!'

'What about the million in bearer bonds?'

'Mike Burgess denies those bonds were in his safe.'

Lorraine looked at me like I'd told her Marie's birth father had shown up looking for custody. 'Why would he say that?'

'You have to help me place Seán at the murder of Emer Davidson.'

'What? Are you mad? I've told you he didn't do that.'

'How would you know, Lorraine?'

'You're a fanatic, just like Seán says.'

'You put him with that arm we found in the pigmeat or I'll put Marie back in the community.'

I wanted to believe I didn't mean it.

'What date and where was he supposed to have hacked her up?' The left side of Lorraine's bottom lip was wedged under her front tooth, the words falling out the other side of her mouth.

'We don't have an exact date, more of a time frame. And we don't have a location. That's why I need you to go through his movements with me –'

'Jesus Christ, Bridge! You don't know when she was killed or where but you want me to finger him?'

Lorraine's hand slipped off the shiny countertop and she fell to the floor in a puddle. Her skin was stretched with shock. 'My child . . .'

My conscience did waver a fraction, but I'd made my decision. Lorraine Quigley would testify against Seán Flannery. I had a sense of something growing inside me, expanding like a hot bubble, pushing all decency to the margins in pursuit of Seán Flannery.

CHAPTER 36

He had sour, beery breath. Something I had never associated with my father. I softened my footsteps as childhood habits rolled back the years and tried to walk away without making any noise on the flagstones in the front hall, but my heeled boots gave me away.

'Bridget!'

My father's voice rumbled towards me like a high-pressure weather front. I walked to his study door and crossed my arms. The umber oak panelling gleamed with beeswax polish. My jaw hardened as we regarded one another. He was wearing some type of khaki ensemble – a pair of shorts, matching top and knee socks, with a complicated-looking belt. He looked absurd.

'How was your walking holiday?' I worked to keep my tone neutral.

'As you enquire, it was a little fraught. More people than I expected and too many joint activities.'

Into which I read the blowsy Mrs Richie Corrigan had been

flirting with other old boys instead the old boy who brought her. I was about to open my mouth but his hand stilled me.

'I don't want some judgemental dialogue from you. I need you to review your mother's care plan. I think she should go into a residential home. I've a good one here, based in Wicklow.' He looked down at his desk and pushed a black-and-gold glossy booklet towards me.

I didn't touch it. The brochure was expensive-looking and promised 'We Care about your Well-being'.

'Mum has full-time carers, they come in shifts during the day, plus Nata is here to do the housekeeping. The only time you ever have to do anything is at night. And I'm not sure what it is you do, as mostly I put Mum to bed and go back to work if I need to.'

'I don't find that satisfactory.'

'I'm not prepared to let anyone else care for my mother.'

'Why do you have to do everything yourself? Why can't you let me help?'

I looked away, but he continued talking.

'It's time she had twenty-four-seven care. And I think you need a change in your circumstances too. After all, what's a woman in her thirties doing living at home? We're tying you down.'

I was a teenager again, back in an exam and had picked the Higher Level paper in error. I could get the gist of what the questions were asking but didn't have the depth of knowledge needed to get through.

'Would you like me to move back into the mews? That's fine, Judge. I'll move out tonight, right after I've put Mum to bed.'

'No, that's not what I mean. I'm getting a carer for your mother at night, but . . .' He sounded petulant and paced around his monolithic mahogany desk. 'Your life has been blighted by her illness. I never see you laugh, you're never off to meet a boyfriend, the only person you have back to the house is that dumpy little country girl. You need to move out. Of this house. Of the grounds. I'm thinking of selling the whole place.'

'Selling?' The word was like a smarting slap from a teacher's ruler.

'Yes.'

'Downsizing . . .'

'Now you're getting the picture!'

And I was.

The Judge looked jovial now – anyone looking in would have thought it was a pleasant, if somewhat low-key discussion. He and I had always kept our animosity quiet, but our issues drawn.

'So you're finally going to leave? You thought you'd put Mum in a nursing home, sell up here and head off to the south of France. Play King George to Beatrice Corrigan's Mrs Simpson?' I enunciated each word softly and placed them like petals at his feet.

'You know nothing, Bridget, and you understand even less.' He stood back and looked skyward. He was mouthing numbers. One. Two. Three.

The tip of my left boot knocked silently against my right ankle. I couldn't stop it. After what seemed like minutes of staring at it, I had to bend down and touch my toe. I wrapped my fingers around the top of my boot to still the motion. When I straightened up I found my voice was light, but at least didn't sound as churned-up as I felt.

'I won't let you sell this house while Mum is alive. I know you have enduring power of attorney for Mum but I don't believe either of us want me to contest any of your decisions in court.'

He nodded, like I'd made an interesting point, one he had

missed, and smiled as though grateful. His bony hand touched the point of his ceremonial quill pen. It was a languid motion but his fingertip whitened with pressure.

'Do you ever spare a thought for Richie Corrigan?' I asked.

My father had the manners to flinch. 'If you'd listen, you'd see I'm trying to get away from all that. Normalise the situation, stop this charade.'

'By divorcing my mother and marrying Mrs Corrigan?' My voice was a decibel above a whisper and shook. I put my hand out to the solid door for support.

'No, not divorce, but if your mother is in full-time care, Beatrice and I might spend some time together in France. We'll try to see if there's something between us. I think she deserves some happiness. I would stay in touch with you, of course, and make sure you had a house of your choosing.'

I looked at the lifetime achievement award the Law Society of Ireland had given my father two years ago. Cast in bronze, it was of Ireland's most famous mythical warrior, handsome Cúchulainn, slumped, dead and tied to a post with a crow picking over his bones. The idea being he had given everything for Ireland. My father had missed the significance of this statue. After all, Richie was on the committee that had commissioned it and my father had picked Richie's marriage to pieces.

'You will not move my mother out of her home. But feel free to bring Mrs Corrigan wherever you wish. As long as it's not into this house. Good night, Judge.'

I closed his fine wooden doors on his fine wooden face and wished I never had to look at it again.

CHAPTER 37

SEÁN

1997

There were no signs on the rundown stone pillars that guarded the driveway. The sagging gates were closed and any indications that a religious community lived there had been taken down. People walked and drove by the heavy walls without realising what lay behind. I scrambled over a side wall, parallel to the main entrance on Griffith Avenue and landed badly. I had underestimated the drop. As I walked out the kink in my ankle, the grandness of the convent's grounds bewildered me. Saint Augustine's didn't look like this. The convent was a meadow of countryside in the middle of a raging city. In the distance a silver brook unspooled around a stone statue of Saint Francis of Assisi.

At the top of the driveway was a granite building with arched windows. Russet ivy grew on the far wall, its leaves moving in the breeze as though a kaleidoscope of butterflies had landed. The wind brought cooking smells too, of freshly baked scones. I knew if I followed my nose that's where I'd find Sister Assumpta. I hugged the perimeter walls to get a feel for the place. The kitchen at the rear of the great stone house had its back doors open, Joe Duffy was on Radio One, enticing some member of the community to share their woes with the public. The nuns were chatting and laughing, half-listening, half-gossiping. A genial air. I crept low into a thicket of honeysuckle.

Sister Assumpta was there. I had thought her ancient when I was a child, but as I had grown up she seemed to have cheated time. Her creamy face was less lined, or perhaps it was the unfamiliar, easy smile. She shared it with her sisters now as they brought great baskets of laundry out to a shed. A clean, soap-detergent smell mingled with the kitchen aromas. The women had stopped wearing habits and their hair shone in the sunlight. They were like a landed flock of banded geese, happy with their lot. A sister sang out a line and the other nuns lifted their voices in song. A warbled blessing, that despite their aging voices held harmony for the few short lines it contained. It made my dull anger sharp. I stood up from my hiding place and one of the nuns gave a startled shout, holding her hand to her breast.

'Sacred Heart of Jesus!'

I waited for Sister Assumpta to see me. She squinted into the late summer sun then nodded, as if I were expected and late.

'Come in, Seán.' She beckoned me over.

Her sisters were quiet. They twitched nervous smiles at me and joked that I'd nearly given one of them a heart attack. They were scared women trying to be brave, a current of fear running through them, earthed only by Sister Assumpta.

'Follow me, Seán,' she said and walked into the kitchen. 'Can I get you tea? Something to eat?'

She stood by an industrial-sized kettle and flicked a switch, then picked a Brown Betty teapot off an immense Aga and swirled the old tea around it, sloshing it down the sink.

'Ready for some fresh stuff now.'

'Am I not good enough for the nuns' parlour?' I said.

'If you'd like. Yes, perhaps that's where we should go.'

She went to the door. 'Sister Scully? We're going into the parlour. Would you bring us tea and a bit of toast when you're ready?'

Without looking at me, she walked through the kitchen door and into the connecting hallway, from red-and-black tiles to lacquered parquet flooring.

The parlour had a spartan feel and smelled of altar candles.

I sat on a lumpy couch when Sister Assumpta invited me to sit. I had expected to be full of hate, but it had burned down on the walk. Now I was empty without the immediacy of my anger. Lost.

'I expected to see you, Seán.'

'Did the Administrator at Saint Augustine's call?'

She shook her head and smoothed a non-existent crease out of her navy skirt. 'No, but you're eighteen and I knew you'd be leaving State care.'

We looked at one another, until the words jumbled up inside me, like the water that was surely boiling in the old kettle.

'You let that monster . . . feast . . .' The words came out in great juddering double-breaths.

She was as startled as I was. I willed my fists to form. To damage her the way I had been damaged. But nothing would come. Just filthy tears. A child's response.

Sister Assumpta's eyes were wide and obedient, eyes made for under a habit or behind a veil.

'Seán, I was wrong. I see that now, but in my defence I was born in 1959. You didn't question schoolteachers or the Guards.

Much less a priest. I took vows.'

Sister Scully rattled in with a tea tray, put it down, and turned to leave, after a look at Sister Assumpta. It was filled with compassion.

My hands tried to bunch into fists again, but I was too shaken. I had planned this confrontation from the moment she'd told me my mother was still alive and honed it every day since. I would throttle her. Twist her scrawny neck until it snapped. Even when I stood up the shakes didn't stop. I made an attempt to cross over to her, to swipe at her, but ended up bumping into the parlour furniture and upending a table with a statue of the Child of Prague. It smashed into two thick halves and I pitched forward.

'Seán, alanna!'

'Don't call me that!' I was furious: at myself for being unable to control my emotions, at her for being able to disarm me, at the mother who'd abandoned me. But convents were built for this kind of pain. The high, arched rooms were formed for suffering. The buttresses that held the vast ceilings in place mocked my puny woes.

Sister Assumpta put her gnarled hand on my shoulder. Arthritis had twisted her fingers to near dislocation. I grabbed her hand and pressed it. She let out a screech of pain. No one came to her aid.

'Who is my mother? Where is she?'

'Seán . . . please . . . you don't have to do this.'

I released her hand. An old woman cowering on the floor at my feet. I felt soiled.

'Tell me about her.'

She put the fleshy part of her thumb up to her eyes and wiped.

'She wasn't like the other girls, not as young as them and she had a man friend.' Here she looked at me as though she had opened a puzzle of sorts. Her shoulders sagged. 'She didn't want children.'

'What was her name?'

'I won't give you that.'

'Did she marry him?'

'No – someone else.'

'Who?'

'He was a lawyer.'

I raised my hand.

'Go on, hit all you want, Seán. I won't tell you any more – not to protect her, but for you. She'd set the law on you, cripple you before you'd even started in life.'

'Did my mother have any other children?'

'No.' A vein in her lower eye lid pulsed.

I didn't believe her.

CHAPTER 38

DECLAN

2002

My parents were arguing in our front room. The whole flat was made of plasterboard, thin as rice paper, so I heard everything from farts at night to their fumbled shagging. Still, I slipped out into the hall and pressed myself against the bumpy wallpaper so I could get closer to them. My father's voice was raised but my mother's sounded like white noise. The silent hissing of a woman who lived sandwiched between two other families her whole life. Mam turned up the television – bloody *Blind Date* with Cilla Black on Saturdays and Mass on Sundays. It was my mother's unwavering routine. Still, my father's dissatisfaction came through the walls and wrapped itself around me.

'Declan's so young.' My mother's voice pleaded my case.

'He's bloody sixteen! He's not a child. He needs to understand his actions have consequences.'

'We don't even know if the baby is his. For all we know his birth mother or father might have passed something on to him that makes him sterile. We've no way of knowing.'

My father harrumphed and my mother shushed him. My mam thought I didn't know I was adopted from some convent in Ireland. I thought she'd be upset if she realised I knew, but I found out when I was making my Confirmation. Everyone had to bring in their birth certificate, but Mam had acted all weird and wouldn't show it to me, handed it into the office herself, so I went snooping around in her stuff. She had my adoption certificate stashed in an old bible. I never said anything to her – she still believed I thought gay meant happy.

'And he had mumps when he was thirteen. Sick as a dog.'

She was trying to make my dad feel sorry for me, now. It was a good tactic – those mumps had made me look like a hamster with a mouthful of walnuts. I closed my eyes and backed down the hall to my room, the bumpy wallpaper guiding me like brail. I knew Mam, she had Dad on the ropes. I'd get off. *Ding, ding, ding.*

CHAPTER 39

BRIDGET

2018

It was the day of my psych evaluation. I was between wanting to see Paul Doherty – just to get a look at his fine broad shoulders – and hating the whole system for allowing O'Connor send me for quarterly evaluations.

I pressed my fingers into the grooves at the sides of my head.

'You okay, Bridge?' said Kay, her kind eyes willing me to be well.

'I have an appointment with Dr Doherty.'

'Paul?' Kay's face almost split from the effort of trying not to smile. She would have said more but Joe Clarke materialised by my desk.

'He's ready for you, up on the third floor.' He bobbed his head and walked off.

I suppose Joe thought he was being subtle, but everyone knew the third floor was where gardaí were disciplined, demoted or fired. That last whistle-blower had spent four months going up and down to the third floor until he was broken. I prayed his fate wouldn't be mine. There was an awkward silence as I left the squad room.

Paul's was the first face I saw as the lift doors opened. He must have been waiting for me and gave a flicker of smile that made my insides contract. I growled at myself for such a silly impulse.

'Everything all right, Bridge? You look fierce. I'm nearly afraid of you.'

He had that tone again, friendly and flirty, that had characterised our first meeting, but then I'd carried the game on too long, not knowing when the playtime stopped. I wasn't going to fall into that trap again.

'I'm fine, Paul.' I laced his first name with formality as though it were his professional title and surname.

'I see, it's like that, is it?' He was still smiling, trying all his tricks.

I wasn't bending. At least I hoped my face wasn't giving me away. One of the Human Resources secretaries looked at me. I towered over her as she sat at her desk, still she bared her teeth at me. A blunt-faced, quarrelsome thing with black glasses who had the hots for Dr Doherty. It was so clichéd I wanted to laugh at all three of us.

'We're in Suite 2,' said Paul and walked in front of me, leading the way.

He wore a shirt and slim-fitting wool jumper, both smelling freshly washed. His thick grey hair was parted at the side and he looked as crisp as the middle pleat on his ironed trousers. Even if I hadn't seen evidence of a wife, it stood to reason someone kept him that tasty-looking. I sat in the small conference room which was overheated and stale from the previous occupants.

'Christ!' he said. 'You can't find a room in this building that doesn't smell like a dog's fart.'

That got a laugh from me.

'And none of the blinds work properly,' he added.

The tension slackened a notch and Paul poured two tumblers of water from a bedpan-sized jug.

'Hope this is fresh. I could rustle up tea or coffee if you'd prefer?'

I liked the idea of Bluntface being put out and having to get me a coffee but opted for the glass of lukewarm water instead.

'It's fine, Paul. As I understand it, this is a thirty-minute session.'

'Yes.'

'And we're not in your office off Waterloo Road?'

His mouth straightened and his eyes became serious. 'No.'

'Can I ask you a question? It sort of bothered me from the last time. You were a garda, weren't you? So you'd know we call one another mules. Why did you pretend you didn't know? And why didn't you tell me you were in the Force?'

'Okay . . . first I did Arts in Trinity, graduated a few years before you . . .'

That got a smile, but I cut it short. It wasn't that type of meeting.

'I joined the Force, was trained in Templemore same as you and worked as a garda while studying psychology at night, then I moved into Human Resources. I'm still a member of An Garda Síochána. Of course I know we call one another mules, but my interpretation of names or events aren't important. It's what the culture and these expressions mean to you that's key.'

He grinned and my shoulders started to ease down from up around my ears.

'Okay, let's start,' I said.

'We have, Bridge. You're here because an accusation has been levelled at you, that you're discounting a suspect in favour of another –'

I cut across him. 'Seán Flannery is involved.'

From the intense look on Paul's face it was the wrong response. The sun pushed at the edges of vertical blinds that were tethered together like a chain gang.

'That's not what we're here to discuss. It's the behaviour behind your actions, not the specifics of a case. The obstinacy and the idea that, no matter what, you're right.'

'I'm not going to go into specifics of the case, but I'll find evidence to back up my theory.'

'Your evidence is not what we're here to discuss. Do you update your management and colleagues, do you ask for assistance?'

'Kay helps me.'

'Kay's your sidekick. From what I hear you have an excellent partnership, but it's not equal. Kay does what she's told. And you're not her commanding officer.'

I picked at a stray cuticle on my index finger. It was ridged and bumpy. 'So?'

'So this isn't a regular session where you discuss what's on your mind. You're being reviewed for professional misconduct and you don't seem to get that.'

'That's not what was said at the pre-disciplinary hearing. Just that I needed help. You're telling me that Joe's trying to dismiss me? Or is Maitland in the UK trying to get me off the case?'

'No specifics, Bridge.'

I locked eyes with him. 'Do you think I can't do my job? Is that what you're going to write in your report for Joe Clarke?'

'I think you have smarts and intuition, but you need to work inside politics. Develop relationships. Rely on your colleagues, update your management. Ask for help. The things you show disdain for. The people you show disdain for.'

'I'm impressed. I didn't think psychiatrists gave out solid information like that, thank you.'

'There's no need to be sarcastic, Bridge. As I said, this isn't a normal session.'

'Is Joe Clarke trying to get me off the DOCB?'

Paul looked down at his notes, as though studying something, and shook his head.

That told me two things: first, there was a plan to get me out and, second, Joe Clarke wasn't my biggest issue.

'Superintendent Niall O'Connor.' I took my time over the vowels sounds.

'Is he in the building today?' said Paul, nodding.

I smiled. It was better than tearing up at the thought of O'Connor deliberately plotting against me. Still, I'd found an unexpected ally in Paul.

CHAPTER 40

I woke to a banging on my front door. I had no idea how long it had gone on for. The room was pitch black and still the banging continued. Great loud thumps. Someone was using the polished brass knocker and lowering it onto the plate with tremendous force. The sound had me transfixed until my father's peevish voice brought me back.

'Bridget, it's the middle of the night! Who's at the front door? Is it the gardaí?'

Underneath the annoyance he sounded scared. I was more irritated at being woken up and mildly curious as to who thought it was a good idea to call around instead of ringing ahead. My furry dressing gown lay at the end of my bed. I stretched for it and got a vinegary smell from my armpits. I had been sweating in my sleep again. The soles of my feet found the cold floor and I pulled on the dressing gown.

I tapped my way downstairs in the darkness. No thought given to light. I couldn't see to find a lamp or switch.

'I'm coming, hold on!'

'Bridget, be careful! Wait for me!' It was my father's voice again, his concern and the darkness left him not especially surefooted. He scrabbled on the landing's parquet floor.

'Go back to bed, Dad. It's fine.'

'No!' came from the darkness above me. *'I'm coming – don't open the door without me.'*

I ignored him and fumbled for the switch of the main chandelier – the light blinded me.

'Bridget? Bridge?' said Liam O'Shea.

I could hear something close to fever in his voice.

I opened our front door and looked out into the night, unseeing. Flash blindness blotched my vision.

'Kay is dead, Bridge.'

I know I started to speak. It was a single sound. Repeated over and over again. A clicking vowel that couldn't get past the dense plains of my tongue. That's why I kept repeating it, trying to force it out of my mouth. There was a woman with Liam O'Shea. I can't say I remember what she looked like, but I heard her voice.

'Quick, Liam! Catch her! She's having a seizure.'

CHAPTER 41

Madness had its own aroma. A burnt solder type of smell with the texture of chewed tinfoil. I had a blistered ulcer on the inside of my cheek that wouldn't heal. I gnawed on it to keep the pain fresh and fierce. I had bitten down during Kay's eulogy and held her children, while Matthew sobbed out Kay's virtues and his own pain.

I had stood in Kay's hygge home when everyone had cleared up the tea things and gone, holding Jamesy like we were on a crumbling cliff precipice. One step and we were lost. Matthew was moon-eyed, spooled in a dream that I guessed included Kay. It was the first time I had been alone with him since he received news of Kay's death and he turned towards me with slow recognition.

'I thought we'd have more time,' he said.

I had no answer to that.

'I have something for you.' His voice sounded dim. 'I found it on Kay's bedside locker the night she died . . . only I didn't know she was going to die. It doesn't seem important now . . . she was always writing reminders for you or putting Post-Its with instructions up all over the place for us.'

He was speaking as if I wasn't there. I put Jamesy in his walker gently so as not to break Matthew's frail concentration.

'It's here somewhere.'

He rummaged around in a kitchen press full of woolly hats, scarves, keys, a change bowl and other stuff Kay's hands would have touched.

He handed me a sealed white envelope – it looked like pilfered stationery stock and I could feel the edges of a Post-It inside.

'Open it when you get home,' Matthew told my wriggling fingers, 'so you have something of her in your own house.'

I'd left then and gone home, vomiting bright yellow bile into the hand basin of our downstairs guest toilet. I spent the following days submerged in a panic-tinged grief, unable to sit still, unable to move, of no use to anyone. Kay's envelope lay unopened as though she might come back for it.

On the sixth morning after she had been murdered I touched the yellow square through the thin white covering then ripped the perforated flap of the envelope.

And fought for air.

Am meeting Seán Flannery tonight. Says he'll only talk to me. Don't lose the head. Feel stupid writing this down — it's not like I won't be back! See you in the morning.

Written in Kay's neat script the evening she died. Tears, screams, suffocation all threatened but I fought that self-indulgence to a standstill. I had a job to do and I packed a bag.

The trip to Birmingham was uneventful, even sluggish, but I was still scared. Kay's death was a hole in the centre of my house, so everything, even brushing my hair, had taken on an anxious quality. I was keyed up for the whole journey. So many things I had to do and all were interdependent. If one went wrong the others would be forced out of sync, pointless. I texted Joe asking for extended leave and bought a ticket for the Stena to Holyhead. I had lost confidence in my own abilities and wrote down my plan on a Post-It just as Kay would do, like bullet points would fix everything. The ferry to Holyhead was fast, plus as a walk-on passenger there were lax passport controls. I hadn't travelled under my Garda identification. Just a regular tourist with an overnight rucksack. 'Visiting a friend.' A change of clothes, basic toiletries, and a small sealed bag that looked to be filled with vacuum leavings. Seán Flannery's DNA. Skin flakes and hair harvested from the coat pinched by Kay, at the raid where we'd found Lorraine pretending to be at death's door from an overdose.

I sat on a padded view chair in the passenger lounge, amid a colour scheme that looked like an upturned child's crayon pot. Prime colours everywhere. The buffet belched out a plastic, cheesy smell that seemed at odds with the advertised gourmet experience.

My headphones weren't connected to anything and made me look like I was wearing ear-defenders. In a way I was. I took out a book, sealing myself off from other passengers and small talk. No one bothered me. Still, Kay's face kept coming back to me, no matter the music bawling around the lounge or the dodgy drunk heroine in my pulpy paperback. All I could see was Kay.

The Irish Sea pressed in on both sides, sucking at the ferry, wanting me to look at its navy hues. White horses rode the icy waves and I lost myself in their syncopated movement, in the clear ridges that made the swell, then turned darker as they dived down. A huge wall of water rose, growling by my side, and I pictured the ferry struggling to rise in a wave of that magnitude. Oddly, I found it comforting. Others strained to look out of windows and made quick Signs of the Cross. I didn't find any fear in death and took the earphones off to better sense the sea, but the moment I did so the world intruded. A man checked tickets, children screamed for a movie to start and two women put the world to rights beside me.

On the train to Birmingham I thought of Chris, and how my actions would have consequences for him. He should have asked me more questions when we went to Emer Davidson's flat. Like why did I want to see the flat at that point? What was I doing in Emer's room for so long? But he had no guile once he had opened up his heart. He rang Emer's flatmate, asking if we could see her bedroom one more time. The flatmate had complained but was happy enough to get some time off work. I had palmed Emer's house key off the keychain in her room. Right under Chris's nose, while he was talking to the flatmate. I had followed Kay's example of subterfuge being best undertaken in plain sight.

The flatmate had keyed in her alarm code as we left. I stood beside her and memorised the four digits. It was just a niggle in my head, a vague possibility if my case fell apart, like the way you look at flames of a fire and wonder at the pain if you were to let them lick you. Theoretical. Kay's death changed all that. I had cornered Chris at her funeral. His face was full of concern for me, but I had urged him to get the Forensic Scene Investigators to check the whole flat again. He looked at me as if my grip on reality was loosening. Told me it would him take weeks to get authorisation for scene-of-crime officers to be redeployed.

Maybe it would, but I knew enough to tantalise Chris with the thought of Declan Swan's DNA floating around that flat. Maybe even a Clintonesque dress stashed in the wardrobe, ribbons of chromosomes with which to wrap up Mr Swan. If I had my blind spots, Chris had his too.

Emer's flat was quiet when I got there. I let myself in and put an automatic hand out to turn off the alarm. It wasn't on. A cold bead of fear lodged itself in my chest. Was there someone here? The place stank of sweet burnt tyres, possibly a party last night. I began picking my steps into the interior. I couldn't stand in the hallway with the door open, a frozen tableau for anyone passing Emer's door – or a beacon for whoever was inside. I eased the door closed and inched along the tiny hallway. Quiet. So far so good. Perhaps it was just a stoner passed out in the middle of the flat. I pushed my footsteps into the bald carpet, feeling bolder with each step.

A floorboard creaked under my foot.

A little pee squeezed itself out and I counted to five to calm myself. The bathroom door was ajar and Emer's flatmate was taking a shower. The girl had her back to me and the sight of her coffee-coloured flesh was intimate and disquieting. I slithered along the wall towards Emer's bedroom. There was nothing to be gained by standing around. The room was as she had left it, bed unmade and in a state of general untidiness with an added layer of dust as though the space mourned her. A dislocated voice in my head dogged me.

What are you doing?

'Don't start with me, Kay. I don't have time and by the way I wouldn't have his DNA only you collected it.'

You know I would never have used it like this. It was to check if

Flannery was on drugs or prescription medication.

'You're trying to justify yourself, Kay, and it doesn't suit you.'

By the bedside, between the frame and Emer's painted wooden locker I took my tweezers and placed flakes of Seán Flannery's skin from the sealed bag. I moved back and shook out microscopic fragments in circles on the floor, in the dead air of the room. Some would stick, others might not. It made no difference. DNA in one single place looked wrong, but scattered fragments looked like a living person had walked and breathed around the room.

As I wiped the inside of the bag on Emer's rug, Kay came at me again.

This isn't you, Bridge. You're better than this. You can get Flannery another way. What about equal respect to all people? Discharging our duty according to the Law? We took oaths, Bridge.

'Quiet, Kay.'

I had an ear cocked and twitched my head. The shower was still running. I kept my voice to a whisper, suspecting Kay was trying to get me to reveal myself.

'I wouldn't be here if it wasn't for you! Why did you have to go and get yourself shot? Couldn't you have just left it to me? What other choice do I have? We have nothing on Flannery to tie him to Emer's murder. And now he's killed you.'

She was sulking. More. A sensation of nettles being touched off my skin, just enough for the sharp hairs filled with poison to pierce the dermis. It wasn't so much pain, as the realisation of what I was doing. Betraying Kay was somehow worse than her dying.

'Please Kay, don't be mad. I can't do this if you're not with me.' I put my head back to stop the salty tears, but they slid down the side of my face and pooled in my ears.

You've used Chris as well.

'I didn't mean to, you know that. I thought Lorraine Quigley could stay here.'

No, you didn't. You were going to do this all along. You just wanted a reasonable explanation for when FSI find your DNA here. Don't pretend you're doing this for me. The moment you saw this place you knew what you'd end up doing.

'All right, I did! Are you happy now? Just for the record I did think Lorraine Quigley might be able to stay here.'

But she was gone. I was left with the nothingness of my own voice, reverberating around the thin walls of Emer Davidson's bedroom. I suspected Seán Flannery had killed Emer, but I knew he'd killed Kay. Shot her down on Shelmalier Road in Dublin's East Wall in the middle of the night. Point-blank range.

A gritty peach smell came from the bathroom. Emer's flatmate was still washing. I slid past the plastic fairy lights tacked onto walls, one ear cocked for splashing water and tuneless humming.

I closed the front door with a small click. I looked at my watch: I had spent six minutes in Emer's flat. I couldn't think about repercussions now and kept moving, making for the train. My head was a sequestered jury, overloaded with evidence and boiling with questions: Why was Kay in Flannery's territory on her own? How had her lured her there? Why wasn't she armed? The lack of answers could only be kept in check by movement.

I listened to my voicemail. Again.

You have one saved message. Received at 01.10 on Monday the eleventh of December.

'Hi Bridge, it's Kay, call me back soon as you get this. Something's come up, it's a bit unexpected. Give me a ring.'

The entire message lasted 47 seconds. I had been sleeping.

Snoring in my bed when Seán Flannery murdered Kay.

The ferry trundled into the night-time Dublin Port, spinning on its axis with so much force the tiny hairs inside my ears thrummed with pain. Before I left the passengers' lounge I folded my worn Trinity scarf and placed it under the viewing chair I had been sitting on: a threadbare atonement to Kay.

CHAPTER 42

'You're going to have to speak, Bridge, just a bit. Doesn't have to be much,' said Paul.

I was at yet another evaluation.

I bobbed my head up and down in an affirmative. Paul's hopeful brown eyes tried to keep my gaze even as his head dropped to mirror my position.

I still fancied him, I told Kay. You'd be well impressed that I'm trying to up my game in the interpersonal relationship stakes.

Would you get yourself a bloke – it was Kay's familiar voice – *Just put it out there that you're up for a bit of dirty sex.*

I laughed out loud.

'Good joke?' said Paul. He gave me a tiny smile.

Kay had moved behind me, with her wide backside perched on Paul's art-deco desk. Paul and I were sitting by the small stove in his office-cum-living-room. It cracked and popped with the smell of burning pine, tree-glue bubbling like hot syrup.

'We're back here – not on Human Resources' floor in Harcourt Square,' I said. 'Are the brass taking a softly, softly approach?'

'Joe Clarke is worried. He tells me you haven't spoken more than ten words this week.'

The grandfather clock in the corner of the study pointed to a sorrowful twenty past eight.

'Do you blame yourself for Kay's death?'

No, it was a joint effort between Seán Flannery and me.

But saying that out loud would make me sound more of a loon than Paul assumed I was. I needed to find the right words. For Kay, not me. I didn't deserve forgiveness but I couldn't keep giving myself the comfort of pretending Kay was alive. Couldn't stay in this dislocated stupor. Couldn't pretend Kay wasn't buried under cold, damp-smelling earth in a cemetery outside Naas. I didn't deserve the comfort of Kay willing me on, like she was still here. That she wanted this cleansing for me. This sloughing off of a dead skin that was growing over my eyes and muffled my ears until everything sounded like a maddened sea punching the shore. I couldn't explain that to Paul. Or that if I closed my eyes I could feel Kay's cool hand was on my arm. Hear her klaxon of a laugh. Smell her. That home-baked aroma of vanilla sugar that she emanated like a shield of normality. The fairy cakes she baked for her children.

My mind shied away from that and kicked like a hysterical horse.

If anything happens to me, Bridget Harney, you make sure those kids are all right and Matthew finds another woman. A good one.

Sweat coursed down my spine and lodged in the grooves of my lower body. I let out soundless screams and knew by Paul's white face that I was scaring him. The silent opening and closing of my mouth, like I'd swallowed caustic soda. Imaginary blisters bubbled up on the tender membrane inside my throat. Paul's chest rose for a moment and I caught a flicker. A tiny movement of his eye that reminded me he knew Kay as well, and wished she wasn't gone. That Flannery hadn't wiped her out.

I stretched a hand out to him and he met me halfway. His hand was dry and warm. Like a dog I wanted to sniff it, as though I didn't trust my brain to know good from bad any more, needed my senses and sinews to work out what Paul was.

Say something, Bridge, anything.

'I'm trying, Kay.'

Paul raised an eyebrow and released my hand, putting it back on my knee the way you might put a chick back into its nest.

'One time, Kay and I went out for coffee. We were in a real posh place off Grafton Street with her eldest. She was a newborn. It had taken the two of us to get this madly expensive buggy Matthew had insisted on buying in through the entrance. It was more complex to park then the Challenger space ship. We sat there gazing at that beautiful baby. She smelled of white chocolate. And raspberries.' I took a deep breath in, to better remember them. 'Suddenly there was a massive shot, like a gun or a car backfiring. Everyone looked around for the source of the noise, at the huge glass window in case it had cracked, at each other in case anyone was hurt. But nothing. When Kay and I had finished our coffee I noticed the tyre on the buggy had burst. The noise was a flipping blow-out on a buggy. Nobody said anything, it was too embarrassing. The baby had slept through the whole thing . . .'

Paul's shoulders shook with gentle amusement.

'We looked like idiots seesawing our way out.'

I was laughing too, but it was mostly tears. 'I don't know why I told you that.' I was speaking to the rich mocha-coloured rug on the floor.

'None of us have much idea why memories pop into our minds.'

'I have to get better.'

'You will, Bridge, just give it time.'

'I feel like I'm being tested and I'm failing. I'm not just failing, I'm falling apart. Kay deserves better than this.'

I was fading from view, being rubbed out by grief. That wouldn't do. I had to at least get back to a semblance of myself. Flannery had to be caught.

'I have to get better, Paul. You have to help me.'

'That's it, Bridge. That's it. We've started.'

I felt Kay's hand on my shoulder.

CHAPTER 43

I needed Lorraine Quigley. Otherwise, even with planted DNA, Seán Flannery might yet find a way out. My phone had a speed dial for the burner phone I'd given Lorraine. Blood thumped around my body at an unnatural rate, leaving me disorientated and my surroundings filmy. Kay had left me and with good reason. I was about to blackmail Lorraine Quigley with her own child. A child I had taken into protective custody. I felt queasy.

'Lorraine?'

'And who else did you expect to pick up this phone, Bridge?'

Despite her circumstances she sounded in good spirits, perhaps the effect of getting away from Seán Flannery.

'I've done something.' The enormity of what I'd done hadn't yet descended on me. It was more like blood blooming in the deep end, while I foolishly splashed in the shallows. 'But it's going to set certain things in motion leading to Seán Flannery's imprisonment and I need you to disappear.'

Lorraine didn't flinch or pause when I told her to run. In a way, it told me everything I suspected about her life. She was prepared.

'Can you get me and Marie out of the country?'

'No. I can't get you anywhere. You've got to do that yourself. Can you –'

She interrupted me again with the same deliberate delivery: 'How long can you keep Marie?'

'As long as it takes. Sister Catherine won't give her up if you're missing. We'd have to start looking at guardianship, maybe Marie's father, but I won't let that happen.'

'You'd better not, Bridget Harney. Or I'll cut you in your sleep.'

I believed her.

'Do you have somewhere you can go? Somewhere Flannery can't find you?'

She sighed. A tiny sound in the face of such a relentless hunter.

'There's a place my aunt has. She's not my real aunt, just a cousin on my mother's side, from Sheriff Street. That's where my mother's people are from.' She puffed out a series of breaths. 'I'm not sure why I'm telling you this.'

I knew. To say it out loud and prove she existed, like that tree that wanted someone to listen when it fell.

'They've got a caravan near Ballygarrett in Wexford. The caravan park itself is derelict – it was sold to developers few years back, but something went wrong. The van is probably falling down around itself. Seán doesn't know anything about it, so for a while it's safe. How long before I have to leave?'

'Two days, no more. As soon as Seán's brought in he'll tell his lads to hunt you down.'

'The Cabra Capos.' The words should have sounded full of

mockery but Lorraine's voice was trembling.

'Flannery needs your alibi. It's the only thing that will save him.'

'What have you done, Bridge? Is there any way you can undo it?'

'No. And I wouldn't even if I could.'

'Are you doing it for Kay? It was in the papers – do you think Seán had her killed?'

Those big, eternal words were wrong coming out of such a disposable, plastic phone.

'Yes.' It was all I could manage.

'Bridge, he'd never do that. Think about it. Seán's too clever to kill a cop. The heat it would bring down.'

'Kay was killed at point-blank range in the East Wall – that's Flannery's territory. It was a clean nobody-saw-nothing case and a decommissioned IRA gun was used.'

I wasn't going to tell her about Kay's note. Lorraine had no right to that information.

'Bridge, Seán stopped using those guns well over a year ago. They were too traceable. You're not thinking straight –'

'It's his way of operating, it's his territory, his lying scumbags that live there! I'll link that gun to him. So do what I tell you. I'm your only defence against him.'

'I know.' Lorraine was sobbing.

CHAPTER 44

The squad room fell silent when I walked in. A bubble of conversation that was belting along before anyone saw me, popped.

'Bridge,' said Liam O'Shea, and he shimmied across the floor with his hand extended.

'Jaysus, O'Shea, you missed your calling. You should've been on *Dancing with the Stars*,' said one of the lads, seated at the back. 'Yourself and Marty would've made great partners.' There was raucous, if somewhat forced, laughter, but a young German Shepherd from the K-9 unit, with huge paws, seated beside my desk, tore a sob from the back of my throat. They had an assistance dog for me. I bent down to him and buried my face in his soft fur. His black muzzle found my face and he licked one of my tears.

'He likes you, Bridge,' said Liam.

'Bridget?' It was Joe Clarke. 'When you're ready will you

come into my office, please?'

I nodded and mutely followed him. Liam mouthed at Joe to take the dog.

The dog circled around the inside of Joe's office sniffing until he chucked him under the chin.

'You sit down, Bridge, and the pup will calm down. I'd say this fella's only had the bare six weeks' training.'

Joe gave a tentative laugh and I sat down. The dog lowered his warm body onto my feet. Joe had aired out his office. It didn't have that cuppa-soup smell or else my nose was blocked from all the crying, I wasn't sure which.

'Bridget, would you like tea?'

'No thanks, Joe.'

'Right so, I'll get to it.' He moved around in his chair as though he couldn't find the centre. 'We were in the middle of a disciplinary procedure, but that's now suspended at my request.'

Even through my motheaten mind, I knew Superintendent O'Connor wouldn't have sanctioned that without Joe going toe to toe with him.

'Thank you, Joe.' There wasn't anything else to say.

'I can't do this in Human Resources speak, so I'll just say it. You seemed fine for a bit after Kay died. I thought the couple of days you took off did you a power of good, but you've . . . you're not well, Bridge. You've been swallowed up by Kay's death and I'm worried. I couldn't put you on active duty.'

'You can't do that, Joe.' I sat bolt upright and the dog whined. 'Who's going to lead Kay's murder investigation? I have to be involved. I was the person who knew her best! I know who did it.'

'Bridge, you know we won't investigate Kay's death. We're all too close. 5C will take that. Jim McGovern's heading it up. He's a good man and will find out what happened. I'm not even the sergeant on the case. It's too personal.' He cleared his throat, as though trying to expectorate our joint pain. He had a sheet of white paper in his hand. He spoke quietly.

'I have your psychiatric evaluation here, Bridge. You can't go back to work right now. You have to take time off.'

'I need to be involved!'

The dog jumped and looked at me as though he were in grave trouble. 'I'm sorry,' I said and looked into his flecked, amber eyes.

'You can't, Bridge. Paul Doherty's recommended you be put on suicide watch.'

'I thought he was trying to help me.'

'He is, Bridge.'

CHAPTER 45

SEÁN

I liked the dark. I was terrified of it as a boy in the dormitories, but I was clever like that. I made my fears my strengths. The sky was the colour of a priest's habit and just as unforgiving.

I'd been watching this house for a couple of weeks. Sometimes I just watched, long after I needed to. I found it comforting. With old blankets and a Vincent de Paul sleeping bag I was invisible in this neighbourhood. I mean, people stared down their noses as I sat outside their local artisan bread shops, but no one really looked at me.

This family had two children: a skinny boy, angry at the world because he was so short, and a willowy girl. She had owlish, scared brown eyes and I liked that. The mother did yoga, had horse-riding boots, a bike rack on the back of her jeep and jogged most mornings with some likeminded shrew. All so she could get away from her family. She wasn't the problem because she was never there. It was the limp father. He hung around, emasculated from all the child care. The boy was too caught up in himself to notice anything other than the next Snapchat.

One night the father went out and I followed him at a discreet distance, not that my efforts were needed. He kept his head down and followed his nose to Glennon's pub, where he met friends. I could see them backslapping each other through the pub's picture window with a gaudy 2018 Six Nations rugby ball painted on it. They stumbled out of the pub hours later, talking of sports none them played. One of them tripped over my inert body and gave me a few kicks. Shouted, 'Benefits run out?' Alcohol peeled back their layers.

Another night I watched from the end of some old dear's back garden. Her dog was as blind as she was, so I sat with the mutt and fed him chopped-up mackerel I'd caught in Bullock Harbour. Dogs love oily fish. I was on my own because I wanted to look at the shy-faced girl, but her mother drew the blind too quick. All I caught was the girl's soft downy arms, her thin vest over a budless chest. It was enough. Perfect.

I waited for another night, until the mother was out. The boy sneaked over the back wall with a bottle of lemon-coloured liquor. He had the keen face of a hunting fox. I lifted the latch on the back door. The family had an old church pew they used as a breakfast bench. It had a burnt-incense smell. You could never get rid of that odour. It reminded me of being sent to clean the sacristy in the Mother and Baby home. Sister Assumpta would lean into me and pat my arm.

'Seán, you're like a ghost. You hover. Father O'Mahony says you and Gavin are the only ones who don't disturb him.'

Didn't matter if he disturbed me.

There was a bowl of fresh-cut roses in the girl's hallway, with charcoal-coloured paper on the walls. I flitted passed their sitting room where the father was wearing a white helmet with the visor down. Blue light emanated from the headgear as he sank deeper into his own virtual world, oblivious to everything around him. I checked the house alarm by the front door, more out of professional curiosity, but no one puts their alarm on when they're in their own home. They should.

Softly, so softly, I found my girl. Round cheeks and sleep-sweet eyes. Pupils pulsed as she watched herself in her dreams. She was in my dreams. I don't know how long I sat there. Only until I knew I'd be back. I'd touch her the next time.

PART 3

BOWLINE

bowline

'bəʊlɪn

noun

1. A rope attaching the weather side of a square sail to a ship's bow

2. A simple knot for forming a non-slipping loop at the end of a rope

CHAPTER 46

BRIDGET

My mobile rang. It trilled with a ridiculous birdsong ring Kay had put on it. The look of irritation on my face every time it rang made her laugh. I stretched my hand out and groped for the phone. My bedroom was the kind of blackness made for slumber, not a shrill alarm and bare feet on a cold floor.

'Yeah . . .' I sounded like a stranger. My eyes were gummed with sleep-wax. Guilt flicked its tongue out to taste my bed whenever I got up, or slithered around my ankles when I tried to walk away. If I had expected to feel no remorse when I framed Seán Flannery I was a fool, or I didn't know myself. Something I was beginning to realise.

'Bridge? It's Chris, we've found Flannery's DNA in Emer Davidson's apartment.'

And like that I was on fire.

I hopped out of bed and pulled back the heavy drape curtains to let light into my room.

'You know I'm on sick leave?'

'Aye, I'd heard. You sound awful – are you up for this?'

'*Yes!*' The word came out like a thunderclap.

'Well, that's something. How do we do this?'

'You'll have to ring Joe Clarke or, better yet, get that arsehole Maitland to call O'Connor. Tell them we have a solid link to gang crime in two jurisdictions and they'll be planning their joint press conferences before you've finished speaking.'

'Right, well, get yourself back to the station and call me the moment you hit your desk.'

'No, Chris. Get on the next plane to Dublin – we'll get Flannery the moment you touch down.'

'Fair enough. When will we get to bring in Declan Swan?'

'Let's wait to hear what Flannery has to say, then we'll question Swan.'

I scrambled into my clothes. I should have showered, but my mind was racing. I spent at least three minutes like a fool, looking for my Trinity scarf. A thin pin of pain to my throat when I remembered where I'd left it.

I threw myself into the kitchen and stumbled over the dog as he danced his way around me, hoping we were going on a walk. Everything drooped as he saw me closing the back door in his furry face.

Mum's ancient gold BMW was sitting in the back garden and turned over first time. I never drove to work, but I wasn't sure whether the bus or train would get me to Harcourt Square fast enough. The idea of waiting in a station was intolerable.

It took a moment for my colleagues to register I was back. Nothing had changed to my eyes. The room still had that goldfish-bowl feel and the oniony tang of body odour. My colleagues were looking at me, waiting for my lead. I looked at Kay's desk. It hadn't been touched, not even dusted, a grave in the middle of a working squad room where space was at a premium.

'Did none of you think to clean the desk?' I put a broad smile on my face and conjured up Kay's bright eyes to help me. The relief was palpable.

'Good to see you, Bridge,' said Liam O'Shea. He was saying something more but it was drowned out by calls from the rest of the team, banging desks and a welcome fit for an Irish lad who'd made it in the Premiership.

You've done it, Kay. You've made them accept me.

'Bridge!' It was Joe. 'Settle down, you lot, we've work to do. Bridge, bring your stuff into my office.'

Not wanting to leave Kay's desk as I'd found it, I wiped it with my sleeve and a line of greyish dust attached itself firmly to me.

'Go on, I'll do that,' said Liam, 'don't keep him waiting. UK have been on to Superintendent O'Connor and he was here before I got in, talking to Joe. Not so much talking as shouting the odds. You could hear them all over the Square.'

I thanked Liam for the heads-up and told myself to breathe. Not that I was worried about Superintendent O'Connor or even that the evidence I'd planted would reveal itself as fake. The problem was me. My grief for Kay was a block of cement inside me and I had to lug it around, while making people think my breakdown was a temporary blip. I eyed Joe's office through a meniscus layer and started swimming up towards him. Kay had to be consigned to memory. I didn't want to see her in the cup on her desk, or her navy curlicue handwriting on the noticeboard.

Joe was sitting at his desk, watchful and waiting.

I was on.

'You look better, Bridge.' He gestured to a chair. 'Would have been good to phone ahead though, let me know you were coming in. You're still written off as sick. Human Resources won't like that.'

Joe slurped a cup of strong tea — he'd never gone in for the hipster coffee from the street vendors that had popped up all over Dublin. The tea smelled like box-hedge trimmings.

'I know, Joe. I should have given you a heads-up and done an interview with Human Resources, then come back next week, but Chris Watkiss called me.'

'Did he now? Well, I can't say I'm sorry. Work is the best cure for anything that ails you.' Joe stretched his neck up and relieved some of the pressure from his shirt collar by running his forefinger in between his jowl and the material. 'I owe you an apology. Looks like there's more to Flannery than anyone's ever given him credit for. Right . . . enough of that.'

I gave Joe a wan smile.

'Let's go then. Read yourself back in and get O'Shea ready to pick up Flannery.' He paused, but got no argument from me.

I raged against it inside, but this was for Kay. I had to appear as if I could trust someone else to get it done.

'Don't worry, Bridge, O'Shea will do it right. I presume Watkiss is on a flight by now?'

I stood up and nodded, unable to contain my satisfaction sitting down.

'Stay away from Superintendent O'Connor until you have this nailed up tight. And Liam O'Shea leads from the Irish side. No buts.'

'Got that, Joe. But I'll interview Flannery, right?'

'Yes, there's no way past that, but I'll be watching the monitors and so will Superintendent O'Connor.'

I accepted the warning and the tacit agreement that I wasn't right yet, but I'd have to do. Deciding not to treat Chris to the joys of my mother's elderly motor, I got a pound car and headed for the zoo that was Dublin Airport.

They were having a bad day in Terminal Two, the automatic doors were stuck open and wind screeched up and down the spacious building. Small birds bounced around the eaves in an alarming manner. I counted the minutes until Chris's large form walked through the Arrivals frosted doors. The moment I saw his grin I hit speed-dial on my phone to O'Shea.

The paddy wagons rolled out to the Gardens. Two Emergency Response Units with Liam O'Shea at the helm. Flannery wouldn't know what hit him.

'I'll bring him in, Bridge,' Liam said. 'By the book, just like you would.'

I wasn't immune to the irony and tried to share a laugh with Kay. She wasn't impressed.

CHAPTER 47

'Sit him down, but keep him cuffed,' I said. There would be no comfort from me for Seán Flannery.

He sat in the bolted-down chair at the bolted-down table, a few sparse feet away from me.

'Is that necessary?' said Richie Corrigan, who always managed to sound like sitting in an interview room was beneath him.

The room had four corner cameras, built-in microphones connected to the wall panel, which I punched and listened for the wasp-under-glass sound that signalled the start of the interview.

'This is Detective Garda Bridget Harney interviewing Mr Seán Flannery, residing in 5 Saint Martin's Gardens in East Wall Road. You were cautioned when you were picked up. Is that correct?'

'Aren't you supposed to say "sir" after that, Harney?' said Seán.

I could play this game all day long.

'Is that correct, sir?'

'That's more like it, Harney.'

'For our records please, Mr Flannery, confirm your name, address, that you were cautioned and understand your rights.'

'Seán Flannery, Saint Martin's Gardens. Yes, I understand my rights. What's this about, Harney?'

His eyes narrowed and his top lip curled, showing his white canine teeth. He slouched down in the seat, his studded belt making a shearing noise against the plastic chair.

'Please answer my client's question, Detective Harney,' said Richie.

I didn't deign to look at the legal mouthpiece.

'Where were you on the night of 25th October 2017, Mr Flannery?'

'That was months ago – do you seriously expect me to know where I was the last week in October? Richie, do something about this! Came round to my gaff as well, unauthorised search. The woman's obsessed.'

'Answer the question please, sir,' I said.

For the first time, Flannery looked cornered. His eyes searched the stark white walls of the interview room, as though his spot on the wall might have failed him.

'Sir?'

'Don't harass me, Harney. I've told you I was at home in the Gardens.'

'Can anyone confirm that for you, Mr Flannery?'

'My missus.'

'Are you married, sir?'

'You know I'm not, Harney. Would mess up my missus' benefits if she weren't a single mother. Got to look after the kiddie.' He grinned. Perhaps he was giving me a not so subtle warning about Marie Quigley.

'All right, sir, let's try another line. How well did you know the deceased Emer Davidson?'

He paused. His narrowed eyes were the shape of slits in a watchtower. He leaned onto his side and let out an ear-shattering fart. Never once breaking eye contact with me.

'I don't know Emer Davidson.'

The air was thick with the smell of rotten eggs. I tried not to swallow. My ears were swollen and blocked. I needed to stay calm. My delivery had to be professional. Nobody watching the interview could have reason to believe Seán Flannery.

'Then how is your DNA in Emer Davidson's apartment in Birmingham, Mr Flannery?'

The veins in my neck throbbed. My voice was light and I hoped it was conversational. Not artificial.

It happened fast. Through the dense air he lunged at me. Even with the cuffs on he managed a swinging kick to my mouth. My bottom lip burst. I rolled my lips together and smeared the blood all around. Then bared my teeth at him, showing my carmine-filled grin.

'You've stitched me up! You lying cunt!'

Uniforms barrelled through the door. Not as fast as I would have liked, but I suppose I had only myself to blame for that. They did a good job subduing Flannery and gave him a right few digs when they saw my face.

'Police brutality!' said Richie. His voice sounded tinny with surprise at finding himself in a violent situation. He hopped around on one leg, as if he were an activist at a rally for misunderstood-rich-guys. One of the uniforms unintentionally caught Richie in the jaw with his elbow. I wish it had been me.

I knew the cameras were recording and turned – so they could get a full view of my mouth. I spat a globule of blood on the table, shiny and veined, then put my hand on the chair to support myself, as though overcome. A little over the top, but I felt Flannery and Richie deserved it.

I walked into the hallway, went to the water fountain and bent to rinse my mouth, spitting pink water into the chrome basin.

'I'm sorry you were hurt, Bridget.'

Richie Corrigan was standing beside me. He looked a bit worse for wear himself. I winced at the lump that was rising on his jawbone, even as we spoke.

'You should get someone to have a look at that. You might have a hairline fracture,' I said.

'It's fine. Is there anywhere we can talk?'

I dismissed him with a wave of my hand. 'It's too early for deals, Richie. Unless Flannery's going to plead to murder and armed robbery? I'll chat all you like then.' I gave him a manic smile.

Richie's mouth turned down and he fidgeted with something in his waistcoat pocket. 'No, it's about your father.'

Richie looked as uncomfortable as I felt surprised.

'It's important, Bridget, please.'

I walked into an empty interview room and sat on the side of the desk. One table leg was shorter than the others, so it pitched forward, startling me.

'Richie, this had better be serious. And not a stalling tactic. I could have you suspended for that. We can keep Flannery for ninety-six hours and every minute counts. This is unprofessional.'

'I know, and if you wish I will excuse myself from the case after this. But your father rang me. He thinks you're ill. That you've suffered a kind of breakdown as a result of Kay's death. And though it pains me, I'd be inclined to agree with him.'

My mouth hung open. I shut it with a clack. 'I will have you suspended, Richie.'

I stood up and the uneven table righted itself, digging a corner into my backside.

'You are not yourself, Bridget.'

'How dare you!'

'I dare because your father has asked me to intercede.'

I put a hand out to steady myself.

'For God's sake sit down, Bridget! Or you'll fall.' Richie took a seat. The skin around his eyes looked chapped. 'This is difficult enough and I recognise that the timing could be better, but you've only yourself to blame for that. You shouldn't have come back on active duty, no matter what was happening to Seán Flannery.'

Richie spoke to me as if we were at home and I was the wilful, disobedient child he'd had quite enough of.

'You've always assumed that Beatrice and your father were having an affair —'

'You're not dragging that up now? In here?'

'*Sit down!*' It was a bark. 'You need to listen and not always assume you know everything.' His hand moved to his waistcoat and the same pillbox shape he'd been fiddling with in the hall. He seemed unaware of the motion. 'You need to know the truth of your parents' circumstances. Your mother and I are . . . were involved for over forty years. Until her illness. She and I were in love before she married your father and we . . . kept in touch.'

My mouth had dried out, making speech impossible.

'You had no way of knowing this, as you never knew your grandparents. Your mother never went back to Offaly, but her parents were unkind people, I'd say made more so by having to scratch a living on twenty acres in the middle of nowhere. Your mother knew real hardship.'

I understood the words, but the fabric of my life was being picked apart, showing heretofore invisible threads. How could Richie know more about my family than I did?

'Elizabeth ran up to Dublin as soon as she finished school. She was a beauty and met your father at a dance in the Shelbourne. Of course, Vincent had to have her. Didn't matter she was ten years younger than him and dazzled by the high life he could give her.' There was a smooth nugget of hatred in Richie's voice. 'Your father came from a wealthy background and had excellent prospects. His career passed mine by in a blur. Christ, he was in the High Court a year before any of his peers! I never blamed Elizabeth for marrying your father. But, as time went by we found our respective situations . . . intolerable. We wanted to be together. Your mother felt your father was too tough on you. Setting you impossible tasks, even as a little child, believing he was building your character through adversity. Your mother thought he was breaking you. She sent him away when you were little, but it was only a fortnight before he had cajoled his way back. He bought you a television.'

Richie held up a hand. I must have looked like I was going to say something, but he was mistaken. Speech was beyond me.

'I thought he wanted her to stay for his career, but I may have been wrong about that, in light of his kindness towards her during her illness. With Elizabeth needing full-time care now,' here Richie sobbed, 'your father wants to take that responsibility from you. My wife also deserves happiness and I've been a disappointment to her. Contrary to your assumptions, Beatrice and the Judge have never been intimate. I'm not sure what he feels for her, but Beatrice has always wanted revenge and I know she'd have left me in a flash if your father so much as crooked his finger. They went on a holiday to Norway recently, but fought about you most of the time.'

There was something hurting in my mouth. Without realising, I had started to chew on the ulcer on the inside of my cheek again.

'What's going on here?' It was Chris Watkiss, his massive form filling the open doorway. 'Are you okay, Bridge?' He turned to Richie. 'What have you done to her? Bridge, are you okay?'

I could hear Chris, but I didn't realise he was talking to me. It was like being at an outdoor movie, watching events being played out in front of me on an enormous screen.

CHAPTER 48

'Bloody rank coffee, Bridge. I thought Dublin was supposed to be the epicentre of hipsterness. That's what my daughters tell me.'

It was raining hard sleet. Great ignorant chunks of ice that wouldn't have looked out of place in the Arctic. I was sitting outside Harcourt Square drinking a harsh-tasting americano Chris Watkiss had handed me.

I snorted back a laugh and got a mouthful of hailstones.

'Are we finished here yet? I know you wanted some air but this is above and beyond. I feel like I'm in the ring with McGregor. I thought it was cold up our way – what kind of weather is this?'

I punched Chris gently on the shoulder. 'Okay, soft lad, let's go back in.'

Chris shoved the main door open and the stuffy heat of Harcourt Square enveloped us.

'You weren't put off by that solicitor, were you? What was he saying?'

I put Richie to the back of my consciousness, even blotted out his features so he became faceless and indistinct. Magritte's bowler-hat man.

'Don't worry, he was just trying to rile me.'

'If he's botherin' you, Bridge, I'll see to him.' Chris had two high spots of colour on his cheeks. 'We can ask him to be removed – you can do that here, right? I despise these solicitors who pucker up to thugs. All for what?'

I thought of Beatrice and her house in France. Money. That's what motivated Richie and I believed Seán Flannery had plenty of it.

'Richie Corrigan doesn't bother me.' The thought of my mother and Richie pinwheeled in my mind like a flaming firework. I doused it. Richie would keep – for now I had to stay focused on Seán Flannery. This was for Kay and it was true what they said. Revenge was best served cold with a clear head and a stone heart.

The uniforms had straightened the upturned interview room when we got back to it.

'Detective Garda Bridget Harney and Detective Chris Watkiss of the West Midlands Constabulary re-entering the interview room. That looks sore, Mr Flannery. Can we get you medical attention?'

I was all politeness to Seán Flannery's busted face.

'You don't look so good yourself, Bridge. Mind you, a split lip suits you. Will you be pressing charges?'

'Detective Garda Harney,' said Richie, 'I want it noted that my client has been assaulted while in police custody. We will be pressing –'

'Shut up, Richie,' said Flannery.

I let Richie's embarrassment sit there, heavy and grainy, like a blob of prison porridge hanging on the underside of a spoon.

'Interesting,' said Chris. 'Crims usually bollock their solicitors in private.'

'You are not allowed to speak, Detective Watkiss.' Richie sounded like a cranky old maid.

'My bad.' Chris held up both hands in mock remorse.

'I want to see what you have, Harney,' said Seán.

'We can place you in the deceased's apartment. You visited Emer Davidson. We don't know on what date, but that's irrelevant. The connection is established.'

'I didn't even know Emer Davidson. Much less killed her. When did she die?' Seán eyes searched my face.

'In the ninety-six hours between 3rd and 6th of November.'

'I was with Lorraine the whole time.'

Did I see a flicker in those dead eyes? I allowed myself the tiniest smile.

'And Miss Quigley can corroborate that, Mr Flannery?'

He fidgeted around in his seat, but his face was unreadable.

'Where's Miss Quigley, Mr Flannery?'

'We have reason to believe due to her ill treatment while in Garda custody —'

I spoke over Richie. 'Let me answer that for you, Mr Flannery. She's in the wind. As is your alibi for the 25th October 3rd, 4th, 5th and 6th of November. Burglary and murder.'

'What's my motive then? Eh, Bridge?' He said my name like it was a swearword and flicked an already tatty thumbnail. He restrained himself from putting the thumb up to his mouth, but his teeth made a gnashing motion.

'Let me see if I have it right, Mr Flannery. Emer Davidson worked for Declan Swan. You met her, somehow found out that Declan Swan was having an affair with her and you both decided to blackmail Declan. Perhaps it was Emer's idea, who knows? But either way, you forced Declan Swan to steal the codes to Mike Burgess's safe in Dalkey and took a million in bearer bonds. Then you decided you didn't want to share. You killed Emer Davidson and hacked off her arms, so you could continue to blackmail Declan Swan.'

Seán leaned in to Richie and they shared a conspiratorial whisper.

'Who's Declan Swan?' Seán spoke in a slow voice, but his eyes were alert and intent.

I pulled up a picture from Declan Swan's Instagram and put it on the widescreen monitor. 'Does Mr Swan use an iPhone? Picture quality is smashing. There you are, in the George Club – he's standing right beside you. #bestcrew.'

'That Instagram account is private,' said Richie. 'Did you get a warrant, Detective Garda Harney?'

'You've no idea whether that account is private or not, Richie. But either way it doesn't matter, once you put a hashtag on the picture it's in the public domain. Anyone can see it. You need to get your advice from a better class of technical nerd. Mike Burgess's boat won the Regatta in Dún Laoghaire during the summer. It's all up under #bestcrew. Nice boat – what's it again?'

Seán Flannery stayed silent.

'It's in the manifesto, Seán. All crew members were logged. You were the navigator and second only to the skipper, Declan Swan.'

'I didn't know him. I just crewed the boat because Swan can't sail. That doesn't prove anything. I've crewed tons of boats over the years.'

'If my client says he doesn't know Mr Swan, he doesn't know him. You can't prove anything you've just said.' Richie looked unsure of his ground.

'I think I can. I have motive, blackmail. I have means, Mr Flannery knowing Mr Swan. And Mr Flannery is a career criminal.'

'That is wholly untrue!' Richie's words came in angry jabs. 'Mr Flannery is from a humble background and I think your own biases are showing, Detective Garda Harney.'

'I think a good barrister will peel back Mr Flannery's "humble beginnings", Richie. All those twists and turns until the jury are hanging on his every word. And boisterous objections by your barrister will only prove to heighten the interest in Mr Flannery's colourful past. Not to mention his financial records.'

'I have no money. I do odd jobs and a bit of sailing. It's all on my tax returns.'

'So it is, Mr Flannery, but a known associate of yours was put in prison just four short months ago for upgrading his girlfriend's house in Rialto. Gold taps, I believe, and a three-hundred-grand extension? Again a gentleman who told us he was an unemployed odd-job man with his primary residence in the Gardens. Criminal Assets Bureau helped him see the light, though. Not like you to slip up, Mr Flannery. One of your own boys.' I made a well-bred moue.

Chris stifled a laugh at Seán's pained face, but it was brief. In an instant, Seán Flannery wiped his face clean of all expression and replaced it with a practised, neutral stare. This was the man I feared.

CHAPTER 49

I didn't go home that night. There wasn't anything at home for me. I was too keyed up to face my father and my mother wasn't capable of reason. With Seán Flannery lying in the cells downstairs being questioned about murder, the Square was the only place I wanted to be. The clock at the end of the squad room ticked on, having no reason to stop. Chris had gone to the Harcourt Hotel to freshen up and I told him to have a bite to eat and get a shower. He had dark circles under his eyes.

I plucked off the pink-framed photograph stuck on the partition Kay and I shared. It was dry and brittle. We were so much younger in that photograph. Long hair in ponytails, up off our collars and our square caps rammed on our happy little heads. Of the three, I was the only one still around. A song skittered around my head – 'Linger' by the Cranberries, a tune Kay, Jeanne and I would have danced to in O'Leary's pub on a Friday evening in Templemore. I closed my eyes.

'Bridge?'

It was Chris.

'Christ, Bridge! It's half ten, I left you hours ago. Have you been here all this time?'

I'd fallen asleep, into a black, dreamless thing. It had left a toffee of bad breath in my mouth and I stank.

'Shall we go to the canteen, see if we can rustle up something? You need a bit of food, Bridge.'

I stretched myself out and pulled my desk drawer open to find a jar of marmalade still alive. Before I could take the lid off and stick my finger in the sugary citrus goo, the door opened.

The night-duty sergeant burst into the squad room. 'Flannery's asked for his solicitor! Corrigan's on his way in.'

Chris and I shared a look.

'Come on, let's get some food into you. I reckon we'll be back in the interview room within the hour.'

'Ring Joe and Superintendent O'Connor.' A horrible excitement started to build inside me.

Seán Flannery put on a show of looking relaxed as he walked into the interview room, but his muscles were twitchy and he sat down too quickly. Richie Corrigan looked grey as Victorian parchment paper and smelled as withered.

'This is Detective Garda Bridget Harney at 1.05 a.m. on 13th December 2017, interviewing Mr Seán Flannery, residing in 5 Saint Martin's Gardens in East Wall Road. Mr Flannery has been cautioned. Please confirm, Mr Flannery.'

'Correct,' said Seán Flannery. He cracked his knuckles. In the ensuing silence it sounded like machine-gun fire.

I stared at him. Looked hard at his face. When had I spent this much time with Seán Flannery? Not since I was a barrister. His eyes, rather than the urine yellow I'd always assumed, were the colour of hardened tree resin. Cold slits behind binoculars, made for directing troops in battle without getting a drop of blood on his own hands.

'My client wishes to make a statement. For this we will want complete immunity, bearing in mind his testimony will convict others. Please consult with your superiors as I am aware you do not have the authority to transact this,' said Richie and tried to pat down his unkempt hair. He looked like the old man he was. Clearly he had retired for the night when Seán Flannery called him back to action.

I looked up at the camera and knew Superintendent O'Connor was in the observation room evaluating us. Chris and I rose to leave.

Superintendent O'Connor was waiting for us in the anteroom near the interview suites. He looked bigger, brighter, more menacing than I had pictured him. I knew by his face niceties were pointless, so I went straight in.

'Can you authorise immunity for Seán Flannery, Superintendent O'Connor?'

Superintendent O'Connor's index finger touched an indentation near his temple, made deep by years of tiny taps. 'I could but I won't. However, you can tell him he has immunity.'

I expected nothing less, but Chris's jaw hung open.

'So Bridge tells Flannery he's in the clear,' he said, 'and when we prosecute him you stand back, Chief Inspector O'Connor, and hang her out to dry, by denying any knowledge of a deal! That's why we're in this little room, so no one can hear you. Well, I'm a witness.'

'Much good your testimony will do and it's Superintendent O'Connor, Watkiss. You're not in England now.'

'Bloody right I'm not — even Maitland wouldn't pull a stunt like this!'

Superintendent O'Connor ignored Chris, instead raised his nose as though sniffing for the prevailing political winds, then looked at me.

'You know the deal, Harney. Take it or leave it.'

'I'll take it.'

'Then stop wasting time and get back in there.'

Chris and I turned away and made for the interview room.

'Bridge, it's career suicide — they'll fire you off the Force for reckless behaviour or worse . . .' Chris's voice trailed off.

I couldn't explain to Chris that I was finished in the Gardaí, couldn't go back without Kay. I knew Superintendent O'Connor would charge Flannery based on whatever he said in the interview. That was the whole idea. So what if I was left swinging in the wind? This wasn't about me.

I was back at my seat. 'Mr Flannery, I can confirm that Superintendent Niall O'Connor will grant full immunity to you based on your statement, if that statement results in a criminal conviction in the murder of Emer Davidson.'

Seán Flannery and Richie Corrigan looked up at the camera in unison. I had a demented urge to shout jinx.

'Go ahead,' said Richie, as though he mattered in this.

'You call the shots, big man,' said Seán Flannery, to underscore the point. 'I met Mike and Anne Burgess last July, at the George Yacht Club in Dún Laoghaire. He had two boats, a Beneteau Oceanis 60, kept year round in Dalkey, and a sweet boat called the *Lady Lydia*, a Volvo Ocean 65 Class.'

To my surprise his features softened, then hardened like the hulls of the boats he spoke of.

'I crew in the George and a couple of the owners have used

me as skipper. The sailing manager recommends me to any visiting sailors, particularly lads like Burgess.'

'What do you mean?'

'No questions, Detective Garda Harney.' Richie was glaring at me.

'Richie, he's not giving a statement about a missing bike. It's a murder enquiry and you've been given immunity.'

Seán Flannery smiled at the tone in my voice. 'She stoops to conquer.'

'Why Burgess in particular?' I said, refusing to be diverted.

'He can't sail. As in, he can barely get from the tender into his own craft. The worthies in the George don't want fools like Burgess destroying the marina, so when he applied for membership they emailed him and told him to get a local crew. Sent him my way.'

It made sense.

'I get a few quid and everyone's happy. I did a bit of crewing for him and he introduced me to his daughter Lydia and her husband Declan Swan. Swan was a fool, all fast cars and women, thought he could sail as well. No idea how to read a nautical map or understand currents, but at least he knew his tacking from his jibbing. Suited me as I spent most of the summer on that boat. I got to know Mike Burgess a bit better, sorted him out with a bit of Charlie.'

'What's that?'

'Surely you know what that is, Detective Harney? Don't you spend your time socialising in the drawing rooms of suburban Dublin?'

'For the benefit of the cameras, Mr Flannery.'

'Cocaine. It gets everything going in the right direction. Needs must, eh?' He gave Richie a leering, theatrical nudge.

It was terrifying in its inappropriateness. I suspected that's what Flannery wanted.

Chris tensed beside me.

'Are you telling me you were supplying Mike Burgess with illegal substances?' I asked.

Richie all but yanked Seán into a hissed whisper, then turned to me.

'Mr Flannery shared a small amount of cocaine with Mike Burgess. It was for personal use and during this voluntary statement – under which immunity has been given – he cannot be prosecuted. I might add you have no right to cross-examine Mr Flannery at this time.'

'No questions will be put to Mr Flannery other than for the purpose of removing ambiguity. Crime Investigation Techniques Chapter 4, section 4.17, subsection –'

'7. Yes, I know the procedures, Detective Garda Harney.'

Richie wasn't as asleep as I'd assumed, but I knew Seán was lying. The toxicology analysis I'd had done on his hair showed no sign of drug use, recreational or medicinal. Seán was a 'just say no to drugs' type of guy and seemed amused by Richie's and my pathetic attempt to out-expert one another.

'Go on, Mr Flannery,' I said.

'Burgess didn't rate the son-in-law, Swan. Thought he was a tit and suspected Swan was playing around on his daughter. Told me he'd pull the rug out from under Declan Swan if he caught him cheating. Make sure he got nothing in the divorce.'

'Mike Burgess told you all this? A deckhand?'

'I was hardly a deckhand, Bridge.' He scowled at me, as if I were a traffic uniform asking him if he owned the vehicle he was driving. 'I ran the *Lady Lydia*, and it's a race boat. No room for amateurs and it's the dog's sailing up to Carlingford. I got her up to 27 knots, that's nearly fifty kilometres an hour, in the open sea. Sometimes the keel would turn forty degrees. It's pretty exhilarating stuff. Can bring people together.'

'So Mr Burgess told you he'd bankrupt Mr Swan. If he found Mr Swan was cheating on his wife, Lydia Burgess-Swan.'

'As good as.'

'What happened then?'

'Finished up the summer sailing season and went back to the Gardens. Burgess and the wife went back to Newnham on Severn, I suppose. We're not exactly Facebook friends. He rang me out of nowhere on the 4th November.'

A sudden, drenching shower of rain beat on the dark window so hard I thought it might shatter. It was the colour of ink, sliding down the window pane. I was jittery and had to force composure on myself.

Seán Flannery looked unfazed.

'Burgess rang me, said there'd been an accident and asked me to sail the Beneteau from Dalkey over to Newnham. He needed help.'

'And?' I tried not to sound frenetic.

'A girl was dead. Burgess said it was Declan Swan's fault, said Swan hadn't meant to kill her. It was an accident and she'd fallen badly. But there was a body and Burgess needed to get rid of it.'

'So he called you for the clean-up?'

'I must have come to mind, Bridge.'

'Go on.'

'I told them to wrap the body in plastic and stick it in the freezer.'

'Why'd you do that?' This was from Chris, his second intervention.

'Detective Watkiss, you are not permitted to ask questions and my client is not to be cross-examined at this time.' Richie's beetle brows were so low I couldn't see his eyes.

Seán Flannery said nothing. He didn't have to.

'Please continue, Mr Flannery,' I said.

'Took me ten hours to get over there. I would have made better time in the 65, but I can't manage it on my own. Severn is a tricky wench to navigate, particularly at night, but the boat had radar and an on-board computer. Still, took some skill.'

Seán Flannery's misplaced pride was galling. Yet, it revealed how detached he was from the horror of what was happening. He truly saw himself as innocent.

'Girl was Emer Davidson.'

'So you did know her?'

'Easy now, Bridge. They told me who she was. I'd never met her before. And you have no genuine proof I had.'

We locked eyes. I knew Seán was telling me I'd hang for planting his DNA . . . but not before Superintendent O'Connor saw him swing.

'Keep going, Mr Flannery.'

'I told Mike I'd dump her body in the Irish Sea on the way back to Dalkey. The wind was up so I made good time, sawed the arms off with a cordless Black and Decker on the way back. About midway between Newnham and Dalkey I dumped the corpse. When I got home put the arms in acetone to get rid of her fancy manicure. Simple as that.'

I found it hard to take, his just-another-day-at-the-office demeanour.

'Why did you saw her arms off, Mr Flannery?' I was spitting but knew to keep the anger from my voice.

'Insurance mostly. Mike Burgess is a powerful man, knows politicians, police in the UK.' He leaned his thin frame over the table. 'I didn't want my name turning up as a prime suspect in Emer Davidson's murder. And Mike had money. He gave me twenty grand in cash when I took the body, but I knew he'd give me more. With the right inducement.'

'So you blackmailed him?'

'Yes, I blackmailed Burgess but, I'll give him this, he's a tough old bird. Wouldn't pay up at first, so I planted an arm in the docks in a pig carcass bound for Birmingham. I rang the *Daily Journal* – your friend Lowry – told him two detectives were selling black-market meat. I said the container would be open and to go right inside, have a good look around, that there was something in particular in there that would give him the scoop of a lifetime. Told him to get it on film. Rang two other paps, told each of them it was an exclusive, told them to get down to the docks. Then you show up! Falling on your arse.' He gave a wide chiselled-jaw grin and shook himself, as if containing his mirth. 'Your self-entitled face roaring at Lowry. I'll take that to the grave with me.'

'How did you know Kay and I would be assigned to that case, Mr Flannery?' I said.

Flannery eyes flickered up to the cameras, like he was looking for something.

'I didn't. And truth be known I didn't give a rat's ass what shades found it. But a severed arm in the East Wall part of the docks, my territory – I knew you'd be down there like a hot snot, looking for evidence it was me, or making it up if you couldn't find any.'

'Let's not get personal, Mr Flannery.' I hoped he would do just that.

'Personal!' He jack-knifed across the desk at me. Only Richie's restraining arm stopped him.

I was so shocked I couldn't even stutter out a word of defence.

'Sit down, Seán,' said Chris, a menace in his voice I'd never heard before. 'Or there'll be no immunity from anything.'

'You always have someone taking care of you, don't you, Bridge?' Seán looked at me with a loathing I could touch.

'And the arm in Centenary Square?' said Chris.

'Detective Watkiss,' it was Richie's whinging voice, 'you are not allowed question –'

'I'll ask what I need to ask about my jurisdiction, Mr Corrigan.' Chris looked straight at Flannery.

'Not difficult. The arm was kept in a deep freeze. Then we boxed it up and one of the lads took it over on the ferry to Holyhead, drove to Birmingham, found a likely courier, spun him a yarn and got him to take it to Centenary Square.' Flannery snorted, amused. 'When the *Birmingham News* got a phoned-in tip from our man, the package was found immediately and reported for twenty-four hours solid on their website. The newspaper thought it might be a bomb initially, but Burgess got the message. He knew what was in that package.'

'But you left tracks. Sea charts, something filed online, or pictures on social media? That's what Kay found, wasn't it?'

I kept my voice neutral. It took everything I had. Even through the darkness Seán Flannery emanated, I could see Kay's light. Feel her soft smile.

'That's why you killed her, isn't it?'

'*Jesus Christ!* Richie! I'm not being fitted up for killing a cop! I had nothing to do with that.'

The duty sergeant barrelled into the interview room and hauled me into the corridor, no doubt on Superintendent O'Connor's orders. He was waiting for me.

'Where's the proof he murdered Kay Shanahan?' he growled.

'We're a professional organisation! I won't let any of my officers take chances or make fools of themselves. We rose from the ashes of the Civil War – for Christ sake we were founded by Michael Collins! I will not let some Detective Garda bent on personal revenge disgrace us. If I could take you off this case now I would.'

He was inches away from my face. I could smell his hungry, rank breath.

'I have to go to Birmingham and question Declan Swan, Superintendent O –'

'We'll talk about your tenure when you return.' He walked away in clipped-heel steps that rang around the hallway.

CHAPTER 50

DECLAN

Our sex was mechanical. Reminded me of building a Lego Technik truck when I was a kid. I knew where each bolt went and how to turn the screw on every nut. It was so unexpected that the feeling was coming from intercourse. With Lydia. I was a high-performance man, never had any issues or complaints – soon as I saw an opening I went for it. It was strange to feel my mind detaching, like the uncoupling of a key from a lock, but the door had to open.

Still, it was better than trying to sleep. I kept seeing Emer's face. The last time I saw her, turning her head towards me, eyes wide. Her neat red lips asking me in genuine surprise 'How?'

I focused on the headboard and calmed my mind, moving it towards the tit pic that tart of a reporter sent me weeks ago. Otherwise I would droop. I wasn't sure which was more alarming: the memory of Emer's dead body or the thought of not being able to keep it up.

Lydia was spreading herself wide and she had a sweet, oily smell. She urged me on with little grunts and praise, but I wanted to be anywhere else. I closed my eyes and tried to hold onto my erection, remembering screwing that reporter tart on my boardroom table. It worked to some extent. I visualised her moaning and pumped my hips, my eyes shut tight.

'That's it, Declan!'

I wanted to tell her to shut up, it was putting me off. I grabbed her round backside and she winced. My watch strap was biting into her dimpled skin, but I was close to climax. It would take me too long to get it back if I missed now.

'Oh Declan!' Lydia started to cry.

I detested women who cried during sex.

I pulled out and grabbed a condom from the nightstand.

'There's no point,' said Lydia.

I assumed her fertility test results had come back and by her tears the results were bad. At least I didn't have to use a condom but her self-pity and histrionics were threatening to make me limp, so I worked quickly. This is the last time, I told myself, the last time I ever have to do this. It was our goodbye fuck. I don't know whether it was relief or ecstasy but my climax was intense, if swift. I closed my eyes and rolled off her.

'I didn't get off! Why don't you talk any more during sex?'

'I'm exhausted, baby, you wear me out.' I wanted her gone, to the bathroom, to the moon. Anywhere, I didn't care.

'Well, get some rest and you can work on me later.' She had calmed down and was making a plan, I could see it plotted on her face.

'I mightn't be able to do it, babes – the stallion comes out to play but the pony goes back in.'

'In your case a Shetland, Declan.'

I looked at her tiny frame and bow-shaped mouth. I hated her. I'd clear out the business accounts by the end of the week and leave.

'I'm sorry, babes.' Lydia gave me an oversize pout. 'Look, Daddy's lifted some of the financial controls and I've made you my agent. I also put more money in my savings account, just like you said. Now, I want you to come to the fertility clinic with me.'

I was weary of her.

'Declan?'

'What?'

'Aren't you pleased?'

'If I knew what you were talking about, maybe.'

Being an agent sounded like being a lackey and I'd had enough of that.

Lydia looked at me with her head turned to one side, pity on her face.

'I'm Dad's power of attorney –'

The door buzzed, drowning out Lydia's voice, an irritating bing-bong chime she thought was classy. She went to check the monitor and her voice, when she called to me, was tight and strange.

'Declan, it's the police.'

It was humiliating being driven in a marked police car. I hunched down and sat back into the seat, trying to make my body small. Some old dears stared into the back of the car when we stopped at a set of traffic lights, etching my features onto their memories in the hope of a *Crimewatch* special. My face burned.

'Mind your step, Mr Swan,' said the portly bizzy to my left as I was getting out of the car. The skinny bizzy beside me tipped my elbow. He was trying to steer me towards the rear entrance.

It was a blowy day and the wind pushed itself up into my face. I couldn't even hang my head in comfort.

'Don't touch me,' I said. I knew my rights. I wasn't under arrest.

Interview Room A75 was an exercise in blandness. The room was cold and had a used-car smell to it. That good-looking Irish bird and her sidekick lump Watkiss were waiting for me. I felt like my pockets were full of stones, weighing me down. My body slowed and I knew if I didn't get to a chair fast I'd stumble. And I didn't want to look scared. I hadn't done anything wrong. Or at least I hadn't done anything I couldn't explain.

'Take a seat, Mr Swan. You know who we are – here's Detective Garda Harney – and I'm Detective Chris Watkiss.'

'I know who you are.' My voice sounded squawky. 'Do I need a solicitor?'

'We're not charging you with anything but we are recording this interview – there's a few cameras up there.' Watkiss nodded towards a winking red eye in the corner of the room. 'And I'd ask you to speak towards the microphone, but it's a good 'un and will pick up most sounds. Now, Declan, you're free to leave at any time or have a solicitor present if you wish. As we hope to elicit information which will open further lines of enquiry or lines of enquiry that may lead away from you, I'll caution you so we start off on the right foot. *"You do not have to say anything, but it may harm your defence . . ."*

He droned on as though it were boring him senseless – I knew it was something he had to complete or nothing I said could be used. It would have been good to call his bluff. Just stand up and walk out – then I'd see the fat lad scrabbling to get me back. It was tempting, but I had questions too and if I looked unwary they might let something slip. I was a canny questioner when I wanted to be. I'd caught out a few wide boys in my time at interviews, inflating their CVs and acting the big man.

'Mr Swan, you're helping us with our enquiries around the murder of Emer Davidson,' said Watkiss.

'Okay.' My body relaxed and I let out a long breath, as slowly as I could, so they wouldn't notice.

'Mike Burgess –'

A hot surge of rage went through me. This was why they'd picked me up.

'I only moved money into my personal account as a temporary measure. Mike Burgess would say anything to discredit me, I've been trying to get him to retire for months now, but he's still holding onto the . . . purse-strings.'

My voice slowed. Their faces registered nothing but a desire to have me split open like an overripe tomato. I shut up.

'I'm not saying another word until I have my solicitor here. Andy Kerridge in Marsden Green. I want him called in now.'

'Of course, Mr Swan. I think I know the gentleman. Interview suspended. Detective Chris Watkiss leaving the interview room.'

He walked out and told some other bizzy to get Andy.

I looked at the blonde and felt a mixture of curiosity and unease. I flexed my arms in an alternate motion, to help me stay vigilant.

'Why are you here?' I asked. 'Why is a cop from Dublin partnering a cop from Birmingham?'

'I think we should leave any questions until Detective Watkiss is back in the room,' she said. 'Technically the interview is suspended.'

She sat like stone. I gave her an appraising stare and she shifted around in her seat. She was uncomfortable and that was good. No Micka cop from Dublin was going to put the frighteners on me. Another block of a bizzy stood in the corner, I presume so she couldn't start anything with me, but I would have liked to see her try.

The thin wooden door to the room opened and the large lad reappeared.

'Can you leave the door open?' I said. 'This room smells like the inside of a training shoe.'

They both smiled and I was pleased I'd disarmed them.

'Good call, Mr Swan,' he said. 'Detective Chris Watkiss has re-entered the room. Can I ask you a few questions while we're waiting for Mr Kerridge. Don't answer if you don't like.'

'Fine.' I had seen enough police dramas to know if you looked helpful it confounded them and I was smart enough to realise if someone was asking me the same question in a different way.

'Do you know a man called Seán Flannery? Based in Dublin?' He had a natural high colouring and I had pity on his wife, waiting for that blotchy face of an evening.

'No.'

'Are you sure, Mr Swan?' Chris handed a phone to me, with my Instagram account and a picture of Flan, one of our sailing crew in Ireland.

'Are you talking about Flan? I thought it was a nickname, that he was named after a pie. His name is Seán Flannery? Was he the lad you were talking about when you came to see me in the Data Centre?'

'Excuse me, Mr Swan? What's that?' said Watkiss.

I cursed myself for running away at the mouth.

'Sorry, is the man I know as Flan your Seán Flannery?'

'Yes, Mr Swan.'

'Okay then, I know him – but he's a cack-handed idiot. Thinks he's ruddy Steve Redgrave.'

'Redgrave's a rower, Mr Swan, but I know what you mean. Flannery's a bit up himself.'

'You're telling me! Thought he owned Burgess's boat.'

'Did he sail with you?'

'No, he sailed for us. He was a deckhand. I was the skipper. Look, what's this got to do with me? I haven't seen him since the summer and I've no plans to see him again. Is this to do with the boat?'

'In a way, Mr Swan,' said Chris. 'Seán Flannery disposed of Miss Davidson's body and sawed off her arms. He maintains you murdered her, said it was an accident.'

'What? No!'

Terror ripped through me. A cold wet feeling. When I looked down, urine bloomed like grey flowers around the crotch of my suit.

'Where were you, Mr Swan, on the 4th of November?' said Chris.

'At home.'

'Your wife says you were away. On a lads' weekend.'

I swallowed, a raw gulping sound and looked down at my trimmed nails.

CHAPTER 51

BRIDGET

'I'm sorry, I know you liked him for it,' I said.

'I did!' said Chris. 'Right up until the daft ha'p'orth admitted knowing Seán Flannery and pissed hisself. Soft lad doesn't even know what Flannery is – thinks he's a ruddy deckhand. And I bloody bet he has an alibi. He must have been with a woman that weekend.'

'He'll crack and tell us who after a while in the cells.'

'Aye.' Chris bit into a chocolate crispy square but didn't appear to taste it. 'Your Seán Flannery has sent us on a right fool's errand. And you know the most flaming irritating thing about this?'

I let Chris vent. We were on the fourth floor in a Starbucks concession and I was impressed that the West Midlands Constabulary were so cutting-edge in their condiments and coffees. I shoved the tail-end of a grilled cheese sandwich into my mouth and chewed appreciatively.

'Swan's is the only case that would stand up in court,' he said. 'He has motive, a pregnant mistress and the prospect of losing Lydia Swan's money. He lied to his wife, told her he was on a lads' weekend. We could lock him up now, even with no corpse.'

Chris looked close to putting his head in his hands.

'Swan has an alibi – listen, Chris, I know Flannery did this. But his story is part truth, part invention. That's what makes him so dangerous. Let's sweat Declan Swan, he might yet be useful. Charge him with Emer's murder and he'll verify Flannery's story or break it without realising it. Either way we get Swan for ninety-six hours.'

'That will feel like a lifetime to a bloke like Declan Swan.' The idea seemed to appeal to Chris.

It took four hours in the cells. We were back in the interview room with Declan Swan. Devoid of tie and shoelaces, he shuffled in as though we'd manacled him and shoved him in a hot box. White-faced, he looked ready to spill his guts. His solicitor sat beside him and looked as bewildered as Swan. The solicitor had the look of a man who specialised in fraudulent accident claims and cheating spouses. He sat in an ill-fitting houndstooth blazer that smelled of camphor.

'Detective Chris Watkiss interviewing Mr Declan Swan. Mr Swan was cautioned earlier and that is still in effect. Detective Garda Bridget Harney from Dublin observing with Mr Andy Kerrigan, solicitor representing Mr Swan. Just wanted to get that out of the way, Declan. Do you need tea or coffee? Anything at all to drink? I've water there in front of you with a bit of ice in it. Take a drink of that, there's a good man.'

I liked the way Chris worked. Declan Swan was bug-eyed with the desire to talk and Chris was making him wait until bursting point. He combined it with a paternal tone as though he had only Declan's best interests at heart.

'No . . . thank you.' Declan Swan turned to his solicitor, the way a child might look at his minder. It was dawning on him how alone he was in this.

'Can I start?' He made a kind of tooth-grinding noise.

'Of course, Declan. Don't rush yourself, close your eyes if you need to and just take me back to the start.' Chris was like a bishop taking confession.

Swan nodded and took a swig of the water in front of him, then eased himself back in the chair. He slouched down a notch and, just as he was told, closed his eyes.

'It started with a phone call from Lydia on Saturday 4th November. I knew by her voice something was badly wrong.'

CHAPTER 52

DECLAN

'Lydia didn't even sound hysterical. It was like she'd passed that stage. She told me I had to get down to Newnham – quick as I could – something awful had happened. I remember my pulse hammering in my neck at the tone in her voice. She couldn't say any more. Instead she was making a high-pitched keening sound.'

I opened my eyes and leaned forward in the chair, moving my gaze from Watkiss to Harney.

'I told Lydia I was coming and jumped out of bed . . .' Heat touched my face at this – I'd said it without thinking. 'I was with a reporter from *Data Centre E-Zine* . . . we'd met when she did an article on me . . .'

I looked at my hands, picking at a fingernail.

'Go on, Declan lad. Does this girl have a name?' said Watkiss and I was surprised to hear some empathy in his voice. Maybe I'd misjudged him.

'Claire Holden.'

I nodded at Andy and he passed me over pen and paper. I scribbled down Claire's details – it was green ink and just spoke of how unprepared Andy was for this. I tried not to think how scared Claire might be when the police called her – but she was strong and we'd discussed this possibility.

'I drove like a madman. Through tolls and on to the M5, not caring if I was caught for speeding. The house was in darkness when I got there, no lights whatsoever. I didn't even see Lydia until she waved. She looked like a frightened child huddled in the doorway. Soon as she saw me, she darted back inside.'

Bridget Harney put her hands, palms upward, on the scarred wooden table, as though beseeching me. I looked at her health and love lines – they seemed cut into her palms.

'I chased after her, but she was gone. The corridor was empty and I ran into the main reception rooms calling for her.' I swallowed. My voice was becoming high-pitched, recalling the fear and panic I'd felt that night. 'I found her eventually. All the Burgesses were waiting for me. In the double-sized living room at the end of the hall. They were lined up in a row. Emer . . .'

I sat back in my chair and looked at the ceiling.

'Take a minute, lad,' said Watkiss and pushed a glass of water towards me.

I couldn't drink it – the glass looked like it was sweating.

'Emer was lying in a heap, at a wrong angle and matted in blood . . . the fucking smell.'

I wrapped my arms around my body, willing myself not to cry in front of grown men and women.

'Lydia was screaming at me not to get too close, but Anne told her to stay quiet, said I could go as close as I wanted to. I wanted to pick Emer up, hold her in my arms. She wasn't just dead, she was so . . . damaged. How could they have done that?'

No one spoke.

'Anne told me the Burgesses had a private detective following me. I remember Lydia saying something like that a couple of weeks before, but it stands to reason it was Anne behind it. You've no idea what she's like.'

'Why don't you tell us, Declan?' said Watkiss.

'Everyone thinks Mike is the man, but he's not. Anne makes the decisions. He's minted but Anne made him put everything in joint names. Doesn't matter he made the money – Anne wants her share. She told me they knew all about my affair with Emer, that I'd cheated on Lydia and had a motive for killing Emer. I didn't kill Emer, but Anne told me the police would suspect me, and she was right, you did. Straight off the bat.'

I looked at Watkiss. He had a big sheep's head on him. I knew he liked me for the murder and he sat there, like a great hulk of firewood waiting to be burned while Harney's hot eyes bored into him.

'Anne told me they were going to cover it up, that some fixer bloke was coming over and the less I knew the less I could tell. She said Lydia would give me an alibi, but I had to go back to Birmingham, stay off the motorways and cameras, no speeding. Then lock myself in our apartment, not even order in food. Leave no traces. I wanted to go to a hotel with Lydia, but Anne said that would be stupid. I'd be leaving an audit trail for the police right after Emer died. I'd make myself a prime suspect.'

'So what did you do?' asked Watkiss.

'Went back to Birmingham like I was told, but I went to Claire's place instead of home. We didn't go out or order in. I was careful, no one saw me. Anne kept calling me a 'daft yampy' and blaming it all on me. I'd no idea they were going to mutilate Emer.'

I looked at the plain interview room wall. It was a washed-out white, the type of paint that doesn't mark and blends into the bricks, almost isn't there. I tried not to think of Emer and waited for their questions.

'Did you know why Emer was in Newnham on Severn?' said Watkiss.

I shook my head. 'No idea.'

'Would it have been anything to do with the pregnancy?'

'Possibly.'

Watkiss waited.

'Maybe Emer was trying to force my hand, get me to leave Lydia.'

'And that would've made you angry, wouldn't it, Declan?' said Watkiss.

I looked across the room at the window: it had started to drizzle. 'Yes, but not in the way you think. Lydia and I have been together for a long time, but I've had . . . other relationships. Outside my marriage. Lydia knows this but somehow we've always managed to stay together.'

'But this affair was different. Emer was having a baby.'

'Doesn't mean I was going to leave Lydia or that Lydia would've left me, despite Anne Burgess's coaxing.'

'Do you know where Emer's body is?' Watkiss looked right into me.

'No. I would tell you if I did. Emer deserves to be buried properly.'

'Do you know who killed her?'

I shook my head. 'I don't know which one of them did it, but it was Mike and Anne. Lydia wouldn't do that to another human being, no matter the provocation.'

I didn't care if Chris Watkiss believed me. He was a suspicious bastard and that would save me. He wouldn't stop until he proved my alibi.

CHAPTER 53

BRIDGET

'Hurry, Bridge!'

Chris didn't have to tell me twice. My legs pumped as we flailed our way out of Lloyd House, through the rear entrance and through the parking bays. The freezing December rain was like razor wire and lashed us.

'You okay?'

Chris's voice sounded like thunder in my ears as I crisscrossed the car park and was almost hit by an oncoming squad car. Her surprised face imprinted in negative on my retinas as I scrambled into the Alpha.

'We have undercover on him!' said Chris. 'Declan Swan won't be unobserved at any point.'

Fierce determination rumpled his usual carefree face. 'It should take him an hour or so to get to Newnham on Severn and he's got a head start. Plus he'll make good time in that two-seater. Still,' he banged on his black dashboard, 'this old girl will give a good account of herself.' He gave me a playful grin.

I nodded. *'For sure!'*

Chris raised his eyebrows at me. 'Everything all right? You're shouting.'

'Am I? Sorry, just excited.'

He was enjoying the chase and I didn't want to ruin it for him. I'd had white noise buzzing inside my head from the moment I planted Flannery's DNA in Emer Davidson's apartment. It had been building, until it sounded like a chainsaw. I couldn't hear Kay's voice over the din, but I knew what she would have said. That my secret was corroding me.

We sped along the M5, suspecting Declan Swan would make for the Burgesses' house as soon as we finished questioning him. We had given him enough reason. It was becoming clear that Seán Flannery wasn't in Newnham on Severn in time for Emer Davidson's death – he was the clean-up guy. So to add insult to mortal injury, I had framed an innocent man. The thought of Flannery cast as an innocent filled me with utter despair.

'We've got the buggers now!' Chris was wired with the scent of a kill.

I knew that feeling, so I was aware of what I was missing.

Chris's two-way radio crackled to life.

'Suspect Declan Swan has pulled into the Burgess house in Newnham on Severn – are we advised to follow?'

Chris punched the button. 'No, stand down, we're thirty minutes out. Only continue pursuit if suspect leaves the Burgess residence.'

He gunned the Alpha. We knew where Declan Swan was and threw on the red and blue lights in the front grill. No siren, but it was enough to clear a path through the traffic.

Chris slowed as he approached the house. The waiting team

showed themselves and through a series of pre-arranged signals they fanned out around the Burgess estate.

Chris and I left the car and started on foot towards the house. We kept to the lawn as much as we could, moving at a steady trot. There was no movement and no one in sight. Only Declan Swan's haphazardly parked car gave a clue that anyone was home.

We skittered across the gravel to the front double doors. They were ajar. Chris put a hand on my arm.

'You're not carrying a gun so stay behind me.'

'Chris, these people aren't dangerous – pathetic for sure, but they won't hurt the police.'

Chris had his SIG Sauer 229 at his side, unholstered and the safety on.

'Bridge, that's your problem all over! You underestimate people – if they aren't Flannery. Burgess and Co might be a crowd of idiots, but they've managed to kill a girl and get rid of most of the body. Plus, in all of the Dublin sailing circles, Mike Burgess connected with Seán Flannery. Like calls to like, and I want to go home this evening, so I'll stay on my toes, thank you.'

I must have looked like I was going to protest. Chris silenced me with a glare and cocked his head like a dog trying to hear a signal. Mike Burgess had a church organ of a voice and we used it as sonar to locate the family.

'None of this would 'ave 'appened if you'd let us go!' said Mike. Disgust loomed large in his voice.

'Are you mad? This is down to him, the half-soaked gawby,' said Anne Burgess, the situation driving her accent back decades.

'This is your mess! You tried to stitch me up for Emer's murder!' said Declan. His voice was high with disbelief.

Chris and I stepped into the massive living room and swung the door shut with a hard bang to announce our presence. All the

Burgesses jumped and swung around to us. Declan stayed rooted to the spot and I had a moment's pity for him. He had existed in certain structures his entire adult life – now those structures were closed to him and he was adrift. He was the colour of cheap sandwich-cheese.

'Declan? What mess are you discussing?' said Chris. He was resholstering his weapon.

Declan looked baffled. He leaned in to Anne for guidance or solace and for a moment I thought she was comforting him but she shoved him away.

'I . . . I don't know,' he said.

Chris gave Declan a wad of silence to chew on, but his mouth was hinged open and flapped with his thoughts.

'I would never have killed Emer. She was having my baby. Emer was dead when I got here.'

Lydia did what looked like a full head-spin to face off Declan. Her left eye twitched.

'Liar! You murdered Emer Davidson then had some of your Lozzell Grove pals to stash the body, but they hacked her up, didn't they? And started to blackmail you! That's why you stole from my father's company. To pay them off.'

Declan sank to the ground.

'Who said anything about stashing and blackmail? You're a bit ahead of us there, Miss Lydia.' Chris stared her down.

'I – I – we know she was hacked up because the arms were found. And it stands to reason they were taken to use for blackmail.'

'Go on, Lydia,' said Chris.

'Stop it!' Anne Burgess stood with her feet apart, ready to fight.

Mike caught her eye and she seemed to deflate.

'It was an accident.' Anne covered her face with her hands.

The air pressure in the room shifted. Mike had opened a window and was lighting a cigar. A line of navy smoke rose in a straight line from it. He puffed and rotated the cigar – it was shiny at the cap with his saliva – and sent billowing clouds into the outside air.

'It wasn't an accident,' he said. 'You lured Emer here, Anne. I should say it was my fault but it wasn't. Emer was an innocent, pregnant with my child and you killed her like she was a stray dog.'

The naked hatred in Mike's voice surprised me. Anne's face folded in on itself, but he continued speaking.

'You got Lydia involved as well, then got that arsehole she's married to down here. To fit him up.'

'Your precious Emer was having an affair with Declan, so how do you know it wasn't his child?' Bitterness gave Anne's voice a crystallised quality. 'Did you ever think of that?'

Lydia shook her head. 'Declan's sterile.'

'What?' said Declan.

'Remember the time I tied you up? I took your semen and had it tested. Results came back last week. Why do you think I kept banging on about a fertility clinic? I wanted a doctor to tell you. You're so arrogant you wouldn't have believed me.' She made a hollow, despairing sound. 'I thought the fertility clinic might be able to help us with a sperm donor. Give us some options. A baby of our own . . .' There was a flicker of softness in her voice, but it changed as she looked at Declan, her eyes becoming shiny and hard as coal. 'You're completely sterile, no rich fruited plains for you.. It's unlikely you've ever produced a working sperm in your adult life. That's what the tests showed. Chronic infertility, so not only could Emer Davidson's pregnancy have had nothing to do with you, but *our Ava* isn't yours either.'

Declan was slack-jawed with shock.

'Enough!' said Chris. 'That has nothing to do with the murder of Emer Davidson. Please continue, Mr Burgess.'

Mike spoke to the view outside the window and I got a sense he had held his story in for long enough. That it had been burning a hole in him, as sure as if he'd pressed that lighted cigar into his skin.

'Anne and I had gone our separate ways years ago, but everything was in joint names. Anne will tell you,' he gestured at his wife, 'that she had me followed by a private investigator who saw me with Emer. The investigator followed Emer, who was ending an affair with Declan. Emer and Declan were finished, but it gave Anne more ammunition when I asked for a divorce. Anne used the photographs of Emer and Declan as her trump card.'

'She was playing you!' It was an angry scream from Anne. 'What – other than your overweening vanity – made you think a girl of twenty-two wanted you? She wanted your money.'

'You know nothing.' Mike dismissed her. 'I told Emer that you wouldn't divorce me and told me to stop our affair. Something I had no intention of doing. Emer and I were expecting a baby and I wanted to make a fresh start. You can have all this,' he poked one finger up at the house, 'but feel as locked up as you would in Broadmoor.'

Lydia moved over to her mother's side and tried to comfort her, but Anne snatched her hand away, making a claw shape with her bony fingers.

Mike didn't look at her. Instead, he continued telling the view down to the Severn his story.

'I knew Seán Flannery and knew what he was. A fixer. Bloke who had a price. So I told him about the safe in Dalkey, gave him codes and times. I put a million in bearer bonds in the safe. I wanted it to be cash, but if Anne saw me carting that much wad around she'd have figured out what I was up to.'

'So Flannery agreed to rob your safe and you left the alarm off for him?' said Chris.

Mike nodded. 'There was a deviation to the plan. I thought of it as I went out that evening. If I switched off the alarm and admitted to it, the insurance company investigators would be off my back. But Flannery was furious, said I'd made it look like an inside job and wanted a bigger share of the take. He took Anne's jewellery and wouldn't give me my half of the money. I was going to give the other half a million to Emer. She was going back to Mijas to have the baby. I was going to join her when I'd sorted out a settlement.'

'You old fool! She was never going anywhere with you!' Anne's body writhed, as though her anger was sloughing off an outer, now redundant layer. She glanced around, looking like she might hit Mike Burgess with one of those ornaments they had bought over the years.

'You didn't know Emer. She wasn't like you.' Mike didn't deign to face Anne.

'Yes, I did, you stupid bastard! She contacted me! Told me she'd disappear if I paid for an abortion and gave her half a million.'

'I don't believe you!' Veins either side of Mike's neck stood out like blue cords as he turned to Anne.

'You're seventy years of age with a head of raven hair. Do you know how ridiculous you look? Do you? How do you think I got her to come down here in the first place? She didn't need persuading.'

'Then why did you kill her if all she wanted was money!'

'It was an accident.' The wind went out of Anne and she staggered to a sofa where Lydia joined her. 'She told me that you were planning to run off with her.' She tilted her head back and choked down sobs. 'Emer Davidson had no interest in you, but she rubbed my nose in it. Said you'd give up everything for her. Told me you'd started to take Viagra – and she knew you were taking angina medication! That combination could've killed you!'

Anne leaned in to a white-faced Lydia. When she spoke her voice sounded dry and defeated.

'I told Emer I'd part-pay her with jewellery and went to get my jewellery box out of the safe. Told her to find a piece she liked. As she was picking over the contents, I hit her on the head with one of those crystal paperweights.' She nodded at a lead crystal orb sitting on a writing table. 'I didn't mean to kill her. I just wanted her . . . gone.'

Chris picked it up. 'It has some weight. Where's the one you used?'

'In the Severn. Flannery told me to ditch it.' Anne was resigned, even calm, now the truth was in the open.

I knew confession was good for the soul. My own lies were picking mine apart.

'What happened after you hit Emer?' I used a soft voice, wanting to keep Anne talking, let her feel I recognised that she had been discarded with so little feeling.

'She staggered a bit . . . then fell, hit her head off the brass fender. There was an awful mess.' Anne gave a dry retch. 'I rang Lydia, but she was frightened when she saw the body and rang Declan. He was so useless I sent him back to Birmingham. Mike contacted Seán Flannery, who told us to wrap the body in plastic and put it in the freezer.'

'Was Emer's bag was in the safe in Dalkey?' I looked into

Anne's defeated eyes.

'Yes, I brought it over, thought we could ditch it in Dublin. I hoped someone would use her card and the police might think she'd run away, but it was taken in the burglary.' She was holding Lydia's hand, her head slumped on her daughter's shoulder.

Later, I would wonder if Anne Burgess used Lydia. As I stood looking at the Burgesses, I wasn't convinced Mike would have helped Anne, if Lydia hadn't been at risk.

CHAPTER 54

There was a smallness to the inside of my heart I had never realised. A finite amount of storage. Rather than expanding to love more people as they came into my care, the cold of Kay's death froze it and my heart began to contract. I didn't even have room for Kay's grieving husband and her children, so mired was I in my self-indulgent sorrow. How else could I explain the madness of betraying everything Kay and I stood for by framing Seán Flannery? Perhaps it was fury. The choking injustice of Kay's death and Flannery's taut but triumphant face. Or just that Kay's death loosed something inside me.

The squad room smelled of pencil shavings, like a classroom after home time, and was just as empty. As I sat waiting for Joe, I lifted my head to let the tears roll down my face. They splashed onto my letter of resignation. It made the envelope transparent and blotted the ink, so that the letters were weeping too. Out of habit, I put my tongue out, looking for the worn lining of my

Trinity scarf. I could taste the cold.

Emer Davidson's case was closed and this was the first weekend the squad room had been quiet for over a month. Joe would be in a foul mood because I'd hauled him in here from home. My brows cinched in, wondering where home was for Joe. Kay would have known that and his wife's name.

'Bridget Harney!'

I jumped clear off the bench.

'This had better be good to get me in from my bed on a rare day off. The last bloody Saturday before Christmas as well.'

I had forgotten about Christmas, another stab of anxiety I had to push down. I stood up and moved back and forth, like an old pigeon looking for a perch. My body was awkward with fear and I bumped into a sharp desk corner.

'Everything all right?' Joe searched my face.

'Bad night's sleep is all.' My eyelids were so swollen you couldn't see the creases.

'Come in.' Joe unlocked his office door.

His voice was gruff, but not unkind, and I hoped he could hold on to that feeling for the duration of our conversation.

'Sit down.'

I couldn't and gave a dry cough – the air had an over-perfumed taste as though the cleaners had emptied a bottle of Mr Sheen into the interior, then sealed the office up tight.

'Well?' he demanded.

'Joe . . . I planted Seán Flannery's DNA in Emer Davidson's flat in Birmingham. I thought he had murdered Emer and Kay and was going to get away with it. I'm sorry. I take full responsibility and I know you have to arrest me. I've given you no choice.'

The words fell out of my mouth like a guilty defendant

muttering his way through a swearing-in. I put the soggy envelope on his desk. It had taken me hours, through night and into the cold amber dawn, to come up with the wording. I hadn't typed it. That would have seemed too callous a way to end the most meaningful eight years of my life. It felt like a death to me. It would be like a death to my father, but I pushed that from my frazzled mind.

'What?' Joe's voice sounded wrong, like someone had chopped him square in the Adam's apple. 'Sit down, Bridge.'

But I couldn't. For a moment Joe's guard came down and he looked exhausted. The puffy bags around his eyes were brought into sharp relief by the morning light.

'Why did you do it? For Christssakes! If anyone knew this would compromise a case, it's you.'

I think it was the quiet of his voice that made me realise I'd got Joe Clarke all wrong. He wasn't shouting or raging against me, demanding my badge and calling for a desk sergeant to take me into custody. Because I had committed a crime. There were no two ways about that. It had eaten away at me, dissolving me cell by cell until I was ready to keel over. Thoughts of being committed to the Dóchas Centre had stayed on the edges of my consciousness like a looping horror-movie trailer.

'I thought it was the only way I could get him.'

'Did you?' There was anger now. 'Did you think that was your only option, Bridge? You couldn't have asked the Technical Bureau to help? Or your colleagues? You couldn't have shared information with them and got a bit of perspective on the situation? You couldn't have spoken to me?' He was standing now and pacing in a tight line behind his desk. 'No, you had to go and give Flannery a get-out-of-jail card. Jesus, what a clusterfuck!'

Joe rubbed his eyes with a thick fist.

'I've never heard you swear before.' My voice sounded small and scattered – it seemed to collapse Joe's anger.

'My mother hated swearing.' His bottom lip rose up, pushed into his teeth and gave him a sad clown's face.

'I'm sorry, Joe. I should've told you or brought in Tech, or Liam. I should never have done a solo run. If I had it to do over again . . .'

But that was wishful thinking and spilled milk, all curdled into one. I would never have it to do over again.

'They could have both of us over this.'

'I won't let them do that to you, Joe. That's why I came in here. You can deny all knowledge of my actions, say you found out when you were doing a sweep of the online casebook. Kay made a note that she'd collected Flannery's DNA, which she did, and I never accounted for it. You found it missing, questioned me then arrested me when you found out what I'd done. You'll be in the clear – more, you'll be saving the bureau.'

Joe was shaking his head in a painful-looking movement. 'You think you'd last, do you? In the Dóchas Centre or down in Limerick? You'd be dead within a year. Why, in God's name, did you do it, Bridge?'

'I think Flannery killed Kay. She left me a note telling me she was meeting him, the night she died. Matthew gave it to me after the funeral.'

'*Jesus Christ, Bridge!* Why didn't you tell anyone?'

'I thought he'd have someone set up as an alibi and beat the charge. The way he always does! I thought we had a better chance framing him for Emer Davidson.' The sheer stupidity of what I had believed took me by surprise when I said it aloud, and opened a vault of tears. 'I'm so sorry, Joe!' Up came a shuddering double breath and I stood there, choking on saline and snot.

'Easy, alanna, easy.'

Joe's eyes were like two currants in a pale pudding. He didn't speak for a bit, then cleared his throat.

'I think you might be right about Flannery murdering Kay. That's the only reason I'm not hauling you down to the cells. But you've screwed us royally. What if Flannery's barrister accuses us of planting evidence in open court? There'll be an investigation of both West Midlands and ourselves. We can't use that DNA, we'll have to lose it.'

'Then we're putting the case forward on the basis of his confession?' I said.

'Yes, and you know what'll happen.'

'He'll recant, say it was forced, tell his barrister we framed him.'

'But we have the Burgesses' testimony as to his involvement and that ties him into the robbery. As long as the Burgesses testify. Christ, what a mess!'

'I know. I should have trusted the team. Not thought myself above them.' The admission was like blow to the back of the legs. I staggered into a chair.

'You think?' Joe's sarcasm poured over me like boiling water. 'You were one of the best officers I had. A true blue. All that's gone now . . . and I don't want your resignation, either. Some pap or God forbid that idiot Lowry will start digging into it. I've had enough attention with Kay's murder. I'll put you on disability, say you're unbalanced after Kay's death. Which is true. And you'll keep your mouth shut until Anne Burgess's case is over.'

He stood there chewing the corner of his bottom lip until all colour had leached out of it.

'This fella Watkiss, he has your back?'

I must have looked confused.

'Where did he collect the samples from? A hairbrush, a facecloth? Where did you put the stuff in Emer Davidson's apartment?'

'I sprinkled it around the room but it seems to have stuck on a rug. They took the rug.' I closed my eyes against what I knew was coming.

'He'll lose the rug if I ask him?'

I looked Joe in his square face and nodded. 'I think so, but it's too dangerous. It would wreck his career. I can't do that to him.'

'I'm hardly asking him knock out the officer in charge, break into the property stores and burn the rug in the station carpark, am I? Evidence goes missing or gets destroyed all the time – look at that state prosecutor who shredded the Seánie Fitz files.'

'What happened to him?'

'Nothing much – it was stress related. Evidence gets mislaid and it's usually human error, not malicious. You'd know that if you'd ever spent time in the property stores. Do you even know what PEMS is?'

'Joe, I know it's the Property and Exhibit Management System.'

'Yes, but Bridge, how many times have you been to the property stores? I know you – Kay would have done all the evidence-logging, you'd be waiting to see it on PULSE. But just because PULSE says evidence is in the property stores doesn't mean it's always there.'

I allowed myself a little smile at the mention of our old routine. Kay's name was balm given the current topic of discussion.

'West Midlands, I believe, use property books as well if the system is down or unavailable, leaving the Officer In Case to update the system when it's back online. If the officer forgets to update the system, it causes more confusion.'

'You seem to know a lot about this,' I said.

'I do! I was in charge of the property stores for the station in Dundalk during the nineties. I've lost evidence, received evidence from the Tech bureau when it should have gone to another station and been involved in cross-border policing where everything from paper weights to trucks went missing or were returned to their owners too soon.'

'So what would Chris do?'

'Go into the West Midlands property store – he'll have more than one case on the go – peel the RFID sticker off the rug, and either put the rug in an evidence pack with similar items that are going back to a third party or put it with similar items scheduled for court order destruction.'

'That would work?'

'I did it myself once by mistake – gave a woman back a set of man's clothes I thought were her husband's but the items were belonging to another case. Sure it was over a month before anyone noticed and by that time the poor woman had burned everything.'

'What happened to you?'

'Not much – I got a bit of a talking-to, but it was a genuine error.'

'Did the case fall apart?'

Joe shrugged. 'We had testimony and eye witnesses, so we were fine. Police are only human, evidence gets misplaced.' His eyes flicked from side to side. 'As long as Chris signs out a couple of different cases he's involved in and moves the rug he'll be fine. Could be weeks or months before they track where the rug has gone – you never know, it might even make its way back to the station in a year's time . . . It happens. But it would be too late for our case. The news would come through Maitland to O'Connor, but I'd manage him.'

'What if the CPS put the forensic scene investigator on the stand? Get him to testify to finding Flannery's DNA?'

'CPS won't do that – the defence barrister would tear into him with no physical evidence to back it up. We have Anne Burgess's confession. That puts Flannery in after the fact. And we have him for the robbery in Dalkey.' Joe moved his mug a centimetre to the left, exposing an arc of tea-stained desk. He tapped it with his forefinger. In an erratic, disquieting rhythm. Then stopped. 'At least, with the confession, the CPS won't have to go to trial – just plead Anne Burgess in open court.' He looked up at me. 'But what possessed you, Bridge?'?'

'I'm sorry, Joe. I've always respected –'

'Enough, Bridget. You don't respect anyone and because of your nobody-does-it-better attitude we're at the mercy of witness testimony and confessions.'

He looked out the knobbly window and was silent for what felt like an eternity. His thoughts played out on his face and seemed to fracture at the end of every cycle, like he was trying to beat a zero-sum game.

'The only thing that will save us is O'Connor, he's been telling the Commissioner he'll solve the case, so he'll have to make it work. He's the one who assigned you to it in the first place.'

'Why?'

'You're a woman. He probably wanted to look progressive to the media and the Commissioner – but who knows how his mind works?'

I looked Joe clear in the eye, a madwoman-at-the-gallows euphoria flooding over me. 'Were you watching Flannery's confession?'

He nodded. 'Course.'

'Do you remember when I asked him how he knew Kay and I would be at crime scene and he looked up at the cameras? Like he was signalling something to someone.'

'I remember him looking up.' Joe's voice was slow.

'Flannery wanted me down in the docks fumbling around, being humiliated by the press. He asked his source to assign the case to me. I think O'Connor is Flannery's source. Lorraine Quigley told me he has a high-level informer.'

Joe was out from behind his desk before I could blink. Rammed up into my face and hissing.

'Don't you ever say that to anyone! D'you hear me? O'Connor would have you . . . wiped out.'

I looked at the network of broken veins in his nose. 'He's getting ready for wife number three and has children in private education,' I said quietly. 'How do you do that on a Superintendent's salary? You suspect him too, don't you?'

'What I suspect and what I can prove are two different things, Bridget Harney. Do not mess with O'Connor – he's a dangerous and violent man.' There was a pleading quality to his voice. He stepped back and put a hand on my upper arm. 'Bridge, please stop taking risks. Lie low until this trial is over.'

He picked up his mobile phone. In the quiet of the office his next question sounded like a gunshot.

'Do you have a home number for Watkiss? I'll need to arrange to meet him.'

CHAPTER 55

BRIDGET

The Sexual Assault Unit was located in an ice box on the fifth floor in Harcourt Square. That's where O'Connor had put me after a month's sick leave. The air conditioning that created swamp-like conditions on the ground floors seemed to have found its purpose with a vengeance this high in the building. You could bring in a pound of butter and it would stay rock hard, even on a hot day in June. Dimly lit and severely understaffed, there was little atmosphere and no banter in the small squad room. Most of the detectives spent their time on the streets, picking up girls, giving verbal warnings to pimps or finding shelters for young women and children who were trafficked into the country. Work I would have been happy to do – if I were let. Instead I was based full time in the office. Field duty wasn't an option according to Superintendent Niall O'Connor. He had told my new sergeant I was to work the tax returns of known pimps and chase down Inland Revenue Affidavits for men who claimed their 'Mammy' had left them money. It was all in the detail, according to Superintendent O'Connor, so he buried me in terabytes of data.

I might as well have been sealed up in a tomb of ones and zeros.

A buzzing desk phone cut through the silence in the squad room. It was an old model so the digital display simply said: 'error code 483'.

'Hello?'

'Hey, Bridge. Paul here. How's things?'

'Bizarrely cold.'

'You ready for our session?'

'For sure. Are we still in Interview Room D on the third floor? Your email invite doesn't have a location.'

'Sorry, I'm not great on the new meeting software. We're in D and I'm here waiting for you. Can I get you a cold drink?'

'It's freezing up here. I'd love an americano if you're offering, but we can pop out to the coffee cart at the end of Harcourt Street and get an iced and regular, if you'd like?'

'Yeah, let's do that. It's boiling in this office. I'll meet you in reception and we'll chat before the session.'

Escape.

Paul stood waiting for me outside the Square. The sun was a high yellow ball in the sky and I realised I'd be sweating shortly. I was in full navy serge uniform topped with a clownish Day-Glo jacket. We must have looked incongruous drifting along Harcourt Street, me with my GARDA sign emblazoned across my back and Paul wearing stylish khaki shorts with a white T-shirt. I tried not to notice his strong arms but looked anyway. Life had few blessings at the moment.

'Can't wear your Trinity scarf?' Paul made a visor with his

hand. I liked that he hadn't worn sunglasses.

'Nah, I have to stick to regulation, but it's gone in any case.'

'You lost it?'

I nodded. 'In a way. Can you believe this weather? I'll have sweated off my make-up by the time we reach the end of the street.'

I sizzled. My face was getting greasy, not the look I wanted for meeting Paul.

'I'll have to talk to Facilities – that SAU squad room's freezing, it can't be healthy. More instances of colds and chest infections from that room than any other.'

'Paul, I think Facilities know that. Might even be why O'Connor put me up there – two of the detectives are on extended sick leave.'

Paul raised an eyebrow, his head to one side. 'How you doin'?'

I laughed. 'Vintage Joey?'

'Yeah.'

He put a hand out and glanced off my arm. It made hope and desire bubble up from wells I thought were exhausted.

'But seriously? Are you okay?' He raised both palms. 'This isn't for Superintendent O'Connor, I'm just asking as a friend.'

'Remind me again, when are the Super's evaluations over?'

'You know it's not as simple as evaluations, right? You've been diagnosed with Complicated Grief Syndrome as a result of Kay's death.'

I felt my insides cleave together. 'O'Connor called it a nervous breakdown at the disability hearing.'

'O'Connor doesn't know shit about psychology and he should be disciplined for using inaccurate terms like nervous breakdown. You listen to me – you're doing great. I reckon by the end of the year you'll be fine. You've had one evaluation a month since your return and this is your sixth, so when we go back into the office I'll start the clock. Halfway there. You'll be finished by December.'

'That's the one where I'm appraised as fit for duty?'

'Yes and no. That's what O'Connor wants you to believe, but if you weren't fit for duty you wouldn't be in the building.'

I liked the way he'd dropped Superintendent O'Connor's title.

'That's some comfort, but I get it – this isn't a tick in the box. The disability hearing was clear: I'm on continual assessment with no assurance that I'll ever get back to detective.'

'Don't lose hope, Bridge.'

He got a weak smile for that and moved a millimetre closer to me. I breathed in his tincture of coconut oil, sandalwood and musky skin. He seemed to tan as we walked, whereas I was like something from the aphotic ocean floor. He looked at me, most likely wondering why I was so pale.

'You look well.' His voice had a low timbre. 'Like a porcelain doll. I'm the colour of a chai-wallah from sitting outside at lunchtimes.'

I snorted with laughter. 'You can't say that!'

He grinned and raised his left hand and slow-crossed his right foot in front of his left foot.

'And what is that?' I giggled self-consciously.

'Jai ho dancing?'

'You oaf!' I punched him on the shoulder and he caught my hand. For a moment I thought he might lift it to his lips, but he released it.

It was so good to be the centre of his attention. He had an open, eager look that made me bold.

'Did you have a good weekend? Do anything nice with the family?'

He raised his eyebrows. 'My mum and dad? They're in their eighties so a good weekend is lunch in the garden.'

I grinned but kept my eyes steady. 'I meant with your wife or girlfriend or . . .'

'Ah . . .who's been talking?'

'No one. I just assumed someone kept you looking so well-turned out.'

My face was burning and it had nothing to do with the sun. I looked down at the ground but Paul chucked me under the chin.

'I'm single. Have been for a bit now. I keep myself well-turned out, Garda Harney. Indeed, that propensity for neatness is something I might have to watch out for according to my ex-wife. I was married, but it didn't work out.'

'Sorry.'

'No, you're not.'

'You've a cheek! What happened?'

'Old story, we were young and unhappy. No children, though.'

That seemed to pain him, so we walked on in silence.

'Meant to say, Bridge, congratulations on the Burgess case. What did Anne Burgess get?'

This I could handle. 'Pleaded down to voluntary manslaughter, loss of control. Nine years, with last four suspended. It's not enough, but it was her first conviction. Her defence played up her model citizen record and she pleaded guilty so the premeditated aspect never made it into court. Also it wasn't a full trial, so Mike Burgess wasn't able to testify against her.'

'Does the court like a husband who testifies against a wife?'

'Doesn't give a toss either way, but I reckon Mike Burgess wanted to.' I raised my face up to the sun. The hell with my make-up. 'Crown Prosecution complimented the way the investigation was run and the casebook. Said it was excellent.

Only took six months from her arrest in December to her conviction last week.'

'O'Connor got Big F.O.T.C. points for that commendation from the CPS.'

'What's Big F.O.T.C. points?'

'Big Friend of The Commissioner points.'

I snorted out a laugh, loving the acronym.

'It's true, he got serious kudos for it,' he said. 'Cross-borders investigation, working with the West Midlands Constabulary and assisting with preparation of the case for the Crown Prosecution Service. There was a cock-up with some evidence in Birmingham but I'm not sure what the repercussions were. From what I'm told it's not the first time evidence has gone missing or been misplaced. Either way it didn't stick to O'Connor.'

Paul didn't notice me flinching. The thought of what Chris had done for me was a source of relief and shame in equal measure.

'Did anyone get reprimanded for it?' I said.

'I've no idea. O'Connor only mentioned it in passing in the Supers' meeting. He doesn't like anything that takes the shine off. To hear him, you'd think he did it single-handed. Minister for Foreign Affairs sent a memo to Harris. He singled O'Connor out at a recent briefing. He's not going to give you any credit, but it might get you off his shit-list quicker. What happened to Burgess and the daughter? Did anything happen about their burglary? I never heard anything more about it.'

'Lydia Swan and Mike Burgess got three years apiece, last year suspended, for accessories after the fact."

'I'm sorry about Flannery.'

I nodded. When I spoke my voice sounded emotional. 'It was always going to be difficult. The Burgesses were too scared to testify against him.'

'How did they explain away the missing body? The arms?'

'Anne said they dumped the body in the Severn and when the first arm turned up in Dublin someone rang her with a blackmail demand. When they didn't pay, the second arm turned up in Birmingham.'

'Anyone believe her?'

'No. But she stuck to her story.'

Paul clasped his hands behind his back, holding his wrist in the opposite hand. 'What about Declan Swan?'

'He refused to testify against the Burgesses.'

'Wow! Why not? I thought the Burgesses set him up?'

I looked at Paul's earnest, handsome face. 'They did, but I'm guessing Swan thinks there's something he can salvage when the Burgesses get out. He's been with Lydia Swan since they were in school – the Burgesses are all he knows. And he likes the money.'

Paul nodded and looked up at a single wisp of cloud fluttering like an old party streamer across the high blue sky. 'What about the DOCB? Anyone talking to you?'

I spread my hands out wide, shoulders raised. 'A little, but they're not sure what to say.'

'Sorry.'

'Don't be, I messed that up all on my own. If I'd opened up to my colleagues and told them how much Kay's death affected me, we'd be in a different place.'

I didn't trust myself to say more. My punishment was to keep the cover-up secret. To lie to everyone that mattered to me.

Paul tensed beside me, misreading the signals. 'You're not responsible for Kay's death.'

I didn't answer, and we walked in silence to the coffee cart, deciding to sit down and share a cinnamon-and-raisin bagel. Paul enticed me with a fluffy iced cappuccino. He took a pat of butter from the cart's counter top. The sun had turned it to ointment. He opened the silver wrapping and smeared the butter on his half of the bagel without using a knife, doing all his tricks, trying to get me to smile.

'Enjoying that?'

'Ah Bridge, you have to let yourself go sometimes. There's this lovely spot on Camden Street, was trendy a couple of years ago, so much so you couldn't get a table, but it's calmed down now. They do a lovely supper. Melt in the mouth tuna ceviche . . . I'm not sure why I'm telling you this.'

I thought I might know. Heat flared in Paul's neck and he changed the subject.

'How's Joe Clarke doing since the move to Gorey?'

'Good, saw him last weekend. My dad and I took the dog down to a beach near Ballygarrett. Well ... I was actually checking a caravan park, looking for Lorraine Quigley.' I shook my head. 'No sign of her. But we called in on Joe. It's an old-fashioned station on the Main Street and they're good guys. Joe's delighted to be away from the politics of the Square. He's renting at the moment but thinking of buying a house down there. His girls are in college and come to them at the weekend, his wife has joined a load of clubs and they've rented out the place in Spain. He's only delighted with himself.'

Paul snorted. Some of the shaved ice broke free of his cup and floated down to the ground like a sweet dandelion clock.

I took off my Day-Glo and uniform jacket and popped the top button on my blue shirt, letting the heat lick me.

'I'm glad. He's a decent skin. When did you get a dog?'

'It's the assistance dog the lads in DOCB got for me. He wasn't cut out for life in the Force, so he hangs around with the Judge most of the time. The Judge's taking more walks and has joined a morning bridge club. Dog goes with him. Suits everyone.'

'Things good with you and your dad?'

'We have the dog in common . . . and it's better. We're both trying.'

'I'd hate to be the poor unfortunate who has to play your father at bridge.' Paul flicked a shiny raisin at me.

I snorted a great gas of air. 'Yes, he's on a roll, fifty-eight games unbeaten.'

'Christ, he must be unbearable.'

I nodded and we both leaned into one another, choking our laughter into our chests.

'How's your mum?'

That was more difficult and a knot of hurt bunched my face. I opened my mouth to release the tension sitting in my jaw. I had told Paul at one of our earlier evaluations that my parents' marriage had been strained and I was lonely as a child. He thought it had something to do with my trust issues. I'd given him a gold star at the end of that session.

'She's as okay as stage three dementia will let her be. She's in a nursing home just outside Wicklow town. Nice place, lovely carers. An English girl called Tess. She's a saint – never seen anyone as kind as her, except perhaps her sister Eileen.'

Paul reached over and took my hand. It wasn't a romantic gesture, but full of kindness.

'That's good to hear, Bridge. And Kay's family?'

He said it calmly, as if he were asking for the sugar, but he was watching me and I felt the pad of his index finger brush the pulse on my wrist.

'They're okay. I take the children one night a week, gives Matthew a break. They love my big stupid bedroom and we all sleep together. I feel Kay right beside me.' I took a gulp of air. 'Not in that mad way I used to think she was talking to me.'

'I know. I'd say she is there and I'm sure she's thankful for your love towards her children.'

Easy tears pricked my eyes.

'It's good to let it out,' he said. 'The sorrow. For what it's worth I think you're doing remarkably well. Any news on Lorraine Quigley?'

My hands spread around my coffee cup like pale tentacles. 'I don't know where Lorraine is. I've checked with her family and friends, even went to her cousin's caravan but she's gone. Marie is safe and I'm working with the cousin on temporary custody.'

'That's a good start.'

I gave him a weak smile. 'It is, but I'm worried about Lorraine. O'Connor has me hemmed in and I need to get back on the streets if I'm to find her.'

My hand went to the place where my Trinity scarf had been for over fifteen years. Nothing but my chin.

'Paul, would you help me find Lorraine, please?' I looked up at the sky as I asked. Seven words. I marvelled at myself for getting them in the right order.

Paul handed me a napkin. 'Bridget Harney asking for help – now that's progress.'

I elbowed him.

'Of course I'll help. You tell me what you need and I'll give it a go.'

'You won't get into trouble, will you?'

'I shouldn't – if I get stuck I'll ask Liam O'Shea to give me a dig-out. Come on, let's get back and do this appraisal for O'Connor. I'll show you what I'm sending in before I email him.'

'Are you allowed do that?'

'No, but what O'Connor doesn't know won't hurt him.'

'Thanks, Paul. I just want to get out from under this shadow.'

'There's no shadow, Bridge. Just a woman working through a few issues. You know you won't always be my patient.'

He was puce-faced, but I thought it suited him. My phone rang and a round face filled my screen.

'Hey, treasure!' said Chris. 'How's everything in Dublin?'

Chris's kindness sat like hot coals and I hoped one day to be worthy of the risk he'd taken for me.

'Bizarrely high temperature, but you didn't ring me to ask about that.'

'No, I didn't. I'm in Spain – came over to tell Emer's mother about the sentencing.'

'How did that go?'

I pictured Chris basking in the dry Mijas sun and was about to make a joke but something in the quality of his silence stopped me.

'Everything okay?'

'I'm not sure. I spoke to Emer's mother. Did you know Emer Davidson and Declan Swan were an item in Lozzell Grove? Mother said she never liked him, thought he was too old for Emer. Said Emer left Spain to go back to Declan as soon as she was eighteen – that's the reason she and Emer fell out. And listen to this, according to Emer's mother Swan got an offer to go up to Cambridge after his A levels, but married Lydia Burgess instead. I thought you had to be proper smart to go there. Doesn't sound like Dozy Declan.'

I had the feeling of being on a too-high diving board. My throat clenched and I'd hung up without realising.

'Bridge?' said Paul.

I raced away, my feet smacking the pavement, my breath

raggedy.

'Wait!' Paul was struggling to keep pace and talk. 'What's happening?'

I shook my head. I'd been shafted, an idiot who'd swallowed a line and all I could do was run, trying to force a plan from my dull mind with physical exertion. I wasn't even sure where I was going.

I launched myself into the stairwell in Harcourt Square and pumped my legs up to the fifth floor.

'Bridge! Wait!' Paul caught up with me, his arms full of my jackets. 'Stop!' He dropped the jackets and pulled me in to him. 'What's going on?'

'Declan Swan, he's not who we thought he was! I've missed something. That was Chris on the phone.'

Paul let out a breath of air. 'Christ, I thought it was your mum or something important.'

The boyish expression of relief on his face made me ache. He danced me around and into a supply cabinet. Left foot, right foot, each step tighter in a circle. Awkward knees bumped into spaces unknown. I heard the door close and felt his mouth on mine, the meaty newness of his taste, our front teeth grazing off one another. We hit into a disused filing cabinet that made an indignant metal groan, our embarrassed giggles a backdrop to his strong hands pulling at my clothes. Hot kisses dissolving in the half-light between us until every part blurred.

CHAPTER 56

SEÁN

It was good to be free. Dublin was a strange city by night. By rights it was a medieval city and so much of its beauty wasn't held in darkness or floating, brightly lit rooms. It was better by daylight when the winking skyline gargoyles were visible. At night their sooty faces vanished and smell of the fires that blackened them filled your hair with charcoal. Tiny black grains that wanted to burrow into your eyes.

I was on my way to a warehouse between the East Wall and Clontarf Road, a small little alcove of a place called Castleforbes Terrace. It sounded so posh, like some English lord's residence. It was anything but. It was a grim row of houses with mouldering bricks. Rats from the nearby docks chewed anything that stood still for long enough. The people were suspicious and beaten down, afraid to look up. Unless to protect one of their own, when they had a feral viciousness that didn't need size or strength. My kind of people.

If you've ever had the misfortune to see a woman attack another woman you'd know they sound like dogs fighting. Hysterical screaming interspersed with teeth-bared yowls. When I walked into the warehouse Lorraine Quigley was doing just that. I had hoped for more from her. It was demeaning. That's part of the reason I will only shoot a woman. Get it over quick. You can't beat a woman. They have no dignity. A man will take his beating in grunts. Women make metallic, rippled noises that vibrate in your chest. Horrible. Lorraine's face was pulp. She stank of sulphur and hydrogen sulphide. Blood and shit.

There was also excitement, as there always is during any blood sport. The illicit, salty excitement of a hidden erection. I'd visit that downy-limbed little girl in Dalkey after I'd finished with here. She was a temptress and my trips to her bedside had been disturbed by Bridget Harney's meddling attempts to frame me. Not any more.

But it hurt me to see Lorraine like this. I cared for her and would have shot her as a point of honour, but her betrayal merited closer attention.

Gavin was working a mindful sweated rhythm with his fists. He was lost in the music and didn't stop when I raised my hand, but one of the other lads grabbed his arm.

'What did you say to Bridget Harney?'

I leaned in to Lorraine, inches away from her single open eye and spoke as I would to a child. I pushed a strand of matted hair behind her ear.

'What did you say to my sister?'

CHAPTER 57

DECLAN

That's the thing about beauty, male or female – people couldn't see past it. No one saw past mine. Perhaps they were so jealous they had to believe beautiful people were stupid. Otherwise how could they feel good about themselves, when they looked in the mirror?

The butler answered the door on my first knock.

'All right, Micka. Took you long enough.'

'Bostin, Shabba man.' I slapped him on the shoulder and we grinned at each other.

I stepped into the hall.

'Can't believe it's all over now,' he said. 'Five fucking years opening doors and clipping cigars for that wanker Burgess, with "What can I get you, Mr Burgess?" or "That's very generous of you, Mr Burgess, thank you". Do you know, at the start of the year, he asked me to call him Sir Michael instead of Mr Burgess. I'm fuckin' serious.'

I threw back my head and roared with laughter. 'Come on, let's go to the humidor.'

We walked down the gaudy hall of Newnham on Severn, where Mike Burgess's hubris knew no bounds. Past the oil paintings of Lydia, her mother and a life-size portrait of Burgess himself.

'Hey, Shabba, I want to thank you, man – for always being my eyes and ears on Mike and Anne. It was the stuff you told me down the years that has put us here. In charge.'

'Don't I know it!' Shabba rolled his eyes, laughing.

He stood in the doorway of the humidor, letting the atmosphere in, ruining the cigars. I picked up a huge Havana and twirled it beside my ear, listening for the crackling sound of a perfect leaf. The smell of sweet cherry tobacco was rich and enticing in the moist room. It was almost a shame to leave the door open and ruin all Burgess's prized cigars. Almost.

'They killed Emer, though.' Shabba's oversize eyes bulged with tears he would have called gutless on anyone else's brindleyplace. Nobody from Lozzell Grove cried.

'I know. That part went wrong. But the money's ours. Fifty-fifty. Lydia made me her agent and she has power of attorney for her father. I can access his money.'

'No, you can't! Don't try and fill me full of shit, Micka. You're not Burgess's power of attorney, Lydia is. Only she can get his money – you're just her agent and that can be rescinded overnight.'

This was new – Shabba thinking things out. But it didn't matter now. 'Rescinded? That's a big word for you, Shabba man. Been readin' up?'

For a moment he looked dangerous, the top boy I knew in Lozzell Grove. I laughed and he relaxed his muscles.

'Chill — Lydia put more money in her savings account, like I told her. There's nearly 2 million in that account — split it 50-50 with you, man. I'm her agent so I can access that money. And she'd have to know what I was up to, wouldn't she, to stop me? The bank is hardly sending updates to inmates care of Drake Hall.'

'But the Burgesses don't trust you — they know you moved money in the company.'

Shabba was full of surprises today.

'Burgess tell you that?'

He nodded.

'You must've got more matey than I realised?'

'Fool might have thought he was my friend, but it wasn't mutual.' He squared his narrow shoulders.

'You're right, the Burgesses don't trust me, but I didn't give evidence against them so they think they own me. I moved 5K just to test the water — I wasn't making any grand escape on that. Nothing actually happened other than the financial controller told Burgess — nothing on the bank's end, no penalty clauses, no phone calls. I'll move more remotely when you're out of the country. Financial controller is so rattled he'll do anything I tell him, terrified the business will go under and he'll lose his job.'

'You're a smart lad, aren't ya, Micka?'

I didn't like the way he said it.

We were walking back through Burgess's hall of fame, Shabba unaware I was leading him.

'I remember you and Emer taking off to London when she was sixteen. Her old mum had the police out looking for her. You were engaged to Lydia at the time but she never found out. Always the sneaky bastard. But you were right about Burgess — he fell for Emer as soon as you put her under his nose.' Shabba rubbed a flaking hand across his eyes – small wonder Burgess had made him wear gloves. 'But I thought Emer was supposed to marry Burgess, mess around with his medication and let nature take its course?'

'That was the plan, but Emer changed it.'

'She changed it?'

'Yes.'

I didn't expand – too much babbling would make it look like I was trying to hide something. Which I was.

'Why? Emer would've got Burgess's money after he died. Problem would've been keeping him alive until they were wed – he was chewing those Viagra. What did she say to you?'

'Emer wasn't one for the long con, Shabba. She had other ideas. Maybe she didn't want to spend a year married to Burgess, or maybe she didn't have the bottle to mess around with his medication, who knows? She got pregnant by him. That was a gamechanger. She called Anne Burgess and offered to have an abortion, if Anne gave her half a million. It wasn't a bad plan but –'

'I thought that baby was yours, Declan man.'

I looked at Shabba. It was so obvious, the resemblance to Ava. I swallowed a hard lump of hate.

'Nah, we had that worked out. The baby was a catalyst, to get Mike to leave Anne faster. But Emer should've let me know she was blackmailing Anne. I could've told her Anne wasn't to be trusted. Can't tell you how surprised I was when she rang me and told me she was on her way down here – the night she was killed. Came well out of left field.'

'So she called you, Declan man, swear to it? That it was Emer's idea, the change of plan?'

'It was all Emer's idea. She was the smart one.'

We had reached the front door. I opened it and stepped

outside. The river glinted in the sunshine. I sat on the low wall at the top of the steps and Shabba joined me.

'Hey, man, where you going to go? Barbados?' I asked.

'Haven't decided where exactly. But . . .' He paused, scratching a nest of blackheads on his jawline. 'You've been good to me, Micka – always good to me, we're like brothers.' His lies left dirty creases in his skin.

'We are, Shabba. Always will be.'

'It's just that . . . Did Anne Burgess know you had an alibi? That you were with that reporter bird?'

I decided honesty, or at least a grain of it, was needed here.

'Yes, I told her when those detectives followed me here. Leaned in like I was hugging her and whispered in her ear. Told her I'd pin it on Lydia if she didn't confess to it.'

'But Anne did it, right?'

'Right.'

'It's just that . . . Emer rang me, you know? Week that Anne killed her, told me to get ready to leave after the weekend . . . not to say anything to you.'

This was news. I had a sensation behind my eyes, of a balloon being fiercely pumped up, until I thought my head would burst. I composed my face and decided attack was the best form of defence.

'Why did she do that? Was you planning to go off together behind my back?'

'No, man!' Shabba's viscous eyes were on stalks.

I eased back a click. 'Look, I told you Emer changed the plan. She was the brains behind the operation. Maybe Burgess said something to her. Maybe he twigged you and me knew one another.'

'Maybe.' He didn't sound sure.

'That would've been a disaster. Burgess wasn't a stupid man.'

He would have suspected you'd be tattling back to me. Remember, I forged all your references, told Burgess I'd got your name from a recruiter. Man, the money I spent on elocution lessons and training courses for you!' I nudged him. 'Burgess didn't know anything about class! Imagine hiring you as a butler!'

'I was good at my job.'

Again the danger under the surface.

'Come on, man, that's all over and done with. All we have to do now is let the good times roll! Where you going now you're rich?'

Shabba was grinning. 'Going to London, buy some clothes and get on a first-class British Airways flight to somewhere hot.' His eyebrows cinched in. 'Just tell me one last time about the night Anne murdered Emer.'

I was getting tired of this. But I wouldn't have to put up with it for much longer. Shabba's time was up.

'It's like I said to the police. Lydia called me to come down. Anne had lured Emer down here –'

'Anne? I thought Emer called Anne?'

My lies were like open shoelaces and I was falling over them. Part me wanted to tell Shabba the truth, that I'd caved Emer's head in because she was a double-crossing bint, but now wasn't the time to rattle him.

'Yeah, sorry, man – said this so many times to the police I'm getting confused. Do you really want to hear all this again? Come on, leave it, man! Let's go down to the river – this is the last time you'll ever have to look at it.'

Shabba made a visor of his hand, shielding his eyes, and looked down to the river.

'Hey, Declan, is that boat pulling in here – near the boathouse?'

'Yeah, Shabba. It is.'

I waved at Seán Flannery.